The Hand of Hamora

The Hand of Hamora

by Jarrett Skaddisson

Other Books by Jarrett Skaddisson:

The Kingblade Chronicles

Saga 1: Tarnadins of the Elder Forest
Book 1: Call of the Danna
Book 2: The Road to Anganor
Book 3: The Sign of the Sengara

The Adventures of Neldon Broadbuckle: Volume I

This Work Is Dedicated
to
Dr. Mary Lou Jones,
who is wiser and more remarkable
even than Yahsi

ACKNOWLEDGEMENTS

Here I wish to heartily thank those who have helped bring this book from my head to your hands with their various skills and talents: Max Garrison for editing and consulting, Ferdinand D. Ladera for cover art, Blaine Morehead for font and cover design, Cornelia Yoder for maps, Dawn Allman for text layout and design, Shang Tea for countless cups of refreshing inspirational tea, and all my family and friends for inspiration and encouragement.

Table of Contents

Maps

Part I:
Harp and Air

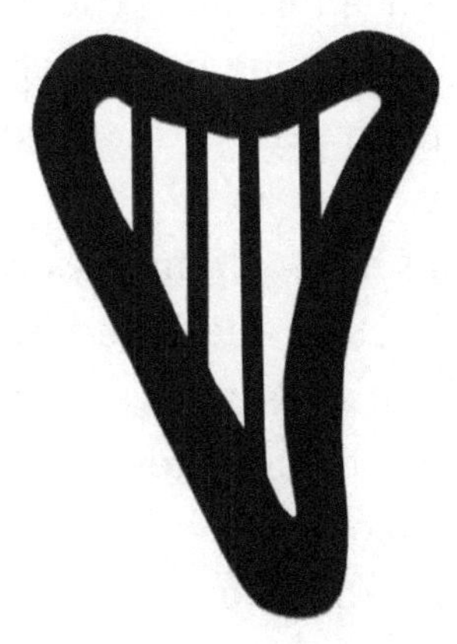

Chapter One

Song of the Summer Stars

ONE COULD HARDLY ASK for a finer feast nor a finer eve to seek the hand of the loveliest maiden in all the land. At least, so Okona thought, for he was nearly certain the Powers of Air, Water and Earth had whispered as much to him. The midsummer breeze was wondrously pleasant, the shining ripples of Takula Lake a mirror of perfection and the many terraced mounds sumptuously green. "This is your day, Okona," they all said.

Okona had sighted his beloved Anisha several times already, but they hadn't conversed yet, as there had been much for both of them to do before the feast's commencement at sunset. Anu Ashori, the Song of the Summer Stars, the festival was called, for it fell at the height of summer. Okona's people, the sturdy, ruddy-skinned Sakooma, were to praise the Summer Stars tonight, so the Stars' blessing might shower them year-round. Last year, their feast must have been especially well-received, it was held, for there had been much bounty. Spread upon a host of blankets atop the feasting mounds, there was more and better food than Okona had ever seen in his life: piping plum stew, rich haunches of venison, no fewer than ten varieties of the finest smoked fish, savory platters of eagle, bear and pelican, all rubbed with wild herbs; also, there were honeyed persimmons, ripe-roasted pecans and hickory nuts, spiced sunflower soups, lavender ponnicberries bursting with the very nectar of the earth, lush blackberries and ever so much more. And everywhere there were clay jars of cool spring water. This year there was even prized, glistening salt from the domes of the Kadora Flats, far to the west.

All around Takula Conflux, in the huge, late-afternoon shadows of the twenty flat-topped mounds, there came the mingled rise of song and merriment. Old folks smoked their pipes of sweet tonga and spoke of cherished legends and days gone by, children capered about in the grass, the well-to-do bartered agreeably, young men competed vigorously in quompi, a game involving notched poles of hickory and stiff leather rings, and nearly everyone had a turn at dancing. Anisha was dancing in a ceremony now, and Okona, who was on his way to join his master tutor, Yahsi, stopped to gaze at her.

A friendly hand landed upon his bare shoulder.

"You're going to ask her today, aren't you?"

"How'd you know, Kimmanic?" Okona inquired, turning his copper eyes to the lean, cheery young man behind him.

Kimmanic smiled. "It's written all over you, Okona. The way you were just looking at her. The way you're wandering aimlessly about and especially the way you've been staring off into the Great Nowhere every minute or so."

Another fellow slapped Okona's shoulder. "Even I can see it," the newcomer laughed.

Okona turned to face his impish neighbor, Jamuni.

"Besides, how else could we explain why you've been so hard at your work this past season? Poor Kimmanic and I have been obliged to have all our fun without you."

"Ha!" Okona returned. "Work of that sort might do you some good, O Jamuni Sleepy-Toad. Besides, I couldn't very well approach Anisha or her father with anything less than exceptional assets and expect a marriage out of it."

"That's the problem with setting your sights on the Sanno's daughter," Jamuni tutted.

"Precisely," agreed Kimmanic. "Old Dhagomi's a generous man, but even he might not be generous enough to regard your assets as 'exceptional.' Except maybe your throwing ability, that is."

"Yes, the things you can do with a simple stone are a wonder," echoed Jamuni. "And your tree climbing is rather impressive too, I suppose. Oh, and you can play a flute like a living legend. But as for everything else ..."

"Come on, you two," Okona retorted. "I know there are other Sakooma who've got quite a bit more to offer, but I have saved up a decent amount, and Anisha likes me."

"Does she?" queried Kimmanic.

"Prove it," Jamuni challenged. "Go and ask her right now."

Okona shook his head, then adjusted the tie holding back his smooth, raven-hued hair in a ponytail. "I've got to play a set of songs with Yahsi first, and Anisha's not finished dancing yet. But after that ..."

"We'll be there to see it." Kimmanic grinned.

"You'll do wonderfully, Okona," Jamuni genuinely assured. "You are right to feel lucky. Today's the day. Fortune is both in the air and in your hand."

"But in the meantime, mind your flute," Kimmanic warned. "Too many sour notes from you and Anisha might have second thoughts."

Kimmanic and Jamuni walked off chuckling while Okona hurried over to where the petite, aging Yahsi, her silver hair in a neat bun, stood with eight other musicians at the foot of one of the mounds.

"Okona, I'm so glad you're here!" she exclaimed. "Baneesh just stopped by and said it was time for us to start."

"I'm sorry, Yahsi, I was—"

"That's all right. No harm done."

Okona nodded, then took his rivercane flute out of a long pocket in the side of his deerskin breeches and raised it to his lips, as Yahsi placed her fingers upon the strings of a small, slender harp. A moment later, the buoyant voices of the entire ensemble began drifting across the lawn.

Shortly, those nearby commenced dancing. Soon, there was a full fling before the band, as the dancers sprang about in formations of various summer constellations: Amwot, King of the Elk, Torokay, the Northern Eagle, and the troublesome, but always terrific, Dongo Rabbit, romping through many a well-loved tale. Anisha, recently finished with her ceremony, was now among the dancers, and she made eyes at Okona several times as she whirled past.

In addition to Okona's flute and Yahsi's harp, there were several other flutes, as well as drums, rattles and rasps. These all played heartily for more than an hour until the aforementioned Baneesh, who, among other things, was the organizer of all the festivities, came by to inform them that the music they had gifted to the heavens was sufficient for now.

To Okona's dismay, Anisha had to rush off to speak with her father, the leader of all the Sakooma. He'd been rather difficult to get hold of that afternoon, for he had nearly as much to attend to as Baneesh.

As Okona was preparing to follow the girl, Yahsi caught his shoulder and said, "Your flute-work was excellent today, Okona. And I couldn't be happier to have chosen you to perform the ode with later this evening."

"Thank you," Okona returned, beaming. "But I couldn't play a note on this thing if you hadn't trained me."

"It has always been my privilege," Yahsi declared. Then, leaning toward him, she said quietly, "And don't worry, Okona. For I believe your talk with Anisha will go just as you desire."

"What talk? Oh, you mean—well, how did you know I—"

"Even a turtle can cross the Southward Sea." Yahsi's amber eyes twinkled. "It may take me a while, but I catch on."

"You're no turtle!" Okona laughed. "Why, I wouldn't be surprised if you could out-clever the likes of Dongo Rabbit."

"I'd take no offense at being called a turtle, and you should be glad your clan bears that name," Yahsi declared. "Turtles are admirable creatures. At least the right kind, anyway. The ones that put their necks out and never give up. The ones that have a direction they need to go and keep going that way, no matter what. But I've no use for the other sort, the ones that shrink back in their shells and just sit there. As far as I'm concerned, they can get what's coming to them. Trampled by a herd of elk or I don't care what. But you're the right kind of turtle, and that's why I'm confident your talk with Anisha will go the way you hope. But only if the Hand of Mahna Shuya is with you, of course. For from that Hand all good things come."

Okona looked around nervously. "Do you think everyone knows about what I'm planning to discuss with her? I mean, I'd only spoken to a few people about it."

"There's no cause for concern," Yahsi assured. "No one told me about it, and I won't tell anybody else. I just know you, and I've seen the way you interacted with her the last several times we've visited here. And I've also noticed you working extra hard this past season. You know, when you've been around as long as I have, you can see where the river's flowing even before you round the bend."

Yahsi looked across the lawn. "Ah, she's just finished with her father! Come, stick your neck out, Okona." She gave him a little nudge.

With only a brief, backward glance, Okona fairly trotted across the lawn to where the girl stood. Her long, black hair was braided in many tresses, a bright silver bracelet was upon her wrist and jeweled anklets just above her bare feet, and she was clad in a deerskin dress which fell to her knees; the dress had many bright, beaded patterns along its hems.

Anisha turned her dark eyes to Okona.

"Anisha, it's so good to see you! For a month or two now, I've been meaning to make it up here to visit, but things back in Hachori have been ever so busy, you know."

"I won't hold it against you." Anisha looked up at him with a roguish smile.

"Listen. I wanted to talk to you about something." He glanced up at the setting sun. "And I reckon the feast is about to begin, but—"

"Blessings to you, Anisha!" called a stout voice.

A tall Sakooma warrior with a painted brow, firm chin and eyes of a fervid brown approached. His leather hunting bag was yet slung over his shoulder from an expedition earlier that day, but he was garbed in festive regalia.

"May the Hand open to you as well, Tencum!" Anisha returned.

"How do you fare, Okona?" the man asked, halting before them.

"Well as ever. And you?"

"Wonderful," Tencum said. "Oh, and Anisha, I'm so glad I found you."

"Okona!" came a cry from the direction of the main feasting mound. It was his mother, Eyuja.

The lad turned to see his parents, two sisters and brother waving to him.

"Come, son! The feast is about to start!" called his father, Panni.

"It's all right," Anisha said, briefly seizing Okona's hand. "We can talk later tonight. The evening is young."

"Of course. Later tonight," Okona promised, as he jogged off to his family, silently cursing this series of disruptions.

Shortly, Okona was seated at one of the blankets on the head feasting mound amidst his family, both immediate and less so. (Although, only his mother's relatives were with them, for that is how things are done among the Sakooma.) From his vantage point some thirty feet above the surrounding landscape, he had an excellent view to the southeast, where many Sakooma, recently finished with their merrymaking, were diverging toward the five feasting mounds spread throughout the compound.

The head feasting mound stood nigh unto the gentle waters of Takula Lake, which bordered the whole northwestern edge of the Conflux. On the opposite side of the mound, to the southeast, was a great plaza, where most of the day's events had been held. To the northeast and the southwest of this plaza were the highest and widest mounds in the whole complex; atop these were, respectively, the Hashoka, the House of Flame and Fume, and the Kamaygo, the Lodge of the Sanno, where the people's leader, Dhagomi, and his daughter, Anisha, dwelt.

But at the southeast end of the plaza was the most revered mound of all. It was the burial place of Takula's most esteemed founder, Hamora, whom the Sakooma credited with sustaining them and keeping them in the good graces of the mighty ones, they who were known as the Powers, for the last two hundred years. And beyond the Mound of Hamora was a high wall of consecrated earth, itself immediately bounded by a ditch, both of which surrounded the entire Conflux and its accompanying lake, marking the area's status as the most sacred site of the Sakooma.

Now, lower and lower the sun melted into the horizon directly to the northwest of the prime feasting mound, so that its final rays shot brilliantly across the lake, which flashed and sparkled like dark diamonds. Okona turned around to watch the spectacle for several minutes, and out of the corner of his eye, he noted Anisha, seated some ways down the feasting strip and on the opposite side, watching it as well.

When the sun had sunk to Baneesh's satisfaction, he, bearing the distinction of chief mediator between the people and the Powers, called for the blessings of these Powers upon the feast; at least he did so for the principal feasting mound, while his associates did the same for the others. He sang passionately to the Summer Stars, then turned to the Mound of Hamora, and his voice rang out, "Praise to thee, O Hamora, mighty forefather of our foremost, and blessed be the earth that covers your ashes. For the benefit of all our people and the splendor of this hallowed feast, I invoke now thy blessed Hand. Ah, the Hand of Hamora! Well wert thou so named. Hamora: 'Blessing!' For such hast thou brought us these many long years. Long may thy Hand continue to bring us such favor! And fortuned are we to rest under its spell."

Baneesh bowed his head, then raised his arms to the sky. As soon as he had done so, the multiple thousands of Sakooma gathered throughout the Conflux launched into their feasting with all the vigor of a summer sunset, of which they had just had a particularly excellent representative.

And such a feast it was! Every man, woman and child reveled in the magnificent quantity and quality of food, the cool evening air, the cheery crackling of the many torches lighting the mounds, the comforting gleam of the evening lights above and the general excellencies of this year's Song of the Summer Stars.

When the deer bones were piled high, bellies were more than satisfied and talk had died down to a soothing murmur, Dhagomi, dressed in a fine kilt of buckskin and a many-patterned blanket, which was draped over his shoulders, got up to address those seated at the main feasting mound. Okona was quite excited to hear his speech and to be at this mound in general, for all the populace were on a rotation, and it had been some years since he had last sat here.

Dhagomi first issued the usual sorts of pleasantries expected at an occasion such as this, then spoke for some time about all the Sakooma's good fortune this past year. Then, as his speech drew to a close, he orated the following:

"My good Sakooma, as I have said several times already, I am beyond blessed to be your leader. And we are all much blessed—and have been for ten generations now—by the Hand of Hamora, the power of our exalted forebear long held in yon mound. Now we come to the formal close of our evening, for we have feasted to the stars and back again. May the Ashori accept our offering. We shall close with an ode to Mahna Shuya, him whom we can never know as we ought, but we must nonetheless not forget. This year, such will be performed by our own Master Song-maker, Yahsi, and young Okona of the village of Hachori, who is becoming quite a Song-maker in his own right from what I hear."

Dhagomi seated himself on a low stool. Then Yahsi and Okona, with due deference, nodded to him, rose and took out their respective instruments.

"The song we are about to play is much older than I am," Yahsi announced. "And that's really saying something!"

This generated much laughter.

"It came to me from the Master Song-makers of my youth, and to them from the Song-makers of old, far up the River of Years. Yea, even back to the age before our own, to the days of our ancient forefather Lakosha, it is said. As you know, in his time, the Stairway to the Sky was broken, so men might no more ascend to the bright and treasure-laden Over-lands. Thus, Lakosha led his children into the deepest north in mourning. And it is from there this song is believed to have come, the North Beyond North, where Air, Water and Earth mingle freely. Although none now living remember who was its maker, many hold it was gifted to man by the Air itself. And this may very well be true, for unlike most every song of ours, it has no words, so none can claim to truly understand its meaning. It remains shrouded in the remotest North."

"In that mystic place, our far fathers wandered, tormented, through the haunted Mists of Shagrash-mula, the Span of the Shimmering Nights, until they entered the world we now inhabit. But the song was said to be the light that guarded them from the perilous spirits of the swirling airs, as they passed hither. It is one of the very few treasures we have from that former, greater world, the World of the West in which Lakosha was born, and it is at times such as this that we may spy the slightest glimmer of That Which Was Lost." The old woman bowed her head.

With the skill of many decades, Yahsi strummed her harp and began to sing. Moments later, Okona joined her with his low, breathy flute, and their song rose into the night sky. Okona played as he never had before, deftly weaving his own notes into Yahsi's wordless melodies of honor to Mahna Shuya, the Light Beyond the Mists. But as beautifully as he played, he still could not help feeling he was missing something; he was playing what Yahsi had taught him, yes, and playing it perfectly. But the song seemed wrong somehow, and he thought perhaps Yahsi was missing something too. These ruminations nearly caused him to play astray, but he held steady, and they finished at last in a slow, melancholy hymn that died away into the night. All were now silent. A deep and inexpressible longing hovered over Takula Conflux, so strongly that everyone on the feasting mound almost felt they could touch it.

Suddenly, the sky was blotted out, as if a great monstrosity had come between the earth and stars. Fear took the crowd, and they began to cry out. But moments later, they were overpowered by a tumult even greater than their own. Thunder roared in the heavens, so deep that the earth throbbed. Terrible flashes of light burst from the blackened sky, and, with a screech, a bolt of sizzling blue leapt to the earth and struck the top of the mound across the plaza, where the Hand of Hamora lay. The whole mound was lit up for a moment in a blaze of bluest fire; then there was a crack. The earth was rent, and the great stone doors sealing the mound's entrance burst into an infinity of splinters. Now all the Sakooma, save one, fell on their faces and covered their heads, whimpering and screaming. The brave heart who alone did not falter rose swiftly from his place and sprinted across the plaza.

The booming gradually faded, and the murk above dissipated, leaving the moon and stars to beam their light once more. But their once charming illumination now seemed somehow defiled.

"It's gone! It's gone! O, ten thousand woes have overtaken us! It's gone!" a voice cried. It was Tencum's.

Okona raised his head, his hand laid upon his bare, beating chest, and he saw Tencum collapsed, grief-stricken, before the open mouth of the Mound of Hamora, with the presently impotent symbols of his strength and skill, his hunting bag and spear, flung in utter despondency before him. All the people were weeping now and Okona with them.

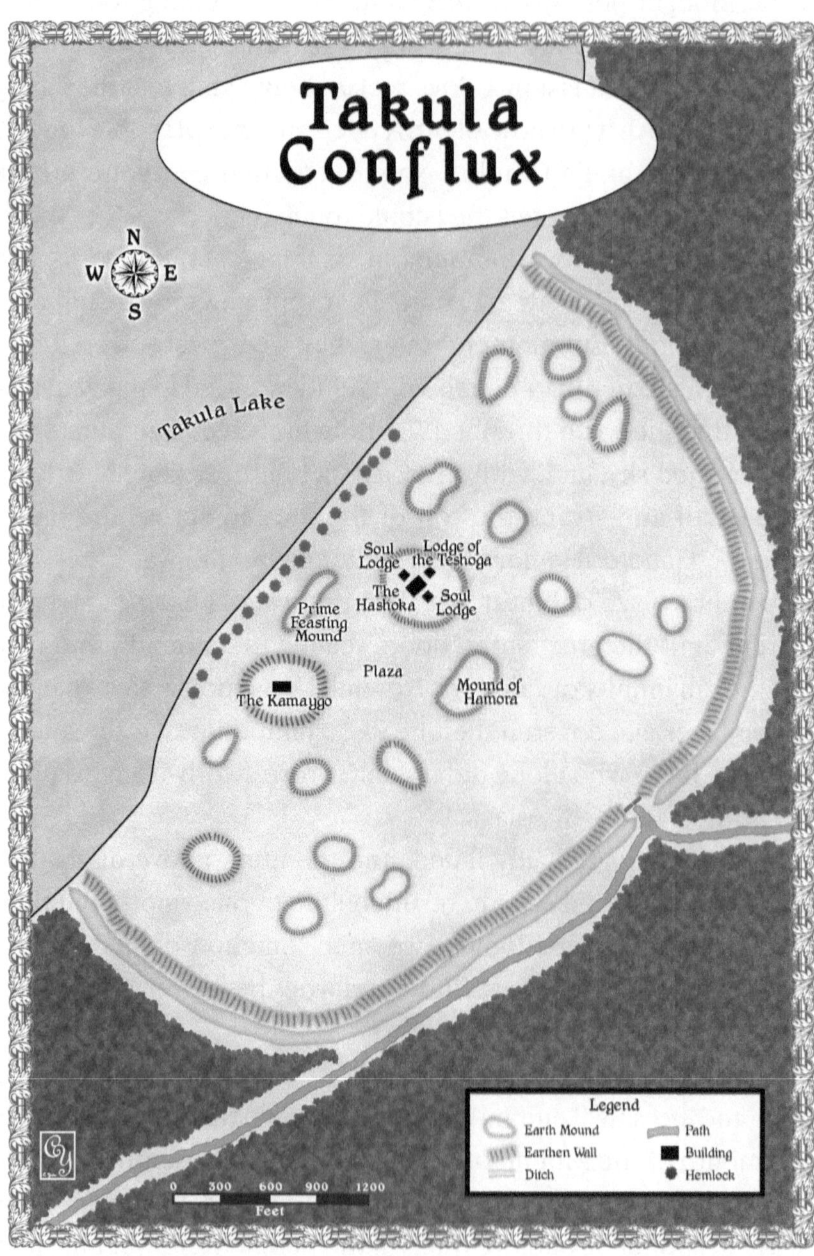

Takula Conflux
N
W E
S
Takula Lake
Soul Lodge
Lodge of the Teshoga
The Hashoka
Soul Lodge
Prime Feasting Mound
Plaza
Mound of Hamora
The Kamaygo
Legend
Earth Mound
Path
Earthen Wall
Building
Ditch
Hemlock
0 300 600 900 1200
Feet

Chapter Two

The House of Flame and Fume

After a while, all the people went to their split-cane mats, either in one of the compound's sundry huts or else under the boughs of the hemlocks near the lake, and fell asleep or at least laid down. For there was unfortunately nothing else to be done. But Baneesh climbed the mound upon which stood the Hashoka, the House of Flame and Fume, and this he entered to work such magic as he could to aid the Sakooma.

Okona had lodged in one of the tall, rectangular, peak-roofed huts the previous night, and here he slept this night as well, though restlessly. His family had been invited there by some friends of theirs who were of the elite few who dwelt at Takula year-round.

When Okona awoke in the morning, he exited the hut and glanced up past its grass-thatched roof at the cloudless sky where a white-headed eagle was circling high above. There was not the slightest sign of the strange storm that had come upon them the previous night. All was still, but the air was heavy.

"Okona!" a voice called. Yahsi was walking toward him, barefoot, across the dewy grass. A simple, elegant deerskin robe ran from her shoulders down to her ankles, and a blue-jeweled necklace hung around her neck.

"Come with me," she said. "There's an important meeting you are to attend at the Hashoka."

"The House of Flame and Fume? I can't go in there!" Okona protested. "Why, you know that's forbidden, Yahsi, forbidden to all but the most distinguished leaders and Magic-makers."

"You may enter if you've been invited, and of course you have or else I wouldn't be telling you to come." Yahsi tugged his arm.

"But who's invited me?" Okona began traipsing along beside her toward Takula's main plaza.

"Mahna Shuya," Yahsi replied.

"Mahna Shuya?" Okona halted, and Yahsi turned to face him. "How could that be? His voice hasn't been heard since before men even entered this world. We can call to him, perhaps, and sometimes he hears, but he calls not to us. Yet you expect me to believe he's broken his long silence to invite Okona of humble Hachori into the Hashoka? Yahsi, it's not like you to weave far-fetched tales."

"You're quite right."

"But Mahna Shuya couldn't have invited me!" Okona insisted.

"Well, there's more to the story, but there's no time to relate it now, and you don't seem of a mind to believe it anyhow. But if you won't accept Mahna Shuya's invitation, as I feared, then at least accept that of a representative of the council—namely, myself. "

"What council?"

"The one that convened early this morning at the behest of our great Teshoga."

"Baneesh?"

Yahsi nodded. "Now come along." She grabbed his hand and dragged him forward.

"Well, if it's the will of the council, then I suppose it's all right. But I don't know why you wouldn't have just said so from the start instead of bringing up this bizarre business about Mahna Shuya."

"I had to at least try," Yahsi sighed. "Now do hurry, for the meeting is about to commence."

Shortly, Yahsi and Okona were climbing the high, terraced mound on which stood four notable buildings. First was the large, high-roofed Hashoka, the House of Flame and Fume, from which smoke rose eternally through a hole in the ceiling as an offering to the Powers of the Air. Behind it, just to the northeast, stood the residence of Baneesh, and on either side of the Hashoka were the twin Soul-Lodges, which no living man but the Teshoga, the people's Chief Magic-maker, was allowed to enter.

Now some sixty feet above the plaza and able to see the vast spread of Takula Conflux as he never had before, Okona shivered as he approached the Hashoka's shadowy, extended entryway. Yahsi pulled him forward, and they passed through oaken doors into the House itself. Several tens of persons were gathered in the relative darkness within.

On the other side of the large, smoke-filled room, sharp-nosed, balding Baneesh, garbed in a long, drab robe, stood on a dais before a ten-foot wooden statue of a man with an upraised right arm. Deep notches were in its forearm; the area beyond this, up toward the hand, was smoother than the rest of the statue, which was covered with knots and imperfections. The statue's face was grim, but turned upward, and had wild, dark eyes. Behind the statue was an altar with a great fire, on which many logs had been laid in the form of a cross. The rest of the room's earthen floor was bare, excepting collections of tools for making offerings and tending the fire.

As Okona's eyes adjusted to the dim interior, he noted others he knew among the attendants. Dhagomi was there, as was Tencum, carrying his weapons and satchel as always (for ever ready for his people's defense was he), along with other great warriors of the Sakooma. Several of the Wise-women were present, and Okona was somewhat put at ease when he spotted his good friend Kimmanic standing under the pillared alcove to his right. Okona himself was led into the back corner of the left alcove by Yahsi.

After several more persons had entered, four of the Deggas, the counselors and chief warriors of the Sakooma, went up and whispered to Baneesh. He then held up his hands and said, "All who were summoned are now present, according to my report. So let us begin."

Baneesh was rumored to have received his mystical abilities as a child from the bite of an enchanted hawk, but this prowess had come with a price, for he was always a little twitchy and often had a queer look in his eyes. But this morning the effect was much more pronounced. His eyes were bloodshot, his face haggard and the twitches more frequent and jarring. "He must have been doing very great magic," Okona thought.

"O, ye brave and wise Sakooma," the Magic-maker said, "I am glad to see you gathered here to receive my words. Through the long watches of the night I slept not, for I was in consultation with the Powers. And much did I sing; I sang to ward death from this place. Alas, I am certain some other was singing against me, and I fear that Magic-maker's work was, in the main, stronger than mine, for I was nearly undone. But at the last, my magic proved the mightier or else some aid unknown swept in. In any event, I have not heard that any of our folk died, even though the cloud which troubled our feast's end had much death in it."

The Teshoga took a clay bowl from a small table before the statue. "Now, I must provide protection for myself to utter the dark things I shall impart to you. For to say these names and relate these matters will bring ill fortune and the wrath of wandering spirits and perchance even summon the evil things themselves if I do not consume this potion." Slowly, he drained the vessel's contents, a speckled concoction of crimson leaves.

"And this yagoni," he said, taking a larger clay bowl, "is for *your* protection. Unfortunately, to hear these things is nearly as bad as to utter them. Luckily, the friendly spirits in the Soul-Lodges nigh to us provide some shielding, which is the reason this meeting had to be here in the Hashoka. But their defense alone is not enough; the potion must be consumed also. Take care to drink only a little though, for there must be enough for all forty-one of you: Dhagomi and the forty who have been called. But do not fear; it is very potent, and a few drops will be sufficient for their purpose."

The bowl passed through all the hands in the room, and when it came to Okona, a mere sip of the black, bitter, burning yagoni was enough to make him want to retch. But he swallowed it resolutely, for he feared the resulting evil if he failed to drink it would be far worse.

At last all had taken their portion, and the bowl was returned to Baneesh, who proclaimed, "All of you were witnesses of the strange tempest that assailed us last night. And I know you have been wondering what it was and how and why it came against us. As to why, that remains obscure. But the answers to the first two questions I now know, for the Powers of the Air have given them to me."

"The storm was wrought by a black spell whose name I will not even utter with such protections as we have taken," he went on. "But a spell it was, and one of far greater potency than any I can conjure. As you saw, it was so forceful as to overcome the deep enchantments set upon the door of Hamora's mound twenty decades ago. It is so powerful, in fact, and so heinous that the beings with whom I have consulted told me it could only have been done by ..." He paused and swallowed hard.

Wiping his forehead, he continued in a lower voice, "By one of the Four Malevolents, the Innakosh, as they were called in ancient days. Four Evils from the Four Spokes of the Earth."

Some of those present, including Okona, had never heard of these beings till now. Yet the breath of every soul in the room was still caught in horror, for the air itself had just shuddered unmistakably with a surge of vile magic.

"You may have heard rumors of them in your dreams on bleak winter nights or from the mouths of the oldest of elders, when some calamity struck. They are four evil Powers who followed us to these hither lands from the world beyond the Mists of Shagrash-mula. They troubled that world too and have such an appetite for depravity that they came even to blight us in this world of Massora, which was already laden with so much sorrow."

"To the east is the Waboka, the Shadow-Stalker, who dwells beyond the great River Anoka in the darkling woods. His body is night and his eyes fire. Woe to all who find themselves in his forest! To the south is the Sharapoc, the Swamp-Demon. Cunning is he and sharp of tooth and tail. To meet him in his own waters is certain death. Westward lies the winged Matora, the Thunder-Bear, swift over forest and plain and merciless to any who cross his nightly haunts. And in the hollows and grots of the north, there lurk the Oolasheg, the Twin Crones of Torment, whose devilries are matchless and whose eyes ever hunger for the blood of men."

Baneesh looked around the room. "Mark me, all! One of these four has taken the Hand of Hamora, and unless we retrieve it, nothing but doom and desolation can be written in our near future."

There was silence for some time, as the company pondered these grievous tidings.

"I said I did not know why one of the Innakosh has stolen the Hand," declared Baneesh at last. "But you can be assured that they did not seize it for charitable purposes. It is extraordinarily powerful and thus could be put to great good, as it has for us, or great evil, as it shall be now unless we can seize it in return. One would need only the ability to access its raw potency to turn it to another use."

"As you all know, Hamora left the whole of his power in it. And he was the mightiest Magic-maker our great land of Sarkanna has ever seen and its finest leader as well, the first and greatest Sanno of the Sakooma. Fortunate we are to still have his blessed lineage with us in the fair Anisha and also for many generations to have been ruled only by those who were wed to his daughter-line. And fitting it is that his image should stand in this House to be venerated." He glanced at the statue behind him.

"As you have heard from childhood, he bargained with the Powers to have his right hand transformed into clear crystal, that he might conquer his wicked brother, whose name is thankfully no longer remembered. He cut off this brother's right hand in battle and drove him and his debased followers into the north, and there he slew them, ending their defiling influence. He fought off all the enemies of the Sakooma from every direction when he returned and established the boundaries of our land. Then, when his time came, the Powers faithfully kept the agreement he had struck with them. And so he entered the mound which bears his name, and there he died, transformed into ash and sealing the great doors in the same instant. And his Hand was eternally locked away for our benefit—until last night."

"But now," Baneesh sighed, "the Hand has been taken, and ruin lies at our very doorstep. I do not have the wisdom to guess what form it may take, only to know that our days are numbered and few. For that was part of Hamora's pact with the Powers as well, that our people should only be spared from catastrophe as long as his Hand remained interred here. It was not that he wished our strength or safety should be dependent on that, only that these were the conditions demanded by the Powers. For nothing is gotten without conditions; nothing is paid for without a price. And the price of nearly perfect protection was the possibility of disaster. Perhaps if you or I had been there, we would not have made that pact, but have any of us the wisdom of Hamora? I have heard that some who are not Sakooma have even called the Hand a curse of sorts. But that is folly! For my part, I think it is a small thing to ask that we submit to the Hand's enchantment for all the benefit we receive in return."

"Obviously, the only thing to be done is to get the Hand back," declared Tencum from the front of the room.

"Aye," agreed Dhagomi from nearby.

"That, of course, is why I had the four Deggas here, the worthy helpers of our good Dhagomi, select our best and bravest to accomplish this task," explained Baneesh. "And that is why the four most gifted of our Wise-women are now present. For each Degga shall go with one Wise-woman and the others they have chosen. And thus we shall have four groups, four Sacred Tens, to seek swiftly for the Hand of Hamora, for time is much against us. One Ten shall go east to face the Waboka, one south to seek the Sharapoc, one west to confront the Matora and the last north to assail the Oolasheg."

"That is your mission," said Baneesh solemnly, looking out upon those assembled. "But you must be warned: even if the Powers of Air, Water and Earth are all with you and you manage to regain the Hand from whichever of the Innakosh has thieved it, whoever takes possession of the Hand of Hamora will be destined for death. For its power is too much for any mortal, and as soon as it leaves his possession, he will perish. That is part of its magic; thus have my Teachers told me. So if you return in triumph, when you lay the Hand upon its rightful altar-stone in the Mound, you will die. But it is only by placing the Hand there that the blessed enchantment can be restored to our people. And yes, I know what I am asking: that you give your own life, whoever you may be, for the whole of the Sakooma. But it is better for one to die than many, for one to give himself so that the many may live. I do not issue this charge lightly. But I know that you are brave and of goodwill. You are Sakooma, the very best of them, and finer folk cannot be found in the whole of this world."

The assembly nodded in grim agreement.

"But keep the details of what we have discussed to yourselves," Baneesh cautioned. "As to what you shall tell your families and so forth, only say that you are going to seek the Hand and bring it back to us. Utter nothing of the Four, nor of the death of he who will bring the Hand home. Add no rain to our thunder and lightning."

Baneesh raised his right hand, mimicking the statue behind him. "Now go, and I will sing a song of protection for you after you have departed. Each must see to his own preparations. The appointed meeting place and time is tomorrow before the sun gets hot at the great crossroads in the fields of Chennipot Chonka. Dhagomi will be there to help you decide which party shall go which direction. May all blessings be upon you as you seek the Hand of Blessing."

Okona and the others all filed somberly out of the building. When they were out of the smoke and back in the morning light,

Okona said to Yahsi, "Baneesh said that everyone in that meeting will be accompanying one of the Deggas. If you don't mind my asking, to which of them am I assigned?"

"Tencum," she replied, glancing over at the famed warrior, who was conversing with Dhagomi.

"Ah. And you are the Wise-woman who is to go with him?"

"I am."

"But why was I chosen? I haven't a reputation for warcraft or bravery or anything like that. I mean, I can hunt all right, but I've not fought in a single battle and can't even—"

"Who are you to question your selection?" Yahsi interrupted. "If it has been decided by higher authority that you're to go on the mission, then you ought to leave it at that. Besides, you'd better not try to pull back in your shell now! For many would leap at a chance to win back the Hand. Also, I think this is the one of the best things that could happen to you. Undoubtedly you believe otherwise, but you'll just have to trust me in this."

Okona looked out at the placid waters of Takula Lake, longing for the vanished delight of the previous afternoon.

"Now, Okona, I want you to enjoy the rest of the day. Breathe deeply of Takula while you may, so at least you will have this to look back to on what may well be a joyless journey."

"I'll try," Okona promised.

Sighing, he went over to Kimmanic and said, "I'm glad to see you'll be going on this quest as well."

"Likewise." Kimmanic gave him a solid pat on the back. "Hopefully we'll be traveling together. I'm with Tencum."

"Me too!"

"Couldn't be better," laughed Kimmanic.

"See you tomorrow, if not before then," said Okona, as he set off down the mound.

When he reached the bottom, he embarked across the plaza, but his eyes wandered up to the Kamaygo, the large, stately lodge where Anisha lived. He had never been up there before, but it wasn't taboo like the Hashoka was, and the thought occurred to him that Dhagomi wasn't there presently, being still at the Hashoka, but Anisha might be there alone.

"Somehow it doesn't feel entirely appropriate for me to just climb right up there," Okona thought, "but I may not get a chance to talk to her again, and a turtle's got to stick his neck out, after all."

With resolve, he finished crossing the plaza and started climbing the crude wooden steps to the top of the far mound. Before long, he reached it and walked up to the shadowed entrance, calling into the hall, "Anisha? Are you there?"

Moments later, the girl, rather surprised, pushed through a curtain in the entryway. "Okona?"

"Yes, I uh ... well, you know, with everything that happened last night, I didn't end up talking to you like I promised."

"Yes?" She stepped toward him.

"I'm supposed to be leaving tomorrow to look for the Hand of Hamora, so I thought I'd better ask you about this beforehand. What I was wondering is if ... well, I've been working rather a lot these past few seasons, and I know I don't have all that much to offer compared to some, but both of us are eighteen now, and I ... I really care for you, Anisha, and ..."

"Oh." The girl's face fell.

Okona stopped, his mouth slightly open.

Anisha looked up at him out of the shadows. "I feel the same about you, Okona. But there's something I need to tell you."

Okona swallowed anxiously.

"Yesterday afternoon, when we were talking ... right after you left, Tencum asked ... you know Tencum ... well, he asked if I would marry him."

"Oh, I see," said Okona, his mouth painfully dry.

"And I ... I said yes."

Okona swallowed again. "That's wonderful, Anisha."

"H-he's a good man, Okona," she stammered, "and I just didn't feel right rejecting his offer."

"You made a good choice," Okona said woodenly. "And you're right. He's a fine man. I assume your father approved it, then?"

"I don't know if they've actually talked about it yet because there was last night, then the meeting this morning, and—"

"Of course," said Okona blankly. "There's been a lot going on. Anyway, I just wanted to tell you goodbye. I wish you all the best."

"The same to you," said Anisha in a pale voice. She took the lad's hand and pressed it. "Goodbye, Okona," she said, then retreated behind the curtain, as the lad withdrew.

Hastening down the mound, he muttered, "Well, I guess sometimes sticking your neck out isn't of much use."

Chapter Three

The Scattering of the Sunflower

Following Yahsi's advice, Okona spent the day as pleasantly as he could in preparation, farewells and leisure, though it was difficult to take his mind off his looming departure. Before the advent of evening, he had amassed all his foodstuffs: several woven bags filled with various nuts, along with a satchel of dried meats and fruit and two hefty waterskins. He decided it would be best to be armed with both spear and bow with arrows, and to this he added a trusty dagger borrowed from his brother, Coryoc. His sisters Yuriba and Annamet made for him a beaded necklace, and his parents spoke their kindest blessings.

Okona did not sleep as well as he had hoped this night, for worries had occasionally awakened him, but his rest was adequate. Well before sunrise, he rose, dressed himself in trousers of a burnt brown, over which he donned a faded, dark-green breechcloth, then grabbed all the possessions he had readied. In the blackness of the hut, his hand fell on his flute. "I really should take this too," he thought, "if nothing else, for my own amusement." He placed it in his trousers' long pocket.

The lad exited the large hut where he had been lodging and went to the southeastern gate of the compound. The sentries wished him well as they opened the portals, and he passed beyond them. As they were closing, he looked over his shoulder at the broad lawns of

Takula and uttered a plea to the Powers that someday he might tread them again. Then, setting his face to the southwest, he followed a worn road running parallel to the outskirts of the compound. Eventually, this veered directly to the west and after that branched off in several directions; Okona took the path that led northwest toward the Kanno River.

He walked at a modest pace, attended by the hum of insects and the choruses of morning birds in the brush and trees bordering the road. By the first hints of the sun's return from the Caverns of Oshaga, the Night-woman, he had come nigh to the river. A walk of an hour more brought him to the edge of Chennipot Chonka, Sunflower Junction that is, which lay six miles northwest of Takula Conflux. Here, fields of tall, gorgeous sunflowers, their enormous heads waving in the morning breeze, spread for several miles along the banks of the Kanno. Okona pressed forward another half-hour through the endless sea of bright blossoms and came to an intersection with another road, where a number of the warriors and wise were standing, conversing quietly with each other.

Kimmanic was there already, and the two conversed amiably while they waited for the remainder of the appointed persons to arrive. Before another half-hour had gone by, the full number of these had joined the band. Among them was Yahsi, toting her harp in a thick leather bag covered by a cloth. She was bare of feet but attired in a russet, barkcloth traveling robe and her customary, blue-gemmed necklace. The old woman and Okona greeted each other heartily.

"Do you really want to haul that thing along?" Okona inquired.

"You never know when you might need some music," she frankly replied.

"Agreed." Grinning, Okona showed her his flute. "But a harp? If you're really set on it, I'd be glad to carry it for you."

"No, that's all right. It'll give me good exercise."

Tencum and Dhagomi were the last to arrive, concluding an intense conversation as they did so. When Okona saw the former, who appeared more prepared than anyone else, laden as he was with his hunting bag, a great knapsack, several smaller satchels and multiple weapons of different varieties, he tried to squelch his resentment about Tencum's engagement.

"Devoted have you proved yourselves already," declared the black-haired Dhagomi when the people had gathered round. "Now, let us waste no time in making the necessary decisions about which of our arrows we shall send along which path. Our four Deggas are Tencum, Homino, Aywish and Orobec. And the four Wise-women who shall accompany them are, respectively, Yahsi, Sheelim, Tannomet and Shoroba. I had originally thought to merely cast gamblers' beans to decide who should go in each direction, but upon further reflection and conferral, I have changed my mind. For there is no reason to leave to chance aught in which wisdom might prove to be of aid. Thus, let us have swift and open counsel regarding who should take which course. Who will go east, who south, who west and who northward?"

"I'm glad we shall have a say in the matter," whispered Yahsi to Okona. Boldly, she spoke up, "Dhagomi, it seems to me the choices should be fairly simple. Whichever party goes south shall have to contend with swamps and backwaters, and Aywish is by far the most gifted in watercraft and swamplore. And to the east lie the Mushatuck. Homino is the only one among our number who can speak their language, having a mother of that stock. Tencum is oft in the westlands for battle against the Chadori and knows well that region. He also knows a fair amount of Kamingo speech and has negotiated trade with the Kamingo before, and, of course, there are many of them up that way. Furthermore, he alone has been as far west as the plains of Taygor, which the westward group shall in all likelihood be obliged to search. Orobec, on the other hand, is on excellent terms with our kin, the Shamoki, who lie northward. And he has spent some time among them in the villages of Sorrequom Ridge. To me, that only makes sense. But if anyone has another arrangement to suggest, I'd be happy to hear it." She looked around.

After a few moments, Homino said, "Your counsel is most sensible, Yahsi."

"Very," agreed Sheelim, the Wise-woman who was to accompany him.

"I would have suggested none other than this myself," voiced the aging Shoroba.

Tencum glanced at the other leaders, then said, "I am in substantial agreement with the plan, but there is one matter I would alter if I may."

"What is it, Tencum?" asked Dhagomi.

"Aywish should, I agree, go to the south. And Homino's skills in Mushatuck make him the obvious candidate for the east. But I desire, just as I'm sure we all do, that everyone's knowledge, situation and expertise be put to the best use. And I am afraid, for my company's sake, that my ill reputation among the Chadori would prove a great detriment and perhaps even fatal. Also, although it is true I have traveled much and far in the west, I have traveled even more often and more widely in the north and would feel more assured of my way in those lands. However, I am more than happy to give way to Orobec if he would prefer to lead the northward band. I know he has been to the Washoma in the west before but not beyond that, and I would not wish to put him in a position in which he felt impeded." He nodded politely to Orobec.

"Well," said Orobec, "I am most partial to the north, but I would not be grieved if I were issued the westward way. Only send me not to the south, for I can abide neither karrawahs nor mosquitoes."

"Fair enough," laughed Dhagomi. "What say the rest of you?"

"I still maintain that Tencum would be best suited to go westward," declared Yahsi. "Yes, he is hated by the Chadori, but so are we all. The difference, though, is that while Orobec has many talents, he has not the experience of Tencum in mastering their wiles. And a wily people they are. I think Tencum is most needed in the west and that Orobec should go the northward way."

Tencum looked at her, then at Dhagomi and said, "I shall do as you bid, O Sanno. Take Yahsi's counsel or mine as you will."

The Sanno paced a few moments, then straightened up and said, "Tencum will go to the west."

"As you will." Tencum nodded.

"Orobec will go to the north," Dhagomi continued, "Homino to the east and Aywish to the south."

"Thank you for leaving all the mosquitoes and karrawahs to me," joked Aywish, clapping Orobec on the back.

"More's the pity," murmured old Tannomet.

"The deed is done, the decisions cast," announced Dhagomi. "Now, embark, my good Sakooma Warriors and Wise. Embark to save our people and our land. And may the Hand of Hamora come back to you and to us. May the Powers be with you all: east, south, west and north."

Those gathered quickly embraced each other and their beloved Sanno and separated into their groups, as Dhagomi set off for Takula Conflux. Then, for several minutes, the four Deggas conferred with each other, after which they joined their respective bands.

Okona was busy celebrating with Kimmanic that they were in the same unit when Tencum cleared his throat. The lad looked over at him.

"I beg your pardon, Okona, but aren't you in the wrong group?" he asked.

"I was told I was in yours," the lad replied.

"You are," Yahsi hastily affirmed.

Tencum turned to her. "What is the meaning of this?"

Yahsi shrugged. "Okona has been chosen to join your group."

"By whom?"

"Mahna Shuya."

"Mahna Shu—did you really just ... But that cannot be and you know it. His voice has been veiled since long ago. Do not toy with me, Yahsi. What you mean to say is that you chose him, eh?"

"As far as a human agent is concerned, yes."

Tencum glared. "The choosing is not of the Wise-women. It was given by Baneesh to the Deggas. And anyhow, Okona, though a very fine lad, is not known for his skills in battle, but in song."

Okona, though burning in shame, tried to stay as expressionless as possible.

"This is true," agreed Yahsi, "but I am not known for my skill in battle either, and yet I have been commissioned to go on this journey. We shall be in desperate need of abilities other than those of a warrior on this mission, considering what we are up against."

"Perhaps, but this is still of no consequence," Tencum insisted. "We have been dispatched in Sacred Tens, and to add anyone to the party would make an Unlucky Eleven. And that would bring dreadful misfortune. I'm sorry, but Okona must return to Takula."

"Tencum, I had no idea about any of this," Okona said meekly. "The last thing I want is to thwart the mission. I didn't mean to cause any trouble, and I'm sure Yahsi didn't either. I've no problem with returning to the Conflux, so I'll just go back."

"You'll just stay right here, Okona," directed Yahsi, "for you've been chosen by Mahna Shuya."

"Cease profaning that name by yoking it to your own plotting," Tencum commanded. "The entire idea that Mahna Shuya had anything to do with this is obviously the highest order of nonsense."

"Even aside from the nonsense—my apologies, Yahsi—we can't take eleven people!" protested Okona. "You know what that will do to us."

The voices of the western band had now become raised enough that some of the other parties took notice and glanced over at them concernedly.

"All right," said Yahsi, putting her hands on her hips. "Dismiss what I've said about Mahna Shuya if you will. But if you two insist on being so stubborn, then *I'll* go back and you'll have your Sacred Ten."

"That you cannot do, my lady," asserted Tencum. "Every group must have both Warriors and Wise. If you return, then we will lack the necessary wisdom to guide our course."

"Well, if I'm so wise," said Yahsi, "then why do you spurn my counsel?"

Tencum gritted his teeth in obvious frustration.

"Please, Yahsi, I—" began Okona.

She took him by the shoulders and said, "Okona, you must go on this mission. You simply must. And unfortunately, now is not the time for a fuller explanation. Let it only be said at present that it really was Mahna Shuya's doing, not my own. If you will not trust him, then at least trust me." She turned to Tencum. "And if you will not allow it, then I swear to you I will make good my promise to return to Takula. You can either have Okona or both of us, but under no circumstances will I journey westward without him."

Tencum looked at the rest of his group, who were shuffling their feet and trying to avoid eye contact. At last, Tencum threw his hands in the air and sighed, "All right, Okona will come with us. And you, Yahsi. But when evil befalls us, as it without question will, then the weight of blame, both now and in the hereafter, will rightly fall on you. But I suppose I must bear some of it, since I've agreed to this madness. But at least I shall try to temper it. I must do some scouting of my own, and then we'll be off to Quinoma Stakes. Wait here. I'll be back in a while."

The southward group had already departed, as had those who were traveling east. Tencum tossed down some of his bulkier gear, though he retained his hunting satchel and an assortment of weapons, and was starting down the road leading west when Yahsi called to him, "Why Quinoma Stakes? Those are much farther north than west."

Tencum returned to the group, his annoyance evident.

"Yes, they are, for we must cross the Kanno much farther up to avoid run-ins with the Chadori."

"Why not cross at Korba Landing, just beyond Chennipot Chonka?" she asked.

"I just told you. To avoid the Chadori."

"Surely they wouldn't come this far east?"

Tencum sighed. "I suppose that shows how much you know about them."

"They wouldn't dare!"

"They would and have. And I've got to go scout right now to make sure they haven't come north of the Kanno; that's something else they've been known to do. Anyway, where would you propose we go if not Quinoma Stakes?"

"Ponca Peak," said Yahsi flatly.

Everyone in the group, even Okona, looked at her in complete incredulity.

"Ponca Peak?" exclaimed Tencum. "That mountain is death! No, I forbid it."

"But if we go to Ponca Peak, we may visit the Seer and inquire who has taken the Hand," returned Yahsi. "And it is the Seer alone who is said to speak for Mahna Shuya, fount of hidden knowledge."

"But none who seek the Seer return!" cried Okona. "Perhaps we could learn who is in possession of the Hand, but it wouldn't do us any good if we were all lost."

"I still say we go to Ponca Peak," Yahsi insisted.

Tencum walked up to her and glowered down at her firm-set face. "Woman, you have already thwarted my counsel about which direction we should go. That I relinquished to you, though I knew it would bring us to greater peril. But still you were not satisfied. I agreed to your marring of our Sacred Ten by the addition of an Unlucky Eleventh, though this will lead us to peril more certain still. But listen to me and listen well. I would not lead our band to Ponca Peak even if its Seer really did utter messages from Mahna Shuya—which, of course, I do not believe; hardly anyone else does either, as you well know. For if anything is certain, it is that that mountain is death. We go to Quinoma Stakes."

With that, he stalked off, calling over his shoulder, "I go to watch for the Chadori. When I am assured our way is clear, I will return."

Watching him depart, Okona said, "Yahsi, I wish you hadn't involved me in all this. And I know it's not polite to say it, but I agree with Tencum and everyone else. We have no business going anywhere near Ponca Peak."

"You're entitled to your own beliefs about these matters, Okona," said Yahsi, "and at the moment I've no intention to argue you out of them. The same goes for your disbelief of your selection by Mahna Shuya. As I said before, there's more to that matter, and we'll surely discuss it when the time is right. But in the meantime, I hope that, even if you don't see why I've done and said these things, at least know they're coming from a heart that cares for you, our little band and the whole of the Sakooma."

Tencum was gone for a full two hours, and of course by that time, the northbound group was long gone, and the bees were buzzing in the summer sun, as they flitted among the tall, coarse stalks of the giant yellow sunflowers.

"We are safe to go the route I wished," said Tencum, as he strode up to them and began gathering the equipment he had left behind. "We still have more than half the day to travel and should make good progress, for the weather is fair. Tonight we camp at Ohkasac Groves."

With these words, the warriors commenced collecting the supplies they had laid down while resting during Tencum's absence. And soon, all set out on the westward road.

A gust of wind blew several petals off an especially high sunflower, and they drifted lazily to the ground.

"Scattered they are," murmured Yahsi, gazing at them, "just like us, set upon the Wind and brought to our own separate paths." She smiled at Okona. "The Wind knows what it's doing," she encouraged, picking up her pace.

Chapter Four

The Unlucky Eleventh

T HAT MORNING AND EARLY afternoon, Tencum's band hiked for several hours along the Kanno. Then he had them wait under a tall row of hickories for two hours more while he did some additional scouting to ensure they were clear of any Chadori presence. After his return and message that all was sound, they continued their march. The wary Degga took a few more scouting trips throughout the day, but these were much shorter in extent. And though the party was grateful he was taking such care to guard them from mishap, none were pleased at the delays themselves.

In the late afternoon, they came to the pleasantly shaded Ohkasac Groves, a large stand of stout, old tarrameg oaks along the quiet banks of the Kanno. Here the Sakooma came in season to harvest tarrameg nuts, one of the most delectable varieties that grew in this region.

A little brook ran down to the river here, and there the party washed themselves and refilled their waterskins before making camp. For an hour, they scavenged for berries, roots and such, then sat down in a circle to enjoy their supper. By that time, evening had fallen, and most were content to lie back on the grass or against the tree boles and listen to the lighter music of the brook and the slower, deeper melody of the Kanno. However, Yahsi drew Tencum aside some distance, and not long afterward, they became engaged in a dispute.

Restless, Okona wandered down closer to the Kanno, glancing up at the pale starlight between the gaps in the foliage. Such reminded him of Anisha, for she was of the Star Clan. Glumly, he sat upon the roots of a broad tarrameg. Hearing someone approaching, he turned to see Kimmanic in the shadows.

"Is something the matter, Okona?" Kimmanic asked. "When you walked off, you just looked ..."

"I'm not the best I've ever been, I suppose," Okona admitted.

Kimmanic sat down beside him. "Did you get a chance to talk to Anisha?"

Okona nodded.

"And?"

"She was already taken the night of the feast. Tencum asked her first."

"I'm sorry to hear that," sighed Kimmanic.

"I know there's nothing to be done about it," Okona said, "so I'm just taking some time to come to terms with that. I expect a good many things may go not as we wish now that the Hand is gone. But I hope there may be a turn for the better if we can somehow get it back."

The two sat in silence for some moments. Then Okona said, "Kimmanic, about this morning—I just wanted to reiterate that I really didn't know I hadn't been chosen by Tencum and was very surprised when Yahsi told me I was. Well, I guess she never technically said that; I just assumed it. Ah, she designed her ruse well. I suppose when I entered the meeting at the Hashoka, each of the Deggas just presumed someone else had chosen me. Honestly, I feel awkward about this whole thing because I know I don't belong and wasn't supposed to have come. And I absolutely don't want to bring bad fortune on the party for being the Unlucky Eleventh, but I also don't want to let Yahsi down. She's done ever so much for me, and in many ways, I am who I am because of her."

"I understand." Kimmanic nodded. "It's a very difficult situation."

Kimmanic scratched his neck. "Actually, I've been thinking that maybe I should go back since you're facing such a dilemma."

"No, that wouldn't do at all!" Okona returned.

"But it would solve your dilemma. The group would be restored to a Sacred Ten, and you wouldn't have to disappoint Yahsi. I could even leave tomorrow morning."

"No, Kimmanic! I actually want to talk to Yahsi tonight and see if I can change her mind. I'm the one who should be going back tomorrow, and perhaps I will even if Yahsi can't be convinced. I just want to help the Sakooma in the best way I can."

Kimmanic put his hand on Okona's shoulder and said, "I would do this for you. You're my friend, after all, and—"

His words were broken by sharp cries from the camp. Tencum's voice rang out above the others, "Ah-ee-aye! Ah-ee-aye! Flee! Peril! Flee!"

Okona and Kimmanic descried through the night, beneath the groves, forms frantically running to and fro. Hearts racing, they sprang to their feet. From the darkness beyond the camp, soft, swift whistling echoed through the shadows of the tarramegs.

"Okona, get back!" urged Kimmanic. Grunting, he shoved his companion farther behind him.

There was a light thunk, and Kimmanic gasped and fell to his knees. A black-feathered arrow was protruding from his chest.

"No!" Okona choked, then turned and fled. Three arrows sped past him, one of them so close it nearly grazed his ear.

Weaving between the tarramegs, bounding like a deer in flight, Okona soon reached the Kanno and veered to the right. Over his shoulder, he spied several man-forms ducking through the shadows toward him. The lad nearly stumbled on tree roots in his crazed retreat, but he managed to steer farther away from the riverbanks into the deeper gloom of the groves.

Abruptly, from the north, there came the screeching jeer of a bluejay. Some of the pursuing shadows turned aside toward it, though three continued after Okona.

The lad exerted every last measure of his strength and burst forward through the trees. But from the shade beneath a huge trunk behind him came a sharply hissed, "Okona!" He turned and saw a small form sitting there. Unthinking, he ran to it.

Squinting, he whispered in disbelief, "Anisha? How did you know it was me?"

"No one else runs the way you do," she replied. "Now, get down here." Grunting, she dragged him behind the trunk.

"Who are they?" she asked, motioning her head in the direction from which Okona had come.

"No idea," he replied, "but this isn't a great time to talk about it. They'll be here any moment!"

Anisha nodded, and they quieted themselves to the utmost.

As two searchers passed them some distance farther inland, they held their breath and marked, with a sudden chill, that these men moved with a canniness not quite human.

Thinking at last that all the enemies had passed, Okona was about to stir when one of the men, naked save a short loincloth, appeared from their right, only feet away. Anisha's arm flew in front of Okona, launching a round stone, which struck the side of the man's head. With horrible speed, he turned and leapt toward them, but Okona had by then pulled his dagger from his side and turned it up toward their assailant. The dagger pierced his chest, and Anisha and Okona stood to battle him. Strangely, the man did not cry out, only made a slight croak deep in his throat. Okona seized the man's bow and flung it some distance away, while Anisha threw all her weight against him, but to no avail, for his balance was impeccable. Okona managed to wrest his dagger out of the man's bosom, but quickly pulled away, grabbing Anisha's arm as he fled, for he sensed a prolonged struggle with this individual would not end in their favor. If nothing else, he was deterred by the lurid glint in the man's eyes; Okona had seen it in the others' as well.

"This way!" Anisha panted, taking his hand and guiding him toward the river.

Soon, Okona knew why she had insisted they flee thither, for he spotted a canoe upon the Kanno's banks. Anisha sprang into the canoe, seizing a paddle, as Okona pushed the vessel out into the water and jumped in behind her. He too took up a paddle, and within moments, they were cutting across the wide Kanno toward its southern banks.

Anisha looked back worriedly at the north shore and cried, "He's coming, Okona!" Furiously, they paddled onward, with Okona looking back as well, both staring at the grim figure readying his bow on the bank. Several arrows hurtled toward them, but they were just far enough out that they only rattled against the back of the canoe. And then, to their great relief, the man collapsed to the ground.

Soon, the pair reached the other bank, hopped out of the craft and pulled it onto the shore, then dashed out of the moonlight and under the shadows of the trees. Now that they were out of immediate danger, Okona noticed the girl's traveling attire; her feet were bare, but she was garbed in a well-fitting, simply-patterned sleeveless dress of deerskin that hung just above her knees.

Still wanting for breath, Okona stammered, "N-n-now, Anisha, just suppose you tell me what you're doing here."

The girl mopped her drenched forehead, replying, "Of course, this isn't the best time for a full explanation, but I'll tell you what I can in short. I came looking for you. You and Tencum."

"Why?"

Catching her breath, Anisha explained, "This morning, I was up very early and had gone down to the Kanno near Takula to make an offering to its waters, asking for success for those assigned to retrieve the Hand, when I saw a strange thing. A fox and a turtle were resting on the bank. Suddenly, there was a howling of wolves, and both creatures went out into the water. Fearing for myself, I hid, and not long afterward, a great pack of wolves came to the shore and started swimming after the fox and turtle. Then, things became stranger still. A glowing starfly appeared, flew out to the fox and turtle, then back to the shore. And you'll never guess what happened then! The wolves turned and clambered out of the water after the starfly, but it escaped into the trees, and there its little blue light was hidden."

"But as for myself," she went on, "one of the wolves was stalking toward me, so I had to flee before I could see what became of the fox and turtle. Anyway, I returned to Takula Conflux and thought about what I'd seen. I concluded it must be an omen."

"An omen?"

"Yes. I am of the Star Clan, as you know, and you are of the Turtle Clan. Tencum, of course, is of the Fox Clan. We have no clan of wolves, I know, but they were obviously enemies. So the meaning was this: enemies would take you and Tencum by the Kanno if I did not intervene, for it was only when the starfly came that the wolves were turned. I knew from this sign given to me by the Powers that I must seek you and Tencum out if you were to be saved. So when my father returned to the Conflux, I asked him which party had gone which way. He told me Tencum's group had gone west, and I assumed from the omens I had witnessed by the river that you must be with him. I took some time to make preparations for my journey, then left the Conflux, telling the sentries only that I was on an errand for my father and saying nothing to any other. I came to Korba Landing and told the boat-keepers there the same: that I was on my father's business. They lent me a canoe, and I took it upriver, watching for your camp, for I knew, again from the omens I had seen, that you must be near the Kanno. Well, I heard cries from the shore, and that's when I landed. And you know the rest."

Okona shook his head in amazement. "Anisha, I really do appreciate you coming after us, but you must go back to your father! It wasn't right for you to sneak off like that, and I am grieved that you placed yourself in such great danger, even for our sakes."

"Be grieved then, but the danger is not over yet, for I must go back and try to save Tencum. I would not that the Fox perish if aught may yet be done. And I do feel bad about departing without telling my father, but he would not have allowed me to leave if I had asked, and then I fear you and Tencum would have been lost."

Okona frowned. "I understand why you want to return to the north bank, but I do not think it wise. Yet I guess, knowing you, that you will not be dissuaded, so at least let me come with you."

"If you wish," returned Anisha, and they got back in the canoe.

Quietly, they paddled back to the other shore, all the while watching for lurkers on the banks. To their relief, they reached Ohkasac Groves in safety, pulled the craft onto the grass and crept under the spreading trees. Okona led Anisha back toward their camp, but when they were still thirty yards distant, they slipped behind a tree, for many figures were standing there, signing to each other with their hands. All of them were clad only in loincloths and all were mute. With dismay, Okona sighted a number of bodies laid out upon the ground. "One, two, three, four, five, six, seven, eight, nine," he counted internally, swallowing hard.

Okona glanced to both right and left and saw more figures still, all silent and signing to each other.

"Only one more of our party lives," whispered Okona. "Perhaps it is Tencum. But there are too many of them, Anisha. I'm afraid there's nothing we can do. Staying here will only get us killed."

Suddenly, the gentle pluck of a harp came from the direction of the river. Okona immediately recognized the tune.

"That's Yahsi," he gasped. "And the song is 'Flee to the River.' Let us heed her warning!" Okona grabbed Anisha's hand, and together they bolted for the Kanno. But the mute warriors came in hot pursuit, having heard the youths' flight.

Yahsi was in the fore of the canoe when they reached the bank, stowing her harp in its bag. Anisha leapt into the midsection and started paddling, while Okona pushed the canoe into the Kanno's dark waters and hopped into the aft. He grabbed his paddle once again, and with his fierce, swift strokes, the canoe darted toward the south shore.

"I could have strangled you two for coming back here," muttered Yahsi, "but I was too far off to call to you safely, and by the time I reached the spot where you pulled ashore, I couldn't see where you'd gone. I thought maybe the song would draw you, and fortunately, I was right."

All of a sudden, she held up her harp bag to shield her face, and only just in time, for an arrow pierced the thick leather and thudded into the harp inside. "Take care for yourselves!" she cried. "Use the pack!"

Okona felt in the hull and lifted up a large satchel, which he used to thwart an arrow that otherwise would have gone into his bosom. "Is this mine?" he asked, astonished.

"Yes, I was able to grab it on my way back through the camp," explained Yahsi.

With the pack, Okona quickly blocked several more arrows, some of which were aimed at Anisha. But the girl stoutly paddled on, and soon they were out of range of the bowmen. Okona shivered as he saw them congregated on the shore, exchanging more signs with their hands before melting back into the shadows of Ohkasac Groves.

Shortly, the three fugitives were pulling the canoe onto the south bank and unloading all their possessions, which included a pack and waterskin Anisha had brought. After concealing the vessel, they hurried into the forest, bearing south by southwest. For they hoped to get some distance from the Kanno during the midnight hours and make it as difficult as they might for their enemies to track them when day came.

With Yahsi leading the way, they wandered about in the night-covered woodlands, all the while mourning their company and striving with the grief that weighed upon their hearts. Sometimes they tramped in circles or odd loops, but always they kept their general course. In the latter portion of the night, they finally halted in an open hickory forest and laid down upon the grass, exhausted in flesh and broken in spirit, but hoping that the Powers would keep them from the silent warriors while they slept.

When first light came, Okona rose and stretched. Yahsi was standing a ways off, gazing to the northwest.

He walked over to her and yawned. "Good morning, Yahsi."

"Good morning, Okona. Interesting, isn't it, that Anisha has joined us?"

"Very. And I suppose it's best if she tells you how and why herself. It's a strange tale, and I don't know that I could do it justice."

Okona, too, stared northwestward.

"About last night," he said, "I'm afraid all this happened because I'm the Unlucky Eleventh. Tencum warned that evil would come, and I knew such in my heart as well. And now, alas, it has proved true, and he and the others have lost their lives on my account. For I counted nine slain, laid in the camp by our foes."

"Do you really believe all that was your fault, Okona?" Yahsi asked, turning to him.

"Don't you?"

"Perhaps the attack did happen because of the Unlucky Eleventh," she mused. "But who's to say it wasn't someone else? All I know is that you were meant to come on this journey."

Just then, Anisha spoke from behind. "A sad morning this is. And the day broods ill if I read it aright, for the sun rises red. But might we return to Ohkasac Groves? Might we at least give our company a proper burial?"

"To return there would be vanity, I'm afraid," said Yahsi, turning to the weary girl. "Much too dangerous. Considering who was attacking, it's no surprise all our comrades were lost. But it's nothing short of a wild wonder that we have survived ourselves."

"Yes, I suppose the Chadori do have a reputation for brutal efficiency," Okona sighed.

"The Chadori?" Yahsi stared at him. "Those were no Chadori! Their garb, their gait, the blank look in their eyes; these all point to one thing."

"But if these were not Chadori, then who were they?"

Yahsi's face darkened. "The Jaggo."

"The Jaggo?" gasped Anisha.

"I thought they were only bogeys to frighten children from wandering off alone!" Okona declared.

"Didn't you notice? Not one of them spoke a word," said Yahsi.

Okona and Anisha looked at each other in dismay.

"So is all of it true, then?" Anisha asked. "The wordless men of the gray and tangled Underbrakes really stalk abroad? Do they really dine upon manflesh? Is it true they are guided as if by one mind? And that they can die but do not feel pain? And they speak with their hands and fire alone?"

"Why shouldn't it be true?" returned Yahsi. "Sometimes folk tell stories without foundation, yes. But magic is much alive in our world, and the bad magic, unfortunately, seems more widespread than the good. And to be sure, there is some uncouth magic laid on them. Moreover, did you not see how these warriors carried themselves? Jaggo they were, sure enough."

"But why have they emerged from the world beneath? And why did they seek out our westbound warriors?" Anisha inquired. "Has it not been many a year since anyone claimed to have seen them?"

"Some decades," said Yahsi. "But as to why they took an interest in our party, perhaps your guess is as good as mine. But I've a hunch the great magic in use of late, with the storm and so forth, has waked them."

"But if those really were the Jaggo, then how did you escape them?" asked Okona. "You were much nearer to the point of attack than I was."

"I had just finished debating with Tencum about our route, and he returned to the camp. Almost immediately, I heard his warning cry and fled. Then, when I saw you running through the trees with those warriors behind you, I gave out a jay whistle to lead them farther from the river and perhaps lessen your peril."

"A fitting call from one of the Jay Clan." Okona smiled. "I thank you."

"It was the least I could do. But as soon as they turned, I hurried back to the camp. It takes more than five Jaggo to catch Yahsi, though ten might have done the trick. Sadly, at our circle, many were already dead; I did not stop to count. But I grabbed your items and my own, for last I saw you, you had not perished, and I hoped that we might be reunited. I went down to the Kanno and followed the bank in the direction you had gone. When I spied you in the canoe coming back across the river, I hastened to meet you, but was not swift enough. And since I did not wish for you or whomever was with you to be taken, I summoned you with song and hoped you would be wise enough to answer the call."

"I never cease to be amazed by you." Okona shook his head.

"But what are we to do now?" asked Anisha. "I would seek to return to my father, for I am ashamed to say I left without his permission. But if the Jaggo are after us, that may well be impossible now. For they know we have come south of the Kanno and are sure to track us. And all the stories regard them as practically peerless in that task."

"Yes, but it is no mean task to follow a trail through the midst of the night, especially one such as we made," said Yahsi. "For one might well go astray. I'll grant that the Jaggo have some magic about them, but unless they are aided by the more terrible of the Powers, I do not think that even with their lesser magic they could have followed us through the dark. And, as you see, they have not caught up to us yet. I think they will have begun their search not long ago, though, for daylight has come. So we must start immediately."

"But if the stories be true, we cannot outrun them, be the distance long or short," said Okona. "Nor will hiding avail us, for they are crafty as a writhing wolmac."

"You are right on both accounts," said Yahsi, as the three went to gather up all their gear. "There's only one thing to be done. We make for Ponca Peak. For unless they have no fear at all—and that I do not believe, for the wicked always fear something—they will not set foot upon that mountain."

"But Yahsi, how can *we* set foot there?" asked Anisha, aghast. She looked up through an opening in the trees at Ponca's distant, rocky summit, upon which a dense fog was descending. "That mountain is drenched in death!"

"And though the Jaggo may fear something, how do you know they will dread that mountain in particular?" asked Okona.

"Any within a hundred miles of the Kanno fear it," returned Yahsi, "and as for us, if it is a choice between deaths, one certain and the other not so, I would rather risk the mountain."

"Yahsi, you are known for your wisdom," said Anisha. "Surely this is a jest!"

The old woman's face remained firm.

"But the mountain is just as certain death as the Jaggo, if not more so," objected Okona.

"Yet it may be our best means of finding out where we may find the Hand of Hamora," returned Yahsi. "And that is why our band was dispatched, is it not? Remember, all are in agreement that a seer resides there, and what use is a seer who cannot be consulted? It must be possible to survive the mountain if it is possible to consult the Seer."

"It is not said that the Seer cannot be consulted, only that those who consult the Seer cannot return to our world," replied Okona.

"And perhaps we shall not," said Yahsi, walking off to the northwest through the hickory trees. The others glanced at each other grimly, then followed after her in the red morning light.

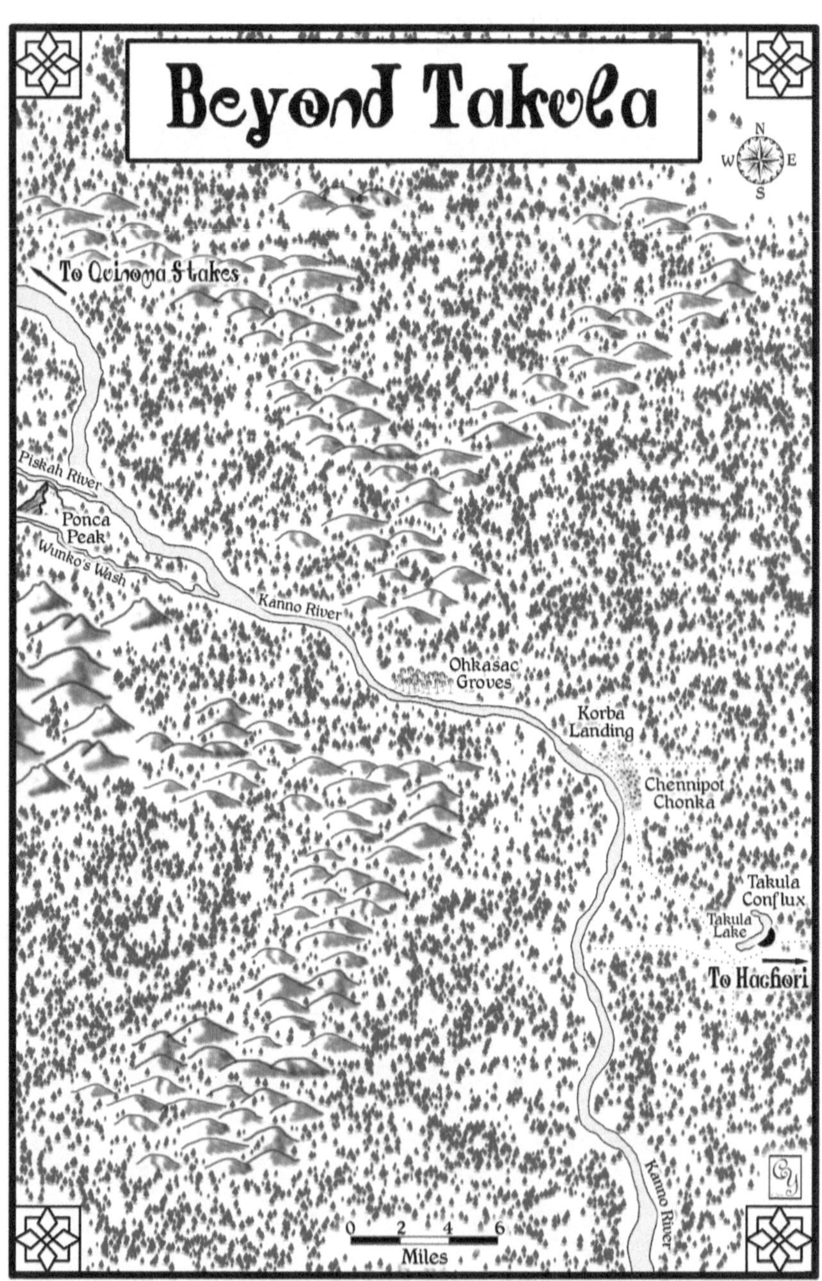

Beyond Takula
N
W E
S
To Quinona Stakes
Piskah River
Ponca Peak
Wunko's Wash
Kanno River
Ohkasac Groves
Korba Landing
Chennipot Chonka
Takula Conflux
Takula Lake
To Hachori
Kanno River
0 2 4 6
Miles

Chapter Five

Into the Thunderhead

THE LOW HILLS TO the southeast of Ponca Peak, through which the trio was treading, were swathed in heavy forest, for which they were quite thankful, as it made one difficult to be spied from a distance. But as Ponca Peak was so much higher than everything around it, rising like a great pyramid a thousand feet from the lands below, they could see it from many points along their route that morning. And, more concernedly (as Okona thought), it could see them. Its sharp, bare summit seemed imbued with senses of its own, and he had a disturbing notion the mountain was watching, with great malevolence, their ill-advised approach. And when the companions came close enough, he imagined, it would be sure to smite them for their folly.

Okona's worries were certainly not helped by the slow advent of gray rain clouds, rising out of the hills of the Washoma, the region to the northwest, to wrap themselves around the upper, pine-clad slopes of the mountain. At first, it looked as if they were only bearing a cold drizzle, but after a while, distant rumbles rolled through the hills, and a more sinister shade tinted the clouds. Then Okona realized, with sinking heart, that these were the angry heralds of none other than Kannikos, the Storm-singer.

"Yahsi, if you intended to lead us to Ponca Peak all along," the lad began after a particularly ominous boom, "why didn't you come more in this direction last night instead of directing us so far to the south?"

"Two reasons," Yahsi called back, as she continued swiftly up the hill they were traversing. "One was that I hadn't quite made up my mind yet. But secondly, and perhaps more importantly, as I'm sure you've heard, Ponca Peak is surrounded by a ring of dangerous spirits at night. I may be foolish enough to dare the summit in the day, but even I could not have been persuaded to near it without the sun at hand."

"Well, it doesn't look as if he'll be at hand much longer, what with these clouds moving in," Anisha glumly remarked, trailing along behind Okona.

"All the more reason for us to hurry," Yahsi advised.

"But the storm has nearly already overtaken the mountain," Okona pointed out.

"I don't mean to be dismissive of a very real problem, Okona," said Yahsi, "but that is presently not the greatest of our troubles. Come, let us hasten! The morning wanes."

As Yahsi drew ever farther ahead of the lagging Okona and Anisha, the latter muttered, "These Jaggo have really run things afoul for us."

"To say the least," the lad concurred.

"Tencum often urged my father to take more lands along the Kanno and in other directions too. He said it would help our people prosper more than we already have but would also provide us with a greater margin for defense. But my father didn't want to involve the Sakooma in any such conflict if he could help it, so he always forbade him to seize more territory. But presently I'm wishing he had listened to Tencum, for if these lands were under our sway, our warriors might have been able to stop the Jaggo at a border farther out. But already we are miles beyond help. And there is no chance the three of us alone will be able to stand against the Jaggo if they come upon us."

"Let us hope, then, that Yahsi is correct and the mountain itself may deter them," said Okona. "I myself have many doubts about this plan, but Yahsi's nearly always right about things. And at the moment, that's all I've got to go on."

"Oh, I do wish we'd been able to save Tencum," sighed Anisha. "We are badly in need of a warrior right now. And I can't help wondering how he would have advised us."

Okona's heart stung at the longing in her voice, but he chided himself, "He was her betrothed after all, and he was a great warrior. Besides, he perished and you did not, so do not envy him. Furthermore, she's available, as it were, once again, but probably best not to say anything about that yet. Too soon ..." But what actually came out of his mouth after these moments of reflection was, "I don't think even Tencum, great warrior though he was, could fight off all the Jaggo. And I don't know what he would counsel us, but I can tell you he'd be completely against going to Ponca Peak, for he and Yahsi quarreled about that very matter yesterday."

Waiting for Anisha to catch up to him, he stopped her, and they both stood for a moment. His voice softening, he said, "I haven't had a chance to properly say this yet, Anisha, but I'm terribly sorry about what happened to Tencum last night, both for your sake and that of the Sakooma. His death has left us a much poorer people."

"Much poorer," agreed Anisha. "And we are poorer still with the loss of all the others."

A short whistle brought them to attention. Yahsi was beckoning forcefully at the top of the slope.

"I suppose we'd better be hurrying along," said Okona, and they hustled after the old woman.

All told, the threesome covered three leagues that morning and a bit more, all without a sign of the Jaggo, and at last, they drew near to the very foot of the mountain. Oddly enough, the storm had not advanced, but only brooded over the peak, as if some command had been given from on high to engulf the mountain alone. The heavens could hardly have given a clearer sign of unwelcome.

"Only a short way more," Yahsi puffed, as they pressed up a forested slope.

Abruptly, Anisha cried out, "They've come! Ah-ee-aye! The Silent Walkers!" Over her shoulder, she had just spotted numerous pairs of dark forms jogging through the widely spaced trees.

"To the peak!" Yahsi urged, and they all sprang forward. Simultaneously, the forms below began racing toward them.

Anisha barreled ahead, but Okona paced himself to match Yahsi's stride and readied his bow, hoping that when the Jaggo came within range, he might at least dispense with a few of them before they swarmed upon them. And perhaps, he thought, Yahsi would have just enough time to escape.

Then, without warning, Anisha shrieked and stumbled. But she immediately gathered herself and continued pounding ahead. Only moments later, Okona and Yahsi came to the spot where the girl had hollered, and they cried out as well. For it was as if they had passed through a wide draft of biting, icy air. Okona caught his breath and began running forward again, though his hair stood on end and he was beset by a lingering chill. As he looked back, the air shimmered, as if for a moment he were seeing all the forest beyond through a reflection in a rippling pool. There was no doubt about it. They had come through *something*; whether truly invisible or no, he could not tell, but whatever it was, it had unsettled him to his core.

Anisha slowed a bit, and the others caught up to her. Then all three stopped to look back down the slope. The Jaggo had also halted but behind where the fugitives had felt the bizarre shock of cold. They were watching them with glinting eyes, but their bows were lowered, and they were slowly backing away.

"Did I not tell you they would not tread upon the mountain?" Yahsi panted.

"But what have we done?" Anisha asked, horror-struck, as she looked down at her tingling hands. "We have crossed into that which is forbidden. Do you not feel it?"

"We were not meant to come here," Okona murmured, looking up toward the storm-menaced summit.

Within moments, a fierce rain began pelting them, for the clouds over the mountain were multiplying and spreading. But those over the summit proper were as dark and as monstrous as ever, losing none of their potency for all the wrath they had lent to the furor spawning from them.

"We cannot climb the mountain in this storm," cried Anisha, brushing her soaked, black hair from her eyes.

"This is no storm of the world," said Yahsi. "Surely you know that. It is a terror to stay the unworthy and the timid. If we are to speak with the Seer, it will be during this storm or not at all. So let us get on with our business. Besides, the less time we spend here, the better. I do not think any one of us should wish to be caught here at nightfall."

"This storm is likely just as bad, if not worse, than whatever the night may bring!" shouted an increasingly drenched Okona over the rising wind. "And anyway, how are we to leave the mountain even if we do survive the storm? For the Jaggo have only to watch and wait for us to come down."

"Let us first see that we make it back alive," counseled Yahsi. "There's no sense worrying about it now. And anyway, we've committed to this already, and storm or no storm, we must seek the summit, for that is where the Seer is said to reside."

"You know, you're crazy, Yahsi," Okona huffed. "But if you're determined to go on, I'll go with you."

Yahsi nodded stoutly and began wending her way up the wooded slope, with Okona not far behind. Anisha shook her head in exasperation but rushed up behind Okona nonetheless.

For the better part of an hour, they made their way up through the thundering woods, which grew steeper all the while and were increasingly populated by lengths of large stones upon which they were forced to scramble in order to proceed. At many places, it was all they could do to stand upright, so great was the incline toward

Ponca's looming apex. The rain came down ever harder till it almost took their breath away, but they were grateful the trees provided at least some protection from the torrent. However, eventually, the woods came to an end, abandoning the three Sakooma at the foot of a naked stretch of jumbled sandstone boulders. Nothing more stood between stone and the black sky. And here there was no shield from the awesome deathbolts of the stormheads, the sky-rending bursts of crooked, crackling fire. Here, the whole face of the mountain shook every time thunder roared from the blackened depths of the storm.

"I'm sorry, but nothing in all this world could induce me to go farther. I will not risk the summit," Anisha swore, as she laid her rock-roughened hands upon a great stone at the base of the boulder field.

With sudden ferocity, lightning bit the slope only a furlong away, and the crack of stones echoed across the mountain.

"See! It is death!" she warned, white-faced, and fell back against a pine.

"The Seer is near!" Yahsi sang triumphantly, gesturing toward the raging gloom of the peak. "But if you will not go forward with me, I must go alone. If I survive, I will meet you on the far side of the summit, the mirror of this spot. Wait for me there! But if the day grows late and I have not yet come, see to it that you are off the mountain before night falls." She removed all her gear and laid it under the edge of the trees, then scrambled into the boulder field.

Okona looked after her, then at Anisha, then at Yahsi once again. The lightning hissed and the thunder rumbled. The rain poured down and the wind wailed. Then, with sudden resolution, Okona flung his equipment beneath the trees and said, "Anisha, I must follow her. Do what you will, and I will think no less of you for it, but somehow, I must see that Seer. I was chosen to seek the Hand of Hamora, after all, and seeing as our whole band was lost, it falls to Yahsi and I alone of the westward-sent to continue the mission. She is doing what she can to that end, and I must as well. I'll see you on the west face—I hope." And with that, he too set off into the boulder field.

Anisha raised her hand in farewell. Then her gaze fell to the ground, as she whispered a plea to the Powers.

It was not long before Okona caught up to Yahsi, and together they pressed on toward the forbidding ridge towering high above them. Now came the real climb, for the talus on this last ascent, a terrifying third of a mile, was stacked so steeply that they were forced to proceed on their hands and knees. Every instant they feared death from above, and on many occasions, they nearly tumbled down the slope from sliding on the rough, wet stones. The wind howled like a hundred wolves, casting rain into their eyes, so it was often necessary to close them and carry on in blindness. The thunder waxed louder and louder all the while, and they seemed now to be fighting their way through the storm cloud itself.

But at last, Okona glanced up through the sheets of driving rain and nearly impenetrable blackness and spied where the mount's mighty crown actually pierced the heavens. They were only a little more than four tens of yards from the top of Ponca Peak!

As Okona drew a long, cold breath and steadied himself for his final push, from the very heart of the storm, a shaft of white fire sprang forth and blasted into the mountain to his right. Both he and Yahsi were flung off the boulders to which they were clinging and onto the stones just below. There was a crunching and splitting of stones, and many smaller rocks rattled down the mountainside. But as Okona sat up, he was astonished to see that where the lightning had struck, there was a clear opening in the mountain, from which a gray smoke, nearly invisible in the downpour, issued.

"Look!" Yahsi cried. "A door! A door in the mountain!"

Hurriedly, they made their way over to it, and sure enough, there was a gaping entrance in the rock. All the boulders had been cleared, seemingly obliterated, and a narrow cave, only tall enough for Okona to stand in, vanished into darkness before them. Breathing heavily, they stepped inside the opening.

"This is undoubtedly the way to the Seer!" Yahsi gasped. "Our desire for an audience has been granted."

Though relieved to be out of the rain, Okona felt the greatest dread he had since first setting foot on the mountain.

"I followed you here against my better senses, but this I will not do," he breathed. "There is something truly terrible in there, worse than everything this storm has thrown at us."

Yahsi peered into the murk. "I do believe you're right. And do not think that I am not just as afraid of it as you are. Ah, that I am, Okona. That I am. Anisha could only come to the foot of the field of stones. I do not fault her. And if you cannot enter this cave, I will not fault you. But fear or no, I must see the Seer, even if you will not. A turtle's got to stick its neck out, after all."

She marched forward into the blackness.

Okona stood on the brink for several moments, with the thunder's pulse in the rock beneath his bare feet. He glanced at the outside world, then put his hands on the walls of the cave, took a deep breath and stepped quickly after Yahsi.

CHAPTER SIX

THE PERIL OF PONCA PEAK

OKONA HURRIED FORWARD TO Yahsi's dim shape treading before him. After passing down the rough tunnel for some length, the duo came to a stone stair leading down into further blackness. Using the bare illumination from the mountain's exterior, they carefully stepped down stair after stair until the passage flattened out again. Here, Yahsi, who was still in front, placed her hands before her and pushed. There was a creak, and dim, red light flooded the stair.

They went past a thick, timeworn wooden door carved with arcane symbols and into a long tunnel lit by flickering oil lamps resting on high shelves on the walls, which bore many cryptic glyphs. At the end of this was a doorway, hung with two deerskin curtains. Trembling, they passed down the corridor and pushed through them. Beyond was a large chamber, which they only surveyed for a moment before the deerskins flapped shut. Now they found themselves in utter darkness, alone in the very heart of the mountain.

Okona and Yahsi held their breath, not daring to move. Then, with a quiet hiss, many candles sprang alight. These candles, set in ancient sconces, lined the walls of the room, which was a twelve-sided, domed chamber, sixty feet across, in the midst of which stood four great, square pillars. These pillars were arranged in a square and topped by thick, square lintel-stones, laid so as to form a square that one must pass underneath to enter the area marked off by the pillars. From the apex of the chamber's dome, a large, unlit brazier was hanging.

A sudden wind filled the room, and all the candles went out at once, only to light again a moment later. This time, the brazier above roared into flame as well, then quickly died to a steady crackle. But now, directly beneath the brazier, in the center of the pillars, stood a stooped figure, half in shadow, half in low firelight. The figure's head was hooded with a blanket, which also covered his shoulders, but his chest was bare. A tattered loincloth was wrapped around his waist, and in his hand was a straight, slender staff.

Okona froze and stared at the figure, wide-eyed.

"Are there no prophets among the Sakooma?" a low voice croaked from within the hood, eerily echoing throughout the chamber. "Was there none other who would speak for Mahna Shuya? Why have you come through such peril to seek my voice? For your peril was and is even greater than you know."

Yahsi, slightly tremulous, replied, "We accord an audience with you worth such peril. And though we know we've come out of our depth, we will admit we do not know how far. Very likely if we did, we would not have come. But here we are nonetheless."

She swallowed and continued, "And as to why we have sought you out and not our own diviners, even he who is greatest among us knew not the answers we desire. There were those who counseled against coming to you, but we have pursued it anyhow, for our people are in grave danger, and it is on their behalf we have come."

The voice spoke again from within the hood, "It is partly because of your concern for your people that the way has been opened to you, a way which has been shut to many others. But also, and more importantly, you recognized me as a mouthpiece of truth, unlike the others who profess to understand mysteries. And the proof of your belief lies in this: you braved death for the cause of obtaining this treasure. For I know that you, O Yahsi, Master Song-maker, have come not only to inquire about the Hand of Hamora, but also something of greater import still, something for which you have long wished to seek me out."

Okona was stunned. He looked at Yahsi, then said to the shadowed figure before them, "You know all about us, then? And you know of the Hand of Hamora?"

"Yes, for there has been some talk of it among my people in this land," was the reply.

"Your people?" the lad queried.

"You are of one kind, we another. But yes, I have a people."

Rather surprised to find himself speaking so freely, but deciding he must have borrowed his boldness from Yahsi, Okona pressed on. "Please, sir, can you tell us where we may find the Hand of Hamora? For that is why we have come. Well, besides, whatever it is that Yahsi has come to ask you about ..."

"Of which Hand do you speak? The Greater or the Lesser?" The figure turned his head toward the lad.

"I'm afraid I don't understand." Okona wrinkled his brow. "I know Hamora had two hands, but why would anyone look for his left hand? For it was turned to mere ash."

"Yes, some years ago now. And his other, as you know, was changed into crystal and given some measure of power. But that Hand is the Lesser. The Greater Hand I speak of is not something that can be held or thieved by the hands of men. And it is not of Hamora the man, but of Hamora itself—you know the meaning of the word: blessing—and it comes from beyond this world."

"I suppose we seek both," concluded Okona after a moment's thought, "for in finding the lesser, we hope to obtain the greater."

"Do you really believe the Lesser will bring you the Greater, Okona Song-maker?" the voice asked, for the first time with seeming emotion, the faintest hint of sorrow.

"Certainly," Okona replied, "for that is what our people are depending on. But we don't know where it lies—east, south, west or north, which is the reason we have come to you."

The figure took a step toward them, which caused them to draw back. Then he declared, "Very well, if it is this Lesser Hand, the Hand of crystal, that you desire, then you must seek in the Kannitaw, the mountains of the north; there you shall find it." He gestured leftward with his staff. Then he directed, "Come toward me, Okona, but do not pass the pillars."

Okona gulped and followed his instructions.

The figure took several steps toward Okona, so that they only stood a few paces apart, and said, so quietly that the lad almost heard the echo of his voice more than the voice itself, "There is a Terror there whose name you have been told, and you shall have to enter its abode. Heed well—avert the hellish rite therein at all costs. Another way you might seek, a way still difficult but seemingly more sensible, but you must turn aside from it and pass into that black realm, hid from Sun and Sky, or all shall be in vain. But take heart; you will not be alone."

"Stretch out your hand," he said, and the lad obeyed.

The figure reached beneath his blanket and drew out an object, which he laid in Okona's palm. It was a twelve-sided, amber-hued shaft of crystal, with one end roughly rounded and the other sharpened to a point. It was small enough that he could close his fingers upon it but thick enough that it comfortably filled his fist. Its honed end protruded beyond his closed fingers and glinted in the dance of flames from above.

"This, O Okona, is a shard of sunfire, taken from the shining peaks in the Over-lands," said the Seer. "You may use it once and once alone, ere it passes again into the Air from which it came. Use it well. And know this: it will only prove of any real use when you truly understand from whence all good things come."

Okona slowly turned it over in his hands. "But what do I do with it?"

"That you will know when the time comes," returned the Seer. "In the meantime, continue to seek. As long as one has life, he may do so, ere Night is fully upon him. If there is naught else left to you and no other way out, perhaps you will be driven to reach up. Reach up! Reach even through rock and stone. And when words fail, do the best you can without them. But if help comes to you, it will not be because you have so done, but because Another has reached down."

Okona, pondering this strange counsel, placed the shard into his pocket and took several steps back, so he was again by Yahsi's side, and the Seer stepped backward to the center of the square of pillars.

Reaching up with both hands to grasp his hood, the Seer inquired, "Tell me, would either of you look upon my face?"

After a moment's hesitation, Yahsi declared, "I will look."

Okona, fearing the Seer might remove the hood immediately, shielded his eyes.

"Very well, Yahsi. You shall see my face. And we shall also speak of that greater matter for which you have come. But Okona, you who rightly fear to look upon me, you must depart."

"Yes, sir," the lad murmured, then turned to go back through the deerskin curtains. But, to his great alarm, they weren't there. A worn stone wall had taken their place.

"How do I—"

The chamber's lights were suddenly extinguished, then leapt ablaze again. Okona turned to see, across the room, a doorway covered by the pelt of an elk.

"Take care not to cross the pillars," the man warned.

Okona walked around the mysterious columns, keeping a healthy distance from them, and so came to the door on the far side.

Suddenly, the hollow echoes of the Seer's voice filled the room.

"This quest will change your life forever, Okona. But apart from magic from the Over-lands, it will not save it."

"What do you mean?" asked the lad, pivoting to face the mystic.

The Seer lowered his hands from his hood, turned slowly to face him and replied, "Your tale will end in nothing but death unless you find what you are not seeking."

Deeply unsettled, Okona could hardly think what to reply. Finally, he stammered, "B-but how can I find something I'm not even looking for?"

"Sometimes you find more than you seek," the Seer replied cryptically, and the lad could almost swear his eyes shimmered beneath his hood.

The Seer turned around once more, and Okona did as well after imparting a last, wary look to Yahsi. Then he pushed aside the elkskin and exited the chamber.

The passage before him was a mirror of the one through which he had entered, but as he neared the end of it, he halted at the sound of a faint, muffled music coming from the chamber he had just departed. It was the limpid plucking of a harp, and the tune was that of the ode he had played with Yahsi at the feast only three days ago. But he was greatly puzzled, for Yahsi had left her harp down on the mountainside, and he knew her playing well, yet something about this performance was different. It was both more beautiful and more tragic at once, and it quickened his heart. The music, soft though it was, took a powerful hold of him, and he longed to return to the chamber. But fear rose stronger still, fear of he knew not what, and he turned away from the ode's haunting call.

Walking swiftly forward, he pushed open an old wooden door at the end of the passage and hastened up a black stair into a tunnel that opened onto the mountainside. Here, the rain still poured down, but the wind was quieter and the thunder much more distant.

Downslope to the west, a small figure was standing where the line of trees began. "Anisha," Okona murmured, and began clambering down the maze of strewn boulders toward her. This face of the mountain proved to be much more manageable than the eastern one and was more like a crooked stair than an unrelenting rise of steeply stacked boulders. Also, the lad felt much braver traversing it, for he was inclined to believe that the greatest danger had already passed.

When Okona reached the girl, he was glad to see she had ported all of their items with her. "Oh, I'm sorry. I didn't even think about you having to carry all our equipment. But thank you so much for bringing it. And you have Yahsi's harp too!"

"It wasn't an easy task, nor an agreeable one," she returned. "Still, I'm glad to have taken that over what you did. I have to ask, though, where's Yahsi? And did you see the Seer?"

Okona frowned. "Yes. And no. I saw all of him I cared to. Yahsi stayed to see more. I hope she's all right."

Anisha pointed toward the summit. "Ah, there she is now!"

Sure enough, Yahsi had emerged from the cave and was picking her way down the tumbled stair toward them.

In a while, she reached them, and, leaning against a scraggly pine, her face ashen, she panted, "Alas! I have seen the true peril of Ponca Peak. It is enough. Let us leave this place."

Both the youths had many queries, but something in her voice told them now was not the time.

The three of them walked as quickly as they might in safety down the slippery stones through the forest. When they came to where earth supplanted stone, they were much gladdened, and Yahsi guided them toward the west, surmising this would be the least likely direction for the Jaggo to be waiting.

"Of course, they might have spread out around the whole mountain, but there certainly aren't enough of them to cover all of it," she remarked.

Eventually, they came to the foot of the mountain, and when they again crossed its unseen boundary, there was another frightening blast of cold air followed by a queer feeling of moisture upon their skin, though this quickly dissipated. The storm's fervor seemed to be spent now that they had left the peak, and the rain deadened to a sprinkle. But still the day was gray and grim.

They had only been walking for several minutes beyond the peak's boundary when the piercing call of an eagle rang out through the dripping forest. They looked in the direction from whence it had come and saw several tens of Jaggo pacing toward them, studying the ground.

"Get down!" hissed Yahsi, and they crouched behind nearby trees.

"We're done for at last!" choked Anisha.

"After all this!" Okona moaned.

"No!" Yahsi gritted her teeth. "There's got to be a way to escape. We've done it before, and by the Highest Hill of the Over-lands, we'll do it again!" She looked around desperately.

Jabbing her finger to the south, she said, "We make for the bottomlands, creeping along as well as we can. And if we're seen, we run. That's all we can do."

"I suppose you're right," sighed Okona.

Anisha nodded, biting her lip.

So, with Okona now in front, they began stealing south through the trees.

They had been going for more than a minute when Okona ventured a glance back, hoping to catch a glimpse of the Jaggo's whereabouts. To his terrible dismay, he realized Yahsi was not with them.

"Why, what's she ..."

At that moment, Yahsi, who was quite far to their north, stood up and waved her arms. "Death to every last one of you!" she cried. "Return to the dark realm from whence you have come!"

"No!" screamed Okona, rising.

"Run, you fool!" snapped Anisha. "Don't you see what she's done for us? Don't let her last gift be in vain!"

Swiftly, she snatched Okona's palm and dragged him southward through the forest. By that time, several Jaggo, hearing Okona's cry, had veered to follow them, while the rest raced toward Yahsi, who was fleeing northward.

Tears streamed down Okona's face, as he and Anisha pounded over dead leaves and pine needles, stones and earth. A continuous whir of rain and branches flew past, as they fled from the foot of the mountain. The couple raced on through the woodlands and into a thicket of rivercane, not daring to look behind and dreading the almost inevitable 'thnick' of the Jaggo's black-feathered arrows in their backs.

But before they realized it, their feet had carried them from rain-drenched soil into shallow, loathsome brown water.

"A quag!" Okona exclaimed, looking about at the knobby roots of the surrounding cypress trees.

Having nowhere else to flee, they splashed on until the water was up to their waists, while hoisting their packs as high as they could. Only then did Okona turn to see the Jaggo bounding toward them.

"There's something moving out there," Anisha murmured, stepping back apprehensively.

Sure enough, farther out in the water, there were ripples in the murky surface, and out of these came broad, scaly brown snouts with gleaming, yellow eyes. These quickly submerged once again.

"Karrawahs!" Okona cried, upon sighting them.

Ten Jaggo had reached the quag's shore by this time, and there they stood, with arrows nocked, pointed at the Sakooma's hearts.

With death both before and behind them, the terrified couple froze and prepared to pass into the Realms Beyond.

Part II:
Flute and Water

CHAPTER SEVEN

KARRAWAH AND QUAGWEEDS

S UDDENLY, A LOUD GRUNTING noise, evidently of another karrawah, came from a stand of rushes on a little island some ways out in the water. The karrawahs near to Okona and Anisha again emerged from the quag-waters and grunted in reply. As soon as the Jaggo heard this and saw the karrawah snouts, their eyes grew wide, they lowered their bows and began stepping backwards. Then, all at once, they turned and retreated into the forest.

Meanwhile, Okona and Anisha, fearing they would momentarily find themselves in the karrawahs' merciless jaws, had backed out of the water. They had just come to the shore when more karrawah noises came from the cluster of rushes. The Sakooma stared out at the shadows dancing under the huge cypress trees, hung with pale-gray moss, but saw no sign of the creature producing the utterances.

Abruptly, the pod of karrawahs melted back into the water, as the prow of a canoe appeared from around the little island with the rushes. Within moments, the whole craft was visible. It was a dugout, hollowed from a cypress tree, and within it sat a man, older than Okona's father but rather younger than his grandfather. His face was droll, but sharp-featured, and he was dressed in a trim deerskin vest and a breechcloth made of mulberry barkcloth. His legs were covered by deerskin leggings, and over his shoulder were slung two long straps, one with a waterskin attached and the other with a curious little box.

"Hoi!" he called in greeting. "You're lucky I was around, eh?"

Okona noticed immediately that his accent was similar to that of the Shamoki, the northerly branch of their kin.

"Lucky indeed!" Okona replied. "And we thank you! However did you manage to scare those things off?"

"The karrawahs? I simply told them to keep away from you or they'd be hearing what from me! I've got them well-trained, you see."

"Y-you mean—" stammered Anisha, as the man paddled up to them. "You sure had me fooled. Sounded just like them! How do you do it?"

"Like so." The man stepped out of the canoe onto the bank, looked at them with a sly smile, rascally danced his eyebrows and, putting his hand by his mouth, produced a loud vocalization indistinguishable from that of a karrawah. Several of the long, brown creatures stuck their heads out of the water a third time, a good deal too close to the shore for Okona and Anisha's comfort. The man tossed them a few fish from the bottom of his canoe, then grunted once more, and away the karrawahs went, slipping beneath the opaque surface of the quag.

"Did you see the warriors at the water's edge?" asked Anisha.

"Sure enough! Jaggo-men by the look of it. That's why I assumed you were worthy of rescuing."

"You know of the Jaggo?" queried Okona.

"Oh, were they really Jaggo, then? South of the river? And how'd you get mixed up with them?"

"It's a long story," Anisha replied.

"Well, we've got us a long afternoon, unless you've got something better to do." The man shrugged.

"Not at the moment," Okona admitted, "although I would like to get away from here before the Jaggo come back. I can't imagine why they left to begin with. They had us right there and could have shot us easier than you can say tigglesquat."

"Oh, that's easy," said the man, climbing back into his canoe. "It was the karrawahs."

"They're afraid of them, then?" asked Anisha, as the man beckoned them to the vessel.

"Yes, though not as one fears beasts, but as he fears the sacred. Karrawahs, now—the Jaggo believe they're divine; that's what folk say, anyway. They take karrawahs as representatives of some higher being, I should guess. And that's why they didn't just shoot you, for that would have been taking away the karrawahs' place to do with you as they pleased."

"You seem to know a lot about the Jaggo," said Okona, who, with Anisha, had by this time climbed into the boat.

"More than some, I suppose. But anyhow, let's clear out of this backwater. I've just got to get my grockberry basket, and then we'll be on our way."

Humming quietly, he paddled over to the bank behind the rushes from which they had first heard his superb imitation of a karrawah and picked up a basket full of small, sky-blue berries. Then he steered out into a narrow channel beyond, and soon they were surrounded by a maze of sluggish waters, dangling moss and mucky islets.

After somewhat more than a quarter-hour of winding through the quag's quiet labyrinth, they came upon a more open stretch of water. Across it was a little island. And upon that island, blending so well with its surroundings that the Sakooma didn't quite recognize what it was until the second glance, was a round hut of grass above and mud below. It had short walls and a high, pointed roof. On the side facing them, there was a low doorway, covered by a blanket of woven grasses. And before the hut, twixt it and the golden water, was a ring of stones in which were a few scattered ashes.

They shored at the island and were all climbing out of the canoe when the man inquired, "Have you taken meat today?"

"Only a little," Okona replied.

"Well, if you don't mind waiting a bit, you can have some more," the man cheerily offered.

"We'd love that," Anisha returned.

Okona and Anisha sat upon the grass, much relieved to rest in the pleasant shade offered by the quag (though they did not care for the marauding mosquitoes there), while the man set about making fire with a bow drill and fireboard, which he procured from his hut. When he had some tinder burning, he built a little fire in the ring of stones and then disappeared into the hut, humming to himself. He returned not long afterward with a stewpot, a vessel of water, some ladles and a few small packages.

Intrigued, Okona glanced into the hut when the mat covering the doorway was pushed aside. It was filled with odds and ends, which almost completely surrounded a single sleeping mat. Its interior walls, largely covered by cane mats, were supported by a framework of poles and beams over which wattle and daub had been laid.

With obvious expertise, the man began cooking, still happily humming. And shortly, unfamiliar, yet enticing, odors rose from the cookpot. The Sakooma watched with much interest as the man added more and more ingredients to the stew. At one point, he took a pinch of something out of the little wooden box that hung at his side and flung it into the mixture. Also, several pieces of meat were cast into the broth, along with various bundles of plants and herbs.

After a while, the man declared the stew finished and went back into the hut once more, emerging moments later with wooden bowls and spoons. After another trip into the dwelling, he came back with clay cups, more water and a little bundle of leaves. These he placed into the cups to make a cold tea, and then he set bowls of stew and cups of tea before each of the Sakooma and himself.

After thanking the man for his hospitality, Okona and Anisha fell to eating, as did their host. The Sakooma, though not expecting much from swamp food, found it surprisingly delightful, even exceptionally so. The stew was rich and savory, containing a number of flavors they had never encountered before, and the cold tea was quite refreshing and perfectly matched to the stew.

They ate in silence for some minutes; then Okona, unable to contain his curiosity any longer, asked, "What's in this stuff? Whatever it is, it's fantastic!"

"'Twas only a trifle, mind you," the man replied modestly. "They call stews like this jibbanic where I come from. The word means 'whatever.' But oh, it's got various things: chiefly, karrawah and quagweeds. A number of different kinds of them, actually."

"You eat karrawah?" asked Anisha skeptically. "I thought they were your pets."

"I wouldn't go quite that far. But anyway, I don't *normally* eat them these days, at least not mine," said the man, stew dripping from his chin. "But there was one particularly mean old karrawah that was giving the others a lot of trouble, so they did away with him. I didn't want to waste good eating, you know, so now we're all benefiting from his bad behavior."

"Who are you?" asked Anisha, after taking a long sip of her tea.

"The name's Wunko, but you can call me Uncle Wunko if you like." The man rubbed his nose with his thumb, touched it to his forehead and then stuck it out toward them. Assuming this to be a greeting, they tentatively did the same.

"And you live here?" asked Okona.

"In the heart of Quimmidog Quag. Just me and the karrawahs," Wunko proudly replied.

"Have you always lived around here?" asked Anisha. "It's awfully close to Ponca Peak."

"Oh, the mountain ..." said Wunko. "Me and the mountain, we've got an understanding; I don't go near it, and it doesn't come near me. Well, I suppose near is a relative term ... Anyway, I've seen some spooky-ish things at night, but I'm apparently removed enough that the peak doesn't take an interest in me. But neither does anybody else, for that matter, seeing as the mountain isn't far off. Anyway, I've only been at this pretty little spot for two years and a bit more. Came the spring before last."

"Where'd you live before coming here?" inquired Okona.

"You're a curious lot, aren't you? Well, I reckon I've lived about everywhere, leastways anywhere down the aisle of the Anoka River. Never been to the big water out east, nor the great mountains in the west, nor the endless flatlands before you get to them, but I've been a whole lot of somewheres in-between. Yessir, I've spent a fair amount of time in the valley of the Hohosha River, one of the Anoka's biggest tributaries. Runs from the east into the Anoka several hundred miles north of here. And I stayed for a time in the chiefdoms of Xiku, Vannabish and Zaranga in the Woods of Much Buzzing; they're up where the Anoka begins its long journey. Oh, the pines are beautiful up that way! And I've also tarried near the shores of Wabashi Igama Chika not terribly far from there, relatively speaking. Ol' Wabashi's not as wide as the Southward Sea, mind you, but might as well be. It just seems to go on forever."

"Where are you from, then?" pressed Anisha.

Wunko chuckled. "You won't rest until you get to the bottom of me, will you? I was born and raised away south, but since, ah, since a number of years ago now, I've been roaming Massora far and wide. I'm a storyteller, you see, and a teller of tales has got to get his tales somewhere, don't he? The more you travel, the more there is to tell. But I wore myself out after a while—that sort of thing happens to people, you know—so when I found this pleasant little quag, I decided I'd stay here a spell until the wind blew me on again. And so far, it hasn't. Now, you've had your fun fishing in my pond. I wouldn't mind fishing a bit in yours. Who are you, and what in all shine of sun and moon got you in such bad straits as to be chased by the Jaggo?"

Anisha began, "We're Sakooma, you see, and—"

"I could tell *that* the instant I saw you! You've got the look, as they say. Besides, we're speaking Sakooma, aren't we?"

"Yes, and you have an interesting accent," observed Okona. "One like that of our brothers, the Shamoki, but with its own unique color."

Wunko nodded. "I learned my Sakooma from the Shamoki, for I dwelt with them a fair while some years back. But of course I didn't learn it as a child, so there's your color."

"What was your birthspeech, then? Tikkichaw, seeing as you're from the south?" asked Okona.

"You guessed it. Swamp Talk, as they say. Deep Swamp Talk in my case. But I haven't spoken any Tikkichaw in years. Try not to even think in it if I can help it. But I'm afraid it's all still up there." He sighed and stared across the quag's cloudy waters. "Anyway, we were fishing in your pond now, not mine, remember?"

"Oh, yes," said Anisha. "Anyway, we're from down the Kanno a bit, Takula Conflux if you know the place. Or at least I'm from Takula, but Okona—"

"Ah, now we're getting somewhere! Okona is it?" He nodded politely to the lad, then went through the business with his thumb again, which Okona awkwardly copied.

"And what's your name, young miss?"

"Anisha," the girl replied.

"Lovely." Wunko greeted her with his thumb ritual, and this she mimicked in return.

"Please continue," he requested.

"Well, we were at Takula a few days back, holding our summer feast," she said. "And then a strange storm struck, breaking open the doors of our most sacred mound.'

"One of the chief ancestors of the Sakooma was a man named Hamora," explained Okona, "and he—"

"Hamora?" Wunko, who had been lounging after a fashion now that he had finished his stew, sat up erect. "Don't tell me the mound that was struck was the one with the Hand of Hamora!"

"How do you know about the Hand?" asked Okona, much astonished.

"You're forgetting I'm a storyteller. And a good storyteller is also a good story collector! Yes, I've heard of the Hand of Hamora. The Shamoki told me about it years ago."

"I suppose we can shorten our explanation then," said Okona. "Anyway, after the storm struck, we discovered the Hand had been taken. So our Chief Magic-maker talked to the Powers about the matter, and the next day, he commissioned a group of forty, thirty-six of our best warrior-men and four of our Wise-women, to go reclaim the Hand from one of four, uh ... beings, the only ones who were powerful enough to—"

"Oh, *those* Four," Wunko muttered ominously, studying Okona's face.

"You know about *them* too?" asked Okona.

Wunko nodded.

"*What* four?' demanded Anisha. "I haven't heard anything about this."

"For good reason," uttered Wunko darkly. "Miss, I advise you to remain in ignorance about this matter as long as possible. They say that to even learn what they are robs a year from a man's life, and to learn their names removes two more."

"Then three of mine are gone already," said Okona miserably.

"Be glad the sun is shining presently." Wunko looked about warily. "For to speak of this after nightfall would almost certainly bring defiling spirits upon us. Come, our talk has touched upon them more than enough already. So you've got to get the Hand back. And I'm assuming you were sent out to help?"

"Yes, I was to go west. My band came to Ohkasac Groves yesterday afternoon, but in the evening, we were attacked by the Jaggo and fled."

"And you fled with him?" Wunko looked at Anisha. "Were you one of the Wise-women, then? Rather young for—"

"Wise-women? Not I," Anisha laughed. "And I wasn't with the band at first. I only joined them at—well, it's complicated."

"Certainly seems to be," Wunko agreed, chewing on a piece of grass. "No matter. Any idea why the Jaggo came after you?"

The Sakooma shook their heads.

Wunko paused to reflect, then said, "With one of those, uh ... beings you mentioned on the move, perhaps the bad magic in this region has been stirred. That would be enough to rouse the Jaggo, I would think. But for now it's a mystery to me too. Anyhow, back to where we were. So the two of you presumably crossed the river somehow and ran down this way to escape from the Jaggo?"

"Essentially," Okona confirmed. "But when we were running toward your quag, we had just come from the Seer of Ponca Peak."

Wunko nearly choked on his tea, then spat it out. "Great wippikats!" he exclaimed. "What insanity possessed you to seek the Seer? You mean you went up the mountain in the storm and everything?"

The lad nodded. "Our Wise-woman Yahsi, the only other of our band who survived the Jaggo's assault, said we needed to ask the Seer where to find the Hand. And I was against it before, but even so, I'm glad we went because now I know where the Hand is, more or less."

"You do?" asked Anisha, astounded.

"Where's this Yahsi of yours now? Still on the mountain?"

"No, she lured off the Jaggo to save us, and now she—she's gone." Okona, his eyes clouding, let out a long, slow breath.

"Oh, I'm sorry." Wunko sighed.

"Okona, where is the Hand?" pressed Anisha. "Where did the Seer say we could find it?"

"In the North," the lad replied, wiping his eyes.

"The North?" Wunko tutted. "Ah, it won't be pretty to face *them*."

"Face *whom*?" asked Anisha, with rising annoyance.

"Remember what I warned you about?" Wunko looked at her sharply.

"Anyway, how well can you fight?" inquired Wunko, after finishing off his tea. "For of course, you shall have to fight along the way, I would guess. Have you any weaponcraft?"

Okona shook his head. "Nothing to speak of. In the main, music is where my skill lies, though I can hunt a little with bow and spear."

"Okona isn't exactly a warrior," explained Anisha, "but you should see him throw a stone! I should think if things came to a battle, he could deal a fair amount of damage with a good supply of rocks."

"Oh, really? Here, then." Wunko tossed the lad a nearby rock. "This I'd like to see."

"Uh, well," said Okona, "I can throw pretty decently, but I've never been in a battle, and I imagine it wouldn't be quite as simple to throw stones at enemies as it is to do it just for fun. But I guess ... well, I'll try to hit the knob on that cypress knee over there. You see the middle one in that set of three?"

Many yards across the pond, three cypress roots stuck up from the water like strange, silent sentinels. Okona eyed the central one for a moment, then hurled the stone at it. The stone rebounded precisely off the knob, then plunked into the pond.

Wunko whistled loudly. "You really *can* throw. And that might well prove handy. Now, do you have a northward route you mean to take and a plan for getting clear of the Jaggo on your way?"

"Not remotely," Okona replied. "And at this point I'm wondering if maybe we should just head back to Takula and tell our Magic-maker what we learned. There's a party already headed north, for we sent parties all four principal directions. Perhaps we could get word to them and even send them the aid of more warriors so they'd stand a better chance of retrieving the Hand."

Wunko shook his head. "There'll be no getting back to Takula now, not with the Jaggo prowling about."

"Why?" asked Anisha. "As far as they know, we were left to the karrawahs, so there's no further cause for them to seek us."

"Maybe not you specifically. But I'd be surprised if they've cleared out of the area altogether. I've never heard tell of them coming south of the Kanno before, so I reckon something out of the ordinary is afoot. Better to play things on the safe side and assume they're still around. There's a fair stretch of miles between here and

Takula, and you couldn't outpace the Jaggo if you did run into them. Also, you'd have to cross the Kanno."

"You have a boat, don't you?" queried Okona, glancing over at it.

"I *do* have a boat, and—say! There's an idea! Not even the Jaggo could track you if you went by water, and there's a nice little river that runs from this quag into the Kanno."

"Would you let us borrow your canoe?" asked Anisha hopefully.

"Certainly not!" Wunko gruffly replied. Then he grinned. "But I'll tell you what I will do. I'll take you back to Takula myself."

"Would you?" she asked excitedly.

"Of course. I use my canoe practically all day, every day, so I can't very well do without it. But if I'm paddling up the Kanno with you, I won't be here to need it. Besides, I know the way up to the river. But also, and most importantly, sneaking past the Jaggo should make for a great story. And the only thing better than telling a great story is being in one!"

"Could we leave this afternoon?" inquired Okona.

"Why not right now?" asked Wunko, rising. "I'll be ready in a few minutes."

He fully extinguished his fire, then went into his hut, humming once more, and came out several minutes later with an array of gear, including a bulging pack. The Tikkichaw indeed seemed ready for an extensive expedition, outfitted with dagger, spear, bow and arrows and also with cookware, a fireboard and spindle and sundry other items.

Together, the trio entered Wunko's canoe to a serenade of insects and the distant grunting of karrawahs, to which Wunko replied in karrawah sounds, as the canoe glided out into the golden afternoon water.

"Don't worry. We'll have you home in no time," Wunko said, as he guided the craft out into the tangle of small, muddy isles and brown, rippling channels.

CHAPTER EIGHT

THE WINGED WATCHER

WUNKO CANOED THROUGH THE wandering waters of the quag until they came to a proper river, which was narrow and overhung with many lofty cypress trees. "Wunko's Wash," he declared, as they entered it. "It may have another name, but I don't know it, so I've taken the liberty of dubbing it. A fine name it is too, if I do say so myself."

Down this river they passed for three hours and a good bit more, cutting through the lotuses basking in the river's slow current and gazing about at the wildlife. Beavers they saw, along with various wading birds, many turtles and fish, a few hawks, several water-snakes, a deer and even another pod of karrawahs. Also, Okona noticed a spot where they had forded this river earlier that day.

As they paddled southeastward, Wunko requested that Okona and Anisha relate the story of their journey. They readily obliged, and as there was much to tell, this helped the time go by more quickly. However, Okona remained vague about much Baneesh had disclosed in their meeting and carefully excluded the fact that he had not actually been chosen to go on the mission and also that he was the Unlucky Eleventh of his Sacred Ten.

The afternoon was coming to an end when the river suddenly opened up, spilling out into the wide waters of the Kanno. A long spit of land lay to their left, and Wunko wanted to pull ashore there for a few minutes to examine the state of things on the river before heading on.

"Your tale is fascinating," Wunko said, as they dragged the canoe onto the bank. "And you've already been through much in such a short time!"

"Hopefully it will be rather less exciting from now on," said Anisha.

All of a sudden, Wunko shoved the others down behind some brush on the bank.

"What is—" Okona began, but Wunko shushed him and pointed up to the graying sky.

There, gliding only a few hundred feet above the Kanno, was a dark form, small in the distance, though it would have been huge up close, thirty feet in breadth and nearly twice that in length. It was a truly monstrous thing, for that is really the only name Okona could put to it. To call it a bird would have been much too kind, though this thing did have wings, horrid and leathery, like those of an enormous bat. Its dark-blue, scaly body was larger than an elk, and its spike-lined tail, which terminated in a vicious point, was of incredible length. A single, curved horn jutted from the thing's black head, and at the ends of its six legs were cruel, curling claws. Its eyes, large and lidded, shimmered red as they surveyed the lands about the Kanno.

"What in the name of the Underbrakes' blackest briars is that?" asked Anisha, nearly breathless.

"A ganoja," Wunko quietly replied. "The Winged Watcher they call him, a sort of river dragon. It feasts upon both the dead and the living and dwells in river bluffs, making its abode in caves filled with the bones of its victims. But until now, I'd thought they could only be found in the heartland of the Anoka, rather far to the north and east of here. What's it doing this far afield, I wonder? But in any event, up that way, in the mid-reach of the Anoka Valley, folk regard it as an omen of death. Also, see how it's flying back and forth over the water? It seems to be looking for something."

"Have you seen one of these things before, then?" inquired Okona, still in awe of the grotesque creature.

"No, I've only heard it described. But that's a ganoja, all right."

Abruptly, the creature swept down toward the river, then glided to the north bank, where it landed near a small cluster of figures. Though these were barely discernible from this distance, it was clear they were moving toward the ganoja and not away from it.

"Might those be ... I do believe those are Jaggo!" exclaimed Anisha, straining to see across the wide Kanno.

"It's impossible to tell for certain from here, but if I had to guess, I'd say you're right, miss," Wunko affirmed. "See those tiny red spots? Loincloths I should think, all dipped in blood."

"So that's where the red comes from," Anisha muttered queasily.

"What do you think they're doing?" Okona asked.

Squinting at the far shore, Wunko replied, "Disturbingly enough, it appears they may be on familiar terms with that atrocious thing. And I know the Jaggo can't talk, but I wonder if what we're witnessing is not some kind of communication between man and monster. It did come to them, after all, and they didn't run from it. It's almost as if it were reporting to them."

"What do you make of it?" Okona inquired.

"I'm not pleased to suggest this any more than you'll be pleased to hear it, but I suspect the Jaggo are enlisting the ganoja's aid, undoubtedly in their hunting. For hunting—man-hunting to be precise—is the Jaggo's main business. And I've more than a sneaking suspicion that it's you two they're seeking."

"Us?" cried Okona.

Wunko nodded. "Somehow, I've a hunch they know you aren't dead. It's held that there's some magic about them, after all, and that they may learn tidings from stray spirits, of which there are no shortage in this area, close as it is to Ponca Peak. Also, it's clear they were set on slaying you in particular, but since you've escaped them, perhaps they've hired a keener hunter even than them to finish the job. Unfortunately, this still brings us no closer to knowing why the Jaggo are pursuing you. It only adds to your list of harriers." Okona and Anisha's expressions grew bleak.

The Tikkichaw continued, "My friends farther up the Anoka tell me the ganoja's power is in river-waters. He is a guardian of them, so he will sense it if you cross. It is said the rivers obey him and that they speak one to another."

He turned to the Sakooma, his face grave.

"I know you wish to return to Takula, but I would not enter the river here for anything in the world. To do so would only mean our end, for the ganoja would be upon us immediately."

"Couldn't we paddle along the south bank until we are some distance away and then cross?" Anisha suggested.

"No, you don't understand; the river itself will know if we have entered it, and it will inform the ganoja. Oh, and at need it can fly as fast as a gale." The Tikkichaw chewed his thumb, then murmured, "Unfortunately, the river is closed to us."

"Then what can we do?" asked Okona.

"I suppose we can either return to my hut or, if you have another idea, then I'm willing to listen. Being in an interesting story is all very fine and desirable but not so much if you perish in it."

Okona and Anisha thought hard, keeping an eye on the ganoja all the while. After a few minutes, the creature flapped up from the bank, then resumed its watch high above the Kanno. Meanwhile, the Jaggo disappeared into the forest.

At last, Okona said, "If there is no possibility of us crossing the river, we can get neither the help I hoped for nor even attempt to get the Hand ourselves."

"What if we went far down the river?" Anisha suggested. "Very far. If we were far enough away from the ganoja, might we stand a chance of crossing?"

Wunko wrinkled up his face. "Though the ganoja may be swift, it would take it *some* time to fly to us. Also, it cannot fly beyond a certain distance from any river, or so I've heard, for it is from the rivers itself that it draws both strength and life. It would be terribly risky, but perhaps it could be done. Maybe we could cross quickly and then get far enough from the Kanno to be safe from its power. You think to go far downstream and then go back up to Takula?"

"Precisely," said Anisha.

"But if we do that, we might lose several days," said Okona, "and unfortunately, getting back the Hand is an extremely urgent matter, both for the safety of our people but also to prevent something really terrible being done with it. I'm willing to dare your plan, Anisha, but I think we need to go upstream, not down."

"Whatever for?" Anisha returned. "To try to get the Hand back ourselves?"

"What other choice do we have? We cannot cross the river here, as Wunko has said. Nor can we reasonably go far downstream and make our way back to Takula, for our news of the Hand's whereabouts may come too late. And we certainly can't go sit in Wunko's hut and let our people come to ruin. Giving up is simply not an option; we've got to see this quest through, no matter what. A turtle's got to ... well, never mind that right now. It's just something Yahsi said."

Okona went on, "I hate the idea as much as I'm sure you do, Anisha, especially because you left without your father's consent and our journey would only lead into greater danger. Yet as all roads lead to danger now, I think we must go northwest and try to cross there. We have to do what's best for our people. And since there is already a group of our best folk headed north, perhaps we can find and join them."

Anisha considered this, then sighed, "All right, we'll at least give it a try. For I, just as you, desire to do what shall most benefit our people. Well then, where should we cross?"

"Aska Karalonga?" suggested Wunko. "That's Kamingo for Crossing of the Broken Crag. It lies in the shadow of Pagoma Rock; you may have heard of it? The Kamingo have many craft there, and if the ganoja were to come after us, I'm sure we'd much prefer having many Kamingo nearby to help us assail it, eh?"

"*Us?*" returned Okona. "There's no need for you to endanger yourself. You've already helped us tremendously."

"Well, if you'd have me, I'd be happy to make your mission mine as well. I've been doing naught for the last two years but sitting around in my quag, and I feel it's time to be moving on anyhow. Also, remember, a storyteller's got to have stories. There's nothing better than being in a story yourself, and I'm sure this is going to be a grand one."

"What do you say, Anisha?" Okona prompted. "Shall we let Uncle Wunko come with us?"

"It'd be unkind not to at this point." The girl smiled. "But regarding your plan, mister, I don't think the Kamingo would appreciate being used the way you intend."

"I'm sure they wouldn't, but unfortunately, Uncle Wunko isn't quite as scrupulous as he ought to be," the Tikkichaw remarked jovially.

Okona thought for a bit, then said, "I reckon there have been worse plans in the world, but this sounds like the best one we've got. It's off to Aska Karalonga, then?"

"Quite," Wunko affirmed. "And you're lucky I'll be along, as I know the way through the Washoma. We shall be obliged to cross a number of miles through it if we are to come to Aska Karalonga. But before we set out, let's hide my canoe here on Talligo Spit, for it did take me a fair bit of work to make it, and I may end up coming back to get it at some point."

So they carried the canoe farther inland on the spit until they found a dense clump of bushes satisfactory for concealment.

Just after they had finished stowing the canoe, Okona, glancing at Anisha, caught a flash of orange on her neck.

"What is that, Anisha?" he asked. "I've never seen you wear it before. And is that agate?"

"My necklace?" she said, looking down and fingering it. "Oh, it's made of hakinu, mined from the Washoma. It's a little fox. See?" She held it up. "And I've only had it for a few days. It was, uh ... it was Tencum's betrothal gift. He gave it to me the evening of the feast."

"You're betrothed? Congratulations, Miss Anisha!" Wunko exclaimed.

"Actually, he died last night," she awkwardly replied, her eyes dimming. "He was one of those killed by the Jaggo."

"I'm so sorry," said Wunko mournfully. "That's very hard, miss, though I'm glad you at least have the necklace to remember him by."

"Yes," Anisha mistily returned, gently holding the pendant.

"You brought your silver bracelet also," noted Okona, nodding at her right wrist and hoping to move from the matter of Tencum as speedily as possible.

"I did," said the girl softly, "although it was supposed to be given to Tencum as the seal for our engagement since it was the most cherished item I received from my mother."

Okona immediately rued his remark, though tried not to do so visibly.

"However, I couldn't bear to part with it, so I gave him her redstone ring of Kannikos instead. But I brought this bracelet as a token of luck, though it doesn't seem to have worked very well thus far. Then again, I don't know how bad things might have been if I hadn't had it. You see, my mother left it behind the day she ... well ..."

Anisha swallowed hard.

Several birds twittered uneasily in the brush, and Wunko looked warily about. "Perhaps we'd better be moving along," he suggested. "I know the ganoja already left and the Jaggo we saw were on the other side of the river, but all the same ..."

The others nodded.

That evening, they hiked roughly northwest along the Kanno, but a little ways inland, and covered some five miles from where they had concealed the canoe. At sunset, when they halted, Okona looked directly west to Ponca Peak, dark against the orange sky.

"Your tale will end in nothing but death unless you find what you are not seeking," the Seer's voice echoed in his head.

"But what am I supposed to be looking for?" he wondered. The pale mists shrouding the summit gave him no answer.

Not long afterward, he lay down near Anisha, between two collections of shrubs. Nearby was a trickling rivulet running toward the Kanno. Its soothing music inspired him to sit up and pull out his flute. However, he had only played a few low notes upon it when a swift tut from Wunko silenced him.

"I'm sorry, lad," said he, while bedding down in the twilight, "but I'm afraid we shall have to do without music for tonight, for we don't know who or what may be listening, and our danger is still much too near. And music, especially of that sort, carries through Air, Water and Earth as other things do not. But there will be a time for song again."

"Hopefully," murmured Okona, as he closed his eyes.

He could hear Anisha breathing not far off, and he whispered, "Good night, Anisha. May your sorrow be less tomorrow than it was today."

"Good night, Okona," she quietly returned.

And with that, lulled off by the melodies of water and wood, Okona passed into slumber.

Kannita w Mountains
Lake Oganosha
Pagoma Rock
Aska Karalonga
Kanno River
Lalaska Point
The Halahna
Banuma Creek
Banuma Falls
Maze of the Marauders
Watamora River
Kalmora Mountain
Kashamee River
The Washoma
Forest of the Fifty Founts

Through the Washoma
To the Lands of the Shamoki
N
W   E
S
Quinoma Stakes
The Pashola Timbers
Kanno River
Piskah River
Ponca Peak
Talligo Spit
Quimmidog Quag
Wunko's Wash
Ohkasac Groves
0   5   10   15
Miles

CHAPTER NINE

THE WAY THROUGH THE WASHOMA

UNDISTURBED DURING THE DARK hours, the trio rose just as it was getting light the next day, and Wunko informed them they must cross the Piskah River that morning. Fortunately, he had constructed a raft some time ago and stored it along its banks, as sometimes he took to leaving his quag and exploring the area beyond the Piskah. However, the raft was stowed several miles inland from the Kanno.

They trekked west by northwest to the spot with his raft, which was just barely big enough for all of them, then paddled across the placid Piskah to the far shore. After this, they continued north and then due northwest.

The first leg beyond the Piskah covered broad stretches of lowland, peppered with modest-sized lakes. There were also several wide valleys, jaunty ridges and, every once in a while, a peak or two. In the higher areas, they encountered both pine woods and prairies, and in the lower ones, forests of tall oaks, such as could be found near both Okona's village and Takula Conflux.

After midday, they reached the eastern edge of the Washoma, a charming region of gentle hills with ridges of sandstone covered in luxuriant hickory, pine and oak, which fell into wide valleys of shale. Here they veered west by northwestward, grateful for the cover of the forested slopes. There were not many streams here, it being the summer, but they did run across various pools, at some of which they were able to replenish their water supply. Elk roamed here, as did deer in abundance and also squirrels, birds and a great many rabbits.

Quite late in the afternoon, they halted their march, having traversed some fifteen miles that day. They could have gone on until nightfall, but the day was hot and humid, and all thought it would be better to rest now and rise even earlier the following day. Also, they wanted a little time to scavenge to replenish what they had already consumed from their packs.

Later that evening, when the stars appeared, they bedded down by a great, hollow oak and slept soundly until just before dawn.

As Okona was collecting his equipment in the semidarkness preceding daybreak, he asked, "Should we be taking any precautions to avoid encounters with the Chadori?"

"I have been already," replied Wunko, fishing through his pack for some morning herbs to chew on. "I've been keeping an eye out for their signs, but it doesn't look like they've been active of late in the area we've been traveling through."

"How near are we to the Kashamee River?" inquired Okona.

"We'll cross it this morning," Wunko replied. "Why do you ask?"

"Oh, it's just that the Kashamee is the northwestern border of our Powers' dominion. And their sway beyond it, though it doesn't drop to nothing, is nonetheless much diminished and fades ever more with every onward mile."

"So I suppose we'll be rather on our own once we've crossed the water," remarked Anisha sullenly.

"Not quite. You'll still have me," Wunko said cheerily, though this did little to hearten the Sakooma.

That morning, they set out north by northwest, roughly following the course of the Kanno but still several miles southwest of it. Soon, they came to a wide valley, and only four miles from where they had camped, they reached the aforementioned winding Kashamee River. Wunko was sorry to inform them that he had no raft ready here. Fortunately, all of them were good swimmers, and also, the river was relatively narrow at this spot. However, they wished to keep their foodstuffs dry, so Wunko contrived three miniature rafts out of stout branches lashed together with wild grapevines. They placed their packs and supplies upon these, and then each individual towed his or her raft alongside while swimming the cool, glassy brown river.

They kept their same course for another four miles beyond the Kashamee, then headed west and just a little north for six miles more, climbing gradually back into the Washoma's uplands.

While there were still several hours of daylight left, Wunko thought it would be wise for them to fully restock their food once again. So all went off in search of nuts, roots and berries and returned with their plunder a while later. However, the Tikkichaw had done better than the others, for he had also in tow a rabbit, a squirrel and a snake.

"These are just what we need!" he exclaimed. "Now, be a good lad and lass and get Uncle Wunko some firewood and brush (the driest you can find, mind you), and I'll make you such a stew as you've never had before."

Humming gaily, he began scooping out a hole in the earth rather near to a tree (which would better disperse the smoke from their intended campfire) and setting appropriately sized stones around it to make a fire-pit.

Meanwhile, the Sakooma walked off into the towering pines to do as Wunko had requested.

When they were some distance from the campsite and had already filled their arms with many sticks and twigs, Okona ventured, "You've been looking rather down today, Anisha. Is anything in particular troubling you or just, you know … what happened?"

"I just wish I would have left Takula sooner," the girl replied. "I knew from the omen that disaster was coming, and if only I'd have acted faster—"

"About that …" started Okona. He was considering saying something about his being the Unlucky Eleventh, for he didn't wish Anisha to be burdened with guilt that wasn't hers. But he quickly decided it was much too shameful a thing to reveal.

"What is it?" She turned to him.

"You really oughtn't put the blame on yourself for the incident at Ohkasac Groves. You didn't know exactly what was going to happen or when, and anyway, you did come and even put yourself in considerable danger to help us. You may not have saved the others, but if you hadn't brought that canoe, Yahsi and I would almost certainly have perished that night."

"But Yahsi perished anyhow."

"True, but it was to rescue us. And I'm very torn up about it, yet I know she wouldn't want me to be, so I'm trying to lay it to rest." His gaze wandered to the ground.

"It wasn't your fault in any way, Okona." The girl drew closer to him.

Okona looked up."And thus it is with you and the attack by the Jaggo."

Anisha turned away. "I so badly didn't want to fail the same way my father did, but I did anyhow."

"What do you mean?"

"It's the reason my mother died." She turned back to face the lad. "When I was a little girl, there was a day when my father saw many wolves in a glade, chasing a starfly. But suddenly a falcon came behind them, screeching. The wolves turned to chase the falcon, and the starfly escaped."

Stifling a sniffle, the girl went on, "Do you understand what it is that he saw? My father was of the Falcon Clan before he married my mother."

"Oh ..." Okona's face fell.

"My father thought what he had seen was quite strange but did not ask Baneesh about it until noon of the following day. However, that morning, only a few hours before they discussed it, was the very morning my mother was shot by an arrow and died. My father heeded the omen too late. And what's worse, we never knew who killed her ... until now."

Okona stared at her. "But it's well-known Hatina's death was the Chadori's doing."

"No one saw who did it, but my father assumed them to be the culprit. He brought back the arrow that slew her and has kept it in our lodge ever since. I think he hoped that someday Baneesh's magic would be strong enough that he could cast a spell on the arrow so my father could speak to my mother one last time in the River of Dreams. But the arrow was black-feathered and of a peculiar make. And it was of a black wood no one recognized."

She went on, "I saw the arrows of the Jaggo three nights ago and also when they chased us into the quag, and I could tell immediately they were of the same sort."

Okona recalled the horrid shaft sticking out of Kimmanic's bosom and replied, "Their arrows do have a unique and rather ghastly look to them. So you think the Jaggo killed your mother? But why her?"

"I don't know. But yes, I've no doubt it was them."

"May the Powers judge them as their deeds deserve," Okona cursed. "And I suppose now I understand why you were so confident about the meaning of what you saw, for it was not terribly unlike that seen by your father. Nevertheless, you didn't fail, Anisha. You may not have saved the others, but coming when and how you did, you saved my life. And for that, I'm grateful beyond words." He looked at her warmly.

The girl smiled in return.

Wordlessly, they finished collecting their firewood and rejoined their companion.

Some while afterward, Wunko had a nice little fire of dried fern and wood going, low and with little smoke. He had even dug a smaller hole to the side that angled into the hole where the fire was to keep the smoke levels as minimal as possible, just in case there were any unwanted persons about who might spot them. And not long after that, he commenced work on his triple meat stew, again adding all kinds of mysterious ingredients, not the least of which came from his special, carven box.

Night fell and the silver stars sang over the wooded Washoma, as Wunko completed his masterpiece. The pines whispered, night birds cooed and the fire burned low, but still warm, as they began consuming the meal the Tikkichaw had prepared.

"Never had a finer stew in my life," Okona complimented between mouthfuls.

"Yes, this is excellent," Anisha concurred.

"And I don't mean this to be rude in any way—quite the opposite—but I wasn't expecting much considering what you had to start with," remarked Okona. "It's almost like you've got a kind of magic."

"No magic here!" Wunko laughed. "Just an old Tikkichaw who's spent a good bit of time hovering over stewpots."

"Uncle Wunko, are you as good a storyteller as you are a cook?" asked Anisha. "Because if so, we'd love to hear one of your tales."

"Well now," Wunko drawled, "although it's true I'm a storyteller, I never said I was a good one. But I guess if you'll be content with such as I can offer, I can tell you a story."

Settling back on a flat stone nearby, for he had been crouched near the fire tending it, Wunko took a great breath. Then, in a tone, bold and earthy, that was instantly captivating, he commenced, "This is a Tikkichaw tale, but I don't know if that makes it worse or better. However, it's a true one, and I think that definitely improves any story. But let us begin."

"Once in this green world there was a boy named Komakop, who lived deep in the swamps of Chachuma, the Tikkichaw land at the end of the Anoka. He was a clever little boy and also skilled and adventurous. But his mother was very ill, and many thought she would soon die. However, the medicine men said there was a cure for her. If she could look upon the immapok, the prettiest flower in the whole of Chachuma, its beauty would restore her. Yet, there was believed to be only one immapok remaining, and it was in the darkest, deepest part of the swamp, where no one ever went because … well, you shall soon find out!"

"Komakop was determined to get this cure for his mother, but his father forbade him to search, for he feared losing not only one, but two of his dear ones. However, early one morning, before the sun had even winked at the sky, the boy stole out of his hut and got into his father's canoe. Then he paddled far into the swamps, deeper than ever he had been before, searching for the last, legendary immapok."

"To his delight, as the sun was setting, he found it growing on the bank of a misty quag, its blossoms all glorious and orange like the very Furnaces of the Earth, as they say. But just as he was about to pluck it and return to his canoe, thinking his mother was as good as healed, he was grabbed by many hands, hands covered in swamp mud! And before he knew it, he was face to face with the owners of those hands: the Momagaw, Mud-Fiends, Cannibals of the Quags. Terrible people they were! The most wickedest, baddest, meanest folk there are! And if you don't believe me, ask your Aunt Kapicha. Coated in mud from head to toe, they took him back to their village and there prepared the pot in which he was to be cast and cooked."

"The Momagaw leader came out of his hut to gloat over the lad, but the boy said—" Wunko now used a voice considerably different from his own and as much like to that of an earnest young lad as one could wish for from one of Wunko's age, "'Mister Momagaw, sir, if you cook me right away, I won't be able to tell you how best to sneak into my village to feast upon my brothers and sisters, who are much fatter than I am and much lazier and slower too.'"

The Tikkichaw continued, in another, far more comical but nonetheless deep voice, "'Whyze would-in you care-o to betray-ah your's own people-ing?' asked the Momagaw. 'We can-in get-o them by ourselves if-fers we want-ah anyway. We don't need-o your's help-ing.'"

Back came the boy's voice. "'I'm probably the wickedest Tik-kichaw there is, and nothing would make me happier than to have them eaten,' said Komakop, though this wasn't true in the least. 'But more importantly, if I'm going to die, I'd rather you have my enchanted gem from the great northern sorcerer than anyone in my wretched, no-good family have it.'"

"The boy spoke so earnestly that this time the Momagaw chief believed him, and he ordered, 'Supposing we not eating-o you right-ah now, you tell-o me howze we getting-ah in your's village. Then we is eating-o you.'"

"But the lad insisted he wouldn't tell them, only show them, for as a Tikkichaw, he alone had the power to remove the village's magical shield of protection when they reached it. This was a very far-fetched thing to say, but the boy was so serious in his defense of this that the Momagaw chief took it as truth and agreed to take the boy back to his village. 'But no-zah tricks!' he warned."

"'No-zah tricks,' the boy replied."

"The following evening, they came to Komakop's village, but just as the Momagaw chief was about to ask him to dispel the shield, Komakop let out the shrill whistle of a padooga bird, which was a warning sign to all his people; then he immediately dove into the swamp, staying far enough under the water that the Momagaw's spears and arrows could not harm him. The people of his village rushed to see what was afoot and quickly began launching their own spears and arrows at the Momagaw. Komakop emerged and went to the bank, as the thwarted Momagaw attempted to flee. But the people of Komakop's village were too many for them, and every last Momagaw was killed."

"And, oh, what a celebration there was! Food and music and dancing and more food and then more music and a whole lot more dancing! You've never seen such a hurrah! Komakop was promptly hailed as a hero, for the wicked Momagaw had long been a trouble to the Tikkichaw. Komakop then led many Tikkichaw to the village of the Momagaw, where they plundered the treasure they had amassed, and most importantly, as far he was concerned, he also plucked the last of the fabled immapok."

"Now, Komakop's mother was on her deathbed when he returned. His family had said their farewells to her, for they assumed he would not reach her in time. But wouldn't you know, just before she closed her eyes for the last time, in walked Komakop with the most beautiful flower you ever did see. And those watching her always said they saw life itself flood into her face that moment. Back she came from the very brink of the Darker Lands. Up she sat and sang and embraced her boy. And thus was she healed."

"But Komakop thought to make yet more use of the flower and rued that such was the last on this earth. So he planted it before his hut, and soon the whole village was covered in the lush orange glory of the immakop, so that even to this day, it is regarded as the most splendid and prettiest little settlement in all the land."

"Word of Komakop's deeds spread, and not long after his mother was cured, he was admitted into the service of the High Katchiwup, the leader of all the Tikkichaw and son of Samoolga, the Sun-lord himself. And the best part is, this tale is only the beginning of Komakop's many fantastic and marvelous adventures."

When Wunko had finished, the world felt heavier and richer, and there was hardly any sound save the crackling of the fire and the song of far-off insects.

"That was a wonderful story," said Anisha quietly, "and regardless of what you think, I believe you're a magnificent storyteller. We've some fine storytellers among the Sakooma, but I've never heard anyone tell a tale like that."

Wunko, blushing, was about to reply when Okona let out a little gasp, for a shadow had just swept down through the trees. There was a soft cracking of twigs, and the lad tensed, as a figure walked out of the darkness behind Wunko. It was a man, dressed in a white shirt of some strange material. He also wore barkcloth pants, and a red blanket was upon his shoulders. The lad looked closely at his face but couldn't place what tribe he was from.

"Hail, travelers!" the man said in a warm voice, as Wunko turned around. "Would you spare a fellow traveler some soup?"

"Certainly," Wunko replied, spreading out his arm invitingly toward the fire, though he shot a sideways, wary glance to Okona and Anisha.

The man seated himself on the ground near the low blaze, as Wunko rummaged through his gear and fetched another bowl and spoon. Thanking the Tikkichaw as he set the hot stew before him, the man set into supping.

"Your accent is even as our own. You're Sakooma, then?" inquired Okona.

The man took several more bites before replying, "I wouldn't put it that way. However, the Sakooma are of particular interest to me."

Okona gave him a puzzled look.

"Where do you come from?" Wunko asked, as he munched on an evening leaf he had pulled from his pack.

"The West," the man replied. "For Wassu of the West am I."

"And where are you going?" inquired Okona.

"We shall see," the man returned. "And you?"

"Over the Kanno," Okona replied.

Then all were quiet for a while. However, the silence was in no way awkward and even seemed fully appropriate for the occasion.

As the stranger was finishing his meal, he said, "If you must know, I, like you, intend to go north. But I've heard tell there is trouble by the Kanno. Yet ..." he paused. "I think the river can still be crossed with the right help. Anyhow, I must cross it, one way or another. Unfortunately, there is more peril beyond the Kanno, away north. So folk say. However, I believe the hills beyond can be reached nonetheless—again, with the right help. One has only to draw from the Well whence all good things come. Narrow at the mouth it is but wide at the bottom."

Setting his bowl upon the ground, the stranger continued, "I've often found in my travels that a helping hand may make all the difference between tragedy and triumph. But as there is more than one hand to choose from, one must be careful, for some hands which are thought to help may actually bring bring a great deal of harm. And if you've taken one of those, well ... you can't grab the Hand of Help until you've let the Hand of Harm go."

Rising, he nodded to each of them in turn and said, "I thank you for your hospitality, but I must be getting on. There will be no sleep for me tonight, and I have many miles to go." And with that, he walked off into the darkness, disappearing into the shadows of the pines to the north of their clearing.

"That certainly was strange," declared Wunko, spitting a piece of his leaf.

"Very," Okona agreed.

Wunko extinguished the fire, and then they all laid down in the midst of the glade. Anisha and the Tikkichaw fell into slumber rather quickly, but Okona laid awake for some time, pondering the stranger's peculiar advice.

Not long after the sun had risen the next day, they broke camp.

"Today we go to Lalaska Point, the eastern end of Kalmora Mountain," announced Wunko. "It's an overlook high above the Kanno, and I want to take a look around there, as it'd be very beneficial for us to know if our enemies are anywhere about."

It was a journey of six and a half miles north by northwest from their pine glade to the aforementioned point, an impressive sandstone outcrop. As they approached it, they were obliged to reckon with the steep eastern slope of Kalmora Mountain. Yet, this hour-long travail was much more agreeable to them than the terrifying ascent of Ponca Peak. And when they reached the top, both Okona and Anisha agreed the climb was worth it, for they were now some eight hundred feet above the river, which wound broadly through the verdant landscape before them, flowing out of the northwest and curving near the mountain's foot to head east, then meandering to the north again farther downstream. The vista was incredible, and the green majesty of the Kanno Valley had never been so apparent to them as it was from this lofty height. The sun flashed upon the Kanno's waters, and all the valley seemed alive with the magic Mahna Shuya had woven into the world when it was first born.

Wunko raised his hand to his eyes and carefully surveyed the landscape, scanning from west to east.

"Oh, dear heavens, no," he moaned. "I very much hope that's not …"

A black speck was in the sky far, far down the river but growing larger every moment.

"Great wippikats! It is!" he cursed, when it had come close enough that all could clearly identify it.

"Take cover!" he commanded, and they all ducked behind one of the great boulders near the rim of Lalaska Point.

"It's like it knows exactly where we are," stormed Okona, "and probably even where we're going. It's not fair. We've been hiking for days to get clear of it, and here it comes soaring through the miles like they're nothing."

"Perhaps it does know where we are and even where we're going, but crossing at Aska Karalonga is still our best hope," said Wunko, peeking out from behind the rock and discovering (with no small amount of deflation) that the ganoja was following the river on to the northwest.

Slumping back against the boulder, Wunko sighed and stared dismally at his lap.

Suddenly, he perked up. "You know, something's just occurred to Uncle Wunko. I was just thinking about what that strange fellow said last night, and I think if we get the right help, we could outdo that old ganoja."

"Oh?" prompted Anisha. "How?"

"Not far from here is an area called the Halahna, which lies atop and descends down Kalmora Mountain. Really quite beautiful it is. And it's hallowed by the Kamingo and even by the Chadori. Well, of course, that goes without saying, since all Chadori are of the Kamingo tribe. But not all Kamingo become Chadori, only the ones drawn by the lure of banditry. But when I said Kamingo, I meant the good ones, not the *marauders*, which of course is what Chadori means in the Kamingo language. But anyway, that's neither here nor there at the moment. The point is that even the Chadori hold the place consecrated, as there's a sacred cascade there, Banuma Falls, that is inhabited by many watamora; those are water spirits venerated by the Kamingo. They've aided me before, and I suggest we give them an offering and see if they will not grant their aid again. As their power lies in water, perhaps they will hold enough sway with the spirits of the Kanno to persuade them to restrain the ganoja long enough for us to cross."

"It's worth a try," said Okona, shrugging. "After all, we're beyond much aid from our Powers now, so we'll have to seek it somewhere else."

After taking a bit of food, the trio headed west through a forest, heavy with the scent of pines, along the ridge of Kalmora Mountain, then began veering slightly south to head down into the Halahna. It was gorgeous, just as Wunko had said, garbed in flowing water and the gayest green of summer, rife with singing streams, bright forests and timeworn boulders with many a tale to tell. Something moving and spectacular was always at hand.

When they had come nearly six miles from Lalaksa Point, they reached the mirthful course of Banuma Creek, which flowed west toward Banuma Falls. Soon, they heard its rush in the distance and maneuvered their way through the forest, climbing up the left wall of the valley in which the creek lay, until they could hardly hear anything over the huge cascade.

Then they saw it, plunging a hundred feet down from a sheer rock face, which was clad with adventurous greenery, into a shining pool below. They themselves were now more than a hundred feet higher than the top of the falls, but due to the steepness of the canyon, they were unable to get any nearer to the cascade.

"Never fear. It matters not whether the offering actually touches the water," explained Wunko. "It is sufficient to cast it into this valley, for all this place is hallowed."

Wunko uttered something in a language the Sakooma did not understand as he took out a leather pouch from his pack and removed several pressed, bright orange flowers from it. These he tossed in the direction of the falls, issuing a petition in the same foreign tongue as he did so.

"May the watamora hear and help us," he said, as he turned to face them.

But no sooner had he done so than he cried out in alarm, and Okona and Anisha were gripped by ferocious hands from behind.

Chapter Ten

Maze of the Marauders

T HE ENSUING STRUGGLE DID not end well for the young Sakooma. Though they strove with all their effort, they could not break free of the fierce fingers, and momentarily, they were face to face with the bearish visages of a host of fifteen men. Ruddy-skinned they were, as are all the peoples of Sarkanna. All were armed with spears and clad only in long, dark breeches, their black hair shaven except for single, long braids that fell behind their heads. Wunko tried diving out of their grasp, but as he was on the edge of a cliff and had nowhere to go but toward them, he was quickly nabbed and brought into submission.

The men began speaking rapidly to each other in some foreign language. Okona guessed it to be Kamingo, based on the speech of visiting merchants he had heard on occasion. Now it was clear these were none other than the dreaded Chadori, the roving Kamingo bandits of southwest Sarkanna.

Evidently having reached some kind of agreement, the Chadori commenced to mercilessly pummel their captives. All three en-dured bruises, bangs, slaps and spitting before they sank to the ground, unable to resist any longer. Then the Chadori knotted their hands behind their backs with strands of twisted foxbane and tied dark cloths over their eyes. After that, they plundered all they found on the prisoners, save their garments. A horrid tightness seized Okona's gut, as they removed both his flute and his gift from the Seer.

"Tóchà, tóchà!" one of the Chadori ordered, and the prisoners were nudged (none too gently) in the smalls of their backs.

Shortly, they were trotting along through the forest. But the captives faltered somewhat frequently, unable to see hazards that lay at their feet. The noise of the falls grew more distant and, after a while, indiscernible. Okona was listening carefully for anything that might indicate what direction they were going, but the shock of the last few minutes had rather disoriented him.

After many stumbling steps (covering about a mile by Okona's tentative reckoning), the prisoners were brought to a halt. Then they were dragged some feet away from the company and thrust upon packed earth.

A sharp voice, the same one who had given the command by the falls, demanded,

"Rákarábu yach-Kamingó'a?"

There was no response.

"Bugà yushnói?"

This time, Wunko returned, "I'm sorry, sir, but we don't speak your language. But if you speak Sakooma, we could understand. Sakooma? You talk Sakooma?"

"Talk Sakooma'a?" the man replied. "Talk! Where from?"

"Down Kanno," Wunko answered. "We go river."

"Here no Kanno," the man said irritably. "Where witch?"

"Witch?" asked Okona perplexedly.

"We haven't seen any witch," insisted Anisha.

"Where witch?" the man asked again, more aggressively this time.

"No witch," Wunko asserted. "No see witch. No know witch."

"You no talk witch, Chadori kill," the man threatened.

"No kill. No see witch."

The man struck Wunko, then said, "You no talk witch?"

"I no can."

"Chadori kill you night."

This time Wunko did not respond, and the man stalked off.

Although unsure if there were any Chadori nearby, Okona nonetheless ventured, "These Chadori are even more awful than stories make them out to be."

"Yes, I'd have thought even *they* wouldn't do a thing like that at the sacred falls," agreed Wunko. "And I do hope the watamora pay them back for it."

"What do you make of all that business about a witch?"

"Please hush, Okona," advised Wunko. "Enemies everywhere and all that. We'll talk about it later if we can. Unfortunately, I think we're in for a miserable afternoon."

Wunko's words regrettably proved prophetic, for the following hours were indeed most unpleasant. The captives' blindfolds were not removed, so they sat long in darkness, fearing to move, fearing to speak. Every once in a while, one of the Chadori would come kick them for sport. Also, the same fellow who had interrogated them before would come back and make further inquiries about the witch. These episodes always ended in them having no viable response, him threatening to kill them and then storming off.

At last, songs of insects and birds signaled that evening was nigh, and the voices of the Chadori grew farther off.

Suddenly, Okona felt his blindfold being loosened. He blinked in the sudden light. It was sunset, and he was beneath a little overhang of rock at the back of a clearing almost entirely surrounded by large boulders. The place was devoid of Chadori, and Wunko was next to him, unbound, tossing Okona's blindfold aside, as he hurried over to undo Anisha's.

"Wunko, what are you ... how did you ..."

"Uncle Wunko's got a few tricks on hand that'll do in a pinch," the Tikkichaw waggishly replied.

Now working on undoing Anisha's cords, Wunko explained, "Night's coming on, and I knew the Chadori would be going for their sunset smoke. So this was our one and probably only chance to get away."

"Sunset smoke?" asked Anisha. "What is that and how do you know about it?"

"I know a lot of things," said Wunko, "for a storyteller's got to—"

"But how'd you get free?" Okona hurriedly interrupted. "And how long do we have before the Chadori get back?"

Wunko came over to remove the binding on the lad's wrists. "I waited till I thought they were all gone and then began making my way toward that fire over there. I'm sure you've heard it going all day. Then I held my cords by the hot stones until I could get them off. Was a tricky and rather painful affair, but it did the job. And as for how long we have, only a minute or two, I should guess. The Chadori love their shoggo. Smoking it at sunset is a longtime custom of theirs, both for pleasure and—well, we don't need to go into all that now. But they'll be back before the sun is down, and as you can see, that's going to be any moment. Now, let's get! I don't know if there's a clear route out of this place without running into them on the way, but regardless, let's creep up that little slot that leads out of the clearing and see what we have to work with."

"What about our things?" Anisha asked. "We'll probably have a rough time without our food and supplies, and I, for one, have some items I'd very much like to get back."

"I'm sorry, Miss Anisha, but I don't think there's any time to roust them out. There's something I'd hate to lose too, but I'd hate more for us to lose our lives."

While they had been conversing, Okona had made his way to the other side of the clearing. There he chanced upon a small, shallow grotto that had been concealed from view until he got to this particular angle. "Why they've thrown all our things in here!" he excitedly declared.

Wunko and Anisha rushed over, and the girl snatched up her silver bracelet and necklace, Okona his sunfire shard and flute and Wunko his little box. Then they took up the rest of their effects and hurried to the narrow slot through the boulders that led out of the bowl in which they had been imprisoned. The path wound between the great stones, which were so close that one could touch either side just by reaching out. They couldn't see a side passage ahead but knew there must be at least one from the echoes of Chadori voices coming from the left.

"If we go down this path, we'll be spotted; I guarantee it," said Wunko, biting his lip.

"There's got to be another way," said Okona. He looked up, then turned to Wunko and Anisha. "How are you at climbing?"

"With our packs and everything?" Anisha asked.

"With or without. Do you think we could get to the top of these rocks? I'm decent with some of the bigger trees near my village, and I know stones aren't quite the same, but I really think this is climbable."

"If it's between this and the Chadori, this is certainly preferable," said Wunko.

"Actually ..." Okona went twenty feet farther down the twisting walkway. "Here. This spot's much better." He beckoned to them.

They followed him into the gloom, for the path was now quite dark, as the sun was giving its last, red light, almost none of which fell into the slot.

"We've all got to climb better and faster than ever we have," Okona urged.

"Miss Anisha, you go first," prompted Wunko.

The girl quickly began clambering up, jamming herself into a crevice cut in the huge boulder, and as soon as she had ascended a few feet, Okona followed, with Wunko picking his way up from behind. It was perilous work, for the cut was very steep and not quite wide enough that any of them could get all the way in; thus, a fall would have brought them tumbling onto the path beneath. But their luck held, and they proceeded higher and higher until Anisha was forty feet up the rock face.

Chadori laughter rang out from below. They fain would have climbed faster, but knew this would prove disastrous, so continued to carefully select their handholds and footholds. While Okona waited for Anisha to find a viable route, many Chadori filed down the path toward the clearing. It would be only moments before their escape was discovered.

Anisha had just cleared the top of the immense boulder when shouts of rage and alarm echoed among the towering rocks. "Yochkunábe! Yochkunábe!"

Okona and Wunko scaled the remaining rock as quickly as they could, then breathlessly joined Anisha, as Chadori poured back into the network of paths leading through the maze of boulders.

"Ah, this is a much better vantage point," said Wunko. "Excellent idea, Okona. From atop this group of boulders, we can see the lay of things and, with the help of fading sun and rising moon, perhaps spot where all the dratted Chadori are. The only trouble will be if there's a spot too wide to jump."

He led them across to the edge of the boulder farthest away from the clearing, then sprang across the gap to another mammoth rock. They did this several more times to reach other boulders, but on the last instance, Anisha nearly plummeted to the floor of the slot fifty feet below. Fortunately, Okona, who was waiting to grab her hand, reached out and helped her up.

"Perhaps we shouldn't do any more of those," Okona recommended. "We've got to get down at some point anyway. Might as well see to it now."

On the back side of this boulder, they found a series of shelves leading down to a slot that continued on to join the network of paths below. They raced down these, then began following another slot they hoped would ultimately lead them out of the labyrinth.

"Chabà!" hollered a voice behind them. They turned to see a stout Chadori, spear in hand, running toward them. Within moments, many other Chadori poured out of various side passageways to join him.

The desperate trio ran like mad, having no choice but to select their route blindly at each twist, turn and opening of new paths. Wunko dashed in front, with Anisha just behind and Okona bringing up the rear, every once in a while looking over his shoulder to see whether the Chadori were gaining on them.

Their hearts racing, the threesome bolted out from between two jagged cliffs and found they had escaped the maze and were running through a forest of stately pines, which were interspersed with mossy boulders.

"Couldn't do that again if we tried," Wunko panted. "But farewell, Maze of the Marauders!"

The party, with renewed energy, tore through the twilit woods, thinking that if only they could put enough distance between them and their pursuers, they might be able to hide. Driven as they were, the fugitives managed to outpace the Chadori enough to use the sloped terrain to their advantage. As they came up a miniature valley, they climbed over the left ridge, then down the other side, so they were hidden from the Chadori's eyes for nearly half a minute. In this time, they began running back down toward the Chadori, only on the other side of the ridge. Thus, when their pursuers came over the ridge and continued onward, they were actually moving farther away from their quarry.

The threesome hurried to the northeast, ever crouching just in case there were any Chadori about. The boulder maze was more or less directly to the north of them now, and they of course had no desire to return there, but Wunko had a hunch Banuma Creek lay to the north, for the land sloped down in that direction. He hoped they might rejoin the creek some distance to the east of the boulders and make their way from there.

His suspicion proved valid, for not long afterward, they reached the creek and followed it back up to Banuma Falls, then some distance beyond that to where they could ford the watercourse. After crossing the stream, they labored on into the moonlit night.

"Is this a better time to ask what that fellow meant by pressing us about that witch?" asked Okona, as they hiked through the forest.

"Certainly is!" Wunko laughed. "And I'm afraid I'll have to let you two in on a rather naughty secret."

"And what is that?" inquired Anisha.

"I happen to know some Kamingo," the Tikkichaw impishly replied.

"You do?" started Okona.

"Not a great deal, mind you, but enough to do some damage. Learned it from two fellows I traveled with for some time a ways up the Anoka. Anyway, much of what our friends were talking about was beyond me, but I did gather this—the Chadori weren't sure who we were, but they did recognize you two as Sakooma, so they took us for a bounty, a bounty set by the Jaggo. I'm sure they would have nabbed us of their own accord anyhow, but they were promised a pretty treasure by the Jaggo for any wandering Sakooma, and the condition was that we had to be alive, I think. Not that we'd be likely to stay alive once the Jaggo got hold of us, but the Jaggo wanted information first, information about the one they were calling the *witch*."

"And who in all the stars is that?" queried Anisha.

"I'm not sure the Chadori themselves were privy to that. They only knew she was a Sakooma who had last been sighted by Ponca Peak, and they wanted to know where she was so they could capture her. So I guess it may be your Wise-woman."

"Yahsi? Why do they think she's a witch?" asked Okona. "She can't do even a bit of magic, except the plain, ordinary and wonderful kind found among the especially wise." He recalled the cheering twinkle of her eyes and smiled. But his joy quickly faded into melancholy. "Anyway, she's gone. Why do they ... oh, I have so many questions."

"Well, I don't have too many answers."

"But how could the Jaggo communicate with the Chadori?" inquired Anisha. "I thought they couldn't talk."

"Don't know. Uncle Wunko's fairly stumped by a lot of things, just as you are. Anyway, let's all quiet down for the rest of the night so we can watch with our ears as well as our eyes. Unfortunately, we'll need to march till we drop just to put as much distance between ourselves and those knaves as we can. But if our fortune holds, we'll be able to get over the Kanno by tomorrow night and leave most of our troubles behind—at least for a while."

"Alas! Much is set against us crossing the Kanno," said Anisha wearily. "There's that dreadful ganoja flying about, but the Chadori will likely be coming after us too, and I wouldn't be a bit surprised if the Jaggo were still tracking us."

"It could be worse," Wunko muttered. "We might already be where we're going. We might already be facing *them*."

"At what point are you two going to tell me who *them* is?" Anisha huffed. "I assume it's whoever it is that's got the Hand of Hamora, but—"

"Anisha, don't you recall what Wunko told you?" asked Okona. "It really is best if we continue to avoid the matter for now. To speak of them will only stir up bad magic, and we've already got plenty against us." He rubbed one of his recently acquired bruises.

"Besides, if we complete our northward journey, you'll find out who *they* are soon enough," murmured Wunko.

This last remark made shivers run down everyone's spines, and such apprehension fell upon the party that they were silent for a long time.

As they were nearing the western crest of Kalmora Mountain, a shadow, like unto some great, long-tailed fowl, sped across the waning gibbous moon. They tried to console themselves by imagining it was only a hawk or the like, but each in his heart knew it was not so.

Nonetheless, burying their dread as best they could, they clambered down the west slope of the mountain with the moon of pale silver watching on.

Chapter Eleven

Guardians of the Kanno

All told, they journeyed another six miles through the night before they were too exhausted to go any farther. Most of this trek was to the west but angled slightly to the south. Luckily for them, the majority of the march was in the flatlands of the Kanno Valley, for the terrain leveled off and remained relatively tame after they descended from Kalmora Mountain.

They slept for a few hours beneath a stand of old oaks at the edge of a meadow, and when light came, they groggily forced themselves to continue.

After journeying five more miles westward, they veered sharply northward for the last ten miles to Aska Karalonga. Always they sought to keep to the woods and under cover rather than crossing open glades or fields. A heavy disquiet hung over them now; each was thinking of the ganoja's shadow against the moon, remembering its searching eyes and enormous, greedy beak, all the while imagining a whole army of Jaggo stealing along behind them, ready to reveal themselves only when they were well and truly trapped between them and the monster keeping watch on the Kanno.

In the late afternoon, the Kanno swept in from their right, its path converging with their own. But there was nary a sign of the ganoja, and their hopes rose. They followed the Kanno's bank northward, and soon the wooden, mud and grass structures of the Kamingo settlement of Aska Karalonga came into sight, along with the imposing Pagoma Rock, the high sandstone crag just beyond it, whose lower section was garbed in woods of hickory, oak and pine. And that made them feel better still, if nothing else because there were quite a few people about. The perilous wilds where they would be defenseless if their enemies came upon them were, for the moment, left behind.

On the shore here rested many canoes and rafts of varying sizes. Scattered groups of Kamingo were at the water's edge, working on nets, fishing spears and baskets. Also, an assortment of colorful blankets were laid upon the ground in open areas between the buildings. These displayed wares of many kinds, and lively chatter drifted up from the traders gathered about the blankets.

As the wilderness-worn trio approached, one of the traders near the edge of the settlement spotted them, and, raising his hand in a brief halloo, called, "Àcho!"

"Àcho!" Wunko returned. "Rákarábu yach-Sákooma'a?"

"I certainly do!" replied the man, grinning. He did have an accent, but they could immediately tell his Sakooma was quite good.

"I'm Trader Teepu," the man declared, saluting them, first with his right elbow, then his left. They returned the gesture. "And did word of my excellent charms and amulets bring you to Aska Kara-longa? If so, I am honored." He bowed courteously.

"By our Powers, what luck!" laughed Okona. "We actually *could* use a charm or two. And a canoe. Just to cross the river though, not to keep."

"Charms and a ferry? I can supply you with both. Come, have a look at the charms first. I've got ones for every kind of problem you could wish to ward off."

"We'll likely need all of them," Anisha mumbled, only half-joking.

"I suppose we might," whispered Wunko, "for it doesn't seem we'll be getting any aid from those watamora back at Banuma Falls, eh? They didn't seem to take too kindly to my overtures." Then, as Teepu was walking off to guide them, Wunko said to the Sakooma, "It's fine if we take a look at his charms, but please say nothing to him of the ganoja—or the Jaggo, for that matter. His interest in helping us might well vanish altogether if he learns what we're trying to ward off. Understand?"

The two nodded.

Teepu led them to the midst of the settlement to a spot where several youths (evidently his sons based on their resemblance) were manning his wares, which were laid out neatly on a large blue blanket. He spread his arm toward the multiple dozens of rings, amulets, bracelets, trinkets and various other bric-a-brac resting upon the cloth.

"What precisely do you need?" Teepu prompted.

"Well," said Okona, "if you have any specifically designed to protect one from the Powers of Water, we'd be glad to get several of those."

"I've the very thing," sang Teepu, plucking three small, light blue stones from the blanket and dropping them in the trio's hands. "You're fortunate because these are the last and best ones I have in stock. Got them from some first-rate enchanters down in the Forest of the Fifty Founts. There's a lot of good enchanters down that way, what with access to so many magical waters. But anyhow, I'd say these should be able to shield you from just about any mischief Water may try to work on you. Now, what were you thinking of offering in exchange?"

The three hesitated, having not thought about this until just now.

"We've got a fair amount of provisions in our pack," said Wunko hopefully. "Would you be interested in any of those?"

"I'm afraid that won't do." Teepu shook his head. "You see, these charms are really quite potent and thus rather valuable."

"We don't have much to offer, for we didn't come here to trade, you see," explained Anisha. "We would like these charms, of course, but I'm not sure any of us would wish to part with our few items of greatest value for them."

"I understand," said Teepu. "Of course, I don't want to pressure you into anything, but if you are looking for significant protection, you'd be unlikely to find something as effective as these for a good fifty miles round."

"Might we confer privately for a moment?" asked Okona.

"Of course!" Teepu replied.

The three stepped aside a number of yards, and Okona said, "I think we'd all agree we must get across the Kanno, for it just wouldn't do to give up after coming so far. But I've no desire whatever to run into that awful ganoja. Yet I'm afraid if we don't get these charms, that's exactly what will happen."

"But Okona," said Wunko, "remember that we're headed back into the wild as soon as we come to the other side of the Kanno. So we really can't afford to separate with any of our gear or weapons. Things will be hard enough as it is."

"Yes, and the only other things we have are items of personal significance," added Anisha. "He might take my bracelet or necklace, but those are mementos of my mother and Tencum, and I don't think I could bring myself to part with them."

"Then I'll ..." started Okona, "I'll offer him my flute."

"But that's your livelihood!" exclaimed Anisha. "And it was made and given to you by Yahsi herself, wasn't it? And she's been ever so important in your life, as much as your own mother and maybe more so."

"I know." Okona hung his head. "And I did not suggest trading it lightly. If we lack those charms, we might well perish, and then Yahsi would have given herself in vain. I suppose Orobec's band is still going to seek in the north, so they may be able to recover the Hand and save our people. But the Seer made it seem there's something I myself need to do away north for this quest to succeed. Anyway, I'm determined to do everything we can to make it to the Kannitaw Mountains, which is where he said we could find the Hand. And if that means giving up the flute, then so be it."

Anisha frowned.

"Lad," said Wunko, "if this flute is important to you, I—"

"My mind is made up." Okona set his jaw. "This is for the welfare of all the Sakooma. We've got to make it over the Kanno, and I think that will only be possible if we have those charms."

"If you're really set on this, there's nothing we can do to stop you," Wunko declared.

"I just hate to see you barter off something that means ever so much to you," Anisha sighed.

"Me too," said Okona grimly, as they walked back over to Teepu.

Almost wincing, Okona pulled his flute out of his pocket and held it out to the trader. "How would this do? It was made by the greatest Sakooma Master Song-maker of our day. Plays wonderfully, and I can demonstrate if you like."

"Perhaps," said Teepu, taking the flute and running his fingers along it. He looked it up and down, eyeing it both from close-up and at a distance.

"All right, lad. The charms are yours," he said with gusto, distributing the charms to each of them.

Okona felt he should have been relieved that the trade had cleared, but he was filled rather with equal parts sorrow and regret. "I'm sorry, Yahsi," he murmured.

"This is a very fine instrument," Teepu praised, as he pocketed it. "In fact, your Master Song-maker's work is the best I've seen. This is indeed a worthy match for the craft of the Forest of the Fifty Founts."

Then he added, "And I'll tell you what; I'll throw in a nice supper and a place to spend the night if you're willing to stick around till tomorrow. What's more, I'll give you the canoe ride you were wanting for free too."

"Your canoe deal we'll graciously accept, but unfortunately, we really shouldn't spend the night here," said Wunko.

"Mightn't we at least stay for supper?" asked Okona, who wasn't particularly keen on rations again for the evening meal.

"Yes, Mister Teepu's offer is very generous," voiced Anisha.

"Very well," sighed Wunko. "But let's cross the Kanno right after."

"Splendid!" Teepu clapped his hands together.

He led them to a largish grass and mud hut not far from the riverbank, and there he introduced them to his wife, Kachya, who was already getting together ingredients for a great pot of stew. A number of sleeping mats were in the hut, and Teepu offered to the party to rest on a few of them until dinner was ready. Grateful for even a short respite, they accepted this invitation, and Okona and Anisha lay down, while Wunko went off to clamber to the top of Pagoma Rock—to have a good look around, he said. The Tikkichaw returned less than an hour later with favorable tidings; the ganoja was nowhere in sight for miles. This news put all of them at ease. Only a short while later, the day found them napping, though none of them had actually intended to fall asleep.

They awoke nearly all at once rather less than an hour before sunset. Dismayed they had slept so long, they rose and discovered that Teepu's family had just finished the preparation of their repast. They sat with the family outside and shared a hearty stew of fish, herbs and bemmica beans. No one in the family but Teepu spoke Sakooma, so he alternated between chatting with his family and his guests. And sometimes Wunko spoke with Teepu or the others in a bit of Kamingo.

When they had each drained several bowls, Okona, Anisha and Wunko stood and thanked Teepu for his hospitality, then asked if he could shuttle them across the river presently. They had been glancing skyward somewhat frequently during the meal and still seen nothing of the ganoja so were hopeful that now, at the approach of nightfall, they might pass the Kanno undetected.

Teepu took them to the water's edge. The last rays of the sun fell upon the massive Pagoma Rock, which cast an enormous shadow upon the Kanno's dancing waters. On the far bank, many pines formed a wall at the edge of the sprawling forest. And in the midst of the river were a host of Kamingo canoes, filled with fishermen busy with their nightly catch. The sky above was dotted with clouds, which had taken on a ghostly, bluish hue. And behind them, the settlement of Aska Karalonga was covered with a twilight hush, only broken by occasional, distant peals of neighborly laughter.

Teepu took the helm of his long canoe, and the others stepped in behind, then helped him paddle out into the river. Past many canoes they went, and Teepu called out to their occupants cheery Kamingo greetings, which they jovially returned.

When they had barely passed the middle of the river, the canoe jostled dramatically.

"Now, what could be—" started Teepu, but his voice was drowned out by a violent splash that erupted just to the left of the canoe. A baneful, blue light commenced to glow just beneath the water there, and a shape began forming under the surface. It was neither shadow nor flesh, but appeared to be wrought of water darker than that of the river itself. Shortly, this water had coalesced into something akin to a mangled wildcat in the head, body and forelimbs, though the back was like unto a fish, with both fins and tail.

Before the party had a chance to paddle away, this thing sprang from the water directly at Okona. Crying out, he raised his oar to ward it off, and the form broke just as would a wave, but wherever it touched his skin and that of the others, there was a loud hissing, and their flesh burned mightily, though no lasting sign of this was there upon the flesh. They all began screaming, for none had been unscathed. But to their horror, the form consolidated once again on the other side of the boat and whirled around. And to their even greater alarm, a second form began to collect itself just behind the canoe's stern.

"Great wippikats! By all that is dark and dreadful," swore Wunko, "they're real!"

"What are real?" hollered Anisha.

"Yakoba!" shouted Wunko, as the first form flung itself at Anisha, who, like Okona, tried to thwart it with her oar. But she also was drenched and burned as it broke, and only moments later, it had amassed once more, just to the left of the canoe.

"Are these what you feared?" howled a terrified Teepu.

"No!" Wunko returned. "The real trouble—"

At that moment came a piercing cry from high above, a blood-curling screech that blared in their eardrums. The ganoja was spiraling down out of the dusk. Fishermen wailed and cursed, and bows and spears were raised.

"Ganoja! Ganoja!" rang out Wunko's cry. "Keshwèna! Keshwèna!"

"How can we kill a thing like that?" Teepu bawled. "And I can't understand how all this could happen if you each have your charms!"

Just then, Wunko was beset by one of the yakoba. Much distracted by the ganoja, he had not been prepared to defend himself and thus was drenched in the monster's wash. Now his whole body burned like fire.

As another yakoba leapt out of the river, Okona held up his oar once more, but the agony-inducing water covered his face nonetheless. Gasping, the lad saw that there were no less than five of these creatures surrounding the canoe.

"Ee-ai, ee-ai!" came Kamingo shrieks from Aska Karalonga. Many men were running on the bank, seizing canoes and propelling them out into the water.

"Those are Jaggo!" Anisha gasped. "Jaggo and Chadori! We are lost! Oh, we are lost!"

All at once, four yakoba sprang viciously from the water, flinging themselves against every one of the canoe's occupants. So sudden and forceful was the onslaught that the craft tilted, and they all toppled out into the river, though the canoe immediately righted itself.

Fighting their way to the surface, the yakoba's victims emerged, soaked and gasping.

A Kamingo scream rang out above the river, as the ganoja released an unfortunate fisherman from his tearing claws. The man, waving his arms, plummeted into the Kanno, and the monster swooped down to snatch another one of his assailants.

"What have you done, that all the fiends of the Underbrakes should be unleashed at once?" demanded Teepu, his voice shaking. "If I had known this would be the reward for my kindness, I would have withheld it!"

"I'm sorry," coughed Okona, "sorry we didn't tell you how perilous it might be. But even we didn't know things would be this bad."

"Small consolation," sputtered Teepu. "Worst customers I ever had! And you can keep that undoubtedly cursed flute you foisted on me." He flung the instrument toward Okona, who quickly swam to grab it. With that, Teepu swam off to the canoe of a fellow Kamingo who had been launching arrow after arrow at the ganoja, which was flying about erratically some distance above the river, dodging the many missiles hurtling toward it.

"Okona!" Anisha cried, struggling desperately to remain above the surface, as a yakoba grasped her leg.

Okona caught her hand and tried to pull her up, but just then, something terribly cold and vice-like seized his own leg. Staring into the depths, he spied an image of himself, shimmering darkly, with open mouth and wildest terror upon his visage, clasping Teepu's glowing charm in his flailing hand. The image was wrapped about with a shadowy tentacle that was swiftly dragging it into a horrid maw of shadow, darker still.

Utterly undone by this sight, he clutched his own charm tightly, and it, too, began to glow a pale blue. But as soon as he had done this, the creature pulling his leg squeezed ever so much more.

"This confounded charm isn't helping at all! It's making it worse!" he cried.

Then, like a thunderbolt, a realization struck him.

"It's the charms!" he yelled to Anisha, still fighting to his utmost against being tugged downward. "The charms are what brought these monsters. I can't explain it, but I think it must be so. We have to let them go!"

"What?" Anisha gurgled, her head only barely above the rolling water.

"It's what that stranger said: we can't grab onto the hand of help until we've let the hand of harm go. Get rid of your charm!"

Okona forcefully cast his into the black river, and Anisha followed suit. As soon as they had done this, the sinking, glowing charms lit up the water below, and the yakoba which had been coiled about the Sakooma released them and darted toward the lights. Within moments, they had devoured the stones and were turning back toward their prey, but there had fortunately been enough time in the interim for Okona and Anisha to start swimming toward Teepu's abandoned canoe.

Meanwhile, Wunko had already regained the craft and, hearing Okona's instructions to Anisha, had hurled his own charm away. Now he extended his hands to the Sakooma and heaved them into the canoe.

"I do believe you're right, Okona," Wunko wheezed. "Those charms seem to be what brought those awful yakoba up here to begin with. And I hope that now that they are gone, the yakoba will also depart. Ah, but I don't think our poor Teepu was trying to trick us nor that there was anything wrong, as such, with the charms. I think they ... well, I don't know what to think. But now that we've let go of the hand of harm, where is the hand of help?"

"Where indeed!" Anisha returned.

There was a loud thump, and the canoe rocked dangerously. The head of a yakoba disappeared under the vessel.

"Perhaps they can still attack, but just can't jump out of the river anymore," Okona said.

"I'm sure they could still give us plenty of trouble," warned Anisha.

"As could that ganoja," Wunko added. "Okona, fire upon him!"

The ganoja, held temporarily at bay by the Kamingo after its initial forays, had nonetheless maneuvered its way downward until it was not far from the Sakooma's canoe. Suddenly, it swept right toward them, its hideous claws outstretched.

Okona and Wunko readied their bows and loosed arrows at the speeding monster, which swerved to avoid them.

"Very close that was," puffed the Tikkichaw.

"Ah-ee-aye! Look to the Jaggo!" shouted Anisha. They all turned toward the settlement just in time to see the Jaggo out among the boats launching a volley of arrows. These clattered against the stern of the fugitives' canoe.

"Start paddling! Only a few strokes more from them and we'll be in their range!" cautioned Okona. All three of them took up oars and manically paddled toward the far bank. The Jaggo, however, were having some difficulty in their pursuit, for there were other vessels from Aska Karalonga in their way, and also, some of the Kamingo were engaged with them in combat.

As Okona, Anisha and Wunko were paddling onward, beyond the arena of mayhem and out into the open water, yakoba kept plowing into their boat, though they were unsuccessful in capsizing it. And the companions concluded Okona's guess may well have been correct, for they leapt no more from the water. However, the trio's skin still burned horribly from the yakoba's wash.

The ganoja had received several wounds from the Kamingo but none so serious as to keep it from flying. Now that the fleeing Sakooma and Tikkichaw were apart from the others, though, it was able to commence a clear dive toward them.

"Anisha, keep paddling," Wunko instructed. "Okona, spears this time!"

He and Okona poised their spears to hurl at the approaching ganoja, though the lad's courage quailed as its open, toothed beak dropped toward them.

"Now!" Wunko commanded, and the spears sailed upward. The ganoja veered aside, though not quite swiftly enough, for although

Okona's point barely missed it, Wunko's struck its left wing. However, the weapon did not quite puncture it and thus rebounded and splashed into the water below. Nonetheless, the monster was rattled by the attack, for it had some difficulty regaining control of its flight. It was then that Okona reached into the bottom of the canoe and grasped a large, smooth stone; it was one of Teepu's varied charms.

"I'm better with these anyway," he muttered.

The ganoja was commencing yet another dive when Okona let his stone fly. Through the air it sang, striking the monster with great force on its right shoulder. Immediately, it foundered, nearly crashing into the water before it was able to swerve upward.

Meanwhile, Wunko and Okona aided Anisha with many vigorous strokes, and soon they neared the river's far bank. As they came to the shallows, the yakoba who were still swirling about them sped off into the black under-regions of the Kanno.

The ganoja appeared at first to be preparing yet another pass at them but seemed then to think better of it, as its flying was slightly lopsided now. With a final sweep of its long, writhing tail, the monster took off into the black vault above. By now, the fulness of twilight had come, and stars, blue and silver, were beginning to wink in the heavens.

Heaving and sweating from their harrowing escape, Okona looked back across the river, from whence came Kamingo shouts and death wails, signaling an ongoing battle with the Chadori and the Jaggo, both on land and water.

"Those were mighty throws, you two," Anisha praised, as they took their effects from the canoe, which was now pulled ashore.

"I meant to get its head," Okona said, "but I'm glad I hit something anyhow."

"And mine was more lucky than mighty, I think," Wunko sighed. "You know, by all rights, we really shouldn't have made it past all those guardians of the Kanno, even with the debacle of the charms aside. Not that I'm complaining! Ah, I do suppose having an entire force of Kamingo aiding us was a significant factor in our success.

And I sincerely hope we can make amends to these people someday and to Teepu especially."

"Yes, I feely simply awful about not telling him what our danger might be," admitted Okona. "And my heart is broken to think that Kamingo have died because of our coming here. The least we could have done was to warn them."

"Sadly, there's nothing we can do about it right now," said Anisha. "In the meantime, we'd better get far away from this accursed river."

"Yes," Wunko urged. "For even now, death is not far behind."

Abandoning their canoe on the riverbank, they ducked off into the forest, aiming north by northeast. Their plan, once again, was to go as far as they could before they collapsed.

After pressing through a little more than five miles of shadowed land, much of which was covered with dense canebrakes, they came abruptly to the shores of a small lake. They were beginning to skirt to the right around it when Wunko pulled them into some rushes and whispered, "Look!"

A huge, gray-brown creature was lumbering out of the woods near the shore on great, three-toed feet. It stepped with two mighty legs, thick as pillars, into the shallows, then placed its thinner fore-limbs into the water and bent down to eat some of the weeds floating on the surface.

The animal was nearly fifty feet in length and had a thick, round body and neck and a rather large head. Its tail was greater in girth than a man's waist and hovered several feet over the water. Many spines stood upon the creature's back. Its immensity, combined with its queer manner of movement, made the onlookers almost question whether it was real.

"What is it?" asked Okona, in awe.

"If I'm not quite mistaken, that's a noolaboo," uttered Wunko. "I've heard tell of them, but never seen one myself. There are rather more of them up the Anoka though. Apparently not nearly as many as there used to be in the old days."

"Oh, some sort of marsh dragon?" said Okona. "Ah, yes, the Sakooma still see them from time to time, especially in Wayawoc Woods, though I haven't."

"It's absolutely wonderful," gasped Anisha.

The Tikkichaw smiled. "Yes. They've been with us since the days of the first man, the one you call Machakam. My people name him Oja. He was their keeper, for they were brought forth on the same day. And in his time, they could talk, it is said. But many of the dragons, like the ganoja, are dangerous now. Yet the noolaboo is not. Well, not especially anyway, at least to our race. But there are fewer and fewer of all such creatures now. I suppose folk may be sad when the terrible ones, the ganojas and so forth, are gone, for they certainly are a wonder, even if a monstrous one, though they might change their minds if they encountered one, as we have. But it will be a loss to the whole world when ones like noolaboo are no more. Yet such is the way of things. Always downward this green Massora of ours will go, until the end. And then, it is said by some, there will be a sudden turning, and things may be made right again. But we live still in an age of heroes and legends, and I fear the lesser men who follow us will not believe even a small part of what we have seen and done."

Taking a last, long look at the calmly grazing noolaboo, basking in the moonlight, Wunko stole off through the rushes, deeper into the woods, and in a few moments, the others followed.

Chapter Twelve

The Terrors of Toshigan Hollow

D URING THE NOCTURNAL MARCH that took the party due north from the lake of the noolaboo, each was largely occupied with his or her own thoughts, reflecting on all that had happened in the last few days and most especially on the terrifying crossing of the Kanno. Each tried to comprehend the puzzle of the yakoba and the charms, for why should the charms have worked the opposite of their design? But for this, tired minds unfortunately proved a poor match. By the time the fugitives had gone another four and a half miles, sloshing through arms of the lake to confuse the trail of any pursuing Jaggo or Chadori, climbing up into a wooded plateau and halting just before a small ridge, they were all completely spent. Casting themselves under shade of tree and stone, they were taken almost instantly by slumber.

All awakened rather later than they had intended the following day. The trees here were tall and broad and so garbed in rich foliage that sun came only to the forest floor in scattered, golden blotches. But they quickly discerned the morning was already several hours under way, and thus collected their equipment in haste and prepared to depart.

"I'm afraid Uncle Wunko may not be much help to you from this point on," said the Tikkichaw gloomily, as he checked the remaining liquid in his waterskin. "You see, I've never come this way before, and most of what I know about it I learned last night from our trader friend."

"Well, what you've got is still likely more than either of us know of this region," remarked Okona, slinging his quiver over his shoulder.

"Anyway, I don't remember any conversation regarding the matter. When did you get a chance to ask Teepu about it?"

"During dinner," said Wunko. "In Kamingo," he hastily added.

"What for? Was there something you didn't want us to hear?" inquired Anisha suspiciously.

"I'll tell you everything you wish to know right now, but I knew both of you were a little on edge during supper—as was I to some extent—and I just didn't want to involve us all in talk about upcoming dangers when we already had ones near at hand."

"Ah," said Okona. "That was courteous of you. What did you learn, then?"

"Only a few details and nothing encouraging," sighed Wunko. "That spot where we saw the noolaboo last night was Lake Oganosha, I'm fairly certain, based on Teepu's description. In, oh, I would guess another ten miles from here, we should come to the Kannitaw Mountains proper. And Teepu's knowledge mostly fails beyond that point, save for the half-light shed by rumors, for the Kamingo themselves refuse to even go that way. Land's overtaken by a curse, they claim. I didn't tell him where exactly we were going or what we were doing, only that we were going north. He did advise us to avoid the Kannitaw altogether if we could help it, or at least the upper vales of the Wakosi River, for there is said to be great evil there. But, of course, that's precisely what we're looking for. Working from legends I've heard over the years, I had suspected we ought to begin our search in the upper Wakosi, and Teepu's warnings only served to confirm that."

"Also, he cautioned strongly against approaching the Wakosi from the south in particular, for there is, among the maze of hills and hollows, a certain spot with a dark and ancient magic upon it. Toshigan Hollow they call it. The trees grow black there, but after nightfall glow as ghosts; they have a strange power to draw travelers thither, where nameless terrors stalk when twilight falls. No man has walked among them and lived, they say, but Kamingo sorcerers have seen the place in their dreams. He couldn't tell me rightly where it was, only that it lies between the Kannitaws' rise in the south and the Wakosi's flow in the north."

"So, are we to make for that very hollow, then?" asked Anisha nervously. "Is that where you think the Hand is?"

"No," replied Wunko, hoisting his pack. "Whatever evil lies in Toshigan Hollow is, I think, separate from what we're seeking, which is rumored to be in the Wakosi Vale itself. So, if it all possible, we should avoid the hollow, especially after nightfall."

The Tikkichaw looked at Okona and said, "And that, my lad, is something I think we ought to entrust to you."

"Me?" Okona started, staring back at him. "Why?"

"Well, you're the only one among us who was actually chosen to go on this mission, and we've come now to a land in which I'll be of no more service than anyone else. You two were kind enough to let me guide you through the Washoma, and we've finished that leg. But I think this last leg ought to be yours."

Okona looked down thoughtfully. Then, after several moments, he raised his head and said, "All right. I'll lead us in these northern lands. But I hope you'll still be available for consultation?"

"Absolutely." Wunko grinned.

"Thanks, Uncle Wunko." Anisha smiled, patting him on the back, as they began hiking toward the ridge to the north.

That day, due to their starting later and still being so wearied by the previous night, they only journeyed eleven miles. The land was noticeably hillier than that of the Kanno Valley, but still, they were only among the foothills of the Kannitaw. They crossed several valleys and streams and a decent-sized plateau, bearing ever north by northwest. In the afternoon, they halted in a forested upland where they hoped to restock their waterskins and gather food until it got dark. After a good deal of success in this endeavor, they bedded down near a creek to a distant chorus of bullfrogs.

The bullfrogs had fallen silent by the next morning when they set out, which was much earlier than the day before. Fifteen miles they crossed this second day, but these were harder, for not long after they embarked, the Kannitaw Mountains began in earnest. Furthermore, there was heavy rain for several hours that morning. All the slopes were longer and steeper here, the ridges higher and the vales more dramatic. Route-finding took quite a bit more attention too, due to the complexity of the land. But Okona still kept their course aimed north by northwest, for in that direction lay the sources of the Wakosi (according to Wunko, who had been told thus by Teepu). Later in the day, however, the way became more accommodating, as they were able to follow a creek through a long, winding valley for quite some distance.

There was a kind of magic here in the Kannitaw, and all three of them felt it definitively. In the lowlands of the Kanno, one could perhaps ignore the presence of the Other-lands, where the Powers dwelt, if he wished. But here the two worlds were brought closer together. And, as the veil was thinner, the enchantments with which that other realm brimmed seeped into the very rocks, trees and waters. Even the air seemed to tingle, if ever so slightly.

Their encampment that night was upon a little shelf above the creek they had followed in the afternoon, overshadowed by the eastern wall of the valley in which it flowed. Though they had seen no Jaggo for two days now and were well beyond the realm of the ganoja, they nonetheless felt a growing apprehension. Something was amiss here, though they could not tell what. But this awareness disrupted their sleep on multiple occasions, robbing them of proper rest.

When the sun rose again, they resolved to cover as much distance as possible, so as to leave this area far behind. They followed the narrow valley of the creek for several miles until they came to a broader vale, and here they began to feel dream-bound, for the air was heavy, as were their legs and eyes.

"It's morning yet. How can we already be dragging like this?" mumbled Okona.

"I feel as if I could sleep for a week," yawned Anisha.

"If we just keep moving, perhaps we can get ourselves back into a proper rhythm," suggested Wunko.

"There are few things so stirring for the blood as a good, stiff climb," said Okona, "so I propose we scale that north wall of the valley and keep going north as straight as we can, no matter what the Kannitaws throw at us."

All agreed to this, so they made their way up a northern arm of the valley until they were forced to clamber up a relatively steep face to depart from it. Once they had gotten to the top (a task which took them a fair amount of both time and effort), they thought their journey might prove easier. But it was not to be so.

To keep a northward course, they ambled through a wilderness of hills and washes, all blanketed in unending forest. They grew wearier by the minute and wondered if they would not be obliged to halt for the day, though they had only trekked a little more than eight miles. But already, it was afternoon.

Strangely enough, Okona was overcome by a sudden sense of surety, an instinct that he knew precisely which route they must take. This did nothing to curb his drowsiness, but at least it gave him hope that their progress was not in vain. Armed with this satisfaction, he guided the others on at a slightly quicker pace.

They descended into a valley and crossed a creek, then scrambled up the vale's wall to the northeast. Attaining a plateau, they trudged on until the land sank several hundred feet into a deep hollow, ringed with steep, pine-clad slopes and high rock walls, save on the west. After a precarious descent, they reached the bottom of this, removed their equipment, relieved themselves and collapsed.

"As the fowl reckon it, little more than ten miles we've come, I should guess," moaned Wunko, "yet I feel as if I could die."

"This is no common fatigue of a journey," swore Okona. "There must be some enchantment on these mountains. Can you not feel the air? It's so ... so ... heavy."

"Oh, by the Powers, no!" Anisha gasped. "Look! Look at the trees!"

Okona and Wunko forced their heads up and gazed about deliriously.

"They're black!" Okona exclaimed. "This must be ..."

"Toshigan Hollow," finished Wunko despairingly.

The dark, twisted trees all about them seemed suddenly to lean toward them, their branches rattling and scraping ominously, though there was no wind.

"How did I manage to lead us here, of all places?" cursed Okona. "And I felt so sure we were bearing correctly, too. How did I miss this? The trees are black in every direction, as far as one can see. Oughtn't I have noticed a thing like that?"

"We were all blinded by the magic of this place, I think," murmured Wunko, "for I can't remember seeing much of anything clearly once we started down off that plateau. And it may well be the enchantment here that made you so confident we were going in the right direction."

"Ah, but the sun is still out," said Anisha. "Maybe, if we can just get out of here by nightfall, we'll still be all right."

"Yes, let's be gone from here while yet we may!" seconded Okona, and they all tried to stand up. But they couldn't. The weight upon them was too strong, so they dragged themselves along the ground toward the direction from which they had come.

But after pulling themselves only a few feet, they knew it was hopeless. Whatever spell was set against them was too potent. They had just expended almost the very last of their remaining energy, and now it was all they could do to keep from fainting.

"This will never do," groaned Okona. "I don't think I could even raise my arm if I tried, and standing would be out of the question."

"I feel as if my entire body is crippled," moaned Anisha.

Wunko only stared across the forest floor, his eyes already glazing over.

Moments later, the sight of the others failed and they knew only blackness.

When Okona's eyes next cracked open, a dying, orange light filled the sky.

"Sunset!" he burst out. He tried to rise and excitedly discovered that he could, though not without much effort.

"Anisha! Wunko!" he whispered. "We've got to get out of here! Night is nearly upon us."

Anisha's eyes fluttered open, and she looked about, dazed. "Why, we're still in ... Okona, we've got to—"

"I know," said Okona, quickly grabbing her arm and helping her stand. Then they both went and aided Wunko to his feet.

"Don't bother with me. Run!" the Tikkichaw urged.

With Wunko loping behind, all three began jogging westward toward the fading sun but had not gone far when eerie, trailing shadows appeared some ways before them, winding through the forest. They were emanating from the earth itself, it seemed, and some of them from the trees.

"Back the other way!" Okona panted, and they sprinted in the opposite direction.

Now they caught glimpses of more shadows to either side of them, forming a long, curving wall, as it were, which was closing in on them from behind. Ever faster they ran, but found they were only going deeper and deeper into the black-trunked wood. The land dipped down before them, and they knew they were entering the very heart of the dreaded Toshigan Hollow. But the way behind them was now thoroughly obstructed by the advancing shadows.

They pounded across the hollow floor, their bare feet thudding on the hard earth. Only a few sickly, red beams remained of the sun's farewell, and already the black trunks about them were beginning to emit a ghastly, bluish sheen. Also, there were whispers in the air, whispers and thin, scraping laughter.

Suddenly, the trio halted, horror-stricken. The way before them was barred also, for there were more wavering shades assembled on the far side of the hollow, pressing toward them through the murk like faceless soldiers. These phantoms seemed to have dimensions of at least height, breadth and width and perhaps another still, for they projected in a most peculiar way from the air. They had forms of a sort, but their boundaries were unclear, for they were always in motion, flowing and fading in and out of clarity. Tattered were they, as if many long, wispy shreds of shadow were dangling from their bodies. They had upper limbs, clawed perhaps, and things like long, thin heads. But entirely wrought of shadow-stuff they were, from their snake-like hind ends all the way up to the peak of their misshapen heads.

The party whirled around once more, but shadow-beings utterly hemmed them in. The three put their backs to each other, and Okona and Wunko took up unwieldy branches from the ground, for they had neither bow nor arrows, having left all of their equipment elsewhere in the hollow. Anisha, too, grabbed a piece of deadwood and held it before her, her heart racing and her breath shallow and swift.

"Back, all of you!" Okona shouted, brandishing his branch, but the phantoms paid no heed. With open claws, they drifted toward the intruders, hissing like a hundred serpents.

The three mortals froze with fear, with sweat dripping down their foreheads and their hands locked around their respective makeshift weapons.

Closer, ever closer, the phantoms came, and when they were only a few feet away, Wunko jabbed with his branch at one, Okona hurled his at another, and Anisha swung hers with all her might at still another. The first two specters were undaunted, for the branches passed through them as if they were merely air. But the one Anisha had assaulted caught the end of the branch with its black fingers and yanked it from her grasp, then flung it aside. Viciously, it swooped upon her. The girl screamed, as its moist fingers closed upon her throat, and Okona whirled to aid her. But another of the spirits gripped his arm, and he was yanked backward, then thrust to the ground. Wunko, hollering, leapt toward one of the ghosts, but it caught him and wrapped him in its horrid body as if it were a great, suffocating blanket.

Okona tried to stand, but the back of his neck was seized by the tight, burning fingers of one of the shadow-beings. On the verge of fainting from this agonizing touch, he shouted desperately, as Anisha was pulled toward one of the larger trees. The specter hauling her passed into the tree itself, as if it had melted into the trunk, and then, to his utmost shock and horror, Anisha, too, dissolved into the trunk. Moments later, Wunko met the same fate. Then Okona knew it was his turn.

Chapter Thirteen

Night Beyond the Nightwater

WHEN THE SPECTER WHO had a merciless hold upon Okona darted into the tree, the lad was towed right behind him. The twilight vanished, and blackness washed over him, as he briefly felt a crushing rush like that of a waterfall, though devoid of wetness. He gasped for breath and groped in the inkiness that surrounded him. His body felt somewhat lighter, as if he could float if he tried, but his feet were touching something like smooth wood. But where his soles met this surface, they tingled unpleasantly.

A sharp pinch from his captor prompted him to face the being, who was no longer a mere shadow but had a much more well-defined body, which was glowing a wan blue. Tall and lean the wraith was, with abnormally long, skinny legs and a gaunt midsection. Its arms were sinuous and writhed like snakes, and its hands cruel, stretched and thin. Its head was also rather stretched and had a wide, tooth-filled mouth and deeply sunken, glowing eyes but no nose, ears or hair.

The creature hissed loudly, then wrenched him after it as it began descending a spiraling stair, visible only in the grotesque light of its body. Down, down the stair went, deeper into the earth, having neither railing nor, seemingly, an end. But at last, the specter pulled Okona down the final step and on through an archway. They were at the edge of a great cavern, which was illumined by the many fearsome beings that populated it, as well as by eldritch, blue lamps of crystal upon its walls. A particularly hideous phantom, like unto the form of the others, though rather larger, sat upon a crude chair of stone, and Wunko and Anisha stood before him, trembling.

Okona was dragged up next to his comrades, then released, though several specters stood so close behind that he could feel their icy breath upon his neck.

"Foolish beyond measure are ye, hapless mortals!" the enthroned phantom jeered in a voice frigid as a wintry night and sharp as a potsherd. "Foolish to seek the Vale of the Wakosi, where only death awaits any who would dare enter. Our Master has long planned the triumph that will soon spill forth from that vale, and there is nothing ye or any other of your race can do to stop it. Ye might well have waited to suffer the terrors that await such as ye, but with your intrusion here, ye have done nothing but hasten your own demise. For now ye shall know the exquisite tortures of the Kishikot!"

There was much hissing of approval from the leering spirits surrounding them.

"First, let them be torn!"

The Kishikot surged upon them, digging their claws into anywhere their flesh was exposed. The cuts were not deep, and they left little visible trace, but the beleaguered threesome felt as if, somehow, these horrific beings' claws were actually getting in and under their skin without tearing it, and the scrapes they made caused pain to shoot through every nerve in their bodies. Had they the strength, they would have wailed at the top of their lungs, but as it was, all they could manage was a solemn wish for a swift and sudden end to take them amidst their torment.

How long this agony went on they knew not, but at last, the Chief of the Kishikot cried, "Now, down Nightwater Stream ye shall go to a place of confinement, a night beyond the Nightwater, where ye will suffer from within—from lack of light, food, water and air and know intimately the complete unmaking of all hope. And then our finest finishers will end ye from without. Your eyes will be plucked out, your limbs torn off and your skin peeled away. And then—death! Off with them!" the phantom cried.

The trio again were seized by the ruthless claws of the Kishikot. There was a brief disagreement among the spirits about what to do with their adornments and personal effects, which the three had not removed when they had collapsed some hours back in the hollow. Okona's sunfire shard was appraised with horror, his flute with loathing and Wunko's box with a snort of mockery, but particular attention was paid to Anisha's silver bracelet, which they conferred much about in their unintelligible, hissing tongue. However, the uncertainty was ended and the effects ultimately left unmolested when one of them said, "You know the Decrees. Souls alone may we disturb. Leave them!"

After being dragged from the cavern, through many tunnels the mortals were led until they came to swift, dark water flowing down a series of broken stone shelves. This stream then ran straight and level into a high, round tunnel that vanished into utter midnight. A black boat was anchored here, a craft carven with monstrous, loathsome images, and into this they were cast. Several of the Kishikot joined them in it and began to paddle into the tunnel's gloom. None of the captives were bound, but they had not the least thought of escape, first because their wardens were beings of the Other-lands, and secondly because there was nowhere to which they might flee. They certainly had no intention of diving into the chill, black water, which might hold a fate worse still than that which had already befallen them.

For hours upon end, or perhaps days it seemed, they sat silent and numb in the boat with their equally silent captors, as the vessel passed through blackness, which ever echoed with the soft dipping of the oars. Many strange caverns they passed, these often lit in ghostly hues and filled with stenches grievous and acrid. Sometimes the Nightwater Stream ran through spaces so high they could hardly see the roof and other times so low they could almost touch the ceiling.

But at last, the nightmarish journey came to an end. Their spectral guardians rowed the boat onto a stony bank and took them through an arch of smooth stone. Beyond it was a labyrinth of narrow halls and stairs, and through this they passed until they knew there was not even one chance in a thousand they could have found their way out again. And there, at the end of a long hallway, was a wall of rock. One of the Kishikot accompanying them uttered something indiscernible to the wall, and it slid aside. The three prisoners were forcefully shoved through the opening beyond and sprawled upon a floor of cold stone. With another command from the Kishikot, the stone moved back in place, sealing with a quiet, devastating thunk. And the last the captives heard of the subterranean world beyond their prison was the echoing of the Kishikots' mocking laughter, as they departed down the hallway.

Long the mortals lay despairing upon the floor of their cell, throbbing from the strange scratches inflicted upon them, slipping in and out of slumber, none having the strength to so much as open their eyes, even when awake. Not that it would have mattered, for the darkness was absolute. But at last they did stir and even sat up. And, after feeling about, they discovered the dimensions of their cell, which were rather small, and each of them leaned against one of the rough stone walls.

"I know this won't make things any better for us, but I'd like to say it anyway," murmured Okona. "I'm so sorry I brought us to this fate. I led the party only three days, and in that time, I went so badly astray as to enmesh us in a fate more wretched than death. Neither of you deserve this, but perhaps I do."

"Okona, don't talk like that," Anisha admonished. "What have you done to merit this end? Fortune was simply against us. We were going, after all, on a very perilous mission and have passed far beyond the borders of where our Powers can watch after us."

"Anisha—and Wunko—there's something I really ought to tell you," said Okona haltingly.

The others waited for him to continue.

"There's a reason Fortune was against us. I'm terribly ashamed to admit this, but I wasn't even supposed to be on this mission to begin with."

"What do you mean?" asked Anisha, and Okona needed no light to know the exact look upon her face.

"I wasn't chosen to come," he quietly responded. "But Yahsi, for her own reasons, told me I was. And so I went to the meeting with Baneesh. But I didn't find out until the next day at Chennipot Chonka that I hadn't been selected. When I learned the truth, I wanted to return to Takula. But Yahsi insisted I stay. There was a dispute between her and Tencum, and at the end of it, he grudgingly agreed that I should come along."

"But each of the groups was a Sacred Ten," said Anisha, "so that would've ..."

"I was the Unlucky Eleventh," Okona confessed despondently.

"Oh," Wunko murmured in the darkness. "That *is* bad. I'm very sorry for you, lad. And for those who were with you."

"Now do you see?" asked Okona. "*I'm* the reason everything's gone wrong since the start. I'm the reason our whole party was slain at Ohkasac Groves and the reason the Jaggo are chasing us. I'm the reason Yahsi perished at Ponca Peak. I'm the reason the ganoja was guarding the river and also what lay behind us getting captured by the Chadori. And I'm the reason things went so terribly at Aska Karalonga, the reason Kamingo lie dead there now, and sadly, I'm also the reason all of us are now going to perish at the hands of these awful Kishikot." His shoulders slumping, he let out a long sigh. "And the thing I want most now is simply to die, which, I suppose, is well enough, since that's what they want for me also."

Neither Anisha nor Wunko said anything for several minutes, so Okona sat there, brooding in shame.

But then Anisha's voice came softly out of the gloom. "Perhaps all those things are your fault, Okona. And that's too bad. It's awful, really. But they're already woven into the world, and you'll just have to accept that. But we're not dead yet, even if we may feel that way. The Night is near, but not yet fully upon us. And there's still a mission to be completed. But we'll have to get out of here first to carry on with it. Can you think of anything, anything at all, that might help us escape? Or how about you, Wunko?"

"I'm sorry, my lady," Wunko glumly replied. "I've got no tricks for a spot like this. Rather out of my league, I'm afraid."

Okona lifted his head. Nothing but blackness stared back. However, Anisha's words had stirred something in him. "You're right, Anisha. We are still alive," he murmured. "And our Night, though near, has not yet arrived. That has to count for something."

Sitting up straighter, he said, "The Seer of Ponca Peak said something about what I might do when there was nothing else left to me and no other way out. He said to reach up, to reach even through rock and stone. And if I do, help may reach down. But how can I ..." He stretched his arm up into the darkness. "No, that's not it. I've got to reach a lot higher than that. But how?"

"What do you have in mind, lad?" Wunko inquired, also sitting more erect.

Okona laid his hands upon his thighs and noted the bulge of his flute in his pocket. "Of course!" he exclaimed, pulling it out.

"The Seer also said that when words fail, I should simply do the best I could without them. I think I might now understand what he meant."

"Anisha," he went on, turning in the girl's direction, "you're right that we're beyond where our Powers roam and past where their aid can reach us. Almost. For there is one who might still hear us, even from the depths of the earth."

"Who?" Anisha asked.

"He from whom all good things come, as it is sometimes said among the Sakooma. Mahna Shuya!" Okona exclaimed, and at this utterance, the spirits of all were roused.

"I know the tales of our people say his voice has not been heard since even before men left the former world on the far side of the Mists of Shagrash-Mula. Yes, the last time he spoke was in a world older still, the First of Worlds, to warn that most blessed of men, Umarna, that the First of Worlds would be unmade when Water swallowed both Earth and Air. Thanks to that warning, Umarna came safely through the ending of that age and into the World of the West. And we've been lost in the gray silence ever since. Yet I don't suppose it matters whether we can hear Mahna Shuya, as Umarna did, so long as Mahna Shuya can hear us. You see, we have yet a treasure from the days of Umarna's son, Lakosha, which is a means of calling to Mahna Shuya, regardless of whether we could hear his reply. And I have that means in my hand right now."

He directed his gaze to the Tikkichaw, though of course before him lay only blackness. "Wunko, do you remember when you said that a particular kind of music carries through Air, Water and Earth as other things do not? The treasure I just spoke of is an ode, an ode to Mahna Shuya, which has been passed down through the ages from ancient days, and I think it might well pass even through solid rock, for there is great magic woven into it. If I play it, perhaps the Light Beyond the Mists will hear; perhaps he will help."

"Perhaps he will at that!" declared Anisha.

"I see no reason why you shouldn't try," said Wunko eagerly.

Taking an enormous breath, Okona set his flute to his lips and blew. Soft and low the music began, then slowly started to grow. Warmer it waxed, as the melody swelled to fill the chamber. The cold stones reverberated with longing and beauty, and the earth itself seemed to have merged with the lad's plea, also crying out to the far-off heights of the Over-lands and the sanctuary of Mahna Shuya that lay worlds away. Desperate and woeful the song became, yet shot violently with hope and determination. Higher the tune rose, unfolding ever more poignantly, until it seemed to pierce the very rock. Then it sank back into an unquenchable yearning. Traces of joy there were, but they foundered and were lost in shadow. Finally, the melody faded into a mournful cry, which echoed long before vanishing altogether.

The prison's occupants sat silently for some time, hoping against all things that something might happen. But, as nothing did, they soon despaired, and Okona sighed, "Alas! Perhaps even that was not enough to reach Mahna Shuya. For we are deep beneath the earth. Or perhaps he has heard but is simply choosing not to lend his aid. But since he speaks not, we will never know."

No sooner had he said this than there came a sound near, yet faint, the music of a gentle trickling.

"What could ..." Anisha began.

"By all that shines in the sky above!" Wunko gasped.

"It's water!" Okona cried. He crawled swiftly toward the sound. But where he thought to encounter a wall, there was a tunnel; he reached out to its walls and ceiling and said, his voice trembling, "Why, this wasn't here before! It's an opening." He ran his hands along the floor again. "And there's water flowing out of it. Dare we hope our song has been heard?"

Part III:
Drums and Earth

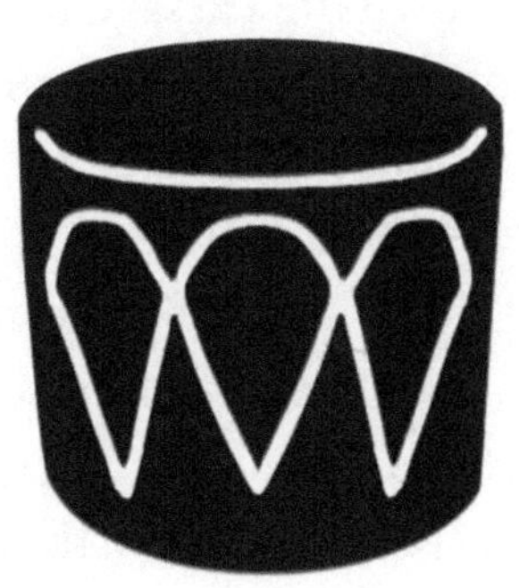

Chapter Fourteen

Valley of the Singing Falls

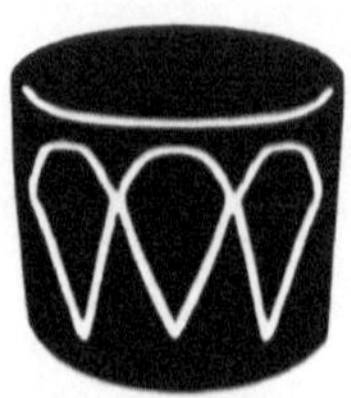

WUNKO AND ANISHA JOINED Okona at the cramped entrance.

"I'm going to see where this goes," said the lad, wriggling into the tunnel.

After proceeding a number of feet, he called back, "It opens up here! And there's more water."

The others crawled down the passage to Okona, who stood and carefully trod on in the pitch blackness until he stepped into a stream. "I sure wish we could see, even a little," he muttered. "Water and darkness isn't a great combination."

"Let's just follow this flow," counseled Wunko, coming up behind him. "Anything's better than that prison back there."

They all stepped into the icy current and splashed down the passage. The water grew deeper, and before they thought to turn back, the torrent became suddenly stronger, sweeping them off their feet. Into the frigid stream they plunged, as it carried them forward with tremendous speed. Sputtering, they soon found themselves unable to touch the bottom and barely able to keep their heads above the surface. On the current rushed, dragging them with it, until their ears were filled with nothing but the roar of foaming water.

Thrust beneath the maelstrom, they were beset by a most peculiar sensation, as if they were being swept upward in some great spout. Up, up they went, with swirling waters all around them. Okona was certain he would drown. But just when he thought his lungs would burst, he stretched up his hand, and a hand seized his own, pulling him mightily upward. Through great force of water he came. The hand released him, and his head bobbed out of the water. Gasping and choking, he saw, for the first time in many hours, the slightest glimmer of light. He was in a stream-filled tunnel, and far down its length, a golden beam illuminated the flashing current, which was drawing him inexorably toward that light.

Moments later, Anisha emerged behind him, heaving and coughing. Okona grasped the side of the tunnel, then helped buoy her up when she reached him. They were swept farther down, and Wunko splashed and cried out behind them. Soon, all three had been carried almost to the stream's exit, and they caught and clung to a protruding rock near the thunderous edge where the stream dashed down several ledges before plummeting down a stony face into a churning pool thirty feet below.

Feeling as if they had just been stampeded by five tens of deer, the waterlogged trio nonetheless managed to drag themselves out of the stream and onto the rock at the cave's mouth, where they took a good while to regain normal breathing.

They were just getting ready to stand when a voice spoke behind them. "Well, even at my age, this world is still full of surprises!"

Okona's heart all but leaped out of him. "Yahsi!" he turned, gaping in utter disbelief. "Is it really you? Have we died after all, then?"

"I should think not!" the old woman returned.

"How can this be? I thought you were ... well, dead!"

"Turns out I'm not—not yet, anyway." Yahsi smiled, seating herself upon a nearby stone.

"Thanks be to all that shines in the Over-lands!" exulted Okona, on the verge of weeping for joy.

"I can hardly believe it!" burst out Anisha.

"Are you then the remarkable Wise-woman of whom my companions have spoken?" asked Wunko. "Very pleased to meet you!

I'm Wunko." He scratched his nose with his thumb, stuck it on his forehead and then extended it to her.

Yahsi copied him, replying, "I'm not sure what's so remarkable about me. But it's true; some have accorded me the title of Wise-woman. And it's nice to meet you too, Wunko. I'm Yahsi. And how came you into Okona and Anisha's company?"

"I happened to be in the right place at the right time to aid this fine young couple in their pinch with the Jaggo near Ponca Peak. And I've been jaunting along on their quest ever since."

"For your care of them," said Yahsi, "we all stand in your debt."

"Yahsi, we have ever so many questions for you!" exclaimed Okona.

"Ever so many!" Anisha seconded.

"And I've many for you," said Yahsi, "not the least of which is what you're doing being spewed out of the earth so very far from where I last saw you. But I suppose we ought to get all of you dried off before anybody questions anybody else. And a hot drink might do you some good as well. You all look as if you've seen a host of ghosts."

"As a matter of fact, ma'am, we have," said Wunko.

"Well!" Yahsi started. "Then you *really* ought to have a warm drink! Now, I've just got to fill up these skins—they say the water from this cave has wonderful properties—and then I'll take you to a more suitable place for recovery."

She took four waterskins, which she had set by her feet, and dipped them into the stream, then made her way out of the cave, with the others following.

They skirted around to the right, clambering down a steep route, and soon they could look back upon the high fall where the stream that had carried them out of the mountain shot over the rock. After making their way down through the forest, they came upon another cascade, twenty feet higher and also louder, more brilliant and grandiose, sparkling like gems in the early morning sun. The bright pool beneath it was rather larger than the one higher up and fed a bubbling creek that ran on to the southeast.

The party followed this creek, and almost immediately sighted a vast grotto in the mighty bluff that stood on the creek's opposite bank. The grotto's length was tremendous, only several tens of feet less than three hundred. The mouth of it was fifty feet high and the depth thrice that. Thin, trailing smoke wafted out of the cave from a small fire in its farther recesses.

Yahsi forded the creek to attain the grotto, and the others came behind her, marveling at the splendor of the vale in which they now trod. Here were an abundance of trees, vibrant and tall, high cliffs, majestic boulders, spreading ferns and laughing water.

The elderly Sakooma took the others to her campfire, which stood on a decently sized shelf at the back of the grotto, which echoed with the rush of the nearby falls. And there, while she readied refreshment, she bade them sit upon the cave's floor, which was smooth, dry and altogether very comfortable. Indeed, there were signs the place served as a habitation, for tools of stone and wood, baskets, pots and other articles for daily living, along with an array of foodstuffs, were stashed against the walls.

The fire began to dry off their sopping garments, as Yahsi went about brewing a tea of various herbs and leaves. When it had steeped well, she gave to each of them a clay cup. From these they drank, and warmth began in their throats, spreading from there to their bellies and all the way down to their toes, driving away the chill of the mountain torrent and even tempering their lingering pains from the Kishikot's tortures. Their weariness was sloughed off, and new strength flowed through them, as their eyes brightened and their minds quickened.

"Have you put some sort of magic in this tea, Yahsi?" asked Okona, as he downed his last drops.

"I can't work any enchantments, Okona. You know that," she replied, busying herself with cooking a thin porridge.

"Well, this stuff is doing wonders," voiced Anisha. "I feel as if I'd just had a full week of rest! There has to be something to it."

"Indeed there is!" Yahsi returned. "It's the water. The Elixir of Nadula they call it. Came from that cave back up there. I filled the pot for the tea with some of it last night. Anyway, this water has the power of healing and of granting an extra measure of strength and vigor. So I was told by a stranger—of whom I will speak more ere long, I'm sure—but I have tasted for myself also and know it is true. It is a great gift to men, for certain traditions hold that this is one of the few places in Sarkanna that still carries the echoes of Tumanila. Not the fullness of it, mind you, but just a taste." She turned to Wunko and explained, "Tumanila is, in the histories of the Sakooma, the ward of peace and unblemished green where our great ancestor Machakam first dwelt before he wandered through the First of Worlds in sorrow to the rising of the sun."

"I have heard of it, madam," returned Wunko quietly, "for I am somewhat conversant with Sakooma tales. Ah, and there is such a blissful locality in the stories of my own people as well."

"Where is this place?" asked Anisha, looking around.

"Nadula Valley," Yahsi replied. "Named after Nadula Creek over there, which starts up at the Singing Falls—the two we passed on the way here—and wanders down through a canyon into the Wakosi River. And this cave is called by some Ambori Kamosa, Roamers' Refuge."

"We're near the Wakosi, then?" Wunko inquired. "Splendid, for that is precisely where we were aiming. Though certainly not by intent, the phantoms of Toshigan Hollow have nonetheless done us a great service."

"Phantoms?" Yahsi prompted.

"Yes," said Okona, and proceeded to describe who the Kishikot were and what they had done to them.

"But you're here now," noted Yahsi when he had finished. "How, then, did you escape?"

Okona spoke of his realization in the cell and the ode he had played upon his flute, as well as the companions' extraordinary return to the world above.

"I don't know for certain, but I think Mahna Shuya must have heard my song and thus granted our plea," the lad concluded.

"The magic of Mahna Shuya is written all over that tale," Yahsi concurred. "And it was his hand, I think, that drew you out of the flood and the others as well." (Wunko and Anisha had related how they, too, had been pulled upward by a mysterious hand right before they had emerged in the cave-stream.)

Yahsi now set bowls of porridge before the three travelers. "It isn't the best of breakfasts," said she, "but I hope you'll find it serviceable enough."

"I'm sure it's delightful," assured Wunko.

Anisha spooned up a large bite of the porridge and swallowed it hungrily. "Yahsi, now that we've told you a bit of our most recent doings, would you mind telling us what you've been up to? And most of all, I'd like to know how you managed to escape slaughter at the hands of the Jaggo."

"I can certainly tell you my tale, though I should like to hear the rest of yours when I'm finished."

"Of course," promised Okona.

"Well, then," said she, "here is the account of my adventures."

"When I attracted the attention of the Jaggo by Ponca Peak," Yahsi began, "I was naturally obliged to flee. So I made again for the mountain, though I held out no hope of outrunning them. But all of a sudden, a great eagle, whose very substance was of fire, fierce and bright, swooped down over my head and toward the Jaggo."

The companions looked at her with wide eyes.

"So much magic there has been of late!" exclaimed Okona. "Anyway, what'd you do?"

"Naturally, I fell upon my face," Yahsi continued, "but the Jaggo ran off in terror. And when I dared to raise my head, I saw only a man, a man in a shirt of white, with a red blanket upon his shoulders. But he was no stranger to me, for I had spoken with him before."

"When?" started Okona. "You see, we also met a men thus clad. Ours named himself Wassu of the West."

Yahsi raised her eyebrows. "This, too, was Wassu! But I'll postpone telling you of my other encounter with him and let you do the same with yours so we can move my story along."

"In any event, this Wassu greeted me and told me both you and Anisha were in safe hands, so I had not to worry about your welfare. Rather, I was needed urgently for a certain task, which was to see that our men who died at the hands of the Jaggo were given a proper burial. He said my talk with the Seer had tested where my heart lay, and that I had passed the test, and that is why he had come to me. Then he touched my forehead, and I was given an extra measure of endurance. This I was to need for the assignment which lay before me."

"That afternoon I hastened back to the place where we had stowed the canoe Anisha brought from Korba Landing. I took it across the Kanno to Ohkasac Groves and was relieved to discover the bodies of our band undefiled, as Wassu had foretold. Eight corpses I found, but Tencum was not among them."

A sudden light came into Anisha's eyes. "You mean he might still be alive?"

"It's quite possible he escaped," Yahsi replied, "for he is—or was—an apt warrior. Or it may be that he did perish and the Jaggo did something with his body. I don't know."

"But I counted nine bodies that night," said Okona, puzzling.

"There's a mystery yet to which we are lacking all the pieces," mused Yahsi. "But where was I? Oh, yes ..."

"In the late afternoon, a Sakooma couple who were on their way back to their village from the feast at Takula came by, and I told them what had transpired and requested aid from their village for the burying of the bodies, for I knew it would be long and hard work. However, I promised to keep vigil over the deceased through the night. They agreed to this and departed, and I began my watch."

"Not long afterward, shortly before sunset it was, I heard two bands approaching, one from the north and the other from the west. Realizing who they were, I hid, for they were none other than the Jaggo. And you know, of course, that the Jaggo are said to remain ever silent. You can imagine my surprise, then, when they spoke."

"What?" Wunko perked up, ceasing from his porridge. "In truth?"

Yahsi nodded. "And what's more, they were speaking Sakooma!"

The others looked at her intently.

"But not as that which we are using now," she continued. "Like unto the speech of my great-grandfather it was, with words and a manner of speaking now fallen from use."

"Very strange indeed. What were they saying?" asked Okona.

"First, the western group spoke of their concerns regarding a Sakooma sorceress whom they suspected might have been commissioned to challenge their master. But of this master, I unfortunately heard naught more, though I have an unpleasant guess as to the identity." Holding up two fingers, she gave Okona a grim look.

He stared back quizzically, as she remarked, "My guess will likely become clearer to you later in my story. Anyhow, I quickly discerned it was me they had taken for a sorceress. And the reason they had deemed me thus was the appearance of the flaming eagle, which they believed I had summoned."

"Ah, that solves one of our mysteries!" said Anisha brightly.

"Yes, we were captured by some Chadori," explained Okona, "who, it seems, had been hired by the Jaggo. And they wanted to know where our witch was. We were uncertain of to whom they were referring, but now it's been confirmed."

"Captured by the Chadori!" exclaimed Yahsi, taking another draft of tea. "You *have* been through quite a business."

"In any event, the northern group told them they would have to trust those they left behind to deal with the sorceress, for they had to all hasten to ambush the north-bound group of Sakooma at Shakola Kora three nights from then."

She turned to Wunko and explained, "That's Shamoki dialect for Stonearch Dell. It's a sacred site, some fifty or sixty miles north of Ponca Peak, which is devoted to the Shamoki's Powers."

"I've actually been there before, but that was many years ago," the Tikkichaw revealed. "The site was well-chosen for reverence. In this world, or at least the parts of it I've seen, I'd wager there are few spans of stone like it—a perfect, low arch of rock, thin but very wide, and undoubtedly spirit-wrought, standing on a steep hillside in the midst of a shadowed wood."

"You've traveled a fair amount, haven't you?" Yahsi inquired.

"More than most, but still less than some," Wunko reservedly returned. "But please, continue with your tale."

"Oh, yes. Well, apparently, the group of Jaggo who came from the north had somehow learned our own Orobec was taking his band to the Shamoki settlement at the foot of hallowed Hanoba Mountain a little under thirty miles southeast of Shakola Kora to get supplies and information and that he would soon be heading to Shakola Kora to make offerings to the Shamoki Powers before hiking farther into the eastern area of the Kannitaw Mountains. I've no idea how they learned all that, but as soon as this information was relayed to the other group, all were agreed they should depart that very night. And so they did, though as they were exiting the Groves, one of them examined the corpses and said, "'Tis a pity, wasting good meat.'"

"What luck it was, then, that they were in such haste," remarked Anisha, whose face had temporarily lost some of its color.

Yahsi took several bites of porridge and a sip of tea, then continued, "I slept near the bodies that night to guard against the creatures of the forest. But the next morning, as soon as the couple from the previous afternoon arrived with others to help with burial, I dispatched one of the fellows with them to a nearby village to fetch me a signal drum as quick as he might, for reasons I'll explain shortly. But I left my harp with another of the Sakooma present and bade him hurry to Takula, where he was to deposit it for my return. But also, and more importantly, I instructed him to bring news to the leaders there of all that had befallen us of the western band and of that which I had overheard from the Jaggo. And Anisha, I also told him to bring news of you to your father."

"I suppose it would at least give him some relief to know where I'd gone and why," said Anisha.

"So I hoped. Furthermore, I charged this fellow to see to it that messengers were sent to Homino's group and that of Aywish—if they could be found—to inform them that the Hand of Hamora was in the north. Well, this young man departed, but as soon as the other brought me the drum I'd asked for, I myself began journeying north toward Shakola Kora. For though I could have taken others with me, none were prepared, as I was, for a journey on a moment's notice. Yet even a moment could not be spared."

"I traveled all that day and the next, as well as much of that which followed. But on that third day, in the late afternoon, I drew near to Shakola Kora. Yet, just as I feared, the Jaggo got there ahead of me and were stationed between myself and the site where Orobec and his folk were supposed to be encamped. So, I used the drum for the purpose for which I had brought it; I played a signal to warn our band there would be an attack that night. Of course, that was certain to draw the Jaggo, so I had to flee. But I had been near a stream, so I was able to wade some way in the water and thus make it more difficult for them to pick up my trail."

"Your foresight in bringing the drum was commendable, madam," Wunko congratulated.

"Age is an excellent teacher," Yahsi returned. "But unfortunately, I was unable to discover if my warning was of any assistance to Orobec or if he had even come to Shakola Kora, for as I mentioned,

I was obliged to flee. Westward I went, even traveling through part of the night. But early the next morning, a troop of hunters came by the place I had slept. Trusting they would not be hostile, I revealed myself and asked if they might spare any provisions, which they did."

"Were they Shamoki?" asked Wunko, holding a yet damp portion of his sleeve over the fire.

"No. Babora."

"Babora? I don't know that I've ever heard of them."

"Neither had I, though I knew there were some nomadic folk, small in number and secretive, that wandered about the edges of the Kannitaw. But Babora these were, and their language was somewhat like unto Kamingo, of which I know very little. But one of them, Chapimu by name, knew rather more Sakooma than I did of Kamingo, as his mother was a Shamoki. He asked what brought me to those remote parts, and I told him I was driven thence in flight from the Jaggo near Shakola Kora. Of these he seemed to know much, yet said little. For apparently the Babora, just as the Sakooma, are of the belief that the more one speaks of evil things, the more he is sure to draw them, particularly if they are already near. And the more terrible they are, the more perilous it is to even mention them."

"Chapimu advised me to head south to escape the Jaggo, for it was from these northern regions that they originated. I asked him more precisely where, and he, with some reluctance, said, 'Where the Wakosi Rises. All that land, once good, is now evil, for that which is foul flows with the river from its very sources.'"

"'Are there none good who dwell there?' I asked."

"'None,' he replied, 'for all that valley is cursed, save one place alone.'"

"I inquired what place that might be."

"'Nadula Valley,' said he. And he told me much of it, some of which I have already related. This valley was long held sacred by his people. Yet, sadly, they had not laid eyes upon it for a count of several generations, so the healing waters of the Font of Nadula have long been lost to men. But he happily reported that at least the

Jaggo may not defile them, for an aura of protection is laid upon this valley that even they cannot pass. For, as I alluded to earlier, it is held among the Babora that it still holds the echoes of that blessed land where the feet of the first man trod before any decay entered the First of Worlds. He told me there were three standing stones here which marked the valley's entrance as one comes up from the River Wakosi. And these, he said, were already set there long before his people came."

"I pressed him for more information about the Jaggo and the place where the Wakosi rises, but no more would he give. So I thanked the hunters for the food and insight they had shared and set out once again."

Yahsi paused to eat and drink, and they all listened in the meanwhile to the mighty music of the falls sounding throughout the grotto.

Yahsi commenced once more, "Now I was faced with a difficult decision: should I try to wriggle through the net of the Jaggo to join Orobec's group or return to the Sakooma heartland to deliver the information I had just learned? Or should I go on alone to the sources of the Wakosi, where I was now nearly certain the Hand of Hamora lay? For it occurred to me that the Jaggo's attacks were not indiscriminate. Perhaps you all see this now as well; they were intentionally going after anyone who was attempting to recover the Hand. Thus, they were likely enough in the service of those who stole it and were sent abroad to prevent its retrieval."

"It all makes sense now!" gasped Anisha. "Yes, I think that must be it. No wonder they were so tenacious in their pursuit of us."

"And I think I have guessed now who you believe commands the Jaggo," Okona said grimly.

"Yes, it is *them*." Yahsi locked eyes with him.

A troubled look crossed Anisha's face, for though she knew not of whom Yahsi spoke, she knew enough to be rightly disquieted. Still, she was to some degree perturbed that she alone was in ignorance about this unmentionable enemy.

"But the Jaggo said *master*, not *masters*," noted Wunko. "Perhaps only one of the two is involved with them?"

"Perhaps," Yahsi replied. "And I did note they spoke of only one. So there may be more to the matter than we realize. Still, I think the two I named not must be involved somehow."

"Anyhow," Yahsi resumed, "back to my account. We already knew from the Seer of Ponca Peak that the Hand would be found in the north, and these hunters had informed me that such was the area from which the Jaggo came. Given the circumstances, I determined I must try to reach the land where the Wakosi began and do what I might to discover the Hand's whereabouts, seeking refuge in the place the man had told me about—if I could find it—until I could learn more of what was afoot. Also, I had hope I would encounter at least you, Okona, again. For, if you recall the words of the Seer, he certainly made it seem you had deeds to attend to here in the north."

Okona nodded solemnly.

"My tale is nearly at an end now," said Yahsi. "All that remains to relate is that I traveled hard west by northwest the remainder of that day and two days more ere I came to the Wakosi around sunset. On my way into the greater valley though, I heard terrifying noises, grunting and snorting, as of great beasts, and saw large shadows moving about in the woods. But something startled these, it seems, for they fled when they had nearly surrounded me. When I got to the Wakosi itself and night fell, I spotted signal fires on the heights about me, though I had no idea what they meant. However, I guessed it must be the Jaggo's work because I was here in the heart of their realm, and legends speak of them communicating with fire."

"Under cover of dark, I forded the Wakosi at a place not far from here. And, as Fortune would have it, or perhaps something more meddlesome than Fortune—" She winked at the others. "—when I was coming up from the river, looking for a place to spend the night, I came upon the three standing stones the hunter had spoken of. I lodged in this valley that night and all the next day, which was yesterday, partaking of its sweet refreshment. And this morning, when I went to draw more water from the cave, out came you three!"

She settled back, took more porridge and tea, then said, "Well, that's my story. Now, how runs your tale?"

Over the next hour, the others told her of their adventures, and she marveled much at these. She had a fair number of questions about the ganoja and the Kishikot, though they had only less than satisfactory answers.

When all was told by both parties, Yahsi said, "As much as this valley has been a blessing to us all, I think we must hurry on. If the Hand of Hamora is somewhere in this region in the possession of some wicked person or persons, as seems likely, then the less time that is the case, the better. For what the villainous will do with increased power we know all too well. So let us set out and search earnestly for our enemies. It will do at first merely to find the Jaggo, but ultimately I believe we must find their master—or masters, as the case may be—to succeed in our quest. Luckily, we still have much of the day before us to investigate this district."

"Then let us drink of this excellent water once more," advised Wunko, "so that we may be at our finest to face our foes. And then let's be off to the Wakosi."

"Actually, we can do better than merely drink now," said Yahsi, "though that we can certainly do as well. For we've the four water-skins I filled not long ago, and those we can simply bring with us."

Everyone thought this a commendable idea, so Yahsi passed around a large pitcher of the invigorating liquid, from which they imbibed deeply. Then they hastily commenced preparations for departure.

As Yahsi, Okona and Anisha were dousing the fire, Wunko gave a sudden, choked interjection. They turned to see him stooping over his wooden box.

"No, no, no!" he cried, flinging the lid shut. "It's ruined! After all these years ..." Abruptly realizing his sorrows were no longer private, he mumbled, "I'm sorry; don't mind me. Carry on." Stiffly, he slung the box over his shoulder.

"Is there anything we can do to help, Uncle Wunko?" asked Anisha gently.

"No, it's quite all right," the Tikkichaw assured. "Everything is fine."

Though all could clearly see how disconsolate he was, none pressed him further.

As they were collecting various items from the cave, Okona remarked, "Yahsi, you said that hunter told you his people had not been here for generations, but it looks from the state of these items—the stocked baskets for instance—as if this place has been used rather recently."

"That was my thought also," said she, "though I couldn't guess by whom."

"This is your pack, isn't it?" asked Okona, as he picked up a sturdy satchel, filled with various supplies.

"Yes, the one I brought from Takula," she said. "But I've restocked it since I arrived here."

"I don't mind carrying it for you," offered the lad, "for mine was lost before we passed under the earth. Besides, then you should be more at ease. You've done ever so much for me in all my days. Please, let me at least do you this small favor."

"Very well, Okona. But I want you to know that you owe me nothing. If I have given you anything, it was given freely. For I also have received much freely."

Okona also spotted Yahsi's drum lying against the cave wall and inquired if she wished for him to take it along, but she replied, "There's no need to haul it around presently. If it were my harp, perhaps so, for I fancy harp rather more than drum. But we shall be in want of strength and speed, so I'll return for the drum when this affair is over, provided things end well."

A few minutes later, they were ready to set out, laden with skins filled with the valley's enchanted water, as well as foodstuffs taken from the cave's much-appreciated, but nonetheless mysterious stock. These foodstuffs Wunko and Anisha were carrying in packs they had taken from the piles of items near the grotto's walls.

Bidding farewell to the cave and the music of the falls, they sojourned down the stream, which sprang and bubbled joyously through the canyon. Soon, they were obliged to traverse a stretch of large, jumbled limestone boulders. And a little distance farther on, the creek ran into a cave in the wall of a great limestone barrier. High above this barrier circled two great hawks, the only creatures they had spied in the vale thus far. Yahsi bade the companions follow her into the cave, and they passed through its entrance, spotting light some fifty feet down the tunnel. Carefully, they pressed on, crossing over the watercourse several times on various ledges. The grotto was quite narrow at the bottom where the creek flowed but rather wider farther up.

At the far end of the cave, the creek tumbled ten feet down into a wide, clear pool, from which it proceeded on down the valley.

"This is the Gate of Nadula," said Yahsi. "And here the vale's enchantment ends."

Yet even if Yahsi had not informed the others of this, still they would have known it. For it was as if they had entered into a different world, a more burdened one. The weight of it was nearly tangible and the air noticeably stickier. And the aura of danger was only too apparent.

The foursome climbed leftward along a ledge at the cave's mouth, then skirted around the pool and crossed back over the creek, so that it lay again on their left. They followed the creek some ways onward, and, passing the three standing stones Yahsi had mentioned, they came to more large blocks of limestone, though these were more spread out than those in the section just before the cave and their faces more angular.

As they walked along, Yahsi and Okona naturally ended up somewhat behind the others, for they were both in heavy thought. When Okona realized he was walking next to Yahsi and the others were some distance before them, he asked quietly, "Yahsi, might you now tell me the story to which you have alluded a number of times—the story about why you sent me on this mission?"

Her amber eyes brightened. "Why, yes! And I think you will believe it now. In fact, one of the main reasons I didn't tell you it before is that you almost certainly would not have accepted it. But I sense you have learned much in your recent adventures."

As they continued along a faint woodland trail running parallel to Nadula Creek, Yahsi explained, "Very early on the morning after the storm at Takula, I attended the initial council summoned by Baneesh that was only for the Deggas and Wise-women. When it was finished, I went down to the shore of Takula Lake just to walk and think. But in the gray morning, an eagle swooped down from the heavens over the water. It glided to the bank, and its shape became that of a man. The man introduced himself as Wassu of the West, then said the time had come for me to seek that which had long been in my heart. 'Seek the Seer,' he told me, then instructed me that, at all costs, I must see to it you were brought upon the mission to retrieve the Hand of Hamora."

"Me?" Okona said.

"'This is the will of Mahna Shuya,' Wassu said. 'Request in that name to Okona that he come, and if he wavers, compel him nonetheless.' And so, as you know, that is what I did."

Okona grew thoughtful.

"I said also to Wassu that you had not been chosen by our own leaders, and he answered that the counsels of Mahna Shuya were higher than those of mortal men. To this I had no reply. But I also told him it was difficult to accept that his message came from Mahna Shuya, for as our people reckon it, he had not spoken to us since before our journey over the Span of the Shimmering Nights. And he said, 'Yes. That is so. But he has spoken much to others. And rejoice that he is speaking to you through me. For sometimes, where the voices of men carry not his light, the voices of such as I do so. But it is very rare and often not heeded. However, someday the voices of men will carry his words hither, and then many will hear them.'"

Okona became more pensive still. "There is much mystery in these words," he said. "And I'm afraid they may have to lie on me for a while before I see any sense in them. Really, what I want most is to speak to Wassu himself about these things, for he is evidently a person of both great magic and knowledge. But ... did he say why it was necessary that I in particular should be sent on this mission?"

"If there was a reason," Yahsi replied, "it wasn't given to me."

They walked on in silence, accompanied by the soft wind in the forest, the chatter of the creek and the song-calls of stray birds. But at length, Yahsi looked about and muttered, "We're getting near the river."

She and Okona hastened to join Anisha and Wunko, and when they had done so, she said, "Be wary, friends. We are but a half-mile from the Wakosi now and beyond the protection offered by Nadula."

"Unfortunately, we are also without any weapons," Wunko sadly reminded everyone.

"Considering what might be lurking in this vale, they might not do us much good anyhow," Yahsi ominously returned.

Just then, as if to punctuate her statement, from away southwest came the distant rumble of dark drumming.

Where the Wakosi Rises

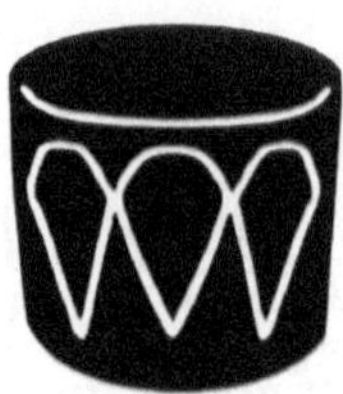

THE COMPANIONS STOOD LISTENING to the drumming for several moments, but abruptly, it ceased. Not long afterward, answering booms rolled from the northeast, rather closer at hand.

"That'll be drum talk," said Yahsi.

"The Jaggo's?" prompted Wunko.

Yahsi nodded.

"I suppose we did leave the valley to seek them out," remarked Okona, "and since the drumming to the north is nearer, oughtn't we go that way?"

"Yes, let's," said Anisha. "But perhaps we should get our bearings at the river first."

All concurring with this, they hurried on to the banks of the Wakosi, warily peering into the woods all around as they approached. The river wasn't very wide here nor very deep, but its bubbling, gray-green waters ran swiftly over many round stones. A steep hill shot up immediately on the far side of the river, but the hither bank was relatively flat for some distance and covered in thick forest.

Wunko turned to Yahsi. "Didn't that Babora you met say that the evil here came from the Wakosi's sources? That would be upstream, to the south. Though the drumming to the north is closer, hadn't we better go the other way?"

Yahsi pondered this, gazing first north, then south. Finally she said, "You speak sensibly, Wunko, but all things considered, it may not be wise to journey to the heart of things until we understand better what we are up against. If we go to the Wakosi's first founts unprepared, we may well come to a quick and bad end. It is dangerous enough to even be in the upper reaches of the Wakosi, this valley which the Babora name Where the Wakosi Rises. Let us not press our luck."

"I couldn't agree more, now that you've put it that way," voiced Wunko. "North it is."

Thus, they turned northeastward, hiking directly along the riverbank, always watching for skulking foes. But after a little more than a mile, at a spot where a creek fed into the river, they stopped and crouched behind some broad ferns, for they had spotted a good many canoes, all designed for two persons each, resting near the Wakosi's western shore. After ensuring no one was nearby, they cautiously approached the collection of boats.

"Jaggo-make," muttered Wunko. "See the karrawahs?"

Sure enough, each of the canoes had a prow stylized to represent the long, broad, bumpy snouts of the quag-dwelling karrawah, complete with sharp, menacing teeth.

"And what have the Jaggo to do with karrawahs?" inquired Yahsi.

"They're sacred to them," Wunko replied.

"Hadn't we better be getting along?" urged Anisha. "I know we're looking for those fiends, but I'd rather we find them than the other way round. And this seems like the sort of place the latter would be more likely to occur."

"Why don't we continue down the river by boat?" asked Okona.

"Theirs?" Wunko queried, nodding at the craft before them. "I don't see why not."

"Won't they notice them missing?" Anisha posed.

"Perhaps, but they may well assume other Jaggo have taken them," offered Wunko.

"Ah, and going on by water might well be to our advantage," said Yahsi, "for we could escape to either bank if necessary. And what better way is there to explore this valley than by the river itself?"

"Does anyone have any idea where the northern drums might have been coming from?" asked Okona. "Were they on this bank or the other? And have we already passed where they were or might they have been sounding from farther downstream?"

Everyone shrugged.

"It's been a while since we heard them, and we'll likely not know where to head until they sound again," said Anisha.

"In the meantime, we may as well start down the river," said Wunko. "After all, the Jaggo wouldn't have boats if they didn't traffic this water. I've no doubt we'll encounter them in some fashion ere long, unfortunately."

In short order, they had dragged two canoes down to the Wakosi. Okona and Yahsi occupied one and Anisha and Wunko the other, with Okona and Wunko sitting in the rear of their respective boats. Thus arranged with the strongest paddlers in the back, the four could proceed with the greatest possible speed and the least risk of anyone growing weary.

The hurrying waters of the Wakosi carried their vessels downstream, and before long, the heights began falling away on their right. But on their left rose another cliff, far more dramatic and looming than the slopes they were leaving behind. This same bluff, tan below and graying to occasional black above, topped with deep, sloping forest, frowned over them for the better part of an hour. During this same interval, the river began to meander in wild loops every two thousand feet or so. At each curving, they feared a party of many Jaggo would be waiting on the shore. But the woods and cliffs were quiet, eerily so, and by now, since they had come so far, they were certain they had passed the place where the drummers were. Yet Yahsi urged them to keep onward, for she speculated there might be Jaggo activity at many points along the upper Wakosi. This suspicion was confirmed when they ran across several more Jaggo canoes beached on their right hand just as they passed beyond the stretch watched over by the bluff.

Not long after these canoes had disappeared around the bend behind them, far-off drumming again reached their ears; it was from the southwest. After it halted, drumming sounded from the northeast.

"It seems they're everywhere in this valley," said Anisha worriedly.

"Yes, and I'd give a good deal to know what they're saying," remarked Wunko.

"I almost feel as if I could understand it," murmured Yahsi. "There's something about the patterns that's not unlike Sakooma drum talk, but it's different enough that it remains a mystery. But if I had to put a guess to it, I'd say it was some kind of summons."

They paddled on another three quarters of an hour, and a bluff more lofty than any they had encountered soared up on their left, a sheer, staggering face casting its massive shadow upon the river beneath. They looked up at it in awe, then gazed farther skyward, eyeing concernedly a circling group of vultures.

"Such eaters of rot bode much evil," muttered Wunko. "It is not without cause people speak ill of this place. There is a watchfulness here and a lingering terror, as if the land itself is in constant fear. And if I didn't know any better, I'd say many of the rocks and trees have eyes—not friendly ones, mind you."

Beyond this point, the Wakosi made a sizable loop south, snaking its way through the imposing heights of the Kannitaw before returning to its general course north and eastward. When they had come nearly another three quarters of an hour beyond the highest expression of the bluff where they had seen the vultures, the land sank on their left and a coppery creek spilled into the Wakosi from the north.

Just as they were about to pass this creek, the anxious stillness of the Wakosi Vale was rent from above by a cold, high-pitched shrieking. Moments later, the shadow of the ganoja swept across their canoes, as the monster began swooping down from far, far above.

"What's that awful thing doing all the way up here?" wailed Anisha.

"Pull off to the creek! Now! Or we're done for!" Okona cried, and everyone paddled like mad toward it.

They had only just dragged the canoes on the bank near the creek's mouth and sprang under the cover of the woods when the ganoja plowed into the Wakosi, squawking and flapping its great wings and flailing its long, hideous tail in the midst of a high splashing of green water. Meanwhile, the companions, with pounding hearts, scrambled into the thickest part of the forest, heading parallel to the creek, which, after a short stint northward, turned sharply west, away from the river. None looked back to see if the ganoja was following them but hoped the closely spaced trees might prove a hindrance to its pursuit. For ten minutes they ran recklessly on before Okona dared to glance behind him. Of their winged adversary, naught could be seen.

"That was that ganoja you told me about, wasn't it?" panted Yahsi. "I've seen all I care to of it, thank you very much. But, Wunko, if you're right about it having to stay close to the water, we may be all right for the moment."

"No we won't," warned Anisha. "Look!"

Back down the creek, from whence they had just come, huge, reddish shapes were moving toward them through the trees. Thick-bodied and strong, these were as tall or taller than a man and easily eight feet long. Long, razored tusks sprang from their mouths, and stiff, black hairs shot up from their spines. Black-hoofed, sharp-eared and white-fanged, they shuffled along, sniffing and snorting, and every now and again raising their heads and glancing in the direction of the three Sakooma and the Tikkichaw.

"I'm afraid you're right, Miss Anisha. Those things—whatever sort of devilries they are—may be onto us," whispered Wunko.

"That sound of theirs is familiar," remarked Yahsi. "I wonder if these were not the shadows that I encountered coming into the

Wakosi Vale. In any event, I don't know how they were scattered before, so I certainly couldn't counsel us what to do now."

"Let's go upland," Okona advised, "for the way they're built, it might be trickier for them to attack if we're among the rocks. But also, I wouldn't be surprised if these beasts could charge at a decent speed if they had a stretch of open ground, so let's try to stay in the most wooded areas on the way."

Everyone thought Okona's proposal sound, so they continued westward, but now also bore south up a steep slope through the forest, soon leaving the creek behind. Yet as they pursued this new course, the creatures followed them, veering exactly as they did, though some distance behind. Neither the companions nor their pursuers moved particularly quickly, for the way was rough, but the chase was nonetheless close, for the fugitives knew that as soon as these creatures actually caught sight of them and were not finding their way with their noses alone, things would be over in short order.

By the time the foursome had fled nearly a half-mile southwest, they had worn themselves out climbing the unrelenting slope, yet had put no greater distance between themselves and the long-tusked creatures. But now their predicament only worsened, for another pack of these same animals was approaching from the northwest.

"Great wippikats! Troubles appear out of nowhere and everywhere in this dratted valley!" cursed Wunko.

"There's nothing for it but to go straight south," puffed Okona.

"But that will take us back toward the ganoja!" Anisha exclaimed.

"So it will, but all the same, I'd rather not wait here to be gored by these things," returned Okona.

So south they went. Very quickly once they had summited the ridge they had been ascending, their possible routes narrowed to a rough path that ran along the foot of a cliff that rose ever higher on their left. This path graded slightly downhill and was interrupted by occasional small junipers growing out of the cliff's base. These they were obliged to climb over, for to their right, the land fell away rather steeply, and ever more so as on they went.

Meanwhile, the two groups of creatures behind them merged and trotted along the path, grunting with increased ferocity all the while, for they sensed their quarry was not far off. The distance between hunters and the hunted closed rapidly, and the companions panted heavily as they looked for any possible way of escape.

Just when they were about to give up hope, the path ran directly into a cavity in the rock, where grew a solitary juniper in the shadows, and there it ended. Then most of them gave up hope entirely, for the thorn-covered slope down to the right had grown too perilous to navigate, and scaling the cliff to the left was quite impossible.

"I suppose we make our stand here," sighed Wunko. "It's been pleasant getting to know you all."

"This can't be the end," said Okona through gritted teeth. He hurried to the juniper and crawled behind it. "It isn't!" he called back, nearly dizzy with excitement. "There's a hole in the rock, barely big enough for us to fit through. But the path goes on!"

Okona crawled through, then Yahsi maneuvered behind the tree, and Okona helped her through the narrow opening. Then came Anisha and lastly Wunko, who had just been sighted by the reddish creatures. These stamped the ground and squealed as they charged toward him. However, he darted behind the juniper and pushed himself through the hole in the rock only just in time.

The beasts struck their tusks against the juniper and pounded their hoofs on the rock, but the area behind the tree was simply too cramped for them, and they wouldn't have fit through the opening anyhow.

"Ha! That's what you get for being too stout for your own good!" laughed Wunko.

"No time for taunting yet," warned Yahsi, "for they may find some other way around. The slope to our right is not so steep on this side of the hole, and if they go back along the trail, they might take some route we missed down and then make their way back up here. And at the moment, we are stuck on the edge of a cliff, you know."

"Not stuck," countered Okona. "The trail continues."

"Yes, out toward the river," said Anisha. "This must be that really immense bluff we saw from below. But the ganoja was just on the other side of the river loop that runs at its foot."

"Well, oughtn't we at least go forward a bit and have a look?" queried Okona. "One can probably see for miles up here. Maybe we'll spy some presence of the Jaggo from afar." Receiving a nod from the others, he started off on the trail, which climbed ever so slightly. The rest followed after one last glance at the enraged creatures behind them, which were still trying to get at the hole blocked by the juniper.

It was not long before the trail bent to face the river. Now the world of the Kannitaw opened wide before them, and they could see far across the age-old mounts in every direction. Here, broad green forest sprawled over mighty, shapened hills, and through it all ran the winding Wakosi, flashing emerald in the noonday sun. From the west it came to the foot of the bluff, then swept away to the south before curving back eastward.

"Look! There are canoes down there!" cried Okona, as he carefully made his way along the path, which was now very narrow indeed, with a precipitous face both above and below.

Sure enough, some three hundred and fifty feet below, five canoes were plying the Wakosi, headed downstream and just about to enter the loop the party had paddled less than two hours ago. Two persons each sat in four of the boats, and in the fifth, which was longer, three. All of these looked to be Jaggo, save those in the last canoe. In the stern of this sat a man, larger than all the others and with a bright red cloak draped over his shoulders. His face was painted a deathly white with streaks of lurid crimson running down it. And even from this considerable distance, his great strength was evident from the way he handled his paddle. This paddle had blades on both ends, and he wielded it in a most curious manner, for he used only his left arm and often pressed the paddle against his upper chest and neck to brace it for his strokes. In the canoe's prow was a figure whose head and shoulders were concealed by a gray, hooded cloak. This figure too was paddling, and there was undoubted brawn in the figure's arms as well. And between these two individuals sat a girl, not more than twelve, clad in a cream-colored dress and with a thin, metal circlet on her brow. She bore no paddle, but sat erect, staring straight ahead.

"Let's try not to be seen," cautioned Anisha.

"Or tusked," declared Wunko, who had just sighted the large creatures they had thwarted only a few minutes ago clambering up the slope to rejoin the path behind them. "They must have found a way around, just as Yahsi feared."

"Hurry!" Yahsi urged, and Okona surged forward along the path.

Their peril was now tremendous, for in places the path was only two or three feet wide, and the drop was a sheer fall of more than three hundred feet down to the Wakosi, while the cliff leered nearly another three hundred feet above them. But happily, their hoofed hunters were unable to follow them any farther, for their bodies were too thick for them to safely traverse the narrowest parts of the trail.

"Whew!" breathed Okona. "And I was just beginning to think it couldn't get—"

He broke off his utterance at the swoop of a huge shadow across the company.

"Not again!" lamented Wunko.

From a height of several thousand feet, the ganoja was descending, with fury in its wings and eyes blazing with bloodlust.

CHAPTER SIXTEEN

SHADOO'S SHELF

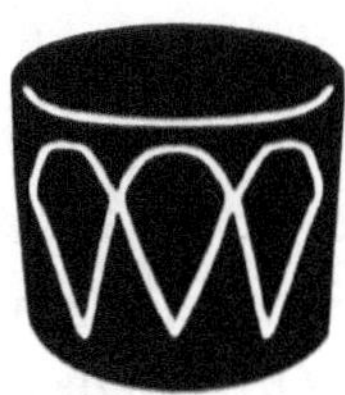

T HEY RUSHED FORWARD ALONG the path, almost heedless of the doom lying only inches from their feet, as they sought to reach a decently sized recess where the cliff hung over the trail, covering it in shadow.

"That terrible ganoja will be here any second, and there's nowhere to hide," panted Anisha, as they came to the alcove.

"No, but at least those confounded Jaggo won't be able to spot us since we're back a bit from the cliff," wheezed Yahsi. "Also, the path isn't so narrow here, and perhaps we'll have just enough room to attempt a fight."

"A fight?" Okona exclaimed. "We haven't got any weapons. And even if we did, there's no way we could survive an assault from that thing. Not here of all places."

"Certainly not."

Okona looked around, puzzled, for a man's voice had made the remark, but it wasn't Wunko's. "Who said that?" he asked.

A wrinkled, bony arm yanked him deeper into the recess. Before Okona could fathom what was going on, he was shoved into a covert, vertical crack in the cliff wall, past which lay a tight hallway, short in length and breadth and running just behind the cliff face. Now he saw that the arm belonged to an old man. Long, tangled gray hair sprouted from his head, and he was dressed in naught but rags: a short-sleeved shirt and loincloth, tattered and soiled.

The man snatched Yahsi's arm and pulled her toward the crack, then hissed at Anisha and Wunko to get inside. As soon as these two had gone through the crack and into the smallish, low-ceilinged cave beyond, where Okona, Yahsi, a sputtering clay lamp and various oddments awaited them, the man himself entered, and only just in time, for the clacking beak and beating wings of the ganoja were by now just outside.

"Ye were very nearly worms for that dreadful bird," he said in a wavery tenor, then seated himself on a rounded rock in the back corner and took a swift swig from a drinking skin.

"Who are you?" asked Okona.

"And where are we?" added Anisha, looking about.

"Shinnemah Shadoo's the name," the old man spryly replied. "Ah, yes, Old Shadoo am I! Shadoo, Shadoo, it's true. And you're currently in Shadoo's Shelf, one of the several illustrious residences of yours truly. And do sit! Please, sit! And feel free to lay down your gear and goods."

The company obliged.

As the threatening sounds from the ganoja continued outside, Wunko declared, "Well, Mister Shadoo, we're all very grateful to you for rescuing us! But why did you imperil yourself to do so? After all, you don't know us from anybody."

"Right you are! But I could hear clear enough ye've no liking for the Jaggo nor the ganoja. And, ye should know, neither have I! Now, if ye'll be telling me your names, we'll get better acquainted."

"I'm Okona, a Song-maker of the Sakooma," the lad said.

"And I, Anisha," stated the girl.

"Wunko, at your service," announced the Tikkichaw.

"And I am Yahsi, old but not yet dead!" said the Wise-woman.

"I know what you mean," Shadoo chuckled. "Seventy and two summers have I walked this Middle Realm, and they lie heavy on a body."

"What's an old fellow like you doing in such a perilous nest as this?" inquired Wunko.

"One might ask ye the same question," the old man returned. "In fact, Shadoo does!"

"As to what we're doing in the Wakosi Valley at all," said Okona, "that's a rather long story. But more immediately, we fled up here, first because of that wretched ganoja out there, and secondly because a bunch of huge, red—I don't know what you'd call them—"

"Chiborka," said Shadoo. "Chased ye up here, did they? Rotten fellows they are, and there's little to rival them on either side of the Vale, save bears every now and then. But they're more perilous than bears as a rule. Compelled by a magic spell, they seek to attack all but the Jaggo. And ye can only really avoid them if ye know their tricks. It's lucky ye found the entrance to my path. Wouldn't have been a pretty sight had they gotten their tusks into ye." He grimaced.

Suddenly, the agitation of the ganoja ceased.

"Is it gone?" asked Anisha, looking nervously toward the entrance.

Shadoo shook his head. "Waiting and listening, I think," he whispered. "But no need to fear. That blighter can fit neither beak nor body in here, or he'd have done so already! Besides, I think I've a way to clear him off well enough when the time comes if need be."

"Now, back to what I asked ye. Why came ye to Where the Wakosi Rises? Doesn't the world at large hold enough death and danger for ye?"

"Plenty," Okona replied. "And we would not have entered this valley except at great need. You see, we're searching for the Hand of Hamora, which is a great relic of our people, the Sakooma. Without this relic in its proper place, the Sakooma will be lost, so we must get it back."

"The Sakooma to me are known," declared Shadoo, "but this Hand is not. Magical, is it? And powerful, I guess?"

"Very," said Anisha. "And our Okona and Yahsi were told by a seer that we would find it here in the mountains of the north."

"Unfortunately," Yahsi remarked, "the Jaggo have made quite a mission out of keeping us from our own. So we came to realize there's a strong connection between the Jaggo and our search for the missing Hand. Also, in the course of our travels, we learned that the Jaggo all come from this valley. What's more, I heard them mention they had a master, so we've concluded it must be this master of theirs who has the Hand and that the Jaggo were assigned to keep any from regaining it. The Jaggo are plenty dreadful alone, so one can only imagine what their master is like and what said person might do with the Hand. For, according to our Chief Magic-maker, it has not only the potential to bring peace and plenty, as it did for us for several centuries, but also lends raw power to those who can wield it."

Shadoo's eyes flashed. "So that's what's got the valley all astir, eh? This Hand must be a powerful charm indeed, for I've not seen the Jaggo so busy and bustling since first I came to this region seven years ago."

He looked long and probingly at each of his visitors, then declared, "Well, I think I've heard enough from ye to know it's safe for Shadoo to share, as our aims are woven closely together. I want nothing more than to free this land from the Jaggo and their master, for this is *my* valley, and I want it back. And I think that to reclaim this Hand of yours, ye will be forced to battle these selfsame villains. Yet ye will likely not succeed in your quest unless ye send their souls to the Underbrakes, for the master of which ye speak is the greatest and wickedest sorcerer this land has seen in a thousand years or more. Too clever he is for ye to thieve it and too powerful for ye to openly seize it while he yet breathes. Ah, yes, he'll have to be done away with."

"*He?*" said Yahsi. "Not *she?* Or *they?*"

"He," Shadoo confirmed.

"But what can we do against one such as that?" Anisha inquired.

"We'll have to take some thought for that, to be sure," said Shadoo gravely. "But the ending of this master's got to be done, for both my cause and yours. Now, I could much use the aid of ye, and I reckon ye could use the aid of me. If it be to your liking, I shall try to help ye gain back the Hand, and ye shall try to help Shadoo do away with the Jaggo and their master. What say ye?" He held out his right palm, facing upwards.

The companions looked at each other, troubled.

"We'd of course covet your help," said Anisha, "but after hearing a little of what we're facing, I'm wondering if we shouldn't return with a whole army."

"I very much doubt we have time for all that," said Wunko soberly.

"What do you think, Yahsi?" asked Okona.

"I think you ought to decide, Okona," she quietly replied. "For I sense your time is drawing near, the time for which you were appointed to this journey. You'll have to make a difficult judgment soon, I expect, but I'd rather you shoulder some of the weight now than do it all at once."

"All right," he breathed. He thought for several moments. Then he, just as their host had, extended his open palm, replying, "Gladly will we accept your aid, Mister Shadoo, and offer you ours as well."

Shadoo grinned, turned his palm over and slapped Okona's open hand, declaring, "Wonderful! The pledge is made. Now, let's get down to particulars."

He leaned toward them, and his voice fell almost to a whisper, as he rubbed his hands delightedly over the dim lamp. "For my part, I shall see to supplying and safety as well as may be, and I'll share with ye what I know of this valley's dark master and his consorts. And when it comes to getting back this Hand of yours, Shadoo's your man! As for the part of ye, ye'll help me carry out whatever plan is necessary to liberate the Wakosi from these filth. For much more can be done with five than one. Unfortunately, for a long time, it's been only Shadoo against the whole lot of them."

"You speak Sakooma quite well for not being one," noted Yahsi abruptly.

"So I do." Shadoo beamed. "And you've guessed right, Missus Yahsi. Not Sakooma am I, but Babora."

"Ah, I met some of your kinfolk not four days ago," said Yahsi. "Away southeast was our meeting, west of a place called Shakola Kora. A fellow named Chapimu was among them."

Shadoo smiled toothily. "Glad to hear the Faithful Forty are still roaming not terribly far from here. Haven't given up yet, they haven't."

"The Faithful Forty?" Wunko prompted.

Shadoo held up his finger and went to the entrance, crept out and then came back and sat down.

"Ganoja's gone," he said. "Or at least not perched on my doorstep. But he isn't far off, I'd guess. Not sure what game he's playing, but we can ignore him, I think, at least for a bit. The same goes for those Jaggo a-water below, for even if they've a mind to find a way up here, it'll take 'em a fair while or longer to do it. But we'll not linger here much nonetheless. Just enough to have a little chat."

After scratching his ears, Shadoo took a nut from his pocket, cracked it and tossed the contents into his mouth. "Well, ye've given me your story straight as ye can; now it's Shadoo's turn to do the same."

"The Babora used to live in this valley, ye see, all up and down it," Shadoo began, "in rock shelters, hunting and fishing—even farming and bird-keeping a bit in the side valleys—and living as happily as any old tribe in this world. But then, fifty-one years ere baby Shadoo first saw the sun, the Chief Troubler himself, the one you've been referring to as the Jaggo's master, entered this land, and his evil witch-wife with him. Well, twasn't long before they started working their bad magic. First it was the animals they turned against us with their spells. Ye know, the bears, chiborka and the like, as if they weren't trouble enough already ... But when that didn't drive my people out, the troublers went to *them*." His eyes fell, and he muttered, "And against such as that, none could stand."

"Who is *them*?" asked Anisha.

Wunko was about to interject when Shadoo hoarsely replied, "The Oolasheg, the Twin Crones of Torment, terrors of a bygone age lingering long past their time."

Okona, Wunko and Yahsi all gasped, while Anisha reeled in shock.

Anisha looked at Wunko and Okona, stammering, "W-was this the name you were guarding against all this time? And if so, have I just lost a year of my life? Or more?"

Wunko stared sharply at Shadoo and reprimanded, "Has living long alone, as I gather you've been doing, completely robbed you of your senses? I myself lived as a hermit for several years, but that didn't—"

"No need to worry, ma'ams and misters," said Shadoo staunchly. "I know what folk say about uttering the name of those terrible beings, but I don't believe it, for I'm not sure such can hear quite as well as generally presumed. They are indeed as monstrous as anything you'll ever meet, but in my experience—"

"But we do believe thus!" protested Okona.

"My apologies," said Shadoo meekly, seeing the lad was in earnest. "I suppose from now on, then, I shall just refer to them as ... the Sisters."

"What's the use?" sighed Yahsi, throwing up her hands. "We've all heard the name now, and each of us has lost whatever years accord with it, if such is really the way of things. And I suppose, as we're all already sitting in the heart of the Upper Wakosi, that adding more danger to our lot is of little concern. Please, Mister Shadoo, continue with your story."

"Very well," Shadoo assented.

"Unfortunately, the Babora were no match for ... ah, the Sisters ... and were forced to flee before more of their number were devoured.

So Kiamosh—that's the master's name—and Shakeega—that's his wife—soon had the whole valley to themselves."

"Didn't you say this Kiamosh fellow came here more than half a century before you were born?" Wunko queried. "And you are now old, so that would make this Kiamosh much older still. Is he not human, then?"

"Can't really say," returned Shadoo. "But yes, he's very old. Yet he doesn't look it! Just as a man in his prime or toward the end of it he seems. But of the year of his birth I've heard no tale."

"Anyhow, he and the witch had this land to themselves for many years, but the Babora roamed not far outside it, always hoping to drive him out and get it back. Sadly, this never came to be. Everyone who ventured in was never heard from again. So eventually, no one even dared it. But the Kannitaw had been the Babora's home for centuries, so they wandered about in perpetual mourning on its edges, making such life as they could."

Shadoo guzzled once more from his flask.

"But then, the evil which had once been confined to the Wakosi started pouring out of it. The Jaggo were seen abroad, and they stalked at night, killing and eating whomever crossed them or else taking them captive to this valley, where things worse still befell them. For Kiamosh to keep on good terms with the Oolash—I mean, the er, well, ye know ... to keep on good terms with *them*, he had to keep them supplied with more and more blood. So the Babora were pushed farther out still. And that was the way of it when young Shadoo came along."

"If you don't mind me interrupting," said Okona, "who or what are the Jaggo? And where did they come from?"

"I don't rightly know nor does anyone else, save maybe Kiamosh," Shadoo returned, "but I've an idea they're wicked warriors whose souls were called up from the Underbrakes by Kiamosh's magic, for they were never heard of or seen before he came here. Anyway, on with my tale."

"I lived the Babora way for some time, hearing about the good old days and this lovely valley, which was our long heritage, but always being told it was futile to try to take it back. But I never believed it, as Shadoo's blood was a noble one. For I was the last in the line of Odamac, the final chieftain of the Babora to reign while they yet possessed the Wakosi. And if I were to give up on reclaiming it, there'd be none left with both the heaven-sent right and the inclination to take it again. But I knew I'd need to learn much before I'd have a chance of regaining this sorrowing land."

"Well, I took a Babora bride and fathered a number of children, and our family lived in various places abroad, as I gathered all the lore about this valley I could, all the while plying different trades. In the plains of Taygor to the west, I hunted the herds of nataki, the great brown beasts, for ten years and five; in Aska Karalonga, I wrought many crafts among the Kamingo; and at the northern end of Sorrequom Ridge, I farmed. And there I left my family seven years ago to at last venture into the Wakosi heartland and devise a means of conquering this land back from the usurpers."

"Many Babora still honored my claim to chiefdom and to this land, but only a modest group of hunters and warriors, the Faithful Forty I mentioned earlier, vowed their willingness to fight the great evil in the Wakosi Vale on my behalf. I accepted their pledge but said I would not call upon them until I was ready to make a decisive strike, for it would be much harder for many to hide here than just one. In the meantime, they promised to dwell ever on the edge of these lands, awaiting my word. I asked none to enter with me, for I knew it would be perilous, and I would lay on no other such a heavy task. So in secret and alone have I dwelt here ever since, moving by hidden paths on both sides of the river and staying at places undiscovered by the Jaggo. A great deal of prying I've done—creeping, spying, skulking and eavesdropping, learning what I might of Kiamosh and those in his service. And thus ye find me today."

He looked up hopefully, "But I sense in your very eyes and in the circumstances under which ye come to me that my trials here are ending. Whether with my death or that of Kiamosh, that I can't say. But I think one or the other shall be very soon. For this business with the Hand seems to be of great consequence, both to ye and to him. Ah, fitting for him that it should be a Hand of all things!" he laughed, then cleared his throat.

"Begging your pardon, Mister Shadoo," said Yahsi, "but we were under the impression from our Chief Magic-maker that it was the Sisters themselves who had stolen the Hand, not this Kiamosh. Well, he didn't know it was the Sisters exactly, but the point is that he reckoned the theft to be work of a certain unnatural caliber, of which the Sisters alone in this area would be capable."

"I see where your puzzlement lies," said Shadoo. "Likely enough the Sisters *were* the ones who stole it to begin with. But they are in no need of artifacts to increase their power. For, as I understand it, their magic doesn't work like that. However, with a sorcerer such as Kiamosh, artifacts are precisely the sort of thing he would be seeking. If ye want my thoughts on the matter, I should say they obtained it for him as a gift for all his ghastly services. As it is a thing of power, Kiamosh will surely use it to master much more than this valley. And if he succeeds, woe to the world! But if we vanquish him first, ye couldn't find a happier man than Shinnemah Shadoo! For then not only would my family be summoned to join me, but the whole of the Babora. Then the valley would no longer languish under the Witch-man's shadow, but flourish bright and fair as it did long ago!"

Now that Shadoo had finished his talk, he sipped again from his flask and nibbled some jerky from one of his pockets.

"Mister Shadoo," Okona said, "running into you has been a tremendous stroke of luck. For it sounds as if you alone possess the lore we shall require to face Kiamosh and the others. We're sorry you've had to lurk like a bandit in your own rightful domain for so many years, but we mean to set that right as soon as we can. If you would but guide us to where Kiamosh makes his lair, we'll help you devise and execute some kind of attack."

"His lair is rather to the south and somewhat to the west of here," Shadoo said, "near the first founts of the Wakosi. The hidden door to the place stands beneath a high cascade in a hollow. Many tunnels there are behind that stone. Only once have I entered them; ah, that was a black and perilous night. Bok Barusha that cursed hollow is called, the Warlock's Hive. And only three miles to the southeast of there, on the other side of the Wakosi, is Kiamosh's temple, where captives are killed and eaten and terrible rites are held. The Jaggo name it Agra Chalura, the Bloodmouth Fall. For a rush of water pours ever through the ceiling of rock there, and men are cut open above and then cast into the fall. I know of no other place like it. It would be beautiful, I think, had it not been taken by them for that dark purpose. And someday it may be again, if it is purged of them. But in those places Kiamosh is found most often. However, presently, I think we needn't go all the way there to find him."

"Why is that?" asked Wunko.

"Because he was just passing by here not long ago," Shadoo returned.

They stared at him.

"Saw ye not the canoes below? Kiamosh was he of the white face with streaks of red."

Anisha gaped.

"Who then was the figure with the hood? His wife?" inquired Yahsi.

"No, the witch died ere I came," Shadoo replied, "though I'm not sure how or why. Laid was she in earth near Bok Barusha, I've gathered."

"What about the girl?" Anisha asked.

"Her I don't know, although I'm rather certain she's one they caught and mean to feed to the Oola—to *them*."

"Are *they* not far from here?" inquired Okona worriedly.

"Not far in owl's flight," Shadoo replied. "But it's a decent step for man-legs, it is. Anyhow, I think we should be getting on and stay at a place I call Shinnemah's Kitchen tonight. It's quite close to *them*, though I shouldn't worry about that if I were ye, for I've stayed there a great many times unharmed. And it will be rather close to where Kiamosh lodges this evening. He means to sacrifice someone to the Sisters, likely that girl—for that's what all the drum-talk today was signaling—but he will not do so until the morning, for he and the Jaggo must do a ceremony in preparation during the dark hours first. But tomorrow morning, let us make the best assault upon him we can manage. At night would be too dangerous, for the dark is firmly on his side."

"But how shall we get out of here with the ganoja about?" Anisha asked, as everyone rose at Shadoo's beckoning.

Shadoo went to the wall and picked up a long wooden tube and several darts, which he waved at the girl.

"You think those will do the trick?" inquired Wunko.

"We may find out shortly," Shadoo answered, as he gathered up a few more items and gestured at the others to collect theirs as well. "I don't know much about this ganoja, as he's only been around these parts a short while. Was only ten days ago I first saw him. Keeping watch for Kiamosh, I presume he is. But with darts like these I've slain chiborka and bears and hill dragons bigger still, and I reckon the ganoja will have second thoughts about attacking if these manage to puncture his hide."

"Supposing the ganoja did somehow warn the Jaggo we were here," mused Yahsi, "do you think they'll be able to track us?"

Shadoo shook his head. "I've been here these seven years and haven't been nabbed by 'em yet. I'm not sure they even know I'm here. Depending on how ye entered the valley, they mayn't know ye're here either. But whatever the case, from this point on, your tracks will be invisible, or close to it, thanks to Old Shadoo!"

With that, he snuffed out the lamp and scurried out the narrow opening of the cave. The others followed, carrying their effects with them.

Outside, they could see nary a sign of the ganoja nor of the three canoes they had spotted earlier.

"Let's get off Kachuma Bluff as quickly as we can," Shadoo urged, as he hurried along the path, back toward the secret entrance through which the companions had first come upon the narrow trail. Soon they reached the hole, and all were relieved to see the chiborka were no longer guarding it.

"Have better things to do than sit around waiting for ye lot, I suppose," remarked Shadoo.

Beyond the hole in the rock, Shadoo went rather more speedily. Age had done little to tame him. Almost like an animal he moved, with balance and wariness in every step. The old hermit took them a little under a mile north by northwest into the woods, helping the others select where and how to walk so as to make their journey more difficult to track. He especially advised them to walk in single file, stepping on rocks and hard-packed earth whenever possible and avoiding thick brush and clusters of weeds and ferns. Also, he was insistent that all remain silent.

They came then to the creek, which they had followed when escaping the ganoja. This Shadoo identified as Sambo Creek, and he took them a mile farther up the stream, curving first northwest and then more directly north. There they came to a wash that entered it from the northeast. They hiked up this a short ways and began climbing the southeastern wall of the valley in which it lay. When they had gained several hundred feet of elevation, they turned northeastward, still ascending. All told, it was a steady climb upward for more than a mile, and this wore on them, for the day was hot, and it was laborious to always be cautious about any traces they were leaving. But ultimately, they came to a plateau, and here the terrain was much kinder.

Though the afternoon was getting on and they had hardly rested, Shadoo's speed flagged not. On the plateau, they went another two and a half miles nearly straight east. Some of this area was covered in grassy fields, where they had to alter their formation, spreading out to keep from all tramping through the same route. But toward the end of the plateau, they came to a forest of close-growing pines.

They wound through these woods and veered slightly north until they came to the brink of a bluff with a wide, wooded valley beyond it. Following the cliff a short distance to the left, they encountered a small stream flowing over a course of rock with several shelves, then tumbling over the cliff in a splashing, forty-foot fall. The cascade plummeted into a forested hollow, ringed on three sides by high walls but opening northward before them toward the greater valley. To their right, the rock lip standing above the hollow overhung a fair amount, forming the roof of a grotto of some depth, which could be accessed from the hollow floor.

Taking care not to slip on the wet stones, they crossed the stream and followed Old Shadoo to a ledge of stone, which ran under a low roof of rock. Shadoo crawled forward along the ledge, and they came after him, crouching to avoid hitting their heads on the rock. At the far side of the ledge, the hollow rose up to meet them via a slope of tumbled boulders. One by one, they lowered themselves from the ledge onto a small boulder and then sprang off onto the slope leading down into the hollow. Now they could see that the large grotto they had noted from above that lay along the eastern side of the hollow actually swept around to its south side as well, continuing all the way behind the waterfall but ending shortly beyond it.

"Welcome to Shinnemah's Kitchen!" Shadoo proudly declared. "A fine little place this is, I say; 'tis sheltered, hidden, has clean, running water most of the time, and if a fellow has want of food, he'll find it aplenty in the valley beyond. The only trouble about it is how near it lies to the Oola—I do apologize—how near it lies to the Sisters. But they've never come to bother Old Shadoo, perhaps because Shadoo's never gone to bother them. Or because this is just far enough beyond their proper roaming grounds. I'm not sure. But on account of how close it is to *them*, it's safe from the Jaggo. This, like all the places I make my lodging, has one thing or another to keep them cleared off. They hold this valley sacred, ye know, for they reverence the Twins, so aren't apt to go trotting about and stumble across this spot."

"You wouldn't happen to stay in Nadula Valley sometimes, would you?" asked Yahsi.

"Nadula Valley?" Shadoo exclaimed. "Why, that I would! Ye know of the place?"

"The Babora I met spoke of it," replied Yahsi. "A mere memory it was to them, but we found it very real and of great assistance."

"Yes, and I suppose now we know why it looked as if somewhere had dwelt there recently," Okona said.

"Recently indeed! I was there but a few days ago," said Shadoo.

Shadoo motioned for them to follow him to the grotto at the far side of the hollow. "Come! Shadoo'll get ye some food. Rain is coming in; I can feel it. But we and our supper'll be nice and dry in my cave."

In a short while, everyone was nestled around a low fire (constructed by Shadoo and Wunko) under the overhanging rock, partaking of bowls of a first-rate squirrel and goomawort soup (jointly prepared by Wunko and Shadoo). The hollow dimmed, and a light rain began, but as the sky grew darker, it spawned an utter downpour. However, the wind blew little, so not a drop of it reached them far back under the shelf.

For several hours, they conversed and became better acquainted with Shadoo, and he with them. They spoke also of goings-on in the Wakosi Vale and related to him more of their adventures. But as evening fell and the rain subsided, they grew drowsy, so Shadoo went to his supply stash farther down the grotto and pulled out woven mats for them to lie upon.

"Tomorrow we strike against Kiamosh," he said, as he spread them out, "so rest ye well tonight."

"Are you not coming to bed yet?" inquired Anisha.

"Soon, soon," Shadoo assured. "But afore it gets much later, I want to have a look at things in the valley, and I've got to give some thought yet to how we might attempt our business on the morrow. After all, it's no mean affair to take on Kiamosh or the Jaggo. And if the Sisters are involved too, it'll be ever so much worse. But 'twould be best to say no more about that while the moon is out."

Looking out at the shadowed forest with bright, darting eyes, he said, "If Kiamosh is allowed to do what he will with that Hand you're seeking, I've a feeling neither we nor anybody else will be able to stop him once he's done it. But I don't think he's done what he aims to yet, for the Jaggo's fires the last week or so haven't been ones of triumph but of watchfulness and preparation. However, the ones I saw last night marked that the preparation is almost at an end. So call on the highest Powers ye can before ye enter the River of Dreams tonight! For we shall need all the help we can lay hands on. After tonight, I tell ye, this realm and those beyond shall clash as they have not for many years in these parts; let us hope the good will prove the greater."

Shadoo soon hurried off into the darkness of the Kannitaw, and the four companions were left alone with the music of tinkling raindrops and the song of the falls, set against a chorus of soft insects, occasionally accented by calls of night birds. Each of the companions murmured pleas to various Powers, but most of all to Mahna Shuya. Then eyelids grew heavy and minds dulled, and there was the sound of deep breathing.

"Anisha," Okona whispered, when he was fairly assured both Wunko and Yahsi were asleep. He was uncertain, though, if she herself was yet awake.

"Yes?" her voice came in soft reply.

"I'm sorry I didn't insist more strongly that you return to Takula back when things first went wrong. For, not to be overly grim, I don't know if any of us will live through tomorrow. And I feel some degree of responsibility for the fact that you will be facing such peril. If I die, the Sakooma will lose only a Song-maker. But you are the Sanno's only daughter, and yours is the last of Hamora's noble blood. And you mean ever so much to so many people." He paused. "And ever so much to me."

Anisha rolled over to face him. "Even if you had bidden me to return, I would not have done so. For do you not know why I came on this journey?" In the pale moon-glow which barely penetrated the shadows of the grotto, her dark eyes searched his face.

Anisha stretched her hand toward him, and he reached out and took it. They looked silently at each other for several moments. Then Anisha murmured, "Good night, Okona," as she withdrew her hand and rolled over.

"Till the morrow, Anisha," Okona replied, closing his eyes, as his waking thoughts mingled with the milky waters of the River of Dreams.

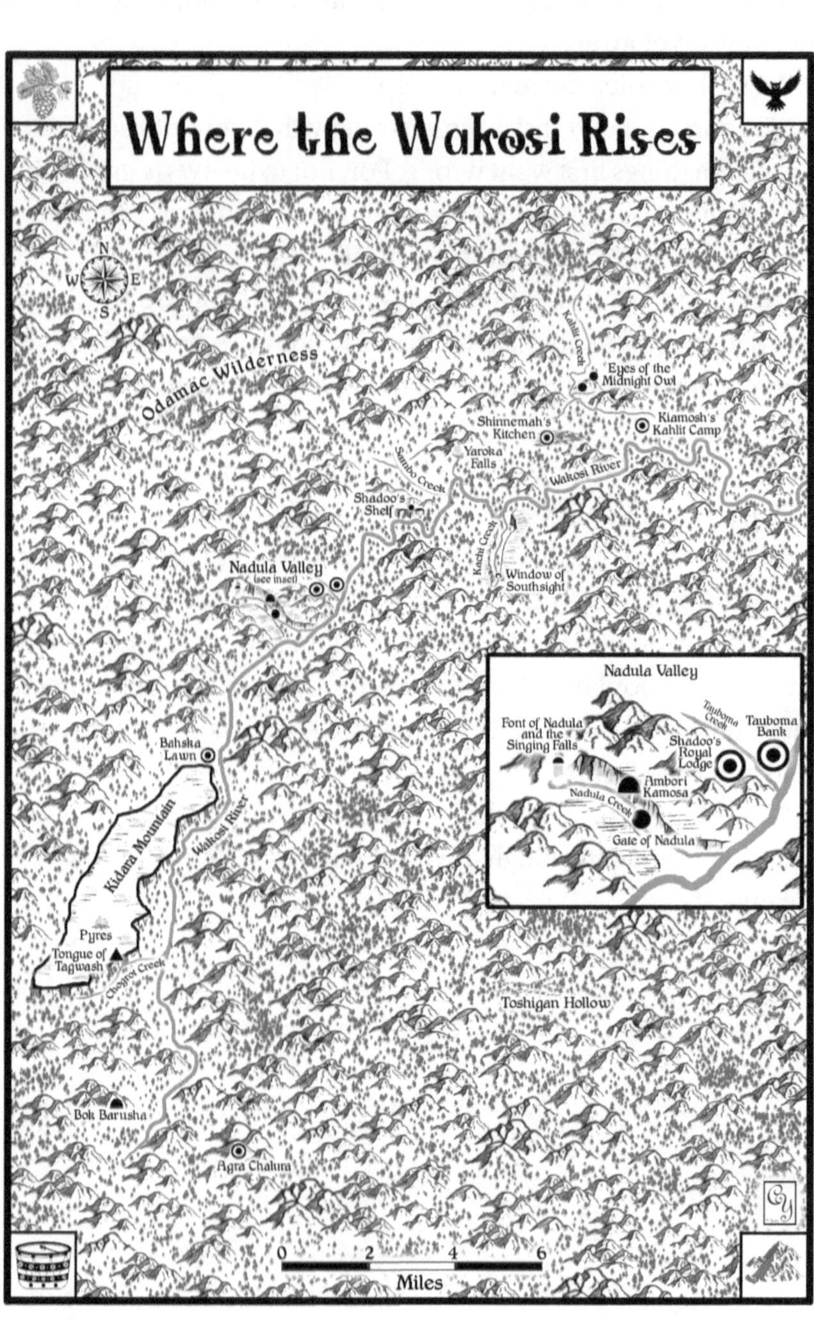
Where the Wakosi Rises
Odamac Wilderness
Kahlit Creek
Eyes of the Midnight Owl
Shinnemah's Kitchen
Kiamosh's Kahlit Camp
Yaroka Falls
Sambo Creek
Wakosi River
Shadoo's Shelf
Kachi Creek
Nadula Valley
(see inset)
Window of Southsight
Bahska Lawn
Kidara Mountain
Wakosi River
Pyres
Tongue of Tagwash
Chogrol Creek
Toshigan Hollow
Bok Barusha
Agra Chalina
N
W E
S
Nadula Valley
Tauboma Creek
Tauboma Bank
Font of Nadula and the Singing Falls
Shadoo's Royal Lodge
Ambori Kamosa
Nadula Creek
Gate of Nadula
0   2   4   6
Miles

CHAPTER SEVENTEEN

EYES OF THE MIDNIGHT OWL

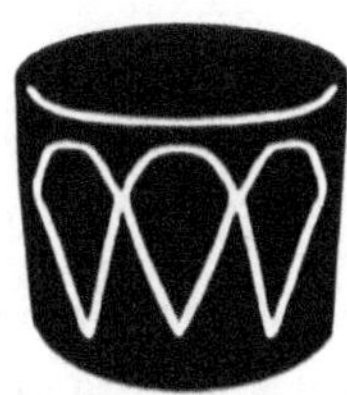

WHEN OKONA'S EYES NEXT creaked open, they were met with the grotto's ceiling, illuminated by faint dawn-light. He shut his eyes once more, and fading images from stray threads of his dreams still clung before him. There was a forest with a stream; a shadow swept through the trees, but the gloom passed, glinting bone whizzed through the air and a man sprang toward him. Okona fled; darkness swallowed him. A hulking form appeared against a red light. But a cleaner, whiter light shone from beyond, and Okona raced toward it. There was a confusion and a blur, then a spur of rock over a wide valley. Okona was weeping. Then his vision failed him, and he opened his eyes once more.

He sat up and rubbed his back, looking around. The others were still asleep, and Shadoo was absent. All was quiet in the hollow, save for a few morning mutterings of the forest. Okona stood and walked under the overhang until he reached the falls. Wishing to fully invigorate himself for the coming day, he undressed and bathed in the cascade's cold, bracing waters. Then he clothed himself and was about to head back to the others when he spied a lone figure sitting on a mossy rock in the midst of the hollow, facing out toward the greater valley. It was Wunko. Okona walked over to him, and, as he approached, he noticed the Tikkichaw's prized wooden box resting next to his feet. Okona sat on a fallen log nearby.

"Morning," Wunko said.

"Morning," Okona returned. "You ready for today?"

"No, but the day is upon us anyhow."

Okona glanced down at Wunko's mysterious container.

"Wunko, if you don't my asking, what all's in that box you've been carrying ever since we met you?"

"The sad remains of my life, I'm afraid," Wunko sighed.

"I beg your pardon?"

"See for yourself." The Tikkichaw flung the box's lid open to reveal a number of smaller latched boxes nested within it. A few of these were opened to display quantities of wet powders or leaves.

"What is it?" Okona asked, peering at them.

"A lifetime's accumulation of rare spices and herbs."

Okona looked at him quizzically.

"Well, you shared your secret shame with the rest of us, so I can hardly consider myself a fair fellow if I don't do the same for you. But I suppose I'd better start at the beginning."

Wunko settled himself more comfortably on his seat. "You remember that story I told you and Anisha back in the Washoma? The story about the boy named Komakop from the swamps of Chachuma?"

"Yes."

"Well, that whole story was true, just as I said. And I can vouch for that because Komakop was my father."

Okona looked at Wunko in amazement.

"Yes, my father was a very great man, held in high renown. And he was a servant of the High Katchiwup, the ruler of all the varied clans of my people. So I was born into his service. And as I had a knack for cooking, I was made one of those who prepared his meals. That went well for some time. But one day, when I was on the cusp of manhood, I erred in mixing the spices for his soup. To this day, I can't remember why or how; it's just one of those things, one of those mistakes we all make on occasion. But this one had tremendous consequences. The High Katchiwup didn't like the soup and said that if I showed so little respect for his position, I had no business dwelling among the Tikkichaw."

"Now, when you're in that position, you can say and do as you please, so no one thought it at all inappropriate that I should be banished right out of Chachuma for making that soup less than it ought to have been. No one except my father. You see, my father tried to persuade the Katchiwup to alter his judgment, but he only grew more set in it, and my father nearly lost his position on account of me. Anyway, I had no choice but to leave the Tikkichaw lands. And I haven't seen my family since."

Okona looked sadly at Wunko, who was staring at the ground, his shoulders slumped.

"I went up the Anoka and began a life of wandering. And since then, I've been north, east and a little west but never back south of Sarkanna. And I've only had two objectives during that time, objectives which I thought might atone for my mistake, at least to myself, even if I couldn't make amends to anybody else. These were to be the best cook that ever I could and to be the best teller of tales that ever I might. For the true tales of my father's deeds were marvelous, but my own story is so dismal it ought really never to be told. So I had to tell better tales than that of my past and be in better ones too."

"As for my quest to be the most splendid cook north of the Southward Sea, I spent decades mastering the preparation of foods of all kinds, but especially soups and stews. And over many years, I collected all the most exotic and flavorful spices and herbs I could get my hands on. These I've always kept in this box here." He nodded mournfully toward it. "But they were ruined—every last one of them—when we came out of the Under-realm. I'm glad we escaped with our lives but am sorry to have lost so many years of labor. I'm thankful, also, that at last I've played a role in a really fine tale but sorry it seems to be coming to a very bad end. This might well be Uncle Wunko's last adventure."

Okona looked at Wunko thoughtfully a few moments, then said, "I really appreciate you telling me your story, Wunko. And I can fully understand why your past has broken you so. But I think you've more than made amends for your mistake. You *are* an outstanding cook. My tongue knows this, and even from the soup last night, I'd say your cooking is just as fantastic even without the aid of these herbs and spices. And what's more, you *are* a mighty good storyteller. My ears know this. And the role you've played in this tale is wonderful and essential. Anisha and I would be dead several times over were it not for you. And lastly, it isn't over yet, even if the end is near. But even if it does end poorly, I'd find myself honored to die alongside you. You've been a good friend, Wunko, and I hope I can be the same to you." Okona looked at him admiringly.

"Thank you, lad." Wunko smiled in return. "You warm a wanderer's heart."

Just then, Okona caught a subtle movement among the trees farther out in the hollow. It was Shadoo. Okona raised his hand to hail him.

Shadoo walked up to the seated pair and said cheerily, "Glad to see ye already roused! But come, let's join the womenfolk. I'd imagine they're waked by now. And anyway, we've got to eat a bite rather quickly, for soon Kiamosh will come forth to meet with the Sisters, and I'd rather be at the juncture before he is to find a good position. By my mind, our best hope is to attack him shortly after their meeting is ended."

Wunko grabbed his box, and he and Okona followed Shadoo back to where they had spent the night. Anisha and Yahsi were awake and conversing. Shadoo hurriedly handed out some jerky, dried fruits and nuts to the companions, and as they ate, he explained what he had discovered, as well as the plan he had formulated.

Sneaking down near Kiamosh's camp, Shadoo had learned there were only a few Jaggo with the sorcerer and that the girl they had seen in the canoe was indeed intended for sacrifice to the Oolasheg. Therefore, he proposed the companions lurk near the customary place where sacrifices were delivered over to the Crones and wait until the transaction had been carried out and the Oolasheg were gone. Then, presumably, they would be occupied with the consummation of the ritual in their lair. Meanwhile, Yahsi and Anisha would go a little ways down the valley to a certain place and make noise to draw the attention of the Jaggo and Kiamosh. Then, the instant they were distracted, Shadoo, Wunko and Okona would fire arrows from hidden positions from multiple different directions to make the Jaggo think they were surrounded. Their goal was to kill Kiamosh first and then as many Jaggo as they could before the Jaggo rushed toward them, at which point they would battle with spears and knives. Yahsi and Anisha were to carry pouches filled with stones, which they were to hurl at the Jaggo.

"It's just barely possible," Shadoo said, "that we might beat them like that. If there were any more Jaggo than those I saw, I think the plan would fail, though we might still do away with Kiamosh. But at least this way we shouldn't have to deal with the Twin Terrors. If they did enter the fray, they'd make an instant end of us. And of course, there's the possibility Kiamosh will be protected by magic. But if that's the case, there's nothing we can do about it. But I know the Jaggo can be killed, though it's difficult. I've killed one myself, I have; 'twas a frightful business. But I still say there's something other-ish about them. They're not just regular men. Anyhow, if everything does go right and we're able to kill Kiamosh and his helpers, I'll wager ye whatever ye wish that ye'll be able to collect that magic Hand from Kiamosh's corpse. For I heard the Jaggo talking last night as if it were already in their camp."

Relieved at least that they had some kind of plan, the party drank of the blessed water of Nadula Valley (and Wunko and Anisha took skins of it with them) and then armed themselves from Shadoo's weapon stock. The men took spears, short stone axes and bows of hickory, along with quivers well-supplied with stone-pointed arrows. Anisha and Yahsi were given bags of throwing stones, and everyone received daggers made from deer antlers. Anisha took also a small pouch of food.

Then, led by Old Shadoo's sure, silent, barefooted steps, the party set out from the sheltered hollow and into the open forest. Following the trickle down from Shinnemah's Kitchen, they made their way toward the heart of the greater valley. This trickle was joined by another stream on the way, and they trekked along the watercourse that led on from their convergence until they had gradually come down many hundreds of feet. Already the day was growing sultry, and sweat beaded upon their foreheads. And each minute, their anxiety grew, for fear they might stumble upon those who lent the valley its terror.

A little more than a mile northeast from Shadoo's secret dwelling, they stopped at a wider creek that occupied the bottom trough of the valley. There, at the old hermit's beck, they hid themselves behind some thick brush a ways back from the water's edge.

"Here lies Kahlit Creek," whispered Shadoo. "This is the place Kiamosh will perform his part of the ceremony. For the Eyes of the Midnight Owl, where the hellish rite will be completed, lie not far from here."

"What are they?" asked Okona.

"The twin entrances to Korashac Caverns, the Sisters' cursed abode. The name signifies that both passages lead to death, as it comes from the Terrors' forms in the Lands of the Living," Shadoo explained. "While the Twin Terrors are under the earth, it is said they appear as razor-toothed hags, hideous in form and face. But above ground, their shape is that of two owls. One is white; Sister Shukina is her name. She is Navina Kayu, Moon Owl, a being of horror and fright. But the other is black; Sister Kwennitch she is called. Midnight Owl, Navina Shoga is she, a being of death and darkness. But bearers of slaughter are they both, for to look in the eyes of either while they wear their owl-shape brings death, instant and terrible."

"Great wippikats!" Wunko uttered.

"So be warned," said the Babora, "the owls fly silently, as, of course, do all of that kind, so if ye see a flash of black or white, turn instantly away and shut tight your eyes. But the white will come first, leading the way and spreading its fright, and the black will follow the victim, bringing death from behind."

"Exactly how close are these entrances?" inquired Yahsi. "Several stonecasts?"

"A bit more than that. But they are near nonetheless, and one more so than the other. To come to the first, one need only go a little more than a furlong up Kahlit Creek, then turn east into a wash. A short distance up that, the Eye stands in the wall on the left. And the other Eye is a half-mile directly north of that, on the other side of the ridge. But let us hope none of us come to either of them, particularly the latter! For it is sealed and can be entered by the dead alone. The other is open to the living, though any who pass through it will surely die. It is used only by the Crones themselves and by Kiamosh to send his living sacrifices to be feasted upon by them."

Shadoo suddenly stiffened. "Look ye! The time is upon us. Be ye still and silent!"

From farther downstream, back toward the Wakosi River, eleven man-shapes and two much larger than men were approaching, moving northward through the forest along the course of the Kahlit. Nine Jaggo, some with spears in hand and others with drums, but all with pelts of wolf-heads upon their own, brought up the rear of the procession. But the sorcerer Kiamosh, who marched at the fore, was readily distinguished by his garb and gait and the terrible look in his eyes. The upper half of a skull, evidently of some variety of smaller hill dragon, rested atop his head, and to this were affixed tall feathers, red and black, standing up straight and running in a line from the forehead of the skull back to where it would have once joined to a neck. Freakishly white was his visage and shot with stripes of angry red. Shards of bone pierced his nose and ears, and a braided silver chain was around his neck, from which dangled many dragon teeth. Long was his cloak and black as a starless winter night, and he held it close about him with his left hand, for where his right ought to have been was only a stump. On the pointer finger of his left hand was a silver ring with a whitish stone, tinged by an eerie, pale blue; this seemed almost to be glowing in the morning light. Bare of feet was he, but bands of dark leather were bound about his ankles.

Behind him walked the girl they had seen the day before, in the same attire and bearing a blank expression, as if her eyes saw not the woods about her but something far beyond them. Her bare feet trod slowly and delicately upon the grass, and there was a fey air about her, a haunting grimness. Hair, long, straight and jet black, fell from her crown to the midst of her back, woven in an intricate pattern, and jewels were netted into it with thin mesh.

On either side of the girl and just behind her, plodding on huge paws, were two great, black creatures of bear kind. These were much larger than any bear the Sakooma or Tikkichaw had ever seen, and when Kiamosh and the girl halted near a collection of stones on the Kahlit's banks, these did as well, standing on their hind legs. More than twelve feet high they stood before placing their paws again upon the ground and clawing anxiously at the earth.

The tall witch-man stood still as a pillar of rock, looking about with dark, sunken eyes.

"They have come," he said in a low, resonant voice. The language was Sakooma, but it was rendered in a poetic manner, strangely measured. "Close thine eyes, each of ye, if ye wish not to leave us."

A cold, silent, breath swept through the forest, and with it came a great shadow, as if a dark blanket had been cast between earth and sun.

Suddenly, a white blur passed through the dim network of tree limbs above the creek.

"Shut your eyes! All of ye!" hissed Shadoo to those about him. And they did, scrunching up their faces to seal them as much as possible. Instantly, icy fear gripped their hearts and crawled upon their skin.

"At last, the time which hath long evaded us is come," Kiamosh's voice declared. "At last, the waiting of many bitter winters and heartless summers is ended. At last, that wrong which lay unresolved for centuries shall be made right, and for this we owe the mighty Oolasheg a fount of unending gratitude. Praise be to the twin wielders of death for their threefold gifts! And praise be to their Master for his power and long-suffering by our side! For he rewardeth much those who are loyal to him, those willing to pay his price. May he grow ever stronger against his foes, and may someday his gracious, silver moon consume the fiery, golden sun, that all may be their own masters, as it ought to have been from the beginning."

"In token of our allegiance to him," he continued, "and that the rite may be completed fully and well, I give to thee, O chosen child, this moon of crystal. Let it guide thee, and thou shalt not go astray."

There was a pause, presumably while this token was being bestowed. Then Kiamosh took a great breath and said, "Go now, last of a lineage long-blessed. Go now to thy destiny and to the black realm, hid from Sun and Sky. For this purpose I now anoint thee."

There was the sound of liquid being poured from a flask.

"Remember, pray thee, for what splendid cause thou bearest this honor, and commit thyself fully to the Powers of Earth. Follow the Sisters faithfully, and it shall go better with thee. And greet her who was dear to my heart when thou comest to that which lieth yonder. Farewell."

"Farewell, O, Kiamosh," said a soft, pale voice.

A tense minute of deep, dull, slow, steady drumming followed. At the end of it, Okona had an irresistible urge to see what was transpiring and opened his eyes just a crack. Almost immediately, he shut them again, for there was a flash of color, a streak of white, darting through the trees upstream. He saw also the girl, who was walking slowly northward behind it.

"Let us return to the Wakosi," Kiamosh said, "for the deed is as good as done, and we have much to prepare for the morrow."

The hidden companions opened their eyes, for the shadow and the wind had faded away just as suddenly as they had come. Now, Kiamosh, the two bears and the Jaggo headed back downstream, walking in a solemn, ceremonial fashion.

"Well, there ye have it," said Shadoo. "He's sent that poor girl to be sacrificed. The Oolasheg are—oh, hang it all—the Sisters are gone, and I don't think we'll ever find Kiamosh with less of a company than he has now, so—"

"Begging your pardon," interrupted Wunko, "but had you any idea those monstrous bears would be with him?"

"I didn't see them last night and was hoping they might not show up. But I knew it was possible they'd be present, for they often are nigh to Kiamosh. Nasi and Tawassi those are, bruin and bruiness, his foremost guards. He never takes them in canoes, for they're too large and much too heavy, but they can easily ford the Wakosi and can run like ye wouldn't believe, so they could have come from anywhere over the dark hours. Alas! Now we shall have to contend with them as well."

"Delightful," muttered Yahsi. Then she remarked, "Say, Shadoo, Kiamosh and that girl were speaking an older form of Sakooma. What do you make of that? Why Sakooma of all tongues?"

"Always Sakooma it is with Kiamosh and the Jaggo, and I've some guesses about it, but they'll have to wait," Shadoo hastily replied. "Our mission is the important thing presently."

"But where is the Hand, I wonder?" asked Wunko. "I would've thought Kiamosh might be carrying it openly or even that it would have played some role in the ceremony."

"Don't know. Don't know," said Shadoo, rising. "But we've got to hurry or our opportunity, already small, will become even smaller.

We go on with the plan as before, with the only change being that we try to kill the bears before aiming for the Jaggo. But of course, Kiamosh is still our first priority. Now, let's get on, for if we dally much longer, we too will like as not end up in the black realm, hid from Sun and Sky."

"Hid from sun and sky," murmured Okona, as the others began moving after Shadoo. "But surely not, for that would only mean ..." He glanced up. A small, bronze-shelled turtle, its neck outstretched, was laboring up the course of the Kahlit.

"Wait!" the lad cried. They all turned to face him.

"I have to go after the girl," he said.

Shadoo's face warped into a look of utmost confusion. "What? Are you moon-bit?"

"It's something the Seer of Ponca Peak said," Okona explained. "He said I would have to avert the hellish rite here and that I must pass into the realm hid from Sun and Sky. The way I see it, this could mean only one thing: I have to go into Korashac Caverns and rescue that girl, whoever she is, from the Oolash—oh, confound it, Shadoo, now you've got me doing it. I mean, from *them*."

All at once, Anisha, Wunko and Shadoo started to protest, but a serene look came over Yahsi's face. She spoke over the others, who fell silent. "Of course, Okona. That must be exactly what he meant. That difficult judgment I spoke of is now upon you. And I think you have decided well."

"I don't," Anisha heatedly declared.

"Neither do I." Wunko shook his head disapprovingly.

"Okona, you can't go off and get yourself killed in our hour of need," Anisha went on. "Besides, didn't you come to get back the Hand, not some girl we don't know from anyone? And we have every reason to believe Kiamosh has the Hand."

"Anisha," said Okona firmly, "what it comes down to is this. The instructions I was given are clear enough. I can either believe them or not, and the same goes for you. I don't want to go. Really, I don't. But now is no time to draw back. For I was told that if I took another way than this, all should be in vain. So I must go; I simply must. If ever there were a time I had to stick my neck out, it's now."

"Well, go then!" said Shadoo. "Every moment wasted makes the success of our attack all the less likely. I am sorry this is the course you are bent on, lad, for you seemed a fine young man in the short time I have known you. But I can't let you spoil my seven years of watching and waiting. I only hope you come to your senses before you reach the Eye."

"Thank you for everything you've done, Mister Shadoo," said Okona. He took off his quiver and handed it, along with his bow and spear, to the old man, explaining, "I appreciate your loaning of these immensely, but I don't know that they'd be of any use where I'm going. Furthermore, I need to move as quickly and freely as possible, and I fear these would only encumber me."

Shadoo, still frowning, nodded.

Okona turned to the Tikkichaw. "And you've been wonderful, Wunko. I do hope you make it back home someday." He put his thumb on his nose, then his forehead and stretched it toward him. Wunko did the same, and they rubbed their thumbs together.

"I wish you all the best, lad," said Wunko.

"Yahsi," said Okona, as he faced her.

"No words are necessary, Okona." She smiled.

Okona smiled in return.

Then, with great bitterness of heart, he turned to Anisha. "Goodbye, Anisha. I wish things could have been otherwise."

"How could you do this?" she asked, as tears welled up in her eyes.

The lad briefly clasped her hand, then tore himself away.

Hastening up the Kahlit, Okona soon passed the turtle. He had come nearly three hundred yards through the quiet woods and reached the mouth of the wash Shadoo had spoken of before he glanced back. His companions had vanished. However, a single, distant figure was walking northward along the east bank of Kahlit Creek. Okona darted behind a tree and squinted to get a better look. He soon realized he had seen that walk, that bearing many times before. It was Tencum! And he was garbed just as when Okona had last seen him. His hunting bag was slung over his shoulder, as usual, though he seemed to be carrying none of his customary weaponry.

Closer and closer Tencum came, and a hundred queries sprang before Okona. However, everything was so jumbled that he laid hold of no proper answers. But he was brought firmly back into the forest before him when Anisha's voice called out from the creek's west bank.

"Tencum!" the girl cried. "You're alive!"

Startled, Tencum rapidly turned to her. "Anisha!" he exclaimed. "What are you doing here?" He hurriedly crossed the creek to her, for the girl had just emerged from hiding in a small thicket.

As she reached him, he took her hand and said, "Anisha, this place is incredibly dangerous. You shouldn't be here."

"We know," Anisha breathlessly replied. "There's an awful sorcerer named Kiamosh, and he's got the Hand of Hamora. And there are two Sisters who are perilous and vile beyond description. And there's a girl who's just been sent to be eaten by them. And—"

"How do you know all this?" Tencum asked. "And does your father know you're here? And who is we?" Suddenly, Tencum noticed the fox necklace around Anisha's throat. "Anisha," he said tenderly. "You still have my gift."

"Oh, the necklace," she said awkwardly, running her fingers down the chain. "Yes, I thought you were slain at Ohkasac Groves, but I was hoping that ..."

"I-I very nearly was slain," Tencum returned. "But the Powers smiled upon me that night." He looked down at her hand in his own and said, "And you have that silver bracelet of your mother's too. For good luck, I suppose? Anyway, who are the others you spoke of?"

As this conversation had proceeded, a vague sense of alarm had grown within Okona. Something was off, he concluded, about the entire encounter, though he couldn't put his finger on what. Presently, though, he thought it best if he and Anisha learn more from Tencum before revealing any more to him. So he stepped out into the open and announced, "There are no others. Only myself and Anisha."

"Okona!" Tencum, releasing Anisha's hand, turned swiftly to face him. "Came you to the Wakosi together, then?"

"Yes," Okona replied, walking toward him.

"Okona, I thought—" Anisha began.

"You both must leave this place as quickly as possible," said Tencum. "It's terribly dangerous here."

"What are you doing here, Tencum?" asked Okona, staring at him.

Tencum stared back blankly for several moments, then said, "Why I've come to fulfill the mission for which we were sent, of course."

"Then let us help you," urged Anisha. "For that is also why we have come. But we'll have to kill Kiamosh to get the Hand back."

"Who is this ... this Kiamosh you keep talking about?" Tencum whirled to face Anisha.

Suddenly, Okona noticed that Tencum was carrying a gray bundle under his arm.

"You were the one in the cloak," he gasped.

"Excuse me?" Tencum turned to him.

"You were in the canoe with Kiamosh," Okona said, narrowing his eyes.

"I don't know what you're talking about," scoffed Tencum.

"Anisha, get away from him," commanded Okona.

"Anisha, I don't know why you would—"

"Don't trust him. He *does* know who Kiamosh is. And if he would lie about that, then—"

"Ah, now I see what this is about," Tencum cut him off heatedly. "Dhagomi mentioned some months ago he thought you had a fancy for Anisha, but this is what it's come to, eh? Mad accusations, all because you're jealous of my betrothal to her."

"As a matter of fact, I am," Okona admitted, "but that has nothing to do with this."

"So now, when we're all in great peril, all you can think about is how to twist things to your advantage."

"Tencum, that's not fair," interjected Anisha. "First of all, Okona would never do something like that. And as for you, I've always known you to be an honorable man, even if a bit hot-tempered, but I would never have expected you to make this sort of wild allegation. Not unless ..." She stopped, then looked up at Tencum's face.

Tencum stared back at her, and there was great pain in his gaze. Almost instinctively, he placed his hand upon his hunting bag. For a bare moment, Okona caught a strange, fierce sparkle in the gap between the bag itself and the flap that had been flung over it.

As if stung by a bolt from the heavens, Okona realized what he had just seen. In an instant, all his troubled shards of thought came together with astonishing clarity. "You alone ran into the Mound of Hamora," he blurted out, "and said that the Hand was gone. And I believe it was. But it wasn't taken by the cloud. You put it in your hunting bag, and you've had it with you ever since."

Tencum immediately grew red in the face. "Why, that's preposterous!"

Anisha looked at him in horror.

All of a sudden, Tencum snatched Anisha's silver bracelet from her wrist and, with his other hand, seized a dagger of bone from where it had been concealed on his left hip and flung it with great force at Okona. The lad sprang aside only just in time to dodge it. Meanwhile, Anisha bit deep into Tencum's wrist and tugged on the bracelet with both hands, wresting it from his clenched fingers.

Tencum strove to lay hold of it once again, but Anisha pulled aside, then reached for his hunting bag. But he swung the satchel out of her reach, and she ducked away barely in time to evade his furious grasp. Springing once more from his clutching arms, she dashed toward Okona, with the flustered Tencum only a short distance behind.

Okona seized her hand, and together, they raced eastward up the wash that entered Kahlit Creek there, with Tencum in hot pursuit. But they had not gone far when a sudden, chilling breeze blew through the woods, which darkened under the same eerie shadow that had covered the valley only a few minutes before. Just before all three of them ceased running and closed their eyes, they spied a black flutter in the trees. After some seconds, Okona again couldn't help himself and opened one eye briefly, just in time to see the Midnight Owl swoop out of sight some yards ahead at a wide ledge of rock some dozens of feet up the slope to their left.

"The owl went up there! It must be this way!" Okona cried, dragging Anisha behind him, as the breeze died and the darkness lifted.

However, Tencum stood frozen where he had halted. And there he cursed his quarry. "May you never again see the sun, faithless fools! Long have I treated both of you well, and yet you turn on me in an instant! Death is all that such treachery can merit."

"Treachery! You're a fine one to talk of such!" hollered Anisha, as she and Okona stopped halfway up the valley wall and turned to him. "You have betrayed not only us, but all the Sakooma. And how dare you try to take my bracelet! Now, give us back the Hand!"

"If you so desire it, come and get it!" Tencum mocked.

"We both know his prowess," whispered Okona. "He'll likely as not kill us, even without any weapons. Oh, how I wish now I hadn't returned mine! We might make use of your bag of stones or our daggers, but then again, he may well have more hidden weapons of his own. I fear it would be wisest to let him be for now. Anyhow, I must do what the Seer commanded. We'll unfortunately have to leave retrieving the Hand to the others. We can only hope they'll learn about his betrayal before it's too late, for we can't get back to them now."

"Yes, I suppose we dare not approach him. But he seems afraid to come to us," Anisha whispered back.

"As would be anyone in his right mind—" Okona glanced uneasily up the slope. "—with the Sisters so near at hand."

"I loved you once, Tencum," Anisha called, "and even when I thought you were dead, I loved you still. Please, Tencum, turn from this madness!" she pleaded.

His face burned, as he glared at her.

"Speak no more to him," Okona urged. "The girl's life hangs in the balance."

"Turn, Tencum! Turn!" Anisha begged one last time, then slipped her bracelet back onto her wrist and scrambled up the rocky wall after Okona.

After they had clambered up fifty feet, they came to a bench of rock. Here, Okona realized the owl must have passed through the gaping maw of Korashac Caverns, which led diagonally down toward the heart of the hill. It was a hole only five feet across, small but dreadful, ringed by sharp rocks, a veritable dragon's mouth. A whispering wind, cold and sorcerous, tinged with the scent of limestone, came steadily out from it, and there was an awful, creaking sound, like the opening of an old, ill-kept gate, just before them. Okona and Anisha, taking each other's hands, took several trembling steps down into the blackness. A suffocation like that of being buried by earth fell upon them, but after a moment, it lifted. There was a creaking once more, followed by an ominous thud. Now they stood upon a downward-sloping heap of tumbled rock. Morning light was behind, but dimmed, as if passing through thin cloth. But ahead was nothing but blackest gloom.

CHAPTER EIGHTEEN

THE EDGE OF THE UNDERBRAKES

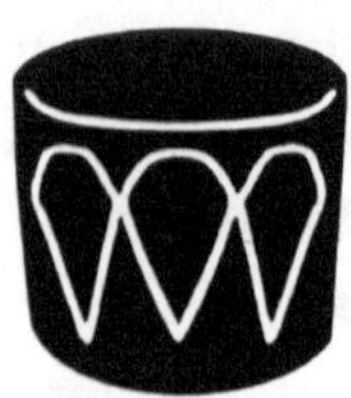

GROPING FORWARD, OKONA AND Anisha used light from the entrance to guide them down the pile of stony breakdown. However, they nearly stumbled into a black pit to their right, a drop-off into nothingness, only pulling back just in time.

Soon they came to the bottom of the slope. After a time, their eyes adjusted to the darkness, and they saw they were in a great hall populated with many formations: columns, stalagmites, stalactites and sundry other features. The hall was some twenty feet high and a hundred feet across; however, they could only guess at its length, for it was lost in blackness.

"We're going to need some better light to find our way around," muttered Okona, "for this place is rather bigger than I expected. Ah, I wonder if the Sisters are in this very room: Korashac's Courtyard, as we might call it." Though he spoke quietly, his voice echoed throughout the hall.

Okona suddenly turned to Anisha and asked, "Why didn't you stay with the others? Now you've put yourself in terrible peril."

"As if I wouldn't be while attacking Kiamosh?" the girl tartly replied. "If it makes you feel any better, the others didn't approve this. They knew nothing of my departure, as I snuck off. But I'm sure Yahsi, if no one else, has guessed where I've gone."

"I really wish you'd stayed with them. At least they have *some* hope of succeeding."

"And you don't think you do? Then why'd you come here?"

"Because it was the right thing to do. But this was to be *my* doom, not yours."

Okona, gazing at the surrounding inkiness, said, "Have you really loved Tencum all this while?"

Anisha looked away.

"Well, have you?"

"I have. But that doesn't mean I had no affections for you."

"A girl oughtn't have a heart that inclines toward more than one man if she's betrothed," Okona woodenly declared. "And I know we both thought Tencum was dead, but that only—"

"Okona, I ..."

"It's all right. Let's just get on with figuring out what we're going to do now that we're in here. Unfortunately, the only consolation we have is that Tencum dared not follow us."

"That two-faced skunk!" Anisha gritted her teeth. "I can hardly believe he's sunk so low as to betray us and all our people."

"I agree it's awful, but we need to concentrate on finding that girl. She can't be far. For if we can't find our way without light, she couldn't either. She *must* have gotten light somewhere."

They began wandering about the cavern, stumbling more often than not. After a few minutes, their feet brushed against something that was most definitely not stone, and they bent down to examine it. It was a supply of cane torches, which had been sorted into multiple bundles. Okona had Anisha pass him her bag of stones to lighten her load, and they each took two bundles of torches, as Anisha said, "It's a pity there's nothing to light these with."

No sooner had she said this than, off to their left, a small, red fire licked up in the darkness.

"Magic, I should think, but we must take what we can get," said Okona, as they made their way over to it. There, in a small alcove, a perfectly ordinary fire was burning. However, its fuel was some strange, dark powder. But they could only conclude, as Okona had posited, that it had been brought forth by some kind of spell. For as soon as they had each lit a torch, the source flame went out as suddenly as it had appeared.

Now that they could see better, they explored the hall with more haste. Off to the left of the entrance, the rock formations were far more extensive and exotic than elsewhere, and here they discovered several pools with small, black salamanders crawling along their edges. Eventually they came to the end of the hall, reckoning it to be some three hundred feet in length. But still there was no sign of either the girl or the Oolasheg.

"Listen!" said Anisha abruptly. "Footsteps! Back there—to the right of where we came in."

They hurried to where she had indicated and climbed down a rock pile to a spot where a walkway ran between the wall on their right and a low table of rock on their left.

They had not been going down the ensuing passage long when Anisha pointed out some queer symbols and drawings on the walls. These had been picked out with stone and painted with a stark black or white, then outlined in a red which once must have been jarring, but was now rather faded. In jagged lines were depicted what Okona and Anisha could only conclude were the Oolasheg, one of them always black and the other white. Though these images were crude, they were nonetheless full of a savage potency. Here, the Twin Crones cavorted through scene after scene of human sacrifice, their stylized, heinous faces ever twisted in diabolical glee, as they slavered with dark, fang-filled mouths and grasped throats with knife-like nails. Occasionally, they were shown as owls flying through darkened woods, with mortals falling before them in agony. But in both forms, bird and woman, and for both Sisters, there were always curious emblems of crescent moons upon their breasts; for the white Sister, it was outlined in black. This same white moon was also painted upon the breasts of all the victims.

Another figure recurred in many of the images as well, an ogre of sorts, and it was often shown ripping people in half or pounding them with great stones.

"Whatever could that be?" asked Anisha, aghast.

"Better not to know, I expect," Okona replied. "But if I had to guess ... see how it's guiding the victims to their demise? Also, see how it has that same skull icon on its neck as there is on that gateway to the Sisters? From that, I'd say it must be a guardian of their lair."

One final figure made multiple appearances at the end of this grim gallery, and this was the most frightening of all. It reminded them vaguely of the Kishikot but was wilder and more wickedly triumphant. Barely mannish it was, but elongated and nebulous around the edges. Its body was twisted and disproportionate, a leering shadow with three red eyes in its forehead and a moon upon its breast.

"Let us leave these abominable things behind," Okona murmured, for he sensed evil seeping from the very glyphs. "It's bad enough they were made to begin with but doubly bad that we have defiled our eyes by them. For it's clear these were painted not in hatred of these beings, but devotion to them."

Turning swiftly away, they passed on.

They came then to a maze of passages and were growing concerned they had already lost their way when a flurry of small, black bats flew toward them. The Sakooma ducked, and the bats continued on out of the passage. But as Okona and Anisha lifted their heads, a dim, flickering light appeared before them.

"Whatever could that be?" asked Okona. "The torchlight of our girl?"

"It does look rather like a torch," replied Anisha. "And it might be her, although ... well, it might not. Should we follow it?"

"We don't know our way around here one bit, and we're likely already lost, so I say we go where it goes. If it is the girl, so much the better. Yet if it's someone or something else, it might lead us to some bad end. But we'll probably come to a bad end anyhow, so what does it matter? We're at the mercy of the Under-realm now."

After lighting new torches (as their old ones were nearly burned out), they commenced following this dim light. However, it often moved a little faster than them and was always beyond where they could see what was creating it. At first, this unnerved them, but they quickly grew accustomed to the idea that the light, whatever it was, could be taken as at least a temporary guide in this stony labyrinth.

The curious light led them eventually to a place where the ceiling dropped quite low. They immediately grew suspicious, for the light flicked out of sight, and they realized they would have to crawl to continue. Okona crouched by the small opening and peered inside.

"I suppose we ought to keep following it," he sighed, "although this doesn't look promising."

Soon, Okona and Anisha were crawling, single file, with their knees planted in separate troughs with a little ridge running in-between. The ceiling was extremely low, so they had to shove their torches along in front of them. However, the opening ran several feet to either side of them. Though this extra space didn't do them any good, at least it made them feel less entombed. They were, nonetheless, concerned about how long this crawling business would go on.

Fortunately, after less than a hundred feet of creeping on their bellies, the ceiling had risen enough that they were able to stand again, though only barely.

"This isn't ideal," breathed Okona, "but I'm glad we're out of the Terrible Troughs."

Anisha shook her head. "Somehow, I just can't picture either that girl or those awful Sisters worming through that hole."

"Perhaps they've taken another route," said Okona. "But seeing as we don't know what that is, or even where *we* are, we'll just have to carry on."

Shortly the ceiling rose even higher, and they traveled through an area with a number of fantastic and weird formations. And, to their great relief, the strange, flickering light reappeared, leading them on.

Not much farther on, on the left, a thick column hung from a yawning mouth above and plunged into a seemingly measureless blackness below.

"It seems to pierce down to the very heart of the earth, where the Dead dwell," uttered Anisha, gaping at it.

"Do not speak of such things," Okona said. "Let us leave this Pillar of the Under-realm."

On through the winding cave they went, igniting new torches as necessary and always following the elusive light, which lurked ever at the edge of sight. Their garments and skin were caked with mud and their knees raw and bruised. Also, both of them had accidentally hit their heads back by the Troughs and still felt a dull throbbing. But they had learned their lesson well and had been taking care to duck whenever necessary ever since.

A short distance past the Pillar of the Under-realm, they were plodding along rather drearily when Anisha spoke. "Okona, why do you think Tencum tried to steal my mother's bracelet? I have my own ideas about it, but ..."

"I'm certain it was no attempt at petty thievery," returned Okona. "Even the spirits of Toshigan Hollow seemed interested in it, remember? Mark me, there's something special about it, something we've missed."

"I've been reflecting on this," said Anisha, "and I think I understand now the connection between the Jaggo and my mother. She was descended from Hamora, after all, and that might partially explain why they were after her, as perhaps she had some link to the Hand. But also, as you said, her bracelet must have some power or significance we haven't guessed, something beyond being a good luck charm, that is. The Jaggo might have desired that something and known the bracelet was in my mother's possession, although, by chance she didn't have it the day they killed her. Ah, and Tencum would have known it was the rightful token I should have given him for our betrothal. The snake! Or the fox, one might say. It sickens me that such was all only a deception! For I've no doubt he simply meant to get it for whatever plot he has with Kiamosh."

"Isn't it peculiar Kiamosh was missing a hand," remarked Okona, "and that is the very thing Tencum was presumably to bring him?"

"Yes, very striking."

"I almost feel as if I knew what all this is about," mused Okona, glancing at some budding crystals in a side niche. "But then there's the matter of the girl we're after. Is she just a regular victim or something more? For, going by Kiamosh's speech, her sacrifice seemed to be of some consequence."

"It's all quite mysterious to me," said Anisha. "I haven't the faintest clue how to unravel it, except for some things about Tencum."

"Now I see quite well what Tencum's been up to," declared Okona. "I tell you, Anisha, when that storm broke open the mound and Tencum rushed in, that's when he got the Hand and put it in his bag. And he always had his hunting bag with him from that point on. Of course, that wouldn't arouse suspicion because he's practically never without it."

Okona continued, with the various threads of Tencum's schemes becoming ever clearer to him as he spoke, "Also, at Chennipot Chonka, after Yahsi suggested our group go west, he pressed for us to go north. Your father mentioned that he had intended to use gamblers' beans to decide which group should go which direction, but he had been persuaded to take counsel instead. It was by Tencum, I'll wager, for he was talking with your father when they arrived at the junction. Undoubtedly Tencum wanted to sway the matter himself, only he didn't foresee Yahsi suggesting what she did before he had his turn. Anyhow, if he had gone north, he would have already been heading this direction. And he even had our western group bear northwest rather than due west. Also, he went to scout ahead, supposedly looking for Chadori, while we waited behind. But I'll bet he really just went off and contacted the Jaggo and told them where they ought to attack. Ah, and the leaders of all four groups spoke together before we separated, so I'd guess Tencum knew where Orobec's group would be headed. And that would explain Yahsi's mystery about how the Jaggo knew Orobec's route. For of course Tencum would want them killed since they were heading north."

Helping Anisha past a particularly slick section of the passage, he went on. "And he even cried out to warn others at Ohkasac Groves in case any escaped, for then he should seem as surprised as them about the attack. Might he, then, have been paranoid about not seeming traitorous to any that survived? And, as for why there were nine bodies at the site that night—well, we know Tencum's wasn't one of them. But when Yahsi returned the next evening, there were eight. What if the ninth were that Jaggo I stabbed that night?"

"He might have been at that," said Anisha. "I suppose his fellows could have removed his body before Yahsi returned. But it still doesn't make sense to me why, if Tencum was with Kiamosh when we saw him in the canoe, he wasn't present for the ceremony with that girl. Also, what was he doing alone by Kahlit Creek? Did Kiamosh know he came?"

"Come to think of it, there's a great deal that's peculiar about all that," agreed Okona.

"Oh, look!" cried Anisha. "Our light!"

Suddenly, their guide-light vanished into an alcove. Okona and Anisha rushed to it.

Here was a hole, guarded by several large stalagmites, that dropped into a hazy blackness. Their familiar, faint glow winked from below, though not the mysterious source of the light itself, which was currently beyond their vision. Since they couldn't see how deep the hole was, Okona threw his torch down. The brand landed upon a stone floor, and with its light, they ascertained it was a straight drop of fifteen feet. Also, they could see well enough there would be no way to get back out of the hole once they had entered it.

"I guess here we really have to decide if we trust that light or not," said Anisha.

Okona stared concernedly at the flickering torch below. "We've committed much to it already. And anyway, there's no way we'd find our way back out of here now. We'll just have to keep following it."

"Supposing this is the right way," said Anisha, "even then, how will we be able to escape with that girl?"

"I haven't a clue. But that doesn't change anything I said." He looked solemnly at Anisha. "Will you enter this Pit of No Return with me?"

Anisha nodded grimly.

"I'll go first," said Okona.

Steadying himself, he crouched at the edge of the hole, then sprang into it, landing none too gracefully on the floor many feet below.

"I'll catch you," he promised, looking up as he stood.

Anisha tossed her brand down to Okona, as well as her water flask and the rest of her bundle of cane torches. Then she too made the leap, landing in Okona's arms. He set her gently on the cave floor, and they looked down the passage. There was the guide-light, barely visible as always. So they gathered up their items and proceeded toward it.

"I really can't believe that girl went through all these dreadful passages," said Anisha, as they set off. "I just can't. And I know she may have taken another route, like you said. But why would she want to deliver herself to the Sisters anyway?"

"Did you not see her eyes?" Okona returned. "There was death in them. She has entered this place, I fear, not of her own will."

They trotted after the strange, ever-retreating glow through many long passages, wide and high enough for them to proceed easily. Then they entered an area with many piles of breakdown. Soon, the Sakooma grew weary of crawling and climbing on the mud-coated, slippery rocks. Still, the subterranean trail went on. However, at last, they entered a large cavern. And, as they had lost sight of the guiding light, they roved about the grotto in search of another passage.

To their initial delight, if nothing else for its novelty, they came upon an underground stream. The water was black as midnight, but its surface shimmered with a light all its own. Intrigued by this, Okona stuck his fingers in it, and murmuring echoes surged throughout the cavern. It was only then they noticed centipedes of lurid hues crawling along the stream's edge. Alarmed, they stepped away and hurried to another part of the grotto.

In their sputtering torchlight, they sighted an opening in the cavern wall, which lay to the left of where they had entered the grotto. They meant to see if it would lead them out of this eerie place but drew up short after glimpsing what lay ahead. Far down the passage was an eldritch, glimmering light. By it could be seen shadows of things like thornbushes. But these were moving, as if shaken by a fitful wind. And gliding among these shadow-bushes were pale, glowing shapes of men. From these came a hollow moaning, as of those forlorn and aggrieved, stricken by loss and sorrow that cannot be mended. And most dreadfully of all, the shapes seemed to be reaching toward them.

Anisha's voice shook. "Have we as the living really laid eyes upon the Edge of the Underbrakes?"

"The whole of these caverns might be dubbed thus," uttered Okona, overcome by terror and awe, "for all this lies on the verge of

Death. Come, turn from this place. It is more than we were made to bear."

Trying vigorously to shut out what they had just seen, they turned and sought another way out of the cavern. Far opposite the passage from which they had first entered, they caught sight of the flickering illumination they had long followed, and they hastened toward it.

More long galleries followed, strewn with numerous piles of breakdown, which they were frequently obliged to scale and descend. And there was one place they had to climb a narrow ridge of rock with steep drops on either side; the Kniferoad they dubbed it.

At length, they pawed up a slippery slope with many remarkable formations. At its crest was a small opening, through which their guiding light had just disappeared.

"I don't like the look of this at all," said Anisha, shaking her head. "It's like being swallowed by the earth."

"Unfortunately, it's our only way on," Okona said resignedly, as he scrambled up to it.

The opening was so narrow that, in order to fit, they had to push their live torches, the remainder of their torch bundles, the bag of stones and Anisha's waterskin and food pouch through ahead of them. Okona even found he had to suck his breath in to squeeze onward. But as in turn he and Anisha went through it, a great measure of their strength was removed, so that they were suddenly much, much wearier.

On the other side, they donned again their items. Here, rock formations spanned the short distance from floor to ceiling, nearly hemming them in. But, summoning their remaining vitality, they crawled through a narrow gap past these and out of their stony prison.

Immediately, they were confronted by a collection of human skeletons spread out upon the floor. Anisha gasped and drew back, as Okona surveyed the grim remains with sinking heart.

"We've been led on a mad and ultimately fruitless chase," Anisha despaired. "And now we're trapped down here with little food and not a great deal of water. And our torches will only last so long. Okona, I don't think I can go on much longer."

Anisha collapsed, and her torch fell from her grasp, burning where it lay. Okona turned to aid her, but he too fell to the ground. And then came the echo of deep drums from far down the passage.

Okona was taken by a swift swoon. Then there was blackness for a long while.

But lo! A hand shook Okona. And a voice was calling, "Wake, wake!" And he did, though immediately, sleep sought to pull him back. He glanced up, and his torch was still burning before him, though about to fizzle out. Hurriedly, he used it to light another. Then he set it down and turned to Anisha. Still slumbering was she, and her face was pale. Grunting, he crawled to her and opened the waterskin, which was still draped over her shoulder.

As the Elixir of Nadula trickled down his throat, warmth and light coursed through him. After breathing deeply, he imbibed a little more. Then, feeling well-roused, he shook Anisha. She didn't respond, so he tilted her head back, then poured some of Nadula's draught into her mouth. She gagged and sputtered, but came to. He bade her drink more. Soon, she too was roused and asked, "Okona! What happened?"

"An enchantment, I should guess. Something bound to that hole we came through, that Black Throat yonder. It was meant, I think, to keep us from ever waking again, like these poor souls surrounding us. Thank the Powers you brought that water of Nadula! Some grace unknown waked me, but I would have gone back to sleep for good if I hadn't taken some of that liquid."

Rising, Okona said, "Your torch has burned out. Get your bundle and light another from mine. Then we've got to get on. There may no point now, for that girl must be far ahead. And I doubt now more than ever that she's gone the same route as us. But we've got to try to catch her anyhow. The Seer said I must stop the ritual that's taking place here. And I still mean to!"

Shortly after they set out, the queer guide-light reappeared, passing on before them. For this they were much grateful, though they still wondered what it might be. From here, they proceeded through more passages, in which they had often to climb and scramble. Ever muddier they grew, appearing now as strange creatures of the murk, slathered in brown and crawling about like animals on all fours. The passage of time was much distorted in here, but if they had to put a guess to it, they'd conjecture they'd been in the caves of Korashac three or four hours (excluding however long they had slept at the Black Throat). But this estimate proved unable to banish the power of earth over them, for they were beset by an overwhelming sense that they had *always* been underground. For all they could tell in their weaker moments, they had always been watching their heads, always straining their eyes and nursing their knees, smeared with muck and cut by stones, creeping about in the hollow silence.

They had been traveling for quite some while when they realized they had emerged into a very large room. It was filled with random heaps of rock, distributed such that they could see no way out of the place.

"Oh, confound it! Where's our guide-light gone?" asked Anisha. "How shall we find our way through this Hall of Hills?

"Explore it, I suppose," said Okona dejectedly, "but if it's a dead end, I really don't know what we'll do."

After a few minutes of wandering, they discerned this grotto was at least as big as Korashac's Courtyard. Then, having searched along the walls and having climbed several high heaps of rock, they ascended a slope of a hundred feet of piled stones, which lay opposite of where they had entered the room. At the top of this, they reached a wide shelf and proceeded on through the cave.

As they walked along, Okona said, "I wonder if, after all, we might have stood a chance of getting back the Hand from Tencum."

"Assuredly not," returned Anisha, "for he is too strong and would have fought bitterly."

"I suppose so. It just strikes me as strange that, though this entire quest was to get the Hand of Hamora back, even with it right there, I turned aside from it so readily."

"Well, when you made your decision to follow the girl, you had already laid aside the pursuit of the Hand. For at the time, we all thought Kiamosh had it. You were pursuing whatever it was the Seer had set for you. You haven't told me much about that meeting, you know."

"I suppose I haven't. There's much in it I don't understand myself. But the Seer did ask whether I was seeking the Greater Hand or the Lesser. The actual Hand of Hamora he dubbed the Lesser, and the Greater I took from his words to be Blessing itself. But it seems I've forsaken the seeking of both Hands for this mad mission. I'm so fogged about everything, Anisha."

"I don't know that I'll be able to clear any of that for you," Anisha returned.

"I'm glad you're with me nonetheless," said Okona warmly. "And there is one thing the Seer said which I think I now understand. He said that when I came here, I would not be alone." Okona stopped and looked at her, and Anisha halted, returning his gaze.

"I would not have been parted from you for anything, Okona," said Anisha.

"Not even to save your own life?"

"Do you not understand even now? I thought you knew why I came, not only here, but on this entire journey."

Okona stared searchingly at her in the flick of their torches.

"I didn't come for the Hand. I came for you. Don't you remember? I told you such that night in Ohkasac Groves. For when you came to me the day after the feast, I realized I wanted nothing more than ..." her voice faltered. "I don't want to lose you," she began anew. "And as long as my thread is woven with your own, I'll do all I can to keep you from death."

"And thus will I do for you," said Okona fervently. "And now that Tencum's been unmasked, I was wondering if ..." He turned away. "I'm sorry. This is neither the time nor the place."

"No, *I'm* sorry. I haven't been fair to you, Okona," Anisha declared. "You were right, you know, right about what you said earlier. It wasn't fair to Tencum when we were engaged for me to keep pining after you. And to tell you the truth, I do wish you had asked me first, not just because of how things have turned out, but because, when it comes down to it, my heart yearns most for you. I did love Tencum, yes, and there was much to admire about him before he became corrupted. But my love for you has always been different. And it still is. And from now on, if you will forgive me ..."

The lad turned eagerly to face her. "Would you then—well, what I mean to say is ... if we do somehow survive this ordeal and everything we hope for comes to pass and the Sakooma are saved and we stand living back at Takula, would you pledge your heart to me? Would you become the wife of Okona Song-maker?"

Anisha stared up affectionately at him and said, "Even if all comes to ruin, still I would pledge that. And I do, Okona Song-maker."

Smiles beamed through the grime on their faces, and they laughed for mirth in this dark place where never such had been heard. Their eyes shone, and, casting their torches and bundles to the ground, they embraced. Long they stood thus, forgetting the Hand of Hamora, the sorceries and plotting of Kiamosh and even the cavernous night that lay about them. And then they stood at arms' length, Anisha's hands in Okona's. Then, drawing close once more, they kissed.

But at last, they looked about and remembered their plight. A moment later, the dooming of low drums rolled through the under-land.

"What are they saying?" asked Anisha.

"I don't know, but let's hurry toward it, for it may concern that ritual we've come to hinder."

Swiftly, they grabbed their live torches and bundles and trotted on.

Soon, both walls and ceiling passed far from them, and their hastening footsteps echoed mightily, more so than they had anywhere on their entire subterranean journey.

"By the Powers," Anisha gasped. "This hall must be simply immense."

"Fate lies heavy here," murmured Okona, as the drums died away. "You can feel it. Let's see what we may of this Dome of Doom before such finds us."

So they wandered through it, looking up in awe at the seemingly roofless blackness. Going right, they eventually came to a wall; very high it was, and they could not see its top, nor its end to right or left. But in the wall was a large tunnel.

In the midst of this tunnel was a light, not that which they had been following through the caverns, but redder, keener and more lurid, like the seeps of some smoldering hell. And within it was a shadow, the silhouette of some large, two-legged being; more than twice the height of a man it was, and perhaps even thrice. Nearly naked, it was covered only about its loins by shredded pelts of elk-skin. Two great burly arms it had and a large, misshapen head with thick, writhen horns. Expelling a thick breath of cave dust, the creature stalked slowly toward them. At that moment they recalled the image in the glyphs near the entrance, the being like an ogre. This, without a doubt, was the very thing from which these awful forebodings were drawn.

Okona and Anisha stood frozen in dismay, as, with a terrible, guttural cry, the thing lurched forward with swifter, thudding steps.

Chapter Nineteen

Rite of the Daughter's Blood

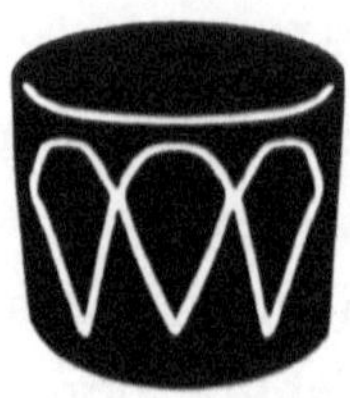

O KONA AND ANISHA BEGAN backing up.

Looking desperately about, Okona said, "Anisha, get away from here. I'll try to engage this thing as long as I can."

"But how—"

"Just go!"

Anisha stepped more rapidly backward, then turned and sped off toward the far corner of the grotto, from which they had first entered.

As she departed, the creature briefly clutched a stone skull that hung from its neck by a rope, then dropped to all four limbs and continued toward Okona. Its pacing was like that of a wolf, but somehow also akin to the stilted crawl of a spider. Meanwhile, with throbbing heart, Okona reached into the bag of stones, drew a sharp rock from his satchel and hurled it at the approaching monster. With a horrible squish, it struck its right eye. Enraged, the beast rushed forward, its huge claws tearing at the cavern floor. Baiting it, Okona waited until the last possible second, then flung himself aside to avoid being trampled.

Bellowing, the creature halted and turned around. In the meantime, Okona fished in the pouch for another jagged rock. As the monster was pivoting, however, a stone struck it on its shoulder. It was then Okona realized Anisha had returned to the area and was attacking it from some distance. Aided by this momentary distraction, Okona cast his second stone, this time at the other eye. Again, the aim proved true. Now some nameless substance oozed down both sides of the monster's face. In a roaring frenzy, the beast galloped toward him, and once more, he was only barely able to escape its thundering limbs.

Spewing out a great, slimy glob of saliva, the monster stood up on two legs and clawed at its eyes, howling and staggering about. Okona was nearly crushed by it before he was able to maneuver to a safe distance away. There, Anisha dashed up to him and said, "Those throws were incredible!"

"No time to celebrate," he panted. "Anisha, I think the tunnel that monster came from leads to where we'll find the girl. For do you recall? The images we saw shortly after we arrived in the caverns depicted it as the Sisters' guardian. But it would be folly to try to enter now with it stumbling about like that."

A half-minute later, the monster tripped away from the entry-way. The Sakooma were about to risk a dash there when the thing stooped and grabbed a small boulder. Yelling mightily, it turned to them.

"Quick! We've got to get rid of our torches," exclaimed Okona. "It might still be able to see enough to spot them."

Hurriedly, he and Anisha cast their brands to the ground and bounded away. This was accomplished none too soon, for the boulder sailed through the air toward the torches, then fractured with a mighty crack as it struck the floor, sending great shards of stone in every direction. The monster pounded over to the spot, growling savagely, while Okona and Anisha raced to the mouth of the tunnel.

Into the passage they fled, finding that it sloped steeply downward not far in. At first, they rued having discarded their torches, but then realized the red light they had seen behind the monster when it first appeared was adequate for them to navigate. Its sources were visible to them now: wall-lamps of red crystal, glowing bright, yet without flame.

Suddenly, the anguished stomping of the monster ceased, but Okona and Anisha tore on. Moments later, the thundering was renewed, this time decidedly coming toward them.

Soon, the passage leveled off, and the Sakooma came to a large, red-lit cavern with many teeth of rock jutting from both above and below. Columns there were in plentitude also and many wild and bizarre formations and crystals. On the floor, splintered bones of men and animals lay scattered about. As the room was somewhat of a maze, they did not see a quick way through it, so they dashed a short distance into its interior and hid themselves behind large stalagmites.

Shortly, the creature came to the cavern's threshold. There it stood, its head raised, alternately sniffing and listening. Abruptly, it stopped, then grunted in satisfaction, bent over and felt along the floor with its giant, six-fingered hands. Okona and Anisha held their breath and sat very still but feared their rapidly pounding hearts would give them away. Closer and closer the monster came, until droplets from its rank breath tumbled upon their necks. A shadow fell over them, as its hand groped out, and they panicked, throwing themselves sideways to escape its grasp.

Roaring, it swatted with its arm, flinging Anisha some feet across the cave. Now it was reaching for her prostrate form, but Okona leapt up and thrust his dagger into the creature's wrist. Foaming and hollering, the beast knocked Okona back against a stalagmite, as Anisha rolled away from the clutch of its other hand. Okona grabbed a large rock, as the monster's right hand, the one he had stabbed, closed about him. In moments, the fiend had raised him to its open mouth and was preparing to tear open his chest with its dreadful teeth, when Okona hurled the rock into its wide maw; it landed directly in the plug of its throat.

At the same instant, Anisha, who had picked up a human thigh bone from the ground, slammed it into the creature's leg, then plunged her dagger into its foot. Furious, it stomped, hitting her with its knee and knocking her to the ground. Simultaneously, it released

Okona, as it was struggling to breathe. The lad only narrowly missed a nasty knock by putting out both his hands and feet.

Meanwhile, the monster tried shoving one of its hands into its mouth to remove the stone blocking its airway, but it was no use. The rock was lodged too well and too deep. It began lurching about, and Okona and Anisha dragged themselves away to avoid being crushed by its great, clawed feet. But as soon as they were clear of it, Okona laid hold of a broken skull and, gathering all his remaining strength, launched it at one of the creature's oozing eyes. It gripped its face, then stumbled forward onto an upthrusted tooth of rock. With a sickening splosh, the monster's belly was pierced by the spike of stone. Revolting sounds followed, as the ogre's body settled and its arms clawed at the stone floor one last time. Then the cavern fell silent.

Okona and Anisha stood looking at each other in disbelief, leaning against stalagmites and breathing heavily for a good long while.

Finally, Anisha managed to gasp, "I thought we were done for."

"Me too," wheezed Okona. "Are you hurt?"

"Some bruises and cuts, but it's nothing that can't wait. And you?"

"The same." He went over to where the monster's lifeless hand lay and pried his dagger out of its rough, ashen-gray flesh. Dark blood poured out of the wound.

Anisha went to its foot and retrieved her dagger as well, and together she and Okona wound their way through the ghoulish cavern. Only one backward glance did they cast toward the monster, whose skull necklace dangled beneath its wrinkled neck. Thankfully, as its head was facing the floor, they were not obliged to look upon its unsightly features, fearsome even in death.

After some quick exploration, they discovered a kind of pathway among the formations, big enough for the monster's tread, that wandered through the heart of the cavern. This led through several windings of this same, large grotto (which was much bigger than they had initially realized) and came eventually to a wide hallway. In this passageway, there was no light, save what was shed by the red crystal-lamps behind them. But they could see well enough that, a hundred feet on, there was a set of wooden gates made of rough-carven stakes, evenly spaced so one could see between them, but close enough that one could fit through little more than an arm. They hastened up to these. Across the two doors, there was laid like a bar a wooden panel with a curious indentation on it. They tried first to push the gates, then pull them, but in neither manner would they budge. Again, they examined the panel, this time searching for some kind of mechanism. Almost at once, the significance of the indentation struck them.

"Why, it's a skull!" cried Anisha.

"The necklace!" they both exclaimed.

"Yes, of course," said Okona. "That thing was a guardian. Those pictures near the caves' entrance showed it with a skull and this gate with a skull as well. The skull must be the guardian's key!"

"I'll get it," panted Anisha, rushing off. A few minutes later, she came racing back with the ogre's necklace. Together, they held the skull to the indentation. Faintly red it glowed, as the gates swung open before them, creaking deeply. Anisha slung the skull necklace over her shoulder, as they passed on into the blackness.

The tunnel went deeper, ever steeper into the earth. Every so often, there were red lamps; still, the majority of the route was in gnawing darkness. Finally, the tunnel leveled off, and here there were no lamps at all. But far, far down the passage, there was another sort of light, the ominous flicker of firelight. And also from that forbidding terminus came a faint, unnerving, slow-paced drumming.

On into the dark they went, pressing toward the firelight. And as they drew closer, there commenced the rhythmic wailing of an aged woman, accompanied by a repetitive, sharp pattern of rattles. The Sakooma, hearts palpitating, came closer still, now crouching and creeping.

At last they reached the edge of a mid-sized, low-domed chamber, which was permeated by a thin, black smoke. In the midst of the chamber was a red fire, licking at the base of a large copper cauldron. And on this beastly vessel were appalling images not unlike those on the walls near Korashac's entrance.

But the cauldron was benign in comparison to those who kept it. Around the fire danced the Oolasheg themselves, two infernal figures, bent with age, but nonetheless swift, strong and spasmic in their movements. Atop their heads were ghastly headdresses of owl feathers; one of the hag's was of white plumes and the other's of black. And around each of their throats was a necklace of pale crystal in the form of a crescent moon. Hideous were their faces and very cruel. She with the crown of black was more grisly than the other, but the second was more disturbing and twisted. The crone with the black headdress was garbed in a tattered mantle of blood-spattered, black animal skin, and the other in one of garish white, also stained with blood, but their dresses beneath these skins were gray. In the hand of the black-garbed crone was a small drum and in that of the other a rattle of bone. The hags' skin was yellow and drawn tight across their bones, and in their sockets, dark eyes glinted like wicked gems. Shard-like were their teeth, filed to fine points, and their fingers were long and grasping, with jagged nails like beast-claws. Barefoot were they, but hair, long and tangled, fell from their brows, black for the black-garbed and white for she clad in white.

Okona and Anisha were nearly paralyzed by the scene before them, but a burst of hope quickened them, as on the far side of the chamber they sighted the girl they had been seeking. Pale she was, even against the ghostly glinting of the moon-shaped crystal charm, like unto those of the Oolasheg, that rested on her neck. The white of her dress showed little now under layers of smeared mud. Standing upright, she was bound by cords of twisted vine to a vertical slab of rock, slightly tilted back. To either side of the girl were two stone tables, and on these were instruments and vessels of abomination: knives of bone for sacrifice, some thick and broad, others long and narrow, many of them serrated; there were also various bowls and pans, dark with flecks of blood. Neither Okona nor Anisha had the stomach to examine the other things lying there.

Okona glanced to either side of the chamber and noted a set of columns, stalagmites and stalactites that formed a nearly unbroken ring near its outer edge. With rising pulse, he realized there was enough room for him and Anisha to move along behind this barrier of stone, largely hidden from the Oolasheg's sight.

Okona motioned for Anisha to follow him, and they began creeping leftward behind the stalagmites that ringed the central part of the cavern, taking great care to move noiselessly and scurry across the places where the ring was broken. All the while, the Lair of the Oolasheg echoed with song and drum, dark and wild, savage and malevolent, the music of the Sakooma's worst nightmares resonating in stones and earth.

As they were making their way around the room, the Crones ceased their diabolical dancing and stood in front of the cauldron. Then they raised high their hands and began uttering some dark incantation in an unknown tongue.

As the hags were angled so as not to be facing them, Okona and Anisha emerged by the slab where the girl was tied and began rapidly cutting her bonds with their daggers.

"We've come to save you," whispered Okona, but the girl only turned her head slightly and stared at him with dreary eyes.

"Please, stay silent," cautioned Anisha, as she worked fiercely at severing one of the cords.

Soon, the girl was cut free, but still she lay flat against the slab, her eyes only half-open. Realizing she would not come with them of her own accord, Okona grabbed her hand and pulled her toward the cover of the stalagmites. Then he put his arm under the maiden's left shoulder. And when Anisha had put hers under the girl's right, they began stumbling back around the ring.

It was a terrible business, and they were terrified that, at any second, they might be spotted by the Oolasheg. But at last, they reached the entrance.

There the girl said loudly, "Stay, strangers! To the Sisters I must go. Where take ye me? And who are ye to hinder the Rite of the Daughter's Blood?"

Instantly, the Oolasheg ceased their singing. And though the Sakooma were not facing the Crones, they felt their eyes lock upon them.

There was a horrible hiss, then a jolt of magic, and Okona and Anisha felt as if their legs were of cast metal. Certain were they now that they would be unable to move if they tried. But at the same instant, both steeled their wills, and try they did. And to their amazement, they wrested free of the Crones' power, hauling the girl with them.

They bolted like mad down the passageway. The tunnel had seemed interminable on the way in, but now it seemed ever so much longer. On and up they went, struggling to pull the girl along with them and always wondering how close behind them the Oolasheg were but never daring to look. Yet at last they neared the light of the ogre's lair. There were the gates!

But with a heavy, creaking crash, the great gates slammed shut before them. Wild with panic, they tried to force them back open. But the effort proved futile. Anisha took the skull necklace off her shoulder and held it against the gate, but nothing happened. She even tried to shove it through the stakes to reach around and press it into the indentation on the other side, but it wouldn't fit, so she flung it to the floor in frustration.

Then came a sound dreadful beyond imagining, the triumphant laughter of the Oolasheg, echoing up from the depths. It was a horrible, soul-scraping cackling, the utmost exultation of primal depravity.

The maiden, who had been released by the Sakooma while they were trying to pry open the gates, was stumbling back down the tunnel, intoning, "To the Sisters I must go. The Rite must be consummated." Swiftly, they grabbed her, but she fought back frantically, and it took all of their effort to restrain her.

"How do we stop her?" Anisha cried.

"There has to be a way to break her enchantment," Okona returned, grunting as he strove with the girl, who seemed now to have strength well beyond her measure.

"But how?" Anisha wailed.

Suddenly, the girl's necklace began glowing and drifting forward, dragging her deeper into the tunnel with it.

"The necklace!" they cried simultaneously.

"Yes, it must be!" Anisha went on. "For the Sisters had them too."

"In the images on the cave walls," continued Okona, "all of the victims had them."

At once, Okona snatched at the charm with such speed and force that the cord binding it broke, and in the next motion, he hurled the moon pendant against the wall, where it shattered. Crystal shards flew through the air, glittering with a white fire, then settled upon the floor, where they died out.

Two high, rending shrieks echoed down the hall.

As soon as the pendant had fractured, the girl bent over double, then collapsed to the ground. Okona and Anisha dropped to their knees to help her, and for several moments, they feared she was dead. But then she began gasping, as if emerging from deep water.

"Who be ye?" she choked, glancing around. "And what place is this?"

"I'm Okona, and this is Anisha," the lad said.

"And we're in the lair of the dreaded Sisters," Anisha explained.

Four glowing points of yellow were approaching out of the gloom. Beneath these were two glinting, white moons.

"The Oolasheg! The Oolasheg!" the girl cried. "Kah-ee-aye! Kah-ee-aye! We die! We die!"

"Ye die! Ye die!" the Crones screeched, as the one in black, her shadowed form now discernible, raised her arms.

"No!" Okona shouted, snatching a stone from his pouch and hurling it at the hag.

A whistling bolt shot from her fingers, and the stone exploded in mid-air with a blast of orange flame. In the light of this, the companions sighted a passage opening on their left, which they had not seen before because it lay in such heavy darkness.

"Quick, this way!" Okona directed, and he and Anisha raced for it, lifting the girl between them. Once they had passed through the entrance, Anisha helped the girl run on, but Okona ducked back into the main hall and lit a cane torch in the burning remnants of his thwarted stone, which rested on the passage floor. Out of the corner of his eye, he saw the crone in black readying another blast, and he dove out of the way only just in time.

Okona dashed after the two girls, who had paused at the top of a downward-leading spiral staircase. Together, all three rushed down this stair, until they came to a level passage, which had a low, arching roof. Into this they ran and soon found themselves bounding through a network of criss-crossing tunnels.

The lay of this maze was very bewildering, and after several minutes, they had lost all sense of direction. Many bones were strewn in these gruesome tunnels, and Okona had rather a mind that these were the private burrows of the Oolasheg, where they actually fed upon their victims. But he could not help wondering if there was something even worse down here.

At multiple junctions, they heard the cursing of the hags in other tunnels and on several occasions even thought they glimpsed their fiendish forms hastening toward them, but ever they ran on, hoping that somehow they might strike upon a way of escape. But they only went deeper into the maze, for the stench of death and the quantity of bones grew, and the passages became narrower and lower. At last, they found themselves at a dead end. And when they turned around, the Crones themselves were obstructing the only exit.

"Ye die! Ye die!" the Oolasheg chanted, their monstrous faces contorted in rage. This time, both Crones lifted their arms, and fire crackled from their fingertips. Though the fugitives had barely room to maneuver, they all sprang aside, and a roaring flame crashed into the wall behind them. The stone split to form a narrow rift in the smoking rock. But, to Okona's amazement, as he held his torch over his head, he saw that the cleft did not end a few feet back, but kept going.

"Get in! Get in!" he yelled, and the girls squeezed into the crack and disappeared.

"Nooo!" the hags shrieked, as they rushed toward Okona, who shoved himself into the crack. Their jagged nails scratched his bare shoulder as he escaped inside.

The opening was quite tight for a number of yards, and the girl, Anisha and Okona, even with turning sideways, all cut themselves on the rock while forcing their way through. Meanwhile, the hags were at the entrance, cursing and trying to make their way in after them. A scream echoed horribly in the labyrinth behind, as, once more, the Crones cast some devilish spell. Fire sped through the narrow cleft after the fugitives and struck the rock. With a mighty rumbling, the rift collapsed in a cloud of choking dust.

At the moment of the cave-in, Okona had just gotten clear of the cleft and into a slightly wider tunnel beyond, where he and the girls were knocked to the floor by the blast. Initially, they covered their heads, fearing the ceiling would come crashing down. But when they realized it was only the opening behind them which had been destroyed, they rose and fled onward.

They raced through this low, rough tunnel for several minutes until they reached the top of a steep, slick slope. So suddenly did they come upon this that, before they were able to halt, they found themselves sliding down it, whooshing over smooth mud ever faster and faster. However, the slope became tamer near the bottom, so they were able to avoid serious injury as they coasted into a level portion of the cave.

Here, when they stood up, a colony of several hundred bats took flight and fluttered off into the darkness.

Okona, who was astounded that his frail torch was still burning, held it up, and all examined their surroundings.

"Have we really escaped the Sisters alive?" Anisha gasped. "Clearly, aid from beyond this world has been with us."

"Indeed!" the girl said in a voice both earnest and well-composed. "For once snared, none break free of the Oolasheg."

"Do you not fear to utter that name?" Okona winced. "Especially when they are yet so near?"

"I am sorry. Of long habit do I speak it. But if ye wish, I will name them no more."

"Your speech is lofty for one your age, and of an ancient kind also," said Anisha.

"Such speech have I heard from childhood, so thus speak I also," said the girl.

"Please, tell us, who are you?" Okona asked.

"Lanoka am I."

"You called the ceremony we foiled the Rite of the Daughter's Blood," said Okona. "If this was its name, are you the Daughter it spoke of, and who are your parents?"

The girl lowered her gaze. "No man's daughter am I, and my mother has left me. But truth, I was the Daughter chosen to die. Yet by strange fate I have been delivered. And who might ye be that have wrought this deliverance? Your names ye spoke before, I know, but I was not so clear of thought then."

"Okona," said the lad.

"Anisha," Anisha declared.

Lanoka nodded to them, placed her fingertips together and touched them to her brow, then returned, "I thank ye greatly for saving my life. And for having the wit to know what it was that held me in the power of the Two. But as they are not far off, let us now depart and hold our talk for later. Know ye the way from this place?"

Okona looked around once more and said, "No, but we'd never be able to get back up that slope anyhow nor would we wish to. And there's only one other way on from here: that tunnel ahead. But before we set out, let's all have some of that water from Nadula."

"Yes, let's," agreed Anisha.

So they passed her waterskin around, and each of them took a long draught.

"I've still got my bundle of torches," said Anisha, when they'd finished. "And you've the rest of yours?"

Okona nodded. "Let's just use one brand at a time, though. That way they'll last longer. We may only have a few hours of light left. Probably six at the most." He frowned, examining the bundles.

"All right. You lead the way, Okona." Anisha laid her hand upon his back.

For the burn of ten full torches, they pressed on through mile after mile of dripping stone passages, most of which seemed to be bearing in the same direction, sometimes falling, sometimes climbing. Still, they had little confidence of whether they were deeper or higher than when they had stood at the bottom of that long, muddy slope beneath the Burrows of the Oolasheg.

As their eleventh and final torch grew shorter and shorter, they all but resigned themselves to a slow, miserable end in the bowels of the earth. But still they went on. After scrambling up several piles of breakdown, between which lay several short, wet passages, they came to a place where the tunnel narrowed. And here the torch finally fizzled out.

No one said anything, for there was nothing remotely heartening to say. But after a few moments, they realized it was not so dark as they might have expected. Indeed, there was a faint, bluish tinge to everything around them. At first, they suspected they had descended into some kind of delusion, but gradually they realized the illumination was genuine, for they could vaguely outline the shapes of both each other and various rock formations. What's more, the light was coming quite clearly from one direction—down the tunnel.

"Why, there really is a light!" exclaimed Anisha. "What could it be? Is it the sun?"

"No, Sun is never cold like that," said Lanoka. "Perhaps it is magic? Or come we to the Underbrakes at last?"

"If so, we should greet them nobly," Okona declared. "Let's go toward it."

So they crawled onward, and the ceiling became lower and lower until they were proceeding on their hands and knees. The light was most definitely brighter now and bigger too. But its color and nature were no less an enigma. Cold air brushed past the party from behind, but they also caught the whiff of a fainter, fresher air ahead, along with the tantalizing melody of running water.

While they were yet some two hundred feet from where the light entered the tunnel, they had to lie on their stomachs to go on. Wriggling forward, with their bellies scraping across the stone, they shoved their equipment along before them. Though feeling nearly suffocated in this cruel throat of stone, they clawed their way on through the hole upon which they had laid all their hopes. Yet every movement came at a heavy price, and they felt it would be impossible to finish their travail before they collapsed in despair and exhaustion. However, after what seemed like an hour, Okona pushed his items one final time before him, then dragged himself to the mouth of the opening through what seemed for an instant like a great weight or invisible curtain of earth. And then he knew from whence came the light. It was the moon.

Using both arms, he thrust himself out of the opening, which lay beneath the shadow of a large slab of rock, and found himself at the edge of a small creek in a narrow, steep-walled valley. Here were many boulders and much hanging greenery, all graced by soft, silver moonlight. He bent down and helped Lanoka out of the constricted cave, then did the same for Anisha. When all three were out in the fresh air and the glow of moon, they raised their arms to the sky and gloried in the the scent of the trees, the sound of singing water and the breath of the cool night air.

"I know this place," said Lanoka delightedly. "And, praise be to the Sky Above, we are now far from the Eyes of the Midnight Owl."

Korashac Caverns
The Way to the Oolasheg

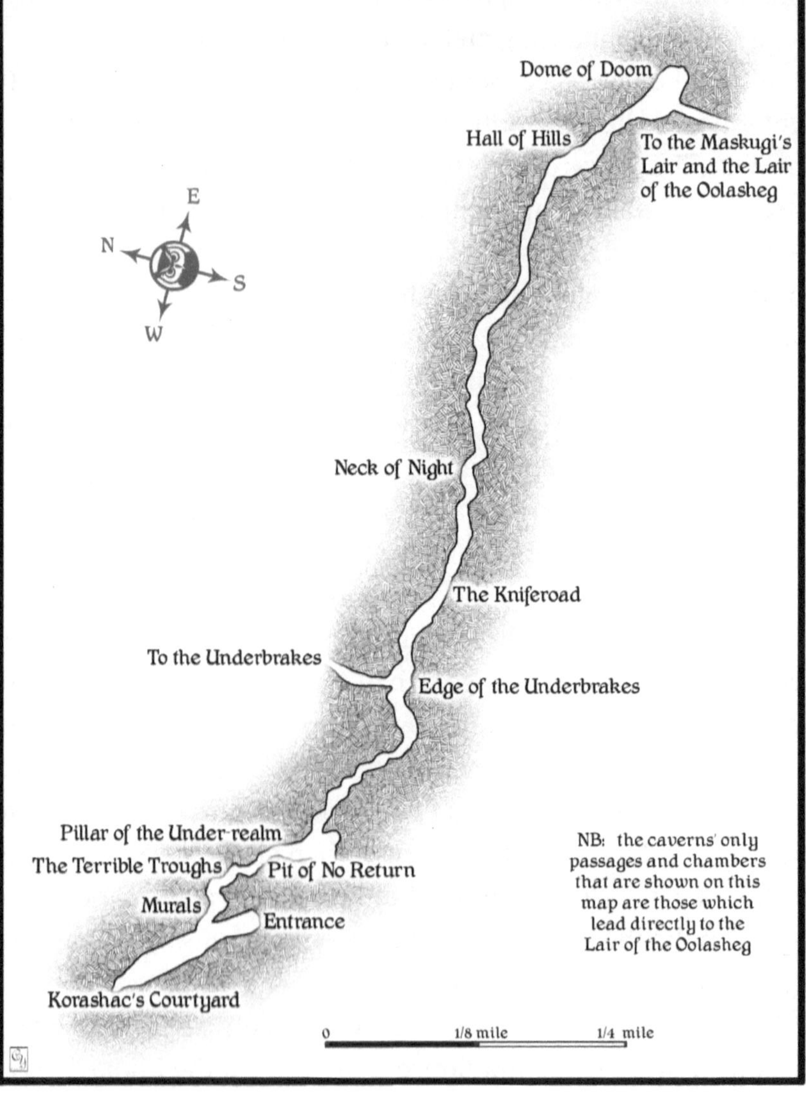

THE SONS OF SAHKU

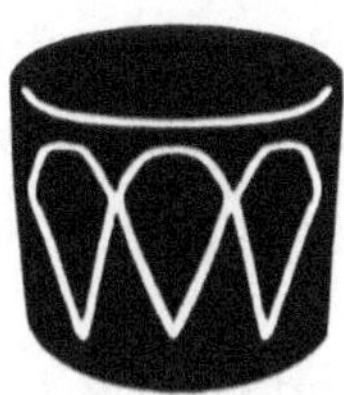

"WE HAVE CROSSED UNDER the Wakosi, for we are some five miles south of Korashac's southern mouth," explained Lanoka, as the others better took in their surroundings. "Here stand we in the upper reaches of Kachi Creek, not far above the Window of Southsight."

Abruptly, she turned to them and said, "As ye have saved my life, it is not right for me to deceive ye. When I said I am the daughter of no man, what I meant was this: he who would be deemed my father is no man, but a monster. For he is Kiamosh."

Okona and Anisha stared at her, astonished.

"A-are you your father's foe, then?" stuttered Anisha.

"Long have I done his bidding," the girl returned. "But I can do so no longer. Now I wish an end to Kiamosh and his evil as much as anyone ever has." She paused. "And I assume ye, too, are opposed to him? For else ye would not have thwarted my sacrifice."

"We are his enemies," Okona said. "However, the real reason we rescued you had nothing to do with him. You see, a mystic near the Kanno told me to prevent the Sisters' ceremony. However, he didn't say why, only that I must."

"Was that what brought ye to the Wakosi, then?"

Okona and Anisha looked at each other.

"Well," said Okona, "I suppose since you are against Kiamosh, we may safely tell you of our mission."

"We are Sakooma from the Kanno Valley," Anisha explained, "and our main business here is to retrieve the Hand of Hamora, which was stolen from our sacred mound."

"Ah," said Lanoka. "It is the Hand that has drawn us together."

"What do you mean?" asked Okona.

"That will take some time to explain. But we ought to journey down to the Wakosi while we speak of it, for from there, more readily may we seek Kiamosh and the Hand, as I imagine ye wish to do."

"We do," said Okona. "And I agree. Let's put our time to the best use we can."

With that, they set out, with Lanoka going before them, making their way down the boulder-strewn creekbed, which was mostly dry. Forest pressed close on either side, but moonlight shone through the gap between the trees, illuminating their stony path.

They had only gone a short distance when Anisha inquired, "Lanoka, how were you turned against your own father?"

"My whole life," said Lanoka, "I had been told it was wise to serve the Sisters of Korashac, for both life and power could they grant. I knew my father had sacrificed many to them, but this idea never disturbed me much, as long accustomed to it was I. But a mere ten days ago, Kiamosh revealed that I, too, was to be offered. Yea, even I, his great treasure and heiress, was to be devoured by the darkness of Korashac. 'Twas for a high cause, said he, and I should consider it an honor. But my blindness was removed that day. Though I am ashamed to admit it, that was the first time I understood how evil these sacrifices really were and how wicked was my father. For only when confronted with my own death did I understand."

"I feared for my life, yet knew there was no escape, for my father's will was set. So when the time came for Kiamosh to look in my eyes and bind me to enchantment in the camp by Kahlit Creek, I resigned myself to fate unfeeling. Once he placed the moon-charm about my neck, all thoughts were dimmed, and I was compelled to take the shadow-road to the Sisters and do their bidding. And I remember little but sound and shadows until ye destroyed that vile charm."

"Ah," Lanoka remarked, looking down the rocky course. "We are nearly to the Window of Southsight."

As they had been descending the creekbed, high rock walls had risen on either side of them, so they were now in a deep, narrow canyon. They went on a short distance more, and towering formations appeared in front of them. But in the midst of these was a large, tear-shaped opening, and through the base of this, Kachi Creek tumbled down many feet into a cliff-walled valley.

"This is the Window I spoke of," said Lanoka, gesturing toward it. "'Tis said if one looks through it from below, he may perchance see there images of happenings far to the south. My father has come here many times to put it to that purpose."

"How can we follow the creek beyond this point?" asked Anisha. "The fall is too sheer."

"There is another way," said Lanoka, and led them up a steep hillside on the right. After they had scrabbled up many feet of loose rock and dirt, the valley of the Kachi opened up before them, its moonlit forest stretching toward the Wakosi, flanked by precipitous, stony walls on either side.

Now they began a long and toilsome descent down the far side of the hill. After a time, they reached the valley floor beneath the Window of Southsight and turned to look up through the opening. The air seemed almost to shimmer there, though they saw no visions of faraway places. A small trickle cascaded from the Window, then flowed on through the valley where they stood. On three sides of them were unassailable, majestic, weird walls of stone. Trees frowned over the edges of precipices above, and scattered greenery clung to the cliff walls. Presently, the vale was covered in shadows, being so thoroughly hemmed in, though moonlight still reached the valley floor in places.

"Let us rest here before continuing," suggested Lanoka, "for the way is treacherous ahead."

The threesome sat upon a cluster of boulders and rubbed their aching limbs.

"Glad am I the candles of the stars light our way," remarked Lanoka, "and also that in this place we are mostly hid from the Pale Eye."

"The moon, you mean?" asked Okona.

"Yes. It is believed the Sisters may see through it. Perhaps even now they seek us."

"Is that why the necklace had the effect upon you it did?" Okona inquired. "Do the Sisters share in the moon's power?"

"In part. But they are only servants of the real power behind the Pale Eye." Her voice darkened. "He they call the Skaggish."

With some trepidation, Anisha repeated, "The Skaggish?"

Lanoka nodded. "The most dreadful being in all the Three Realms. From the highest of them he came, but he plies most often in our Middle Realm."

"As it was told long ago in Sarkanna," she continued, "the Bright Face, Sun, was the lamp of Mahna Shuya, given to warm and sustain the world. And there was only Day, no Night, in the first epoch of man. But after the days of the hero Umarna, man quarreled with Mahna Shuya and was driven from the World of the West. So through the Mists of Shagrash-Mula to our own age he fled. At that time, as punishment to man in his exile, half the day was given to a wicked warden, the Skaggish, who made the Pale Eye from part of the Bright Face. That is why the Bright Face is dimmer in our latter days than once it was."

"When man reached these hither lands, the Skaggish set Moon to rule the Night. And it is to the Skaggish and the Night that all evil creatures owe their allegiance. So the Sun is of Mahna Shuya and good, while Moon is of the Skaggish and evil. However, in the teachings of Kiamosh, it was Mahna Shuya who was vile and the Skaggish who was glorious. But now I see it was all a lie. For the service of the Skaggish is always performed with deceit and bloodshed, greed and selfishness and vengeance."

"Our people still carry knowledge of some of that which you have spoken, but of this master of the Moon, we have no lore," Anisha said.

"I can guess why he was forgotten," remarked Lanoka. "To banish knowledge of him may not be wise, though it may be more pleasant."

"So this being—whose name I suppose we ought not to utter if he's all that terrible, if you would do us the courtesy, Lanoka—this being is far worse than the Sisters?" inquired Okona.

"As ye wish. And yes, he is their master. Perhaps ye saw the scribblings upon the stone when ye entered Korashac? Those were made by ancient worshipers of him and the Sisters. If ye studied them, ye would have seen an image of him there; a terrible shadow is he. It is he who gave plans to seize all of Sarkanna to the Sisters, and these they gave to Kiamosh."

"So that is what Kiamosh intends," muttered Okona.

"Until just now," Anisha remarked, "I'd forgotten the strange thing the leader of the spirits of Toshigan Hollow said about the victory of their Master flowing from this valley. Do you think the evil one of whom you just told us is the Master of whom he was speaking?"

"Ye were ensnared by the Kishikot? And yet escaped?" Lanoka stared at them, amazed.

The Sakooma nodded.

"The Powers are indeed with ye! For the Lord of Shadows, he whose name ye wish me not to speak, is their Master also."

She went on, "When Kiamosh first came to the Wakosi and began serving the Sisters, they besought aid from the wardens of Toshigan Hollow to guard the valley's southern flank. The rest of the borders were already well-protected by creatures called chiborka, which were under an enchantment by Kiamosh. But both the Kishikot and the Sisters were working according to the Lord of Shadows' design of protecting Kiamosh so his power might grow unhindered."

"There was another being in those tracings near Korashac's entrance," said Okona, "one we encountered in the caverns. Like an ogre it was. Do you know of it? And I take it this thing was also in the Shadow's service?"

"All evil things are, as I said, though some by closer degrees than others," Lanoka returned. "The Maskugi it is called, a monster loyal to the Sisters that acts as their guardian, as it has done for a great count of years. But what it is or whence it came no one knows. How eluded ye him to reach me?"

"We slew him," Okona answered, "though not without difficulty."

Lanoka's eyes grew wide. "Verily ye are blessed! And great grace of the Skies is yours. Ye must have had mighty aid also at the Neck of Night, cursed with a spell of unbroken sleep that only bearers of the moon-charm may hold at bay. For there is no way to the Maskugi but through that black place."

"Unfortunately, we did slumber there," said Anisha.

"But a voice called to me," Okona said, "so I woke and then roused Anisha. But we've no idea how long we slept nor who or what awakened me."

"Of that, I know no more than ye," said Lanoka. "But regarding the time, I can perhaps help ye a little. The Sisters' ceremonies end with sacrifice at sunset, when Night is on the rise, so ye may have slept for many hours if ye came in shortly after I did. I lingered for some time at the wall of images, meditating on them, but after that continued straight on, save for halting briefly at the entrance to the Underbrakes, hoping to speak to my mother's spirit. But my terror of the place was too great, so I departed quickly."

"What route did you come by?" Anisha asked.

"In my ken, there is but one way to the Oolasheg, one out of a thousand that would lead one astray. But I was guided by my moon-charm until I came through the Neck of Night. And beyond that, I was led also by the Sisters' drumming, a summons for death. But how came ye to find this singular route unaided?"

"We didn't," Okona said, "for we did have aid, at least for parts of the journey, in the form of a strange, guiding light."

"I wonder what that could have been," said Lanoka.

"We have no idea," Anisha said, "but it nonetheless guided us where we wished to go. We were fortunate also to have magic fire and torches from the entrance."

Lanoka nodded. "The fire is of the Sisters for the service of victims, only lighting when one approaches and going out after a torch is lit. And the torch bundles are replenished by Kiamosh from time to time."

"Who is Kiamosh, in truth?" asked Okona. "And where did he come from?"

"That shall take a bit of telling," Lanoka replied, rising. "Let us pass the most difficult part of the creek, and then I will tell ye his tale. And when I have done that, it should also answer your question of how the Hand of Hamora has drawn us together."

After taking a bit of the food Anisha had brought, they continued down the narrow valley. Several hundred yards on, past a mess of humongous, moss-clad boulders, their way curved to the left, as the land fell sharply to their right. Shortly, the trail led them to a cave, four feet high and ten across, that cut through a jutting tower of rock. They crawled through this to a ledge on the other side that hugged the bluff. Taking care to keep back from the edge, they followed this to the left, curving around a great, overhung, hollow in the rock until they stood almost facing the cave through which they had just come. Then, with Lanoka's careful guidance, they began down-climbing toward the valley floor far below. It would have been a tricky business in the daylight, but in the dark, it was ever so much more so, and at various points, a fall could have proved fatal. Okona and Anisha relied heavily on following Lanoka's exact route and movements, and thus came many feet down without incident. The last twenty feet of the descent was especially steep, but a length of corded rope was there to aid them, tied to a tree and dangling to the valley bottom. This, according to Lanoka, had been set there by Kiamosh for his use in visiting the Window of Southsight.

Once they had come to the bottom of the rope, they stood in a narrow canyon, ringed on three sides. Moss and ferns covered the high canyon walls. To the south was a waterfall, spilling through jagged stones, from which the creek flowed on through the valley. Here they each took a few sips of the water of Nadula, then began trekking along the creekbed. Soon, they noted a large, dark opening in the wall to their right, thirty feet up, and out of this poured a small cascade. Beyond this, the narrow canyon continued. Unfortunately, the way became more slippery and difficult to manage, though the formations no less fantastic.

As they passed on through the darkened valley, Lanoka said, "I promised I would give ye Kiamosh's history. Now, here it is."

"The beginning of my story I suspect ye already know, for it is a tale of the Sakooma's early days and has likely enough been kept alive around your night-fires. But I shall tell it anyhow, in case there is aught ye are lacking, and weave Kiamosh's thread into it when the time comes."

"Ten generations before our time, there was a nomad and warrior named Sahku. From the north he came, from where forest meets plain several hundred miles from here. With him was his wife Machila, a worker of petty magics, and also many relatives, all descended from a man living several centuries before that. Sakoom was he, from whom the Sakooma take their name. But Sahku was the Sakooma's leader at the time. And when he and his band came to where Takula Conflux now stands, they halted and set up an encampment."

"Shortly after they arrived, Sahku and Machila brought forth their first child, Kiamosh. And five years afterward, they had a second son, Hamora."

Okona clapped his hand to his head. "So Kiamosh is the older brother whose name has been forgotten among us! And it is he whose right hand was hewn off. We were always told he was slain by Hamora."

"Thou guesseth aright," said Lanoka. "But slain he was not, as ye now well know. However, it is known in the Wakosi that Hamora spread the falsehood about his death, along with many other falsehoods. Yet Kiamosh let it be, as he found a suitable use for it. If he were accounted as dead, the Sakooma would not regard him as a threat. Thus was he able to plot his revenge in secret."

"But if Kiamosh was born even before Hamora, he must be ancient," Anisha said.

"Two hundred and seventy-six dances of Sun," Lanoka declared.

"But how?" Anisha cried.

"As my tale unfolds, that ye will understand."

"Ye may recall tales of the Year of the Pale Sun, when the land was darkened from the black smokes, the winter was fell, and famines commenced throughout Sarkanna and the lands beyond. This began when Kiamosh was ten, and a Sakooma prophet of those days proclaimed that, as ten was a notable number, such evil commencing that year boded a black future for the lad. Alas! For the prophet's words proved true."

"In Kiamosh's thirty-seventh year, Sahku died in battle against the Mushatuck, for at the time, the two peoples were warring over a breach of honor. And as he had no daughters, the birthright came to Kiamosh as the elder son. But Hamora, in a scheme to seize this, made a pact with the Matora, the Thunder-Bear, a being as powerful as the Sisters, but living to the west of Sarkanna. Like unto a giant, winged black bear is he, cloaked in storm-fire."

"It is recounted among us that Hamora received the Hand from the Powers. But the one you speak of is one of the Four Evils," gasped Okona, "every bit as depraved as the Sisters. And yet Hamora had traffic with it?"

"And must you say its name?" Anisha added, wincing.

"I will not utter it again," Lanoka promised. "But yes, Hamora even bound himself to it. The substance of this pact was later discovered by my father in conversance with the Sisters; it was that Hamora would serve the Lord of Shadows then and forever, but in exchange for this, the being whose name ye wish me not to speak, the Western Thunder as we may call him, would give him what he sought—power. So he transformed one of Hamora's hands into smooth, blue crystal, though still with movement as a hand of flesh. This Hand gave him three great powers, one each of Earth, Water and Air. First, the strength of Earth so that at any moment he wished, he might be as strong as ten men; second, the terror of Water, for he could summon a water-storm from above; and third, the fury of Air, for he would be able to command his own mighty wind."

"We have always been told the Hand gave Hamora power," Okona said, "but the knowledge of what kind has not been preserved among us. However, most often we speak of it as providing protection to our people. But if it had these powers also ... "

"Then presumably they're what Kiamosh intends to gain from it," finished Anisha.

"Exactly so," Lanoka confirmed. "Now, once Hamora had the Hand, he returned to the camp at Takula. Keeping his Hand hidden, he challenged Kiamosh to single combat for the leadership of the Sakooma. When Kiamosh refused, since the leadership was his by right, Hamora called him a coward. This Kiamosh would not abide, so he attacked him then and there. But Hamora cut off Kiamosh's right hand with the Stone of Sahku, their father's stone axe. Kiamosh then saw his revealed Hand and knew that Hamora had an unfair advantage. He called his followers to attack Hamora, but Hamora carried them away with wind and struck them down in a storm. Then Kiamosh cursed Hamora, pledging that he would someday kill him, those he loved, and every one of his descendants. He further swore that he would someday regain mastery of the Sakooma and their land, and that not even death would keep him from this. Then he fled for his life. Hamora sent out parties to search for him, but never did they find him."

"Hamora was ever troubled about Kiamosh for the rest of his days. However, as part of his original pact with the Western Thunder, he had been assured his people would be protected from enemies after he died. For by the Thunder's magic, he would enter the mound and be turned to ash, though his Hand would remain. And this would shield them from attacks by such as his vengeful brother and even prevent foes from approaching the mound itself. And its door would be sealed by the Thunder's spells. Hamora was also promised his spirit would be carried to the Over-lands for his noble sacrifice on behalf of his people. But at the age of six tens and eight, Hamora went to the Underbrakes like all other men, for the Thunder had not the power to grant this pledge."

"We have always believed Hamora was a hero, but the true story proves him rather a villain," Anisha remarked.

"At least he did take some measure of protection for the Sakooma," Okona said, "but in all else, he was a scoundrel."

"Ah, but Kiamosh was no better," said Lanoka. "For through his long life, I should say he turned out much the worse."

As they had been talking, they had been treading on through the ever-lush valley. They had already passed many stunningly-shaped rocks and a waterfall running down a great staircase of rock. There were, in fact, many small waterfalls all down the creek, and their starlit beauty was only marred by the difficulty they made for route-finding, since they obliged the party to find narrow ways along the creekbed's edge, often over (and sometimes under) obstacles of tree and stone. Though there was a natural inclination for them to seek higher paths, Lanoka kept them close to Kachi's edge, for she had told them back when they were taking refreshment that, though the higher paths might be easier, they were more dangerous and would be even more perilous at night.

"What became of Kiamosh after he fled?" Anisha inquired.

After drinking from a small cascade, Lanoka continued her tale. "Kiamosh went far, far to the northwest, hoping to find and cross the Span of the Shimmering Nights to return to the World of the West. For there he meant to avenge himself on Mahna Shuya for allowing Hamora to thieve his domain, for he knew not of Hamora's pact with the Western Thunder, and Hamora had falsely declared that Mahna Shuya had gifted him his Hand. Kiamosh's seeking for that fabled place brought him far up the Shamuri River, which feeds the Anoka from the west several hundred miles north of where the Kanno meets it, and is every bit as long as the Anoka, they say."

"In Kiamosh's fortieth year, he came to the Shamuri's upper reaches, where he encountered a powerful witch named Shakeega. Of a distant tribe called the Hadkanaash was she. He was much enamored of this ambitious woman, for he saw in her magic a means of gaining his revenge. He was taken also by her beauty, of which there was a terrible secret. Prolonged youth and fairness exquisite was hers, aye. But it had been obtained through the sacrifice of several of her children and committing herself, as Hamora had done, to the service of the Lord of Shadows through one of his servants."

"I know little more of the lesser power with whom she struck this pact than its name and, vaguely, its shape. The Omaka it was called, a thing of the lake in some great, serpent form. From it she had received a magical artifact in exchange for her fealty to the Lord of Shadows. This was a silver ring, set with a bright moonstone, and it was the source of lengthened life and youth for her and any others to whom she extended it. However, its use, little by little, sapped her strength. The ring bears the name of the Coil of the Omaka. A twining serpent is engraved upon it, and its stone came from the golden prairies of Nebara, which lie west of the Shamuri some eight hundred and fifty miles up its course, while its silver is from the high mountains of far-off Tarbomu, the land of Shakeega."

"Now, it was not Kiamosh alone who was smitten. Shakeega was also wooed by Kiamosh and much admired his ambitions for conquest. So after they had wed and dwelt together for several years, she employed the Coil's powers to preserve his own youth and life."

"So that's how Kiamosh is still living after all these centuries!" Anisha exclaimed.

"Did Shakeega then return to Sarkanna with Kiamosh to take revenge on Hamora?" asked Okona.

"Eventually. But first, they went to a region known as the Mistwoods, a vast forest of evergreens near the Great Western Water, farther west even than the homeland of Shakeega. In Kiamosh's forty-seventh year journeyed they thither, for they had heard of mighty spirits and warlocks there who could train them in spellcraft greater even than that known by Shakeega."

"For a hundred years they tarried there, increasing their skill in black magic, before they returned to Tarbomu. By then, all those they had known in that region had died. They had outlived several generations, and the fear and awe of them among the Hadkanaash was great. But they lingered not there; rather, they spent the next six years traveling in and around the Anoka Valley and later the valley of the Kanno, gaining knowledge about Hamora and the Sakooma. During that time, Kiamosh discerned what had happened with Hamora and the Hand and learned about his pact with the Western Thunder. He also learned that, not long before, in the fifty-first year after Hamora's death, construction had begun in earnest on some of the more impressive mounds at Takula, as well as the wall that borders it. And to his displeasure, much better was its guard then than in earlier days."

"Though Kiamosh's and Shakeega's magic was strong, they would risk no chance of defeat. And being unable to overcome the protection afforded by the Hand of Hamora, they withdrew to an area some distance off to forge a plot to conquer the Sakooma."

"In Kiamosh's one hundred and fifty-third summer, he and Shakeega entered the Valley of the Wakosi. With their magic and the aid of the Sisters of Korashac, they drove out its inhabitants, the Babora. Then, with the valley all to themselves, Shakeega began to use the Coil of the Omaka in a manner she had learned of in their time in the Mistwoods, which was to breed their own army. Together with Kiamosh, she used it to bring forth children of strength, touched by magic. These we know as the Jaggo."

Okona and Anisha nearly stumbled upon hearing this.

"Wait ..." cried Okona. "All the Jaggo are sons of Kiamosh?"

"Aye. Born were they, always as twins, in fairly continuous succession over more than one hundred years. That is why there are more than two hundred of them."

"And they're all male children?" Anisha puzzled. "How could this be?"

"Shakeega ordained it thus by the power of the ring, for males would be more apt for their army of warriors. And the many Jaggo were kept alive, strong and youthful by Shakeega's ring, for she was mighty indeed in magic after her long training. Still, they may be slain. Yet, as many of them have lived longer than most men, they are more greatly practiced. Also, they are enchanted, as can be seen in their movement and balance. Thus, only few of them have fallen."

"So much about the Jaggo makes sense now," Okona declared, "why they all look so similar, why they hail only from the north, why they are mortal and yet in many ways uncanny ..."

"Long have they blighted these lands," Lanoka lamented. "At whiles, my father would send them out to kidnap victims for the Sisters, so he might stay in their good graces. But the Jaggo were instructed to only attack at night and never speak in others' presence outside the valley, lest their Sakooma origins be discovered. For he wished none to know that he yet lived, so his revenge might be the sweeter when he revealed himself. And the fact that they spoke Sakooma as it was long ago might arouse suspicion, for as Kiamosh still spoke the language of his youth, such is what he imparted to his children. But if ever they had need to communicate with outsiders, such as for inquiring where prey had fled, they could employ a form of sign language used by merchants up and down the Kanno. Kanno Hand Language it is called, and Kiamosh himself had taught it to the Jaggo, for it had been rather unchanged since the time of his youth. But the Jaggo have their own hand language as well."

"Ah, Kanno Hand Language must have been how the Jaggo communicated with the Chadori that kidnapped us," Anisha declared.

"Yes, that must be it," Okona agreed, "for at least one of the Chadori would be likely to know it." He then remarked, "Sorry for the interruption, Lanoka. Please continue."

Lanoka navigated over a fallen limb blocking their path. "After Kiamosh's two hundred and fifty-ninth year, no further Jaggo were born, for Shakeega was then unwell. Her long use of the ring had drained her sorely. So she abstained for several years from having any more children. Yet Kiamosh urged her to bear more, so she conceived another. By that point, she had already given the ring over to Kiamosh, and it was he who used it to keep himself, her and the Jaggo alive. But still her health waned; the ring had taken a deadly toll. And when the child was born, she died. That was twelve years ago now. And I am that child."

"You?" Okona gasped. "A daughter of both warlock and witch?"

"Yes," the girl sadly replied. "But not in magic was I birthed, as were the Jaggo, nor is my life bound to the ring, as is theirs. For I was conceived only when it failed my mother. And that is also why I am a girl; Shakeega no longer had the strength to use the ring to ensure I would be a male. And as I was the only girl and the last of those borne by Shakeega, Kiamosh treasured me as a final memory of her. Thus, never have I been permitted to leave this valley, for fear that aught should befall me."

The party fell silent for some while. But on they followed the dark and difficult waters of Kachi Creek, winding past outcrops of boulders and descending many small waterfalls. The valley broadened to some extent, but the way was still generally arduous.

At length, Lanoka spoke again. "Now we come at last in Kiamosh's history to the events that directly concern ye and I."

"After Shakeega's death, Kiamosh grew ever more eager to enact his revenge. And though the Jaggo were many, they were not yet enough to overrun Takula. And still were the Sakooma guarded by the Hand of Hamora. Yet he could not attack them to get at the Mound of Hamora nor was his magic strong enough to enter it even if he stood before it. Around the time when he and Shakeega had first entered the valley, they had gone to the Sisters to inquire about obtaining the Hand. But what they wished in return was a pledge more terrible than Kiamosh was willing to pay. So ever he looked for his own means of entering the Mound."

"But then, last summer, the Jaggo captured a Sakooma warrior, whom they intended to sacrifice to the Sisters. He had been caught scouting alone in the lands to the east of here. However, he promised Kiamosh whatever he desired if only he would spare his life. Kiamosh ordered that, if the Mound of Hamora were opened, this warrior obtain the Hand and bring it to him. And he laid a curse of death upon him if he should fail to keep his word."

"Tencum!" Anisha cried, her face paling.

"That was his name," Lanoka returned. "And I perceive thou knowest him. A traitor he has proven to ye and all your kin."

"We learned as much just before entering Korashac," Okona said drearily. "But tell us: how did Kiamosh manage to open the Mound?"

"Now that he had one who had sworn to bring him the Hand if the Mound were open, his thirst for vengeance became utterly desperate. Thus, he finally conceded to the Sisters' terms they had laid out long ago. He pledged them whatever terrible thing it was they sought, and in exchange they would grant him three favors, although he would have to pay a price for each."

"The first was that they would use their magic to break the protective spell on the Mound of Hamora. This was bestowed twelve days ago, as I should guess ye already know. Kiamosh, depraved fellow that he is, had waited until the Sakooma's most celebrated day of the year to strike. The Sisters stood before the Window of Southsight, with the lay of Takula rippling therein, and their storm passed through that fay portal into the Sakooma heartland to shatter the Mound's enchanted door."

"The second gift was the service of a ganoja, a bluff dragon. From the mid-reach of the Anoka he came hither on swift wing the day after the assault on Takula. And upon reaching the Sisters, he was raised above his kind. For he was given the power to understand the speech of men, though he could not reply in kind. His purpose was to at whiles patrol the Wakosi and also be the sentinel and visible terror of Kiamosh all along the Kanno. And in this vigil, he might receive aid from the secret knowledge of water spirits in and near there."

"And the third boon was that, by the Sisters' power, the Hand of Hamora would be affixed to Kiamosh's empty wrist, so that its power might be his."

"And what of the prices?" asked Okona.

"The first was that terrible pledge of which even I know not. And the cost of the ganoja was the blood of a hundred men, which Kiamosh obtained through the Jaggo from folk living beyond the Wakosi Vale. And the third ... the third price was me."

Okona spoke slowly, horrified. "It is a dreadful thing to count the lives of a hundred men as nothing to achieve wicked ends. But there is another, more hideous degree of evil to regard one's own child, whom he ought to protect and nurture, as ... as ..."

"Now ye see how the Hand hath brought us together," said Lanoka gravely. "For Kiamosh's lust for the Hand turned me against him, and his theft of it brought ye hither. So we are both his enemies on account of the Hand and enemies of the Hand itself."

"We are no enemies of the Hand," corrected Okona. "We simply wish it back where it belongs."

"Didst thou not hear what I said of how the Hand entered the possession of mortals?" said Lanoka. "We all suffer much from the dealings of these sons of Sahku."

"Of course," agreed Anisha. "And the Hand is a dangerous thing, but it could also be used for much good, as it long has been."

"Nay, there is no true good in it. For know this: the Hand is wrought of sky-fallen moonblood, the very essence of Moon's evil. Moon is the Eye of the Lord of Shadows, and the Hand is ultimately his. To venerate the Hand is to venerate him, whether one is aware of the connection or not. Perhaps he hath protected thy people for many years, but in exchange, ye have been kept in bondage to him."

"The Sakooma? Slaves to *him?*" Okona laughed incredulously. "Never."

"I know a good deal about both magic and the Lord of Shadows," Lanoka solemnly returned. "And I tell ye that all who reverence the works of evil Powers are, without exception, in bondage to those same Powers. And all relics of theirs, even those which work some good, do so at a cost. Think upon the Coil of the Omaka. It lengthens life, but enslaves those under its power, so that their life is not really their own. The Hand protects the Sakooma, but they are also beholden to it. Ye have risked your lives to rescue it, which means ye count it dearer than life. Would ye die for a mere thing of crystal, even enchanted crystal? If so, ye only prove my words true."

Okona and Anisha were silent, for neither could think of any reply to this.

After a while, Okona said, "What then, if you were in our place, would you do regarding the Hand?"

"I should hope, above all, that ye would not be so foolish as to return it to the Mound of Hamora and again enshrine your dark servitude. Best would it be if the Hand were destroyed, but if not, at least let it be taken from Kiamosh and hid from the grasp of man. Alas, there is only one thing that can destroy moonblood: sunfire. For only Sun can vanquish Moon. But very rare is sunfire from one Great Water to the Other."

"Sunfire?" Okona blurted out, with rather more animation than he intended.

Lanoka turned to him. "Yes?"

"Nothing," Okona hastily replied, deciding firmly against revealing that such a rarity was in his possession. Despite Lanoka's warning, he was determined that the Hand should be regained, not destroyed, for such would be an utter betrayal of his entire mission. He could only use his sunfire shard once, anyhow, and certainly the Seer would never intend for him to employ it as a means of intentionally failing his own quest.

"How do you know of this sunfire?" asked Anisha. "And where can it be found?"

"Kiamosh has spoken of it in loathing. Much of it there is across the Great Western Water, it is said, but only a few precious shards lie here in the east, on account of the Lord of Shadows, who desires that men should never lay hands upon it. So I fear we must forsake any hope of ending the Hand's power altogether. Only may we seek to wrest it from Kiamosh."

"Has Kiamosh already joined the Hand to himself, then?" asked Okona.

"Nay, though he shall seek to do so less than a day from now. But as I became not food for the Sisters, I suspect they will regard his debt as unpaid and will not aid in melding the Hand to him. But I know not if, in desperation, his own power is sufficient to do it. And he may be able to access some of the Hand's powers even without joining it to himself. So he is still a great danger."

After clambering down a boulder after Lanoka, Okona inquired, "Did Kiamosh ever speak of what he intends to do after the Hand is fully his?"

"Many times," she replied. "As the Lord of Shadows bids, he will seize control of the Sakooma and their lands, then all of Sarkanna and perhaps even beyond. And as he does so, he will spread open veneration of the Skaggish—your pardon, the Lord of Shadows—along with observance of many profane rituals. Unfortunately, some of these are already established in other places, such as the sacrifice and devouring of other men."

"When does he intend to make the Hand his own? Is there still enough time to stop him?" Anisha asked.

Lanoka looked doubtful. "The ceremony of the Hand was to be held ten full days and ten hours after a day had passed from its departure from Takula proper, the time of which Kiamosh learned from your Tencum. For that first day stood as an offering to the Lord of Shadows. And in the sacred allotment that followed, the Hand might be purified from the power of Takula. So that would put it at the middle of the afternoon on the day that draws nigh."

"That leaves us only about twelve hours." Okona frowned. "Where is the ceremony to be held?"

"The Tongue of Tagwash. 'Tis a little under three tens of miles from here by the way I should take us. A great tongue of stone it is, thrust out high over Shagora Gorge, a valley that runs west of the Wakosi. Less than a mile from the river the Tongue lies, and nigh unto Kiamosh's lair, a place called Bok Barusha."

After carefully making her way over a collection of slippery stones, Lanoka said, "He chose the place for its magic. For in that valley there was once great sorcery. Of old, the Tagwash was a monster, far bigger and more dangerous than the Maskugi, yet like unto its kind. Long ago, it was directed by a warlock to conquer the Wakosi Vale. However, by the efforts of a hero and his band of friends, in that very valley, the warlock was slain and the Tagwash turned to stone. But his Tongue is yet visible, jutting out from the side of the mountain. And the warlock's body is buried somewhere in that vale. I think Kiamosh means to draw upon the lingering remnants of power of the ancient warlock and also the Tagwash itself."

"If it's as far as you say from here," said Anisha, "how can we make it in time?"

"It is very far," Lanoka admitted. "And the way is not a gentle one. Also, we three have already journeyed much. So perhaps we shall come too late."

"Maybe our companions are on their way there already," Okona said hopefully. He turned to Lanoka and explained, "There were three others we left near Kahlit Creek when we entered Korashac."

"But we don't know what happened to them," returned Anisha. "And though I hate to even think of it, they may have been killed. And since we don't know if any other aid will come, we have to make every effort to get there ourselves, though what we could do even if we did come in time, I don't know."

The trio halted and plopped down upon wet stones, much disheartened. And there they sat numbly for several minutes.

"After all this ..." Okona sighed at length. "To have come through so much only to—" He broke off, then thought for a moment. "Anisha, how much water is left in your flask?"

Gently, she shook it. "A fair amount, I should say."

"The Elixir of Nadula has aided us before," Okona exclaimed, rising. "Let us trust to it once again, while it lasts. It just might carry us all those leagues in the little time we have. For I don't believe the Powers would have let us live through all this if there was naught left for us to do."

"You're right, Okona," Anisha said firmly. "We have to at least give it a try."

Lanoka smiled. "Glad am I there is some hope the wickedness of these sons of Sahku may yet be mended, and glad would I be to play some part in the mending."

Roused by the tang of hope, the threesome each took draughts from Anisha's flask.

"Lead on, Lanoka," Okona urged, as they set off down the creekbed.

"I shall guide ye as best I can," the girl returned. "Let us hope it shall be enough."

Now, as the pale night waned, as shadows they passed silently down the moonlit run of Kachi Creek.

CHAPTER TWENTY-ONE

DRUMS IN SHAGORA GORGE

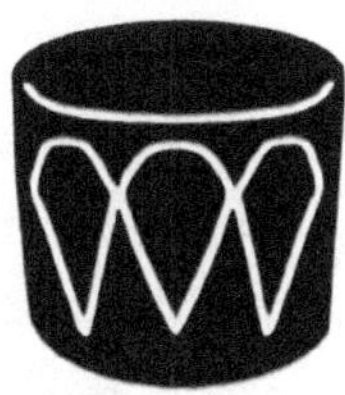

PATCHES OF WARMING, MIDAFTERNOON light fell upon Okona and his companions, as they hurried eastward along a forest trail, cluttered with stones and roots, near the rim of Shagora Gorge. An eerie quiet lay upon the woods, stirred by neither bird nor beast but only the lightest rustle of a breeze.

Over league after league of wild trail they had come, upstream along or near the Wakosi from the lower reaches of Kachi Creek until they had reached a point four miles southwest of the entrance to Nadula Valley. Then they had veered away from the river, taking a little-used track six miles southwest through raw, mountainous country, and now they had nearly completed a final mile jogging southeast to the northern wall of the gorge. Early along their route, they had gathered some packs, food and weaponry (arrows, bow and spear for Okona and daggers for all) from an unguarded Jaggo outpost. There they had each traded their mud-caked garments for fresh ones of similar make, as they had discovered a cache of clothing the Jaggo had plundered from outsiders. On a few occasions, they had halted to rest, though only briefly. And on each of these, they had partaken of the Elixir of Nadula, until their supply was entirely empty. Yet weariness, though near, had not yet descended upon them, for mighty was the magic of Nadula's waters.

Just as the woods thinned and they caught their first real sight of the gorge, a low, dreadful thud echoed through the forest, rising from the bottom of the vale.

"Hark! It begins," Lanoka said. "The Jaggo are summoning the spirits of the valley."

More hollow, dark drumming followed. Thirty strong the drums were, Okona guessed, and their heavy tones were only made the more sinister by the valley's echo. The beat was slow and uncannily steady, and already the companions could feel something amiss in the earth beneath and the air about them.

Suddenly, there came the jarring thump of a higher drum, though from what direction it was impossible to tell, on account of the many echoes. But this higher drum was most definitely unaligned with the beat of the deep drumming. In fact, it was downright disruptive, and grew ever more so, as it had no sense of meter of its own. Its strikes were utterly random, even frantic and deranged. But then it became more regular and positively festive, though still completely disjunct from the low drumming, which had now started to become disordered.

"Why, that other drummer must be Yahsi!" exclaimed Okona. "I know that rhythm; it's one she herself made. I think she's trying to interrupt the Jaggo."

"It's working!" Anisha said excitedly, for the evil tingle had vanished from earth and air.

"She does well." Lanoka smiled. But her grin quickly disappeared, as she pointed down the trail. "Look! We have done it. We have caught up with Kiamosh. But see how many Jaggo are with him!"

Even at a moment's glance, it was clearly more than seventy, all armed and fearsomely decked in wolf pelts, head and all, with the pelts' wolf-heads resting upon their own. What's more, the two giant bears, Nasi and Tawassi, were also in the company, which had halted nigh to the edge of the gorge. With a surge of loathing, Okona spotted Tencum, toting his hunting bag, next to Kiamosh.

Of course, there would be no mortal chance of stopping Kiamosh with so many defending him. Nonetheless, determined to at least get a closer look at the situation, the three laid their packs aside and hastened forward, taking care to remain out of sight.

Meanwhile, Kiamosh, brandishing a great stone axe, raged, "Mockery! Insolence! Sacrilege! How dare this rogue drummer make sport of this hallowed place! Hark, Jaggo! Three tens of ye, find this flea-bitten squirrel at once and slay him. How came he to this vale I know not, but this meddling bodes ill. For it portends that folk are privy to what shall soon take place here. And it may be there are more than this upstart about. Slaughter all ye lay eyes upon! I go to the Tongue."

While the thirty Jaggo who had just been dispatched were hurrying off, Kiamosh set his axe upon the ground and took a long, curved, pale-yellow horn from his belt. Upon this he blew, issuing a series of low grunts, borne aloft by a sudden wind.

Kiamosh was still sounding the horn when an arrow zinged by less than an inch from his face, and a spear-wielding figure swung down from the trees on a long rope, kicking the warlock's head and knocking the horn from his lips. Kiamosh went sprawling. At that very moment, another figure, spear in hand, jumped out from behind a boulder some distance off the path and uttered a wild cry. Still more figures, armed with bows and spears, sprang from behind this boulder and others. Arrows were singing and spears whistling toward the Jaggo before they had time even to raise their weapons.

Though some Jaggo and the great bears immediately tried to aid Kiamosh, they were forced to back away from their master in order to avoid being skewered in a shower of projectiles.

After his initial shock, Okona recognized a number of the attackers. Shadoo it was who had swung into Kiamosh, and Wunko had been the first to leap from behind the boulder. Also, to his tremendous astonishment, the Sakooma leader Orobec and the eight men who had gone with him to seek the Oolasheg were among the throng, though their appointed Wise-woman, Shoroba, was not among them. As for the others, he had no idea who they were or from whence they had come, but it was gloriously clear they were enemies of Kiamosh. With a cry of delight, Okona readied the bow he had gotten from the outpost that morning and launched several missiles into the midst of the Jaggo. Then he hurriedly slung the bow back upon his shoulder. "Stay back!" he ordered Anisha and Lanoka, as he bounded toward the fray, spear in hand.

Meanwhile, the ambushing warriors were running toward the Jaggo, who were drawing together to make a tight defense. While they were thus occupied, Shadoo had dropped from the rope and was now standing above the prostrate Kiamosh, preparing to pin him with his spear.

"Die now, foul troubler of the Vale!" he shouted.

But Tencum lunged toward Shadoo, so that he was forced to spring aside to escape his grasp. Roaring, Kiamosh leapt to his feet, and he and Tencum both grabbed for Shadoo. But the old Babora nimbly ducked away.

Many Jaggo had been stricken in the initial assault, but all yet living, even those who had been grievously injured, still fought maniacally against the sudden assault of Wunko and the warriors with him. Within moments of crashing into each other, the battling forces were locked in a melee of blood, screams and fury. And into this maelstrom hurtled Okona.

Several times thwarted from laying hands on Shadoo, Kiamosh whistled for Nasi to aid him. The great bruin drew away from mauling his opponents to rush toward his master. But while he was still some yards off, Shadoo flung his spear at the bounding Nasi, piercing his shoulder, so that he foundered. One of the warriors who had emerged with Wunko, seeing Shadoo's plight, rushed to him with a blowgun and darts. Nasi roared and stood upon his hind legs. In one bellowing leap, he would have been upon Shadoo, but before he could reach him, the latter blasted a dart into Nasi's chest. Howling, the bear shuddered and toppled backwards, crushing several Jaggo in a rolling fit of agony.

A handful of Wunko's warriors strove to slay Kiamosh, but he was well-defended by Tencum, who had grabbed a stray spear from one of the fallen Jaggo. However, some of these attackers managed to disarm Tencum of his spear and rush past to the warlock. But Kiamosh proved unnaturally good at dodging. Shadoo himself made another attempt on the wily warlock with the spear of a deceased Jaggo, but this too, Kiamosh eluded. The warlock sought to reclaim his axe, but as it lay within the bounds of the battle, he soon abandoned it and broke away with Tencum, who hastily grabbed his spear, to continue down the path.

Noting their departure, Okona struggled to reach the edge of the fray. Over and over he jabbed, blocked and dodged, yet his foes were unyielding. And in the midst of all the turmoil, he lost his bow. He was also parted from his daggers, as he thrust these deep into several opponents. At last, with a furious thrust of his spear, he managed to kill one of the Jaggo obstructing him, then duck under several enemy blows to escape the fracas entirely. However the others were now too enmeshed in the thick of things to disengage so easily.

Panting, Okona tore down the path, throwing off his quiver so as to be unencumbered. Shortly, the trail passed along the brink of the cliff, and Okona saw his destination, the Tongue of Tagwash, a thick, gray, outthrust crag suspended a hundred feet above the vale. Beyond it, Shagora Gorge intersected the Valley of the Wakosi three-quarters of a mile to the east. Two thousand feet across the gorge was from north to south, and at its bottom lay a creek trickling down to the Wakosi. A thousand feet west of the Tongue, the gorge turned to run south by southwest, and that way (which was narrower than the section leading toward the Wakosi), it ran on for more than a mile. But the entire vista was centered on the Tongue, and even from where Okona was, he could sense dark enchantment emanating from it.

Only moments after Okona spotted the Tongue, Kiamosh and Tencum emerged from the forest and stepped out onto it. And at that same instant, the higher, taunting drum, which Okona had taken to be Yahsi's, ceased. Now the Jaggo below were able to realign their strokes, and they returned to their slow, relentless thumping.

Okona's heart skipped a beat, as he feared Yahsi had been slain, but he had no choice but to hurry on down the path.

"Now, O Tencum Hand-bringer," Kiamosh announced, "we have come to the place of power. And here I shall draw upon the ancient strength of the Tagwash, upon which we stand, and the magic of Chogrot, the great warlock of old who is interred below. Also, now that our drumming is pure once more, I may be aided by the spirits of the gorge itself. But fear not these powers, for thou art under my protection."

"Raise thou the Hand," he instructed, and Tencum did so. Perfect in form, brilliant and pale-blue it was, glinting in the sun.

Still, the sounds of conflict between the Jaggo and those who had ambushed them echoed through the valley.

"Do not release thy hold upon the Hand until it has been united to my body," the warlock warned, turning his deep, black eyes upon the uneasy Tencum. "For if thou dost, thou shalt perish. Only by my magic once the Hand is my own can I make thee live. For thou knowest that to lose the Hand would bring thee death were it not for my intervention."

"I understand." Tencum nodded.

"Swearest thou that the time of departure from Takula thou hast told me is true? For the joining of the Hand unto me must occur ten days and ten hours after that departure, in addition to the day I offered to the Skaggish."

"I spoke truly, my lord," Tencum replied.

Kiamosh smiled cruelly. "The time has reached its fulness, then."

Just then, Okona rushed out from the trees, calling, "You shouldn't have given that day to the Lord of Shadows, Kiamosh. For now today is your Unlucky Eleventh!"

Tencum stared at him, incredulous, as the color ran from his face.

"I'm not a ghost, Tencum, in case you're wondering," Okona declared.

Kiamosh turned his black gaze upon Okona. "Thou shalt be shortly, cur! Who art thou—thou who wouldst dare speak thus to the Lord of the Wakosi?"

"Okona Song-maker of the Sakooma, one of those sent to retrieve the Hand of Hamora. For it is to the Sakooma it rightfully belongs."

Kiamosh snorted. "The Hand, like power itself, belongs to whoever can take it. And if thou wishest to seize it, let us see thy prowess!"

"You don't stand a chance, Okona," said Tencum, fingering his spear.

"Kill him now," Kiamosh commanded, "that we may proceed."

"I cannot be slain by a mere spear now that I have passed through death," Okona asserted, hoping his bluff would, at the very least, buy him some time. "For you saw, O Tencum, what it was I faced and conquered. And if you try to kill me, death shall come back on you tenfold."

Tencum hesitated.

"This is all idle smoke," Kiamosh scoffed. "Heed him not."

Tencum remained unsettled.

"You have betrayed your own people, Tencum," Okona charged, "and in so doing, lost yourself. What do you think to gain by joining this madman?"

"He shall have the favor of the most powerful sorcerer in Sarkanna and be made regent of the Sakooma under my governance," said Kiamosh. "And together, we shall conquer lands far beyond the Kanno and spread the glories of the mighty Skaggish. And what hopest *thou* to gain if thou shouldst prevail, Song-peddler?"

"Peace for myself and my people. For what more could one ask?"

"Much," Tencum snapped.

"Do you really think the Sakooma would suffer your leadership, knowing you betrayed them?" Okona pressed.

"They bowed to Hamora quickly enough, usurper though he was," Kiamosh rejoined.

The warlock studied Okona's face. "Knowest thou of this already? Strange. Long has it been forgotten among the Sakooma."

"My allegiance is not to Hamora," Okona asserted, striving to master his troubled expression, "but the Sakooma."

"Bah!" Kiamosh spat. "What are the Sakooma but Hamora's fawning toads!"

"Tencum," Okona pleaded, "do you not realize what you have done? The heavens themselves will surely rain vengeance if you do not turn. For the Sakooma, along with every tribe under the sun, have always held that traitors are doomed."

"You're a fool, Okona," returned Tencum, scowling, "and you should never have come here. Remember, you weren't even chosen to set out."

"I was—by Mahna Shuya himself. And I believe he himself will strike you down."

Tencum raised his spear skyward and cried, "Let him try! If the heavens are against me, why was I allowed to take the Hand in the first place? And why were we permitted to bring this thing to the very brink? I defy both the heavens and Mahna Shuya! Kiamosh has done so for centuries now, and yet he lives. Even without the Hand, he is more powerful than you'll ever be. You cannot defeat us, and you know this. Perhaps you have passed through death. But still you are no warrior nor magician. What can you do to oppose us? Warble on your flute?"

In a single, rapid motion, Okona snatched up a stone from the ground and hurled it at Tencum, striking his wrist, so that he dropped the Hand of Hamora.

"I would have struck your head, Tencum, and ended you now," snarled Okona, "but for the sake of Anisha. For she loved you once, and there was a time when you were a good man. But now you are as good as in the bowels of the Underbrakes."

"Enough!" Kiamosh roared. "Take up the Hand, Tencum, and place it where it belongs."

The speed of the Jaggo's drumming suddenly increased, and the pattern became more varied.

Before Okona had a chance to rush forward, Tencum pressed the Hand of Hamora against the nub at the end of Kiamosh's right arm. But, to the astonishment of all, nothing happened. Tencum pressed the Hand again, this time harder.

"It works not thus, thou fool!" growled Kiamosh, shoving him away. "Something is amiss. The Oolasheg promised that at this time, at this very place, *they* would provide the power needed to affix the Hand."

"The Oolasheg are under no obligation to keep their promise if thou keepest not thine own," a voice called. It was Lanoka, who had just joined Okona near the entrance of the Tongue. Fell was her gaze, which was fixed defiantly upon her father.

"What?!" Kiamosh bellowed. "Is this thy doing, Song-boy?"

"Where is Anisha?" Okona whispered.

"Alas, we were separated in flight as Jaggo pursued us," Lanoka whispered back.

"I said is this thy doing, Song-boy!" Kiamosh roared once more.

"Yes," Lanoka answered. "Okona is my deliverer. And he hath shown more courage than ever thou hast. Ever lurkest thou in caves and hollows beyond the reach of men, while thou sendest beasts, warriors and spirits to keep the world at bay. Hamora was right to call thee coward."

"Hamora!" Kiamosh raged. "Speak on his behalf again and thy peril shall be great indeed!"

"I speak not for him, for he was both coward and villain. But thou hast exceeded him in both measures. In all thy long life, thou hast degraded thyself ever further. It was not enough for thee to spill the blood of thousands. Thou wouldst have had thy own daughter devoured to have thy aims! Thou hast committed countless atrocities against heaven and men, drunken man-blood, made pacts with the darkness, lying prostrate before Crones and Shadows, all for the sake of power. But thy beloved Skaggish and Oolasheg cannot save from the terror that awaits such as thee! Someday it will come to them as well, for Sun must conquer Moon."

"Blasphemy!" Kiamosh's fury grew uncontainable. "Insolence and blasphemies! And thou, Lanoka, knowest it is a lie; Moon shall conquer Sun, for he is stronger."

"Such foolishness hast thou repeated enough to at last believe it. It was the Skaggish who was driven from the Over-lands, not he who drove out Mahna Shuya. And in all the ages, he has never regained that land; and even all his mighty efforts to fight Sun here make no mark upon Mahna Shuya himself. That is why thou, even as the Skaggish, must dwell ever in fear! But call now upon the abominations thou servest and see if they will save thee. Yet know all thy schemes have been unwoven by the rescuing of a mere maid."

Hot blood poured into Kiamosh's face, and he clenched his fist with such force that his knuckles grew pale. "Death is too good for thee, wretched child! What madness hath turned thee into such an insufferable brat?"

"Save thy breaths, sapless churl," Lanoka mocked. "For few are left to thee. Thou shouldst do well to simply toss the Hand over the brink, for it is useless to thee now. Aye, thou hast not the power to join it to thyself. Indeed, what art thou without the Oolasheg?"

Kiamosh's face hardened, and he hissed, "Thou knowest well my power is great."

"Not greater than that of Shakeega, and even she would not have been foolish enough to attempt uniting the Hand to herself without great aid."

"My magic has exceeded her own," Kiamosh retorted, "and I *shall* have the Hand even if the Oolasheg assist me not."

The fervor of the Jaggo's drumming increased, and the rhythms became even wilder than before.

"To attempt the magic alone will slay thee!" Lanoka warned. "Seeking power that was never meant to be one's own is what slew Shakeega. But if thou art so much greater than she, then prove it."

"No!" Okona protested. "Do not provoke him! Once he has the Hand—"

"Show us who thou art, Kiamosh," Lanoka demanded. "King or coward?"

His face contorted in wrath, Kiamosh seized Tencum's arm that was grasping the Hand of Hamora and moved it toward the end of his own handless arm.

"Kiamosh shall show ye!" he screamed, as piercing, blue beams of light erupted from the Hand.

Accompanied by the continuing tumult of battle from afar, the earth shuddered, the air crackled, and the relentless drumming of the Jaggo became a continuous rumbling. As Okona stared in horror, a pale light gleamed from the moonstone ring upon Kiamosh's left hand. Tiny cracks appeared in its gem, as licking, blue flames shot out from it and over to the Hand of Hamora.

With a rending crash, a bolt of bright, blue fire roared down from the sky and struck the Hand. Okona and Lanoka, tumbling backward, raised their arms to shield their eyes. When they had gained their feet again, Tencum was lying upon the ground moaning, and Kiamosh stood before them with both arms bared and his right wrist neatly joined to the pale-blue, crystalline Hand of Hamora, which was giving off a sickly glow. But his face was grown twisted, as if soundness of mind had departed. Sallow now was his skin, and his eyes windows into an abyss.

"See what he hath done?" Lanoka whispered. "Look upon his ring. He may have power, but he will not last long. And every use of the Hand shall only drain him more. Thus it is with all dark magic."

Kiamosh raised his hands to the sky and said in a hollow voice. "Behold ye Kiamosh, ruler of all Sarkanna! Behold him who hath the fury of air, terror of water and strength of earth."

He looked upon Tencum, still stricken upon the ground, and said, "Hark, O Tencum! Thy life is now sustained by me. Thou hast chosen well. See now what becomes of the enemies of Kiamosh."

In the valley below, the Jaggo's drumming broke out of the rumble and passed into a pattern swift and savage.

"Air first!" Kiamosh shouted. "I call upon the wind, my own wind, to banish my enemies!"

At once, a fierce gale commenced, driving against Okona and Lanoka. Kiamosh laughed scornfully, as they were pushed back toward the trees. However, Lanoka latched onto a tree trunk, and Okona threw himself to the ground, managing to grab a thick root before he was thrust far into the forest. However, his spear was snatched by the gale and blown back into the woods. Grunting, he strove to drag himself toward Kiamosh, going hand over hand upon the root.

"Thou wishest to come to me?" Kiamosh taunted. "So be it!"

Immediately, the wind reversed direction, but both Lanoka and Okona held fast. Tencum's spear rattled off the Tongue and plummeted into the valley below, but Tencum yet clung to the rock, crying, "My lord, what are you doing?"

"If thou art strong enough to serve me, thou wilt withstand the wind and prove thy worth."

"Be warned, Kiamosh! Thy end is near!" Lanoka hollered, clasping her tree ever tighter.

"Nay, thine!" Kiamosh declared, as the wind increased in strength and fury.

Lanoka dropped to her knees and used a system of roots to crawl deeper into the forest. Meanwhile, Okona was seeking his own means of escape when a vine plopped down next to him. He looked up to see Anisha standing some feet farther into the woods, holding to a tree with one hand and the vine with the other.

"Come on!" she urged.

Okona quickly grabbed the vine and crawled toward her. When he reached her, he found he was past where the wind originated, so he rose, and together they pressed farther into the forest. Kiamosh, himself immune to the wind and too drunk on his newfound power to notice their departure, had been looking skyward, crying out in exultation in some peculiar language over the tumult of the Jaggo's drumming.

"Ah, but there is more," Kiamosh crowed. "The terror of water is also mine!" He held up his right hand to the sky and closed his fist. Within moments, the sky began to darken, and where the air had once been clear and cloudless, grim thunderheads rose.

He turned then toward the forest, and, seeing that Lanoka and Okona were gone, he cried, "Fled have ye? Ye cannot hide from the power of Kiamosh."

Soon, storm clouds had swallowed up the valley. Rain came in heavy sheets, and with great crashes, streaks of lightning sprang into the forest behind the Tongue. Thrice they hit only several yards away from the fleeing Okona and Anisha.

"I don't know if he can control those things," Okona panted, "but we're not going to last much longer here even if he can't. You go on. Go back the way we came. I want to make at least one more attempt to stop him."

"I'm not leaving you," Anisha insisted, flinging her drenched hair out of her eyes.

Just then, Kiamosh's wind rushed once more, and both were knocked off their feet. It dragged them several yards before they were able to catch a tangle of exposed roots and resist the gale.

Then Okona spotted, back west down the path, several Jaggo battling with warriors from the ambush. But two of each party were caught by the wind and blown over the precipice, screaming. And one of the Jaggo still atop the bluff was struck by a burst of lightning.

Suddenly, Anisha's hands slipped from her root, and she was pulled along by the gale toward the cliff. Okona quickly released his own hold and was dragged after her. Just as she was flung off the edge of the bluff, Okona caught her hand, and he himself seized a sturdy root only just in time.

"Hold on!" he cried, striving with all his might against the tempest. He knew he would lose his grip in but a few moments, and he could see awareness of this growing in Anisha's terrified eyes.

Unexpectedly, the wind ceased, though the rain and lightning drove on, accompanied by the frantic drumming of the Jaggo.

Anisha's dangling feet found the side of the cliff, and Okona hurriedly pulled her up.

"Watch out!" Anisha cried, as she gained the brink.

Two Jaggo were stumbling toward them.

Anisha flung one of her daggers at the chest of one and then sprang forward, plunging her second dagger into his breast, while Okona punched the other's snarling face. The Jaggo staggered onward, seeking to retaliate. However, the Sakooma pulled aside, as both their foes lurched forward, grasped vainly at them and plummeted off the cliff.

"Something's happening to them," Anisha said. "That shouldn't have been so easy."

"They're getting frailer," Okona exclaimed. "Of course! Their lives are tied to Kiamosh's ring, and he's greatly weakened it by putting on the Hand without the help of the Sisters."

Suddenly, there was a high, terrible shriek. A dreaded and by now familiar shape was speeding through the storm, heading directly for them.

"I thought that thing could only stay over rivers," Anisha gasped.

They whirled to flee into the forest, but Anisha tripped almost immediately upon the uneven ground. Okona bent to help her up but knew it would be too late now to escape the ganoja.

But just then, a spear sailed through the air and lodged in the ganoja's breast. Flailing, the monster crashed mightily into the side of the cliff. With an unearthly wail, it plunged onto sharp stones in the valley below.

Okona and Anisha looked up through the rain, gasping, to Wunko standing before them.

"Oh, Wunko!" Anisha cried joyously.

Okona smiled. "What a tale that will make! Wunko the Ganoja-slayer!"

Wunko hurried forward and helped them to their feet. "What in the Three Realms is going on?! It's as if all the vilest vaults of the Underbrakes have cracked open."

"Kiamosh has taken the Hand," said Okona, "and with it he's brought this storm and the wind that keeps tearing through here."

"Is he responsible for those also?" Wunko pointed to the blackening squall over the vale.

There, shimmering shreds of dark blue were swooping back and forth amidst the thunderheads. Staring at them in horror, Okona realized they were specters with arms and heads, complete with wide, toothed mouths.

Ever more feverish grew the drumming of the Jaggo, as these wraiths began drifting toward the mortal onlookers. And behind the phantoms appeared a colossal, gray, clouded form, vaguely man-shaped and with glowing red eyes.

"Great wippikats!" Wunko exclaimed, as they began backing away.

But from behind them came a voice, beautiful and clear. It was singing, and the music seemed to be carried on a wind of its own. Okona was astonished to see Yahsi some yards behind them, her hands upraised, as she sang with utter abandon the ode to Mahna Shuya, which he had performed with her at the Song of the Summer

Stars. But this time, the song had not mere melody, but words also, though Okona did not understand them, for they were in a language strange to him.

As Yahsi's song pierced the approaching blackness, the spirits quailed, moaning and raising their wispy arms to cover their faces. The gray giant behind them shook, and the storm itself seemed to waver. And as the music proceeded, the phantasms began to disintegrate into the haze from which they had appeared. Soon, the storm had swallowed them entirely, as the drumming of the Jaggo foundered and fell away into silence.

Without warning, a bitter wind blasted the four atop the bluff, and Yahsi's voice was lost. Each of them grasped a tree to keep from being driven off. Several moments later, the gale died.

The sound of tramping feet came from the northwest, for multiple groups of Jaggo were running toward them.

"Quickly, to the Tongue!" Okona called.

Swiftly, he, Anisha, Wunko and Yahsi raced eastward toward the stone prominence where Kiamosh still stood, commanding the skies.

Okona glanced over his shoulder as he came nigh to the Tongue and spied Shadoo, with many warriors behind him, hurrying to intercept the Jaggo before they could reach Okona and the others. The lad looked forward to the Tongue. Kiamosh was striding to its point, crying out some incantation to the storm clouds. Tencum, though weak-kneed, was standing several yards behind him.

The three Sakooma and the Tikkichaw halted some feet back from the Tongue, and Okona whispered, "They're both almost finished. See! There is a ring upon Kiamosh's hand, and the stone in it is what's keeping him alive—and Tencum too, perhaps. But Kiamosh has nearly broken the stone through what he's done. We need only to get him to finish himself off, and this will all be over. And I've thought of a means to do it. But I want you three to stay back, because it may be very dangerous."

"I at least shall go with you," Wunko insisted. "There ought to be two of us, for there are two of them."

"Wunko, really I—"

"Please, lad." Wunko looked hard at him. "It doesn't matter much to me if my story ends here, only that it ends well."

Okona put his hand on Wunko's shoulder and smiled grimly. "Very well. We both shall go."

"Okona, don't do this," Anisha demanded, grabbing his arm.

"I must," Okona firmly returned. "I love you, Anisha. More than anything. And I would never forgive myself if you perished on my account. If all else comes to ruin, I wish that you at least might be saved."

"Heed him, Anisha," Yahsi declared. "Let not his peril be in vain."

Reluctantly, Anisha drew back with Yahsi, as the old woman pulled her farther into the trees.

Blinding sheets of rain pounded Okona and Wunko, as they stepped onto the Tongue. Wunko pulled out a knife of bone from his belt and offered it to Okona, but the lad closed the Tikkichaw's open fingers around the hilt and said, "You keep it. Hopefully my words will prove sharp enough."

Okona went a few steps farther than Wunko and called, "Lanoka's words shall now prove true, Kiamosh, for in but a moment, death will find you."

Kiamosh whirled around and spat, "Livest thou yet? I should have taken more care to slay thee, I suppose. Hardy art thou. But no hardihood shall save thee from my stormfire." The warlock stretched his hand upward.

"Have a care, Kiamosh!" cried Tencum. "Look at his eyes. He means some trick by this. I know not what, but do not give him what he wants."

Fuming, Kiamosh glared at Tencum. "Asked I for thy doltish counsel? I have nothing to fear from this wretch."

"If it is as you say," taunted Okona, "then finish me off, and be quick about it." His eyes darted to the moonstone upon Kiamosh's finger, which was now almost wholly fractured.

"So, Lanoka has told thee of my secrets, has she?" Kiamosh muttered. "And thou thinkest to wield them against me. Think again! I need no stormfire to slay thee. I have the strength of ten men and shall finish thee with my bare hands. Tencum, see thou to the other."

Tencum moved to obey, as Kiamosh took heavy, purposeful steps toward Okona. Meanwhile, Wunko took several quick steps back and to the right so as to give Okona more room to maneuver.

"What? Hast thou no more arrogant talk?" jeered Kiamosh, as Okona, too, began backing away.

Suddenly, Okona felt a slight warming at his waist. He reached into the pocket of his breeches and felt the angled surface of the shard of sunfire.

"I will risk no hurt to the Hand," he thought. "But if Kiamosh is persuaded I might ..."

Swiftly, he drew out the shard.

At once, Kiamosh halted. Seeing this, Tencum did likewise. Wunko gave Okona a quizzical look.

"Sun shall conquer Moon," Okona said menacingly. "If you come any closer, Kiamosh, your life is ended."

"How came that to thee?" Kiamosh demanded, his face paling.

"It was gift, a gift for this very hour." Okona took a bold step forward.

For a moment, Kiamosh wavered. But then he grew more ferocious than before and hissed, "Thy trinket will not save thee, boy. One strike of my hand and thy body is broken. And think, too, upon this: if thou shouldst perchance destroy the Hand, how shall thy beloved Sakooma fare?"

Now it was Okona who wavered. But the lad knew he must cast his decision without delay. A fiery abandon rose within him, as he replied, "Perhaps they will come to ruin. But if you are not slain this very day, a fate still worse will befall them. So I will gladly bear the cost of destroying the Hand if but you may be forever vanquished. So come, Kiamosh. I am ready!"

"So be it, wretch," Kiamosh growled.

Tencum rushed forward and grappled with Wunko, quickly disarming him of his knife. This clattered onto the Tongue, and Tencum kicked it out toward the point. Meanwhile, Okona and Kiamosh remained several yards apart, circling perilously. Okona knew he would have to make a move soon or else he would be trapped near the tip or one of the sides of the Tongue. But he was terrified of coming within Kiamosh's reach, so he racked his mind for some means of gaining an advantage against the cunning warlock, who was rubbing the fingers of his right hand together, as if he were going to wield its magic at any moment.

Abruptly, Kiamosh leapt forward and swung his fist, only narrowly missing Okona, who ducked. Several times, Kiamosh made attempts on the lad, but each time he avoided them. Meanwhile, Wunko and Tencum were locked in combat. The normally brawny Tencum, weakened by his link to the ailing magic of Kiamosh, only just managed to match Wunko's strength.

Okona was now rather close to the jagged end of the Tongue and had just dodged another one of Kiamosh's swipes when he saw Lanoka running toward him with a great stone axe. "Cut off his hand!" she shouted, flinging the axe toward his feet.

Tencum thrust Wunko from him and hurried to snatch the axe, which had landed some feet behind Kiamosh and thus out of Okona's reach. But Okona dove past Kiamosh, only by an inch evading the grasp of the warlock, who tripped and fell in his effort.

Yet Okona came too late, for Tencum had already seized the weapon and was preparing to bring it down upon him.

Just then, Anisha bolted out of the forest, her arm raised in protest, and cried, "No, Tencum! Please! No!"

Tencum hesitated, as Okona stood and held out his shard toward Kiamosh, who had also sprung to his feet. Anisha raced onto the Tongue, her arm still extended, and Wunko hastened to stand near Tencum, yet just beyond the range of an axestroke.

"Why heedest thou this stupid, meddling wench?" yelled Kiamosh. Snatching up Wunko's idle knife, which lay near his feet, he cried. "Die, waif, for thy interference!"

With horrific force, he flung the dagger at her breast. But just as it reached her, there was a flash and a crack, and the weapon shattered into ten thousand fragments. Anisha cried out in pain, as the bracelet upon her wrist began glowing like fire.

Kiamosh turned his dark eyes upon Anisha's outstretched hand, and they narrowed with repugnance as they locked upon the silver dangling there.

"Thou! Thou art the heiress of Hamora." He stepped toward her, as the light of her bracelet faded away.

"Kill her not!" cried Tencum ardently. "She is the one I love, the one you promised me."

"So thou art Anisha, daughter of the Sanno," Kiamosh said with terrifying malevolence. "The hated blood of Hamora runs in thee. Thou art his final living heir, and in slaying thee, I shall finally keep my vow to that black-souled brother of mine."

With an eldritch cry, he raised his Hand skyward, and the heart of the storm crackled and glowed, as did the Hand. But Tencum sprang forward, roaring, and swung the axe through the driving rain, hewing Kiamosh's wrist. A rush of unseen potency burst in all directions from Kiamosh, accompanied by a deafening crack, a boom and a blinding flash of blue light. Okona, Anisha, Wunko and Lanoka were thrust to the ground, as the Hand of crystal dropped to the tip of the Tongue, and Kiamosh screamed, tumbled backward and was lost over the brink. With a heartrending cry, Tencum crumpled to the ground.

Part IV:
Music with Words

Paths of the Powers

OKONA, CHEST HEAVING, LAY prostrate upon the Tongue, with rain pelting his back. Strangely frail he felt, but at last he managed to lift his head. The tumult over the valley was breaking up and the rain softening to a drizzle, as a bold shaft of sun pierced the rack to beam upon the Tongue. Far above, a lone eagle circled the golden ray, then glided away southeast.

The lad pushed himself up to a crouching position, then turned to Anisha. With some difficulty, he crawled over to her stricken form and laid his hand upon her shoulder. She stirred and looked up at him.

"Are you all right?" Okona panted.

"More or less," she weakly replied, "though that last bit was rather rough."

Grunting, Okona rose to his feet and looked around. Wunko was aiding Lanoka to her feet, and Yahsi was approaching from the forest. After a deep breath of the clearing air, Okona grabbed Anisha's hand and pulled her up.

"Thank you," she said.

"No. Thank you," Okona returned, "for saving my life. I am deeply in your debt."

"All Sarkanna is in yours. That was a tremendous thing you did, you know, confronting Kiamosh like that. Yours may not have been the hand that slew him, but without you, he would not have been slain."

"The same could be said for all of us here," said Okona. He looked at each of his companions in turn, then at Tencum's fallen form. "But alas, he who did slay him will rise no more."

"Has he departed, then?" asked Wunko.

Anisha went and stooped to examine Tencum, who lay face-down. Laying her hand upon his back, she sat motionless for some time. At last, she muttered, "He has."

By now, the clouds had almost fully dissipated, and the valley was as it had been before the tempest, save that there was a lingering damp and a lush rainbow arced across the heavens.

"And what of Kiamosh?" Yahsi inquired.

Okona carefully approached the knifed tip of the Tongue, then bent and looked down. At the edge of the forest, upon a jumbled collection of rocks, lay Kiamosh's splayed, one-handed corpse.

"He too is slain," Okona announced.

He looked at Anisha. "But how are you not dead as well? That dagger was aimed right at your heart."

"I'm just as baffled as you," she replied. "But though not dead, I do have a rather nasty burn." She held forth her wrist.

Lanoka, approaching them, said, "Anisha, I knew not thou wert the daughter of the Sanno! For in my presence, my father never uttered thy name; only 'the Sanno's daughter' did he name thee. As we came hither, I never looked upon thy bracelet closely, but if I had, I would have known it at once. Okona, sawest thou not her bracelet aglow? Therein lies the secret; she weareth Bashula's Bangle."

"Bashula's Bangle?" Anisha repeated quizzically.

"An enchanted heirloom of the House of Hamora. Since Kiamosh swore to kill Hamora, those he loved and all of his descendants, Hamora was very worried about the safety of his family, particularly his daughter and heiress, Bashula. As he himself had already paid dearly for the Hand, he urged his wife Aloobish to make her own pact and get protection for herself and their daughter from the Matora—thy pardon, the Western Thunder. This she did, swearing fealty to the Western Thunder and the Lord of Shadows. For this pledge, she received Bashula's Bangle, dubbed thus in honor of her daughter. Very powerful it is, for it protects from any weapon made by the hand of man, save be it wrought of black canoba wood, for against such the Western Thunder hath no power. That is why the dagger killed thee not, Anisha. But as with all magic, the Bangle came with a cost. Though it doth preserve the life of the wearer, its use scarreth the one who wears it."

"I suppose it's better to be scarred than dead," remarked Anisha. Peering at her wrist, she added, "Ah, and now I understand why it has this engraving of a winged bear and lightning. That has always puzzled me."

Lanoka continued, "Aloobish bequeathed this bracelet to her daughter, Bashula, who passed it on to her daughter, and so forth, down through the centuries, for each of these was the direct heir of Hamora. For Aloobish had warned her daughter that Kiamosh might return even from the Underbrakes to seek Hamora's heirs, so she and those who came after her should always be protected against him."

"How is it that you know this lore and I do not?" inquired Anisha. "I should think it would be the sort of thing my mother would have told me."

"Undoubtedly she would have in her own time. But likely she said nothing of it before she died because she thought thee too young to be troubled about being haunted by some blood-bent relative of old. But as for me, I heard the Bangle's lore from Kiamosh, and he such from the Western Thunder himself. From him also he learned of the Bangle's weakness against the peculiar canoba wood of the central Kannitaw. This is why the Jaggo always carry weapons and especially arrows made of it, for they hoped to someday obtain the bracelet for Kiamosh if one of Hamora's heiresses could be caught outside Takula. For he learned also from the Western Thunder that it was Aloobish's intention that it should pass down Hamora's direct daughter-line through the ages."

Anisha looked sadly at her bracelet. "I have often thought that if my mother had brought this with her, she wouldn't have died that day. But to know that it wouldn't have saved her anyhow ..."

Looking up, she inquired, "Lanoka, did Tencum know of the bracelet's secret?"

"Not to my knowledge. Or at least, he was not aware of its specific power, even though he knew there was some enchantment about it. Aye, for my father charged him to obtain it for him in exchange for further reward. Tencum revealed to Kiamosh that he desired to marry thee and believed thou wouldst give him the Bangle as a betrothal gift if thou wouldst accept his proposal. And Kiamosh emboldened Tencum by vowing that he would ensure thou wouldst be his wife if but Tencum would do as he asked. But of course, Kiamosh had no intention of keeping this promise, for he wished thee dead."

Okona, glancing at the lifeless warrior, said, "Tencum fell immediately after cutting off the Hand. Was his life bound to it, then?"

"Very likely," Lanoka answered, "but it was bound also to Kiamosh's ring, I'd wager. When Kiamosh lost the Hand, both his magic and his life failed. And with his perishing, all those sustained by the ring will have perished as well. Tencum here lieth, and all the Jaggo and Kiamosh's bear guards will have died also."

At that moment, out from the eaves of the wood behind Yahsi advanced Shadoo with Orobec and some of his men, along with a number of others.

"Shadoo!" those upon the Tongue exclaimed in unison.

"Oh, you were marvelous!" cried Anisha, rushing toward him with the rest of the companions.

"Shadoo couldn't be happier to see all of ye!" the old Babora laughed. "For after our unfortunate parting at Kahlit Creek, I thought I'd never see ye two again. But here ye are! Kiamosh is done for, I presume? For his accursed stormcloud has lifted."

"You presume correctly," Wunko said. "The villain lies vanquished in the valley below."

"Oh, happy day!" crowed Shadoo. "Not only the Wakosi, but all Sarkanna is saved. 'Tis the strangest thing, but I'm pleased to announce that all the Jaggo and both monstrous bears are dead too."

"See, it is as I believed," said Lanoka. "Once Kiamosh died, all those kept alive by his ring would perish."

"More magic?" burst out Shadoo. "Right perplexing it all is."

Okona turned to Orobec and exclaimed, "Orobec, how is it that you and your companions are here? And Shadoo, who are these with you? Without all of you and that magnificent ambush, we wouldn't have stood a chance."

Before anyone could respond, Shadoo called out several statements in a foreign tongue, and many of the men behind him closed their eyes. Shadoo then translated his words into Sakooma as, "Beware, all of ye! The Oolasheg approach! Shut your eyes and don't open them until I say so. For if ye should chance to look while they're looking back, ye shall perish!"

In the very edge of Okona's vision, twin flashes, one of white and the other black, sped across the valley from the east, where lay the Wakosi, toward the valley floor beneath the Tongue. Okona shut his eyes tight and waited, listening. An eerie silence fell over the whole vale, and the darkness of closed eyelids grew darker still. But after several minutes, this greater darkness lifted, and the stillness was rent by the far-off screech of an owl.

Shadoo said something, again in another tongue, then rendered it in Sakooma as, "Ye may look upon the world again."

All opened their eyes.

"What were those two doing here?" asked Anisha.

"Look beneath the Tongue," said Lanoka, "and I think ye shall see."

Wunko went to the Tongue's tip and peered down. Clearly disturbed, he looked back at the group and announced, "Why there's hardly anything left of old Kiamosh. Nothing but bones now."

Lanoka said grimly, "I fear I know now what Kiamosh pledged to the Sisters."

"That he should be devoured by them?" asked Okona.

Her only reply was, "The fate of his flesh is far kinder than that of his soul."

An awkward silence followed, but Shadoo soon broke it, declaring, "Okona, you asked who these are who are with me. They're the Faithful Forty of which I told ye, those who swore to come aid me when the time for open battle was at hand. But alas, many have just been slain. Those left to us are the Faithful Fifteen."

"And," said Orobec, "as for how we are here, by strange circumstance I encountered these Forty in the wild, and together we came hither. Later, I'm sure, we shall speak at greater length of how all that came about. But presently, there are sorrows to attend to, for many of them were lost, as your Shadoo said, and five of our Sakooma perished as well."

"Tencum also is slain." Okona gestured to the Tongue.

"Is he?" said Orobec. "Well, Yahsi told us what a traitor he was, as such was discovered by Shadoo's spying yesterday morning. Let's give his corpse the fate it deserves and toss him to his wicked warlock. Come, men!"

At once, Orobec and his men strode out onto the Tongue.

But Okona ran after them, caught Orobec by the shoulder and said, "Please hold, Orobec, and hear me out. Tencum is a black-hearted traitor. This is true, and I will not deny it. But let us at least honor him as the slayer of Kiamosh, for it was he who cut the Hand from him. Yes, he was turned at the last, for Kiamosh sought to slay Anisha, but Tencum loved her yet. Also, I ask that we honor him for the good he once accomplished among the Sakooma. For you know, as I do, that he did many valiant deeds for the sake of our people. So I do not ask that we honor him for what he is but what he once was and what he did at the last."

Orobec stared pensively at Tencum's corpse. For some time, he did not respond. But finally, he sighed, "Very well. We shall not cast his body as carrion nor shall he be food for the forest like the Jaggo. But we have no proper tools, nor a suitable place to bury him. And we can ill afford the time it would take. For these reasons, even others more honorable than he shall be given to a pyre and not earth."

"Then let his body also be burned and his remains cast in this valley where he died," Okona suggested.

"So be it," Orobec declared. "But he shall be burned separate from our comrades, for they should not be sullied by his remains. But we will burn him first for no other reason than that it was he who slew Kiamosh."

Lanoka had joined them upon the Tongue, and, out near its tip, she picked up the axe that had hewn off Kiamosh's Hand.

"Oh, how could I have forgotten!" cried Okona. "The Hand! That's what all this was about, after all." He looked by Lanoka's feet, puzzled, and said, "But where is it?"

All nearby looked around anxiously.

"By the Powers, no!" Orobec gasped.

Okona turned and followed Orobec's gaze back to the entrance of the Tongue. There stood Anisha, with Tencum's hunting bag, holding the Hand of blue crystal.

"Nooooo!" Okona screamed. He fell to his knees, and all the Sakooma were aghast, as they stared at the girl. But Anisha stood, unmoved and expressionless.

Okona rose, rushed to her and cried, "Oh, Anisha, why didn't I tell you? Why didn't I tell you? Whoever touches the Hand and then releases it or has it taken from his possession shall die. Now, if you place it back in the Mound to restore the Sakooma, you will perish. But if you keep it, then our people are destined for disaster. Cruel are the Paths of the Powers! Cruel is the road they have laid!"

"Okona," Anisha gently replied, "I knew all this already, for I overheard my father speaking to some men about it the day before I left Takula. I know what I have done, and I have intended all along to value the interests of the Sakooma above my own. That is why, when everyone had their eyes closed, I went and took the Hand.

But also, to give my life would spare another. You see, I had to take it before you did."

Okona again sank to his knees, then buried his face in his hands and wept.

While yet on the Tongue, Anisha placed the Hand in Tencum's bag, which she slung over her shoulder. No one spoke any further to her about the matter, for none knew what to say. However, as her doom remained foremost in many of their minds, a gray solemnity gathered and hung over the whole company, even Shadoo's Babora comrades, to whom he had explained the matter. Okona himself was too numb to reflect coherently, and Anisha was overtaken by a quiet melancholy. Thus, neither spoke any word to each other for quite some time.

After singing several hymns of praise to the Powers for their victory, Orobec's men lifted Tencum's body, and they, with the rest of the company, went a mile and a half northwest back up the trail by which they all had come. Along this stretch, Okona, Anisha and Lanoka retrieved their packs from where they had set them, and Shadoo's and Orobec's men gathered several useful items from the slain Jaggo. Also, the living lovingly positioned the hands of their deceased comrades upon their breasts.

When the company came to the start of the trail, they continued around a half-mile north along the summit of Kidara Mountain. (This summit ridge ran for several miles from southwest to northeast.) And there they stopped at a small clearing, where Orobec and his men laid Tencum, for they and the Faithful Forty, prior to the ambush, had stowed their gear in another clearing close by. There it was watched over by the Wise-woman Shoroba, who had accompanied Orobec to the Wakosi; however, knowing she would have contributed little to the ambush, she stayed in the clearing so she might still bring warning to Takula if the battle went ill.

When the matter of collecting fuel for the pyres arose, Lanoka informed the troop that Kiamosh had large stores of wood in the area, for he had several sacrificial altars atop Kidara Mountain. She thought that, all told, there would be sufficient stock to adequately burn all thirty-one bodies of their fallen.

"Long have Kiamosh's stores been used for vile purposes," said she, "but at last they may be put to some honorable use."

Due to the heavy toll the day had taken, Shadoo recommended that only Tencum's pyre be erected that night, since it would be the smallest. Then, the following day, they could retrieve the rest of the bodies and start building their pyres as well. All were agreeable to this plan, so they followed Lanoka to the stashes of wood and began constructing Tencum's pyre in the clearing where his body lay. Okona labored at this task with particular devotion, for he found it a welcome distraction from his tormented swirl of thoughts about Anisha. The girl herself remained largely stoic, though now and then he caught glimpses of the crushing anguish that lay hid behind her brittle mask of quietude.

As the work went on, the afternoon melted away, and the sky changed to sweeping red. But at last, all was made ready. Okona, Anisha, Yahsi and all the other Sakooma moved their hands across Tencum's body, from his head to his feet, then did the same to themselves. Finally, Anisha removed her mother's redstone ring from Tencum's finger. She then pressed her fox necklace into his lifeless hand and closed his cold fingers about it.

Upon the pyre they laid him as the sun was setting in a glorious blaze. As Orobec's men were unable to find any of Tencum's personal weapons (Lanoka explained that Kiamosh would have made him leave these behind to participate in the ceremony on the Tongue), they placed a spear, bow and arrows from their own supply upon his breast. All these had been made at Takula during the daytime and were thus deemed fit to ward off spirits of the Night.

Orobec invoked the grace of the Powers, then set flame to the pile of wood. Dancing flames licked up, as the company sat respectfully upon the grass before the pyre. Okona took out his flute and played a low dirge, and the music echoed mournfully over the mountain.

When he had finished, Anisha sang an old Sakooma lament. Though the song was about Tencum, all were also touched by grief at the nearness of her own parting, for the bag bearing the Hand lay at her side, even as a veritable coil of death hanging about her neck. But also, none could fail to weep at the beauty of her voice and the poignance of the verse, the end of which ran thus:

"Strength broken, life stricken, light swallowed by depths of earth,
Songs ended, mirth stilled, hands limp, eyes sealed forever;
What thou wert is not forgotten; what thou art is lost in the Falls of Time.

We honor thee for deeds done in service of good,
But no more shall kin hear thy footfall,
Nor shall spear flash or arrow sing.

Strange and sad are the Paths of the Powers,
That thou shouldst from us so soon be taken.
But we, frail men, must take the paths we are given.

Shun the shadows, go neither right nor left,
Pass on, tread the bridge, stumbling not,
And may a place for thee be waiting."

When Anisha finished, she too sank to the ground and wept. After she recovered and sat, legs crossed, upon the grass, Okona went and sat beside her, staring at the crackling flames.

As twilight settled more deeply upon the Kannitaw, Lanoka joined Okona and Anisha before the pyre.

"'Tis a great pity his honor was marred so near the end," she sighed.

"Yes. But at least his final deed was noble," said Anisha, gazing at the blaze slowly consuming his body.

"I knew him little," said Lanoka, "but ever he seemed conflicted to me."

"How do you mean?" asked Okona.

"When he reached us with the Hand a few days ago, he was clearly satisfied with his success, but I sensed also he was troubled, even afraid. Strangely, he was cloaked and hooded when he arrived, as one wishing not to be seen. And he insisted on remaining thus until we came to the camp by Kahlit Creek, for by then, he presumably believed Kiamosh's triumph could not be averted."

"You know, we saw him close to the entrance to Korashac, as we told you," remarked Okona. "However, he wasn't at the ceremony there, which we thought was odd."

"He wasn't permitted to attend," Lanoka explained, "for he hadn't gone through the proper rites to enter the Sisters' sacred precincts. Thus, his weapons had to remain by the canoes, and he himself in the camp."

"Why do you think he was by Korashac, then?" asked Anisha.

"Before the ceremony, he had inquired if someone else could be used as a sacrifice instead of me. My father told him in no uncertain terms it must be his own daughter. I perceived in this (and it is only a guess) that Tencum was upset at the thought of me, yet a child, being eaten by the Sisters. Perhaps he snuck down Kahlit Creek to see if he could convince me to run away instead of becoming a sacrifice."

"Maybe he really did mean to do some good there, then," sighed Anisha. "But then he encountered us, and all that was disrupted. He even tried, as I mentioned, to steal my bracelet."

"I am sure he meant to give it to Kiamosh," Lanoka said, "for he had already quite committed to serving him. So while perhaps seeking to do good, he was ensnared by evil. He was, as I said, very conflicted. He wanted to become lord of the Sakooma but did not wish his people to be hurt. He wanted Kiamosh's ceremony to be successful but did not wish for me to be sacrificed. He wanted everything but must have known deep down that if this he should not get, he would get nothing."

"I wonder if Tencum shall make it over the Final Bridge," said Anisha quietly.

"Who but the Powers can say?" Okona said grimly. "In the end, he will take the path they have laid for him."

After a while, everyone departed, save two of Orobec's men who remained behind to tend the pyre. The rest sojourned to the nearby clearing where the company had laid their supplies. There the Faithful Fifteen had made camp and built twin campfires, and around these inviting flames in the darkened forest the company sat and ate a modest dinner.

Yahsi, Wunko and Shadoo wanted to know about Okona and Anisha's adventures, so, together with Lanoka, they related what had befallen them.

When they had finished, Okona inquired, "What about you? What became of you after we separated at Kahlit Creek?"

"Well," said Shadoo, tossing some twigs on the fire, "we snuck after Kiamosh's company to ambush them but soon came upon a large number of Jaggo who had joined them. I knew at once we couldn't battle so many, so I suggested going on to Kiamosh's camp and doing a bit of listening. That I did, and there I learned about your Tencum's traitorous doings and also the place where Kiamosh was going to fix the Hand to himself. So I recommended we get there ahead of him and set up another ambush, for he should probably think himself more secure then than ever and thus be least prepared."

"We went back to Shinnemah's Kitchen for supplies and from there retraced our route from the previous day to where we'd started up the wash leading to the plateau northeast of Sambo Creek. Sambo Creek, ye know, is fed by three washes at that juncture. But instead of following Sambo back downstream, we went west up the westernmost wash of the three to another plateau to keep clear of the Jaggo. Then we journeyed south to Tauboma Bank, where Wunko told me ye had gotten in canoes. And then, wouldn't ye know, a short distance upriver past that, who should we encounter but the Faithful Forty and your Orobec and his men!"

"How fortunate!" exclaimed Anisha. "But how did the Faithful Forty know to come if you never summoned them?"

"Chapimu ..." Shadoo nodded to a tall, lanky Babora sitting next to him.

"Well, miss," said Chapimu, "it's like this. After we met your Yahsi in the wilds near Shakola Kora, we went toward that site to investigate, for she mentioned the Jaggo had chased her from near there, and we wanted to confront them if we could. But by chance, early that same afternoon, we ran into your Orobec and his troop."

"Yes," said Orobec, "for we had heard Yahsi's drum-talk and escaped to the west of Shakola Kora. Anyway, these good Babora told of us their encounter with another Sakooma that morning: our Yahsi. Naturally, the matter of her flight from the Jaggo arose, and we readily discerned these were whom she had been warning about."

Shoroba carried on his account, "Chapimu relayed to us some lore about the Jaggo and their connection to the Wakosi. We in turn told the Babora of our mission, and in discussion, we concluded it was the Jaggo who had stolen the Hand and that they had undoubtedly taken it back to the Wakosi."

Orobec resumed, "The Forty informed us they had pledged to liberate the Wakosi, and, on account of our quest's significance, they took our venture as a sign the time had come for them to enter the Vale and confront the evil there. And by Shoroba's counsel, we all departed at once."

"However," Chapimu said, "we weren't certain where to go within the Vale to look for Shadoo other than to seek Nadula Valley, as he seven years ago told us he would. Unfortunately, we didn't know the exact location of that blessed vale, except that it was along the Wakosi's upper reaches and was marked by three stones. We also remembered ancestrally the general shape of the Upper Wakosi. Happily, that was enough to at least give us some kind of guide."

Chapimu, stooping from the log where he sat, traced a representation of the Upper Wakosi in the dirt.

"We bore northwest to avoid the guardians of Toshigan Hollow, and in this we succeeded but still had to battle several chiborka to pass through the Vale's fences. Also, we were much slowed once we neared the river on account of the unfamiliarity of the territory and in our striving to not be discovered. But we did eventually intersect the Wakosi. And there we sighted the ganoja and were much alarmed, for none of us even knew what it was. We were also wary of the Jaggo, so decided to keep some distance from the river until we had come nearer to its sources."

"Thus, we curved southwest, up onto a plateau a mile or so south of the river, then went due west to encounter the Wakosi closer to its origins. Very nearly we missed Nadula, for we forded the river only a few miles north of it and then continued south along its west bank. But fortunately, Shadoo caught up with us as evening was getting on."

"Aye," said Shadoo. "Anyway, I led them all on to Nadula Valley. That night, we made our plan and collected supplies, setting out early the next morning to reach the Tongue of Tagwash before Kiamosh and his company. Then we arranged everything for the ambush."

"About that ambush ... Yahsi," said Okona, turning to her, "was it you who was drumming to disrupt the Jaggo?"

"It was indeed," Yahsi laughed. "Brought the drum from Nadula I did, though I had to abandon it when some Jaggo came searching. Come to think of it, I've got to retrieve that drum tomorrow."

"How did you know when to start playing?" asked Anisha. "For if you had begun any later, Kiamosh's company would have halted past Shadoo's ambush."

"We had a signal arranged," Yahsi returned, winking at Shadoo.

"I've two hawks," Shadoo explained, "Tiba and Taboba, who normally stay in and around Nadula, but I brought them along and released them at the right moment from high up in the tree to fly over the valley where she could see them farther down the bluffline. I expect they've flown back to Nadula by now."

"Say, Okona, I've a question for you," said Wunko, leaning toward him. "Whatever was it you were holding that had Kiamosh concerned? You know, there at the end of the fight. Some sort of magical device?"

"Oh, that," mumbled Okona. "Well, it was a dagger of sorts, that's all. Nothing special about it, but I think Kiamosh thought there was. He was already a little suspicious about me, since I'd mentioned that I had passed through death, by which I was referring to Korashac Caverns, though I didn't clarify that to Kiamosh."

Okona guessed that none of his close companions, for various reasons, would be fooled by this answer, but he by no means wished to explain how he had chanced the destruction of the Hand. But the thought suddenly occurred to him that if he had gone through with things and actually destroyed the Hand, Anisha's doom would have been avoided. His gut tightened.

From Wunko's expression, the lad discerned he was not convinced by his fib, but the Tikkichaw graciously shrugged it off. "Ah, well, good thinking on your part to play upon his fears. Anyway ... Lanoka, I'm asking you this because you seem the most likely to know about it, but what did Kiamosh blow that horn for? Summoning more Jaggo?"

"No, to call the ganoja," Lanoka replied.

"But how did it come near the Tongue when the river doesn't flow past there?" asked Anisha. "I thought ganojas were restricted to rivers."

"It's not that they can't leave rivers at all," Lanoka replied, "but the less water by which the ganoja travels, the weaker it is. A stream, Chogrot Creek, runs through the valley of the Tongue, but I do not think the ganoja drew its strength from that. Rather, it retained its might by flying in the great rain Kiamosh had conjured, for it had swallowed the whole valley."

After taking a brief draught from his flask, Shadoo rose from his seat and said, "I'm sure we all have many more questions we'd like to discuss tonight, but we really ought to be visiting Slumberwood to be fresh for the deeds of the coming days. Tomorrow, we've many bodies to carry and fires to start building for them. The day following, we can finish up the pyres. And the day after that, Lanoka, as we discussed earlier, I'd like you to guide me and a number of the Faithful Fifteen through the tunnels of Bok Barusha, for we've some defiling of Kiamosh's evil to do. Also, we've got to plunder the treasuries. The rest of ye may go north to Bahska Lawn by the Wakosi and rest while we do so, for we intend to bring treasure back to ye for your aid. Also, ye are all warmly invited—and I hope ye'll attend—to my ordination as rightful chief over the Wakosi Vale."

"Well ..." said Orobec.

"This is really something we ought not to miss," Yahsi candidly declared.

"We do have to be hastening back, but ..."

"It'd mean ever so much," said Okona, "as Shadoo's done a great deal for us."

"All right," said Orobec, rising. "We shall attend, but we'll need to hurry back to Takula with the Hand shortly after."

"Grand!" Shadoo clapped. "That's to be held at Yaroka Falls, and as soon as possible. Grieved am I that the Paths of the Powers have parted us from many of our company and that other misfortunes have come of all this." Here he glanced ruefully at Anisha, whose eyes wandered to the ground. "But those same Paths have also led us to victory great and glorious. Now we must accept what we've been given, both good and bad. Hard and well have ye fought, so sleep magnificently tonight. Ye've certainly earned it."

Soon, all had laid themselves upon the ground near the fires, save Orobec's men who kept vigil by Tencum's pyre and several of the Faithful Fifteen who took watch by the campfires.

The following morning, all the Sakooma in the company took Tencum's charred bones and proceeded back down the trail to the Tongue of Tagwash.

When they reached the Tongue, Orobec said, "Here Tencum of the Mighty Arm fought and died, and here he slew the dread Kiamosh and the Jaggo also. So let his remains here be cast." These were given to Okona and Anisha, who threw them off the Tongue.

Down into the valley the bones clattered, as Anisha said, "Farewell, Tencum."

"Farewell," Okona whispered.

As Once It Was

AFTER YAHSI HAD COLLECTED her drum, the Sakooma returned to the camp on Kidara Mountain. Then all, Sakooma and Babora alike, began in earnest aiding with either the transporting of their stricken comrades' bodies back to the funeral clearing or else the preparation of the pyres there. In these tasks Wunko diligently aided for the sake of his companions. When Okona inquired about his plans, he said he intended to stay in the Wakosi Vale at least until Shadoo's ordination, though was undecided where he would go after that.

It was long, hard and thoroughly unpleasant work, but by day's end, all the corpses had been brought to the clearing, and a good start had been made on the pyres. Also, Lanoka had guided some of the party to a nearby supply station of the Jaggo, from which they obtained many foodstuffs to add to the camp's provender.

The next morning, they continued construction of the pyres, but the whole day was spent ere the bodies were all atop these and flames set to wood. Songs were sung in both Sakooma and Babora, and great was the mourning but also the praise heaped upon the departed. When the funerary ceremonies had ended, all slept once more on Kidara Mountain, save those attending the pyres.

The following day at dawn, the remains of the fallen were placed in a heap at the edge of the clearing and covered with stones. Shortly thereafter, Shadoo, Lanoka and eight of the Faithful Fifteen departed for Kiamosh's lair of Bok Barusha, which lay only three and a half miles south by southeast of the camp. However, on account of the terrain, they were obliged to take a somewhat longer way around to the west.

All the others, including Okona, gathered their effects and headed north along the summit of Kidara Mountain until they reached its end. It was five and a half miles all told before they had descended the mountain and halted upon a green lawn, dotted with pleasant shade trees, on the west bank of the Wakosi. This was the Bahska Lawn of which Shadoo had spoken. And here they made camp.

Later in the afternoon, Okona was struck by a solitary mood, for Anisha's fate weighed heavily on him. So he milled about the lawn for a while, cast stones in the river and wandered aimlessly in the woods. As he was crossing Bahska Lawn on the way back to camp, he spied Yahsi standing alone under a tall oak.

"Hello," he mumbled, as he walked up to her.

"How do you fare, Okona?" she asked.

"The last few days have been hard. And today's not been much easier. It's really a pity because I should be overjoyed that Kiamosh is slain and the Hand regained, but the whole business with Anisha ..."

"Anisha meant to do what she did. It was something she had intended all along."

"I know," Okona sighed. "But if only I'd taken the Hand right away, then—"

"Then your days would be numbered and few," Yahsi finished.

"Better me than her," Okona sullenly replied.

For some time, they stood side by side, gazing silently at the gray-green waters of the river.

Then Okona said, "Yahsi, I know I've said this several times the past few days, but I can't thank you enough for saving us from those terrible spirits. What were they anyway?"

"Lanoka and I spoke about them several days ago. The great, gray one was the Tagwash and the smaller ones spirits of the valley itself."

"Lanoka also mentioned some warlock that Kiamosh was going to try to draw upon. Was he not present?"

"Chogrot? No, for as Lanoka tells it, he's gone to the Under-brakes, just as has Pamori, the hero who slew him. But Chogrot is certainly having the poorer time of the two."

"How were you able to drive all those spirits off with your singing? Also, what prompted you to sing?" Okona inquired. "The tune I recognized, of course, but I never knew it had words. Yet none of them could I understand."

"Their retreat was the song's doing, not mine," Yahsi explained. "For it contains the great tale of Mahna Shuya, of which those spirits hate and fear the proclamation. As for what inspired me to sing, I can only say that I was strongly moved to do so, perhaps by the song itself or the one whom it honors. The song speaks of the world-making of Mahna Shuya, man's exile from the west, and most importantly, the promise of Mahna Shuya's deliverance. For there is an express hope that the estate of man may someday be as once it was, that he may be restored to joy and purity. But there is also much sorrow in the melody because it relates how we must languish in exile until Mahna Shuya is ready for such deliverance to unfold. A wind came, almost certainly from Kiamosh, and silenced me before I finished the song, but thankfully even what I sang was sufficient to terrify the spirits. Also, the reason you could not understand it was that it was in the forgotten speech, not uttered for nearly three thousand years, from which Sakooma and many other tongues have descended, the head of the river from which many streams have flowed."

"If the words are as ancient as all that," said Okona, "how did you come to learn them?"

"The Seer. For that was the matter I stayed to inquire about. I always felt certain the ode must have words, and it troubled me that I knew them not. I thought he might well know them, and he did. In fact, he produced a harp and performed the entire ode for me. And when he had finished, he explained the words and their meaning. By some magic, they were locked into my mind, and I have not forgotten them since."

A gentle breeze played through the boughs above, and Okona half-wondered if there were traces of Yahsi's song in it. He thought about inquiring exactly what the words to the song were but decided such would be more proper for her to share of her own initiative.

"Okona," said Yahsi.

He looked over at her.

"When you were on the Tongue, you drew out something that gave Kiamosh pause; Wunko mentioned it the evening of the battle. By my eye, it was the shard of sunfire, was it not?"

"It was," Okona admitted, blushing. "I felt it heating up in my pocket, and when I took it out, it was all aglow."

"What about it alarmed him?"

"It, uh ... well ..."

Yahsi looked at him steadily.

"It has the power to destroy the Hand," Okona sighed. "I learned as much from Lanoka, though she didn't know I had a shard of sunfire with me. For several days now, I've wondered whether I oughtn't to have destroyed the Hand after all, for then Anisha wouldn't be consigned to death. But then again, the whole of the Sakooma would be destined for ruin if I'd done so."

"The Seer said you'd know what to do with the shard when the time came. Do you think perhaps its awakening was signaling that such was its time?"

Okona shifted uncomfortably. "You believe I've missed it, then? Well, I can't very well destroy the Hand now, for both Anisha *and* the Sakooma would be lost. But why should the Seer have meant for me to destroy the Hand at all? I simply can't believe he would have had me intentionally unmake the very object of all our efforts. Maybe all I was supposed to do was use it to ward off Kiamosh."

"I think if you really *knew* what you were meant to do with it you wouldn't be guessing."

A troubled look crossed Okona's face. "Perhaps not."

Yahsi laid a hand on his back and said, "Remember, the Seer said it would only prove of real use once you truly understand from whence all good things come. If you understand that already, I am certain you will soon know what you must do with it."

She gave him an encouraging look, then walked off toward the camp.

Okona lingered under the oak a while, pondering her words, then went to the river and washed himself, after which he returned to the camp with the others.

Night came, and they supped. Then all went to bed, save a few of Orobec's and Shadoo's men, who kept guard in case chiborka or other hostile creatures should come along.

The companions spent much of the following day mingling about the lush green of Bahska Lawn. The weather was fair and the temperature mild, and the Wakosi babbled happily. But Okona was still mantled with gloom and spoke little to anyone, especially Anisha, for every hour his regret of not destroying the Hand grew. But whenever guilt settled upon him, he would chide himself for not thinking foremost of the welfare of his people. And then he would go back to wishing that he had simply taken the Hand right after it had been cut from Kiamosh. Lastly, he would remind himself there was no use fretting about it, since what was done could not be undone, and then his whole cycle of anguish would begin anew.

Late in the afternoon, Shadoo and those who had gone with him arrived. Few details about Bok Barusha would either he or any of the others give, although Shadoo did say, "A more vile place I have never seen. And I hope no one ever comes upon it in all the ages to come. Anyway, after defiling much and plundering all that was worth plundering, we sealed it as best we could so that none should look upon it again."

"But see here," said he, opening one of the sacks they had brought back with them. Inside it were a large number of pouches, small enough to fit in a man's hand, and he dumped the contents of one of these into his palm.

"Glittering stones!" he exclaimed. Many flakes of silver lay in his hand, but also a great quantity of tiny, sparkling white gems. "Lanoka says Kiamosh got them from a sorcerer somewhere in southern Sarkanna, southwest of the Forest of the Fifty Founts. Kayuna she said they're called. Anyhow, I've brought enough of these pouches for everyone here to have one, and I daresay ye all shall be fairly well off with them. Silver and kayuna! Whoiee!"

Giddily, he passed out little treasure sacks to all present, as the jolly host of a feast delights to shower his guests with his finest food.

When he had finished, Shadoo said, "Tonight we'll be off to Tauboma Bank, and in the morning we'll canoe down to Yaroka Falls, where the royal ordinations of old were always held, and there I shall reclaim this valley. And ye all shall share in my joy!"

With the help of all, they broke camp and marched north along the river for five and a half miles until they came to Tauboma Bank, which was the landing where Okona and the others had taken canoes when they had first ventured down the Wakosi. There were still many canoes here, enough to accommodate the whole company of twenty-six.

Some distance back from the river, they made camp for the night. Most of the Faithful Fifteen had turned aside at Nadula to get more supplies and food for the ordination feast, which was planned for the following day. However, they had also (at Shadoo's request) obtained provender for the homeward journey of the others. And this quantity was augmented by their helping themselves to a nearby depot of the Jaggo. These men came later in the evening, just in time to join everyone for supper. Then the whole company slept under the stars.

The next day at dawn they quickly disassembled the camp and set out in canoes for Yaroka Falls, which lay somewhat more than seven miles downstream. Okona again shared a canoe with Yahsi, while Anisha went with Wunko. Shadoo traveled with Lanoka, for they had much to discuss.

Okona was profoundly uplifted passing the places they had seen before, for now their watchfulness and dread was replaced by serenity and majesty.

After a while, though before the sun had reached its zenith, they reached the mouth of Sambo Creek, where they had left the Wakosi to flee from the ganoja. They canoed for several minutes past this point and then pulled off on the north shore. The Babora quickly unloaded supplies, leaving some upon the shore, where those departing the Wakosi Vale after the feast could put them in their vessels when they set out for home. Most of the other supplies they ladened themselves with in order to transport them up to the falls.

For nearly half an hour, Shadoo guided the company through the forest, first northwest and then northeast, along a creek and past several merry cascades. But as they continued, mighty bluffs rose on their right and left. At the trail's end, a bluff soared before them as well, and from this tumbled a majestic cascade more than two hundred feet in height. Its glinting silver waters danced and shimmered in the wind, and several tall, thin, bright-leafed trees stood guard along the the water's steep, descending course out of the great hollow. There was a health and wholeness about this place, and merely breathing its air was enough to make everyone smile.

Shadoo departed for several minutes, and when he returned, he had shed his tattered garments for apparel most splendid: a shirt sewn with many intricate patterns and breeches of like make, as well as a band of beads, decorated with eagle feathers, which rested on his brow.

Upon the old Babora's arrival, singing commenced among the Faithful Fifteen. It was music of a regal sort and rang magnificently throughout the hollow. Many songs of various moods followed: odes of exuberant, nearly uncontainable joy, slow and reverent hymns, mystic ballads filled with longing for the days of old and adventurous shanties for glorious days yet to come. Last came a song quiet and gentle, almost as a lullaby.

Speeches followed from both Shadoo and prominent members of the Faithful Fifteen. Afterward, the warriors built small fires and waved torches and green branches in fascinating patterns. Then came the final and most solemn portion of the ceremony.

The Faithful Fifteen stood facing Yaroka Falls in a semicircle around the pool at its base, while Shadoo stood in the pool itself and faced them. All the others stood respectfully behind the Faithful Fifteen, as Chapimu proclaimed, first in Babora, then in Sakooma for the benefit of the guests, "Long have the Babora waited to reclaim this land while it languished under the curse of the One-Handed. But praise be to the Skies, for the evil one is at last vanquished and the darkness lifted from the valley. Now, O Shinnemah, O Shinnemah Shadoo, heir of Odamac, the rightful chief of old, I, Chapimu, and these good Babora with me, do, on behalf of all Babora longing for their homeland, swear fealty unto thee."

Chapimu dropped to one knee and continued, again rendering his words in both languages, "Just as the oath was given of old, so do we give it once again. By breath of Air, way of Water and heart of Earth, we are yours to command according to the decrees of the Powers."

The fifteen Babora raised their spears skyward and shouted mightily. The hollow resounded, "Asho hageera'u yau Shadoo. Tama Shadoo-ko! Tama Shadoo-ko!"

Chapimu echoed it once in Sakooma. "Shadoo is lord of the Vale. Hail to Shadoo! Hail to Shadoo!"

"Hail to Shadoo!" cried those behind the Faithful Fifteen.

Shadoo gazed upon them, beaming, and his eyes sparkled.

After Chapimu had poured some of the pool's water upon his head, Shadoo strode out of the pool and stood upon its bank.

"Friends," said he in Babora when they had grown quiet, "Shadoo should not be lord of the Vale were it not for ye and those who nobly gave their lives in battle. And it is to ye that this Vale truly belongs. Long may it flourish, and may its glory be as once it was. May beauty and peace and prosperity fill it for a thousand years to come!" He then repeated his words in Sakooma.

He looked about at the Faithful Fifteen and said, returning to Babora, "Each of ye shall be given jurisdiction of a portion of the valley under me for your loyalty and service. Also, ye shall bring me wise counsel and do the same for my sons who rule after me. And your names, along with those standing behind ye, shall be learned by all the children of the Wakosi for generations to come, in order to honor the great deeds ye have done."

Shadoo raised his hands, palms open. In both Babora and Sakooma he declared, "Now begin the days of the Wakosi's glory reborn! Let us feast!"

At this command, the Faithful Fifteen went and retrieved the many victuals they had brought with them. All sat upon the ground in two long rows facing each other, and Shadoo sat across from Okona, Anisha, Yahsi, Wunko and Lanoka so he might better converse with them. Luscious berries there were and fruit and nuts in abundance, as well as sundry varieties of spiced, dried meat. And all drank of the Elixir of Nadula and were refreshed. Laughter and song rang in the hollow, and the sun shone brightly, gracing the silver falls with gold. The afternoon drew on, and all hearts were happy and content, reveling in the sweet fruits of victory.

Then, at last, Shadoo stood and said, first in Babora and afterward Sakooma, "Once again, I cannot thank ye enough, friends, for all ye have done. And let it be known that, for your shared valor to free this Vale, there shall be lasting friendship twixt the Babora and the Sakooma."

He continued, translating once more, "Now, I wish to make an announcement. This maiden before ye, Lanoka, played no small part in the defeat of Kiamosh, for she it was who led Okona and Anisha to the Tongue of Tagwash and revealed to them the secret of Kiamosh's ring. Also, at the battle itself, she strove with her father and brought forth the axe which ended him. From this, it is evident she has turned from the blackness of her past."

In Sakooma, he said, "So now, my dear Lanoka, if you would have it, I extend to you the offer of being adopted as one of my children. I have already five sons and four daughters, but should you accept, you shall be the fifth daughter, the Auspicious Tenth of my children and a princess of the Vale." He stretched out his hand to her.

Lanoka smiled warmly, took his hand, stood and said, "I thank thee, O Great Shadoo. I am not worthy of this, though I have changed both heart and mind and do here fully renounce all the evil I did and tolerated. Yet, because my lordship asks, yes, I shall accept."

Chapimu translated what had just been declared, and everyone cheered and cried in acclamation, as Shadoo embraced Lanoka.

"Now," Shadoo said, returning to Babora, "my Faithful Fifteen, I ask that ten of ye hasten to the various groups of our people and bear them tidings of all that has taken place here and bid them come to this valley and share in our happiness. And may one of those ten go to my family in the far north of Sorrequom Ridge and tell them it is at last time for us to be reunited. By the time they arrive, I shall have a lovely lodging prepared a half-mile west of the Wakosi, on the south bank of Tauboma Creek. For there shall be my seat of governance.

And when ye return, we will begin restoring and purifying this vale. We've chiborka to kill, more unholy sites to desecrate and a fair amount of evil to undo. But our rest is near at hand, for with all the Babora laboring together, we shall drive the last remnants of darkness from this land in short order. Then may all the Wakosi be even as fair as Nadula!"

"We shall leave ere nightfall," promised Chapimu, and he and others of the Faithful Fifteen stood and began making preparations for departure.

Shadoo translated to the others present what had just been discussed.

"I'm afraid we must now be going as well," said Orobec dolefully, "though I'm ever so glad we stayed for your ceremony."

"I shall be taking my leave also," said Wunko, "but wish you the greatest success and happiness." He clasped Shadoo's hand.

"Thank ye four especially," Shadoo said warmly, as he embraced Yahsi, Wunko, Anisha and Okona in turn. "May Blessing follow ye wherever ye go. And ye shall always have the favor of the Lord of the Wakosi. Ye are welcome here anytime."

"Thank you," said Okona, grasping the old chief's hand.

"Goodbye," added Anisha.

"All the best," Yahsi chimed, as the foursome turned to exit the hollow.

Before they departed, Okona and Anisha went up to Lanoka, and Anisha said, "We're ever so happy for you, Lanoka, and hope that you shall ever be happy also."

"Thank ye again for saving my life," the girl said. "I will always think of ye fondly." She smiled. "In the Wakosi, for the present, Sun has overcome Moon. Someday I pray it shall be thus in all the world."

The girl looked away a moment, then back at them, and said, "I have kept my peace on this matter until now, but I cannot in good conscience have ye depart without saying at least something about it." She spoke more quietly now. "I wish that things had not gone as they did with the Hand, but I know it cannot be altered. And

I understand what your intentions are for it and why, but if I may be so forward, I would advise ye to do almost anything with it but return it to the Mound—for both the Sakooma's sake and your own. Ye remember, I am sure, what I told ye about its nature."

Anisha nodded. "Yes, and we appreciate your warning to us both then and now. But I simply must deliver the Hand back to its proper resting place." She laid her hand reverently upon Tencum's bag resting at her side. "It is the will of my people, our leaders ... and of myself also."

She glanced at Okona, but he offered no sign of either support or discouragement.

"I understand," Lanoka politely returned, though her disappointment was evident. She bowed her head.

"One more thing," she said, raising it. "Here." She picked up a stone axe, which she had brought with her to the hollow. "This is for thee, Okona."

"The axe that slew Kiamosh? Why?"

"It belongs rightfully to the Sakooma, but to thou especially, for at the last, it was thou who battled Kiamosh, even though it was Tencum who killed him. This is the Stone of Sahku, the weapon of Kiamosh's father, with which Hamora cut off Kiamosh's hand of flesh. Kiamosh brought it with him to the ceremony, for he intended to smash it on the Tongue to ritually display his final victory against Hamora. The Jaggo had stolen it from a previous Sanno when he was bearing it out in the wild. Anyhow, during the battle, I saw one of the Jaggo carrying it, but as that Jaggo was slain, I was able to collect it, thinking it would be a fitting instrument to bring about Kiamosh's demise."

"Well, since you offer me this great gift so graciously, I cannot but accept it, although I only do so on behalf of all the Sakooma," said Okona, taking the weapon from her hands.

"Goodbye, Lanoka," said Anisha, and embraced her. Okona did as well, and then he and Anisha turned and departed the hollow.

"Farewell," Lanoka called.

In less than half an hour, they were back at the river. As Shoroba was tidying up some equipment and Orobec and his men were loading the supplies provided by Shadoo into the canoes, Wunko approached Okona, Anisha and Yahsi in the midst of the gravel bar, where they were checking over their packs.

"Have you decided what to do, Uncle Wunko?" asked Okona.

"You'd be more than welcome to stay with the Sakooma as long as you like," offered Anisha. "I'm sure my father would happily provide food and lodging for you."

"I very much appreciate the offer," Wunko returned, "but I've got to see to a certain piece of business before I do anything else."

"And what is that?" inquired Yahsi.

"Making amends to the settlement of Aska Karalonga. Lives were lost there during our crossing, and I have to accept some responsibility for that, for it was my suggestion to go over the Kanno there, and I knew our crossing might well draw the ganoja. Anyhow, I intend to share some of my treasure. I know glittering stones are no proper recompense for the lives of men, but I still want to do what I can to assuage their loss."

Wunko picked up his pack from where he had laid it before they sojourned up to the falls. As he shouldered it, he said, "As I'll be going to Aska Karalonga, unfortunately it is here we must part ways. For I shall be heading back up the Wakosi, and you all, I guess, will be going downstream if you're taking the quickest route to Takula. For I mean to go to the Wakosi's sources, likely passing right by the Tongue of Tagwash, and then heading straight for the Kanno, thus avoiding Toshigan Hollow, which I l now know how to accomplish, since Lanoka informed me of its precise location. Hopefully I shall have no trouble from the chiborka when leaving the area, since Kiamosh's spell upon them is ended."

"We're sorry to see you go," said Anisha glumly.

"But we understand," Okona added. "You've got your own story to live, and I suppose we've got ours. But I'm ever so glad the two came together for a while."

"So am I," Wunko declared. "There's something particularly delightful about being on the other side of the darkness and danger, having somehow survived it all, and being able to look back on it, to reflect on it with those who passed through it with you." He looked warmly at the youths and placed his hands on each of their outside shoulders. "You've been marvelous to me and for me, Friend Okona and Miss Anisha. You and this quest are precisely the medicine this old Tikkichaw needed." He nodded to Yahsi. "And Miss Yahsi, it has been a great pleasure to share this adventure with you as well. Such a trove of wisdom, cleverness, fire and determination as you possess is beyond rare, and I am blessed to have shared life with you, even if only for a few days."

"The blessing is mutual," Yahsi assured.

"Any idea where you'll go after Aska Karalonga?" Okona inquired.

"Oh, I thought I'd return to my quag for a while. But after that, who knows? Now I've got a truly extraordinary tale of my own to tell, and there are many lands where I've never set foot, just waiting to be explored."

Wunko glanced at the canoe in which he had come downriver. Then, looking back to the companions, he said, "Well, goodbye. I shall never forget you, for rest assured, your tale will be told far and wide by yours truly, as best as I can render it."

"Goodbye, Uncle Wunko." Anisha clasped him in both arms. Then Okona and Yahsi each embraced him and said their farewells. After that, Wunko took his share of supplies from the pile and loaded them in his canoe, while Okona, Anisha and Yahsi assisted with the readying of provisions for the Sakooma.

Wunko finished his preparation before they did and so began paddling up the Wakosi. Okona looked up as Wunko was making his way upstream, and the Tikkichaw raised his hand in a final farewell. Okona returned the gesture just before he disappeared around the bend in a flash of the westering sun.

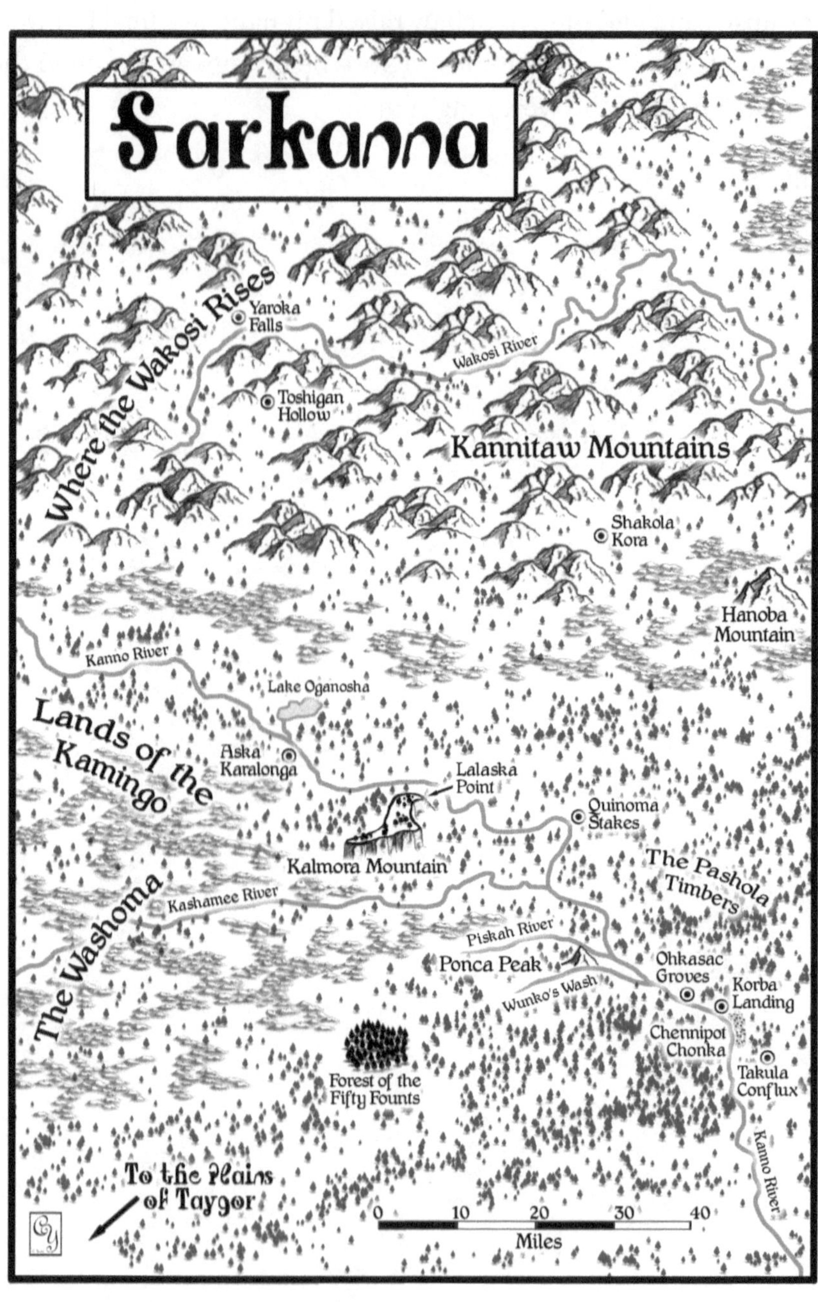

Farkanna
Where the Wakosi Rises
Yaroka Falls
Wakosi River
Toshigan Hollow
Kannitaw Mountains
Shakola Kora
Hanoba Mountain
Kanno River
Lake Oganosha
Lands of the Kamingo
Aska Karalonga
Lalaska Point
Quinoma Stakes
Kalmora Mountain
The Pashola Timbers
Kashamee River
The Washoma
Piskah River
Ponca Peak
Ohkasac Groves
Wunko's Wash
Korba Landing
Chennipot Chonka
Takula Conflux
Forest of the Fifty Founts
To the Plains of Taygor
Kanno River
0   10   20   30   40
Miles

To the Shamori River
N W E S
Sorrequom Ridge
To the Honosha River
Roaming Range of the Babora
Wakosi River
Lands of the Shamoki
Wakosi River
Wayawoc Woods
Lands of the Sakooma
Anoka River
Hachori
Lands of the Mushatuck
To the Soothland Sea
Wakosi River

The Lay of Lakosha

B Y THE TIME OKONA and the others Takula-bound were ready to set out, the afternoon was already mostly spent. Thus, they only paddled a few miles before making camp on a gravel bar beneath a great, gray bluff. As each was still full in heart and stomach from Shadoo's feast, they slept magnificently under the stars.

Over the next several days, they paddled steadily down the Wakosi, which bore generally east, though meandering. Cliffs, cascades and woodlands of staggering beauty ever surrounded them, mingling with the river's gentle song. On many an occasion they were so awed by this remote ribbon of Sarkanna that they wondered if they had crossed into the Other-lands.

For Okona, this whole portion of the journey seemed but a dream, timeless and beyond the circles of the world. His many adventures, both glorious and terrifying, faded almost to figments, as if he knew of them from legend but hadn't lived them himself. But, as he shared a canoe with Anisha (who sat, mostly in silence, in the prow), just before his feet lay Tencum's hunting bag and within it, the Hand of Hamora, a solemn reminder that the quest had been no dream after all. The lad tried to avoid thinking about what was to become of Anisha and was grateful no one ever mentioned the matter. Nonetheless, a gray shadow began to steal over him, for each day that brought them nearer to Takula also hastened his beloved toward her grievous end. And as his melancholy grew, Okona was reminded ever more of Lanoka's final advice, which vexed him almost more than anything else.

On the evening of the third full day since they had left Yaroka Falls, they pulled ashore on the Wakosi's south bank. Nearly sixty miles they had come downriver, and here Orobec intended to turn southeast to the sacred site of Shakola Kora to make offerings of gratitude to the Shamoki's Powers. Even though the Upper Wakosi and the victory there was beyond these Powers' jurisdiction, Orobec's highly consequential encounter with the Faithful Forty had occurred in these same Powers' domain, and thus he credited them with the fortuitous meeting. From Shakola Kora they would journey on to the trading post, Quinoma Stakes, before returning to Takula.

The company had been pleasantly relieved while the canoes bore their burdens, but the next morning, as they would be traveling by land from then on, they distributed their remaining provisions among themselves and embarked southeastward through the Kannitaw Mountains.

It rained on and off over the next few days, but the scenery remained brilliant, though not quite attaining the grandeur of the Wakosi. Occasionally they added to their food supply from the wilds as they went, but Shadoo's provisions, which were exceedingly generous, were already sufficient for them to reach Quinoma Stakes without restocking.

In the late afternoon of their sixth full day after saying their farewells at Yaroka Falls, they came to Shakola Kora, almost three tens of miles south of their departure point from the Wakosi. It was just as Wunko had described it: a magnificent arch of stone, thin yet wide, standing mysteriously upon a hill covered with darkling forest. Orobec and his men set flame to portions of food beneath the arch and chanted their thanks to the Powers as twilight fell. Shoroba, Okona and Anisha joined them in this, though Yahsi lingered a ways off. However, as Okona sang, he felt a strange sense of queasiness, as if something were amiss, though he could not place what. Unable to shake his disquiet, Okona discovered his praises had fallen into half-hearted mumbling, and he quietly withdrew.

As he paced some distance from the campfire, his gaze was drawn up to the enchanting summer stars, winking between the trees. Suddenly, the events of the feast at Takula nearly a month before came rushing back to him. A desperate longing pierced him, a yearning for the world as it had been before the Hand had been taken. But knowing such could never be recalled, he went to the sleeping place he had selected earlier, lay down and fell into slumber.

The next three days, the company continued toward Quinoma Stakes, bearing due south, but angling very slightly to the west. Four more tens of miles they covered, and the journey went by more quickly, since, not far south of Shakola Kora, the heights of the Kannitaw grew ever tamer until they disappeared altogether and became only a wall of hazy hills behind them.

In the early evening of the third day out from Shakola Kora, they came to the stout walls of Quinoma Stakes. Only a half-mile from the banks of the Kanno, which lay to the west, wooden palisades formed a wide oval that could only be accessed via a single portal on the east, where some of the place's occupants always stood on watch. As they approached this gate, welcoming lights of cookfires beckoned from within the compound, blazing away among the many tall, peaked, dome-shaped grass huts where both residents and visitors lodged. The company was ushered into one of these huts near the rear of the compound and bedded down for the night on the woven mats provided therein.

The following morning, Orobec proposed that they rest at Quinoma Stakes the entire day, for they had pressed hard through the wilderness. Also, they might trade for more supplies here, since their stock was now rather low. The next day, they could continue toward Ohkasac Groves to pay their respects to the Sakooma interred there. After that, they could return directly to Takula.

Everyone found this proposition agreeable, so Orobec and his men went to barter for provisions using northern copper and southern seashells they had brought with them from Takula, while Shoroba conversed with a cousin of hers who happened to be visiting the compound, and Anisha and Yahsi went for a walk by the Kanno. Okona opted to wander about Quinoma Stakes to see the broad variety of goods offered for trade.

Everyone gathered again for lunch, and Orobec related that he had encountered a Sakooma messenger who was headed to Takula and would bring tidings of their soon arrival there. The fellow had been overjoyed to hear of their success and was going to bid other messengers to bear news of the Hand's return to all the villages near the Conflux. Orobec also mentioned to Anisha that he had said nothing to the messenger about her being the one who had taken the Hand, for he thought it would be deeply inconsiderate to have her father learn of this if she were not present.

Following lunch, the company napped for a time. After that, they dispersed once more to explore the compound and its surroundings. Okona, however, remained at the hut. There he grabbed some sunflower seeds out of one of the many storage baskets affixed to the wall and sat on a mat before the fire, munching away, deep in thought.

"I see you crossed the Kanno," a voice said.

Okona looked up. On the other side of the fire sat a man in a white shirt, with a red blanket wrapped around his shoulders.

"Wassu!" Okona exclaimed. "It is Wassu, isn't it? I didn't hear you come in." He glanced at the elk-skin-covered doorway.

"Small wonder. When thoughts are heavy, the senses may dim."

"How did you know I ..." Okona stared at him. "Are you really the same man whom we met in the Washoma? And was it you who spoke with Yahsi also?"

"Have you any reason to believe otherwise?"

"Well, no, but it's fortunate you've come because I very much wished to speak with you about some things."

"Oh?"

"You know, it's the strangest thing," said Okona, tossing a handful of sunflower shucks into a nearby bowl he had been using for such disposal, "you showing up here or even showing up at all, but somehow, it also seems perfectly natural. It's almost as if you knew I wished to speak with you."

Wassu appraised him coolly through the thin, coiling smoke but gave no reply.

"Anyway, may I ask why you're here?" Okona inquired.

"I would give you counsel, if you would have it."

"I would. But first, and I hope you won't think me too forward for asking this, would you mind telling me why you commanded Yahsi to bring me on the search for the Hand of Hamora?"

"She herself has already told you such. You were chosen by Mahna Shuya."

"But why?"

"Even I do not know the answer to that. There is only one who does." His eyes flicked upward.

Wassu leaned forward. "But now, to my counsel. Beware, lad, for even though the Hand has been retrieved, your tale will still end in death unless you find what you are not seeking."

Okona gave him a queer look. "Strange ... you speak the words of another, the Seer of Ponca Peak. But even after all this time such words are no clearer. The Seer said my life would be changed, and it has been. But I have found nothing that I did not seek, so I am no closer to escaping death. For that is what you're implying, is it not? That I might avoid dying before my time?"

"Nay, that you should not die at all."

Okona drew back, astonished. "But how can—"

"To put it more precisely, it is my hope that you should only die once, not twice."

Okona cocked his head.

"What is death, Okona?"

The lad paused a moment. "The sundering of flesh and breath. The breath goes on, leaving the flesh behind."

"Yes. Death is a sundering. But more may be sundered than flesh and breath; that is what we may call the First Sundering. Alas, there is a Second Sundering, for even the breath may be sundered from the Light."

"I'm afraid I don't understand."

"Perhaps not yet. But a gift was given to you, Okona, the gift of a warning, of seeing what awaits you if you do not escape the Second Sundering."

"Wassu, I haven't the faintest clue what you're talking about."

"What did you see in the murk of the great river? Learned you nothing from your crossing of the Kanno?"

"At Aska Karalonga, you mean?"

"How did you escape death there?" Wassu looked at him intently.

"By casting away those charms, I suppose."

"To what charm do you yet cling?" Wassu's gaze grew more probing still.

"None. I threw them all into the Kanno."

Wassu's eyes did not waver.

"Is there something more, then?"

"You can't grab the Hand of Help until you've let the Hand of Harm go."

"That is what I did at the Kanno, yes," Okona mused, "though precisely what the hand of help was is not apparent to me."

"You and your folk attribute great luck to ten and its opposite to eleven. But I tell you that naught comes from such as these, nor from the founts of Fortune, which are but an illusion; rather, all is from the Hand unseen. Recall all that has befallen you, lad. This Hand has aided you your entire journey, and not only you, but many others as well, some who cling to the Hand of Harm even tighter than you. Your Baneesh knew another was singing against him. Kiamosh it was, but the Hand of Help delivered both Baneesh and your people from the warlock's curses. And your Yahsi came not through the net of chiborka guarding the Wakosi merely by chance. Also, when you emerged in the waters of Nadula, a Hand there was that drew you out. And the same Hand shook you by the Neck of Night and bore also the light that guided you through the darkness of Korashac. And it was by this Hand your own brand long kept blazing while you were bound in slumber there. Moreover, it was this Hand that imparted to you the shard of sunfire, though you failed to wield it rightly."

Okona knitted his brow. "Was it the Seer, then? For it was his hand that gave me the sunfire. And when you say I failed to rightly wield it ... the Seer said I would know what to do with it when the time came."

"First, the Seer is but an extension of the Hand of which I speak, as am I. We ourselves are not the Hand, though our hands may have served as such in this realm, giving you a gift, pulling you from the water, waking you at need. Also, you should know that the shard, having no power of speech, signaled you as well as it might, but you heeded it not."

He stared hard at Okona. "Did you not know what you must do with it?"

Okona, much discomfited, turned away.

"Did you not?" Wassu persisted.

Sighing, the lad hung his head. "It is too late, then."

"Perhaps not. In fact, that is one of the reasons why I have come."

Okona looked up.

"Do you know the tale of Lakosha?" Wassu asked.

"More or less. Lakosha was one of the seventy sons of Umarna and the father of the people of Sarkanna. It was he who led his children in flight from the broken Stairway to the Sky up to the deepest north. And he it was who found the road through Shagrash-Mula."

"Tell me, Okona, where do stories say all the best things may be found?"

Okona reflected. "Not here in Massora, but in the Over-lands."

"And did Lakosha have access to such things?"

"Yes, but when the Stairway to the Sky was broken, they were lost to both him and all men forever."

"Not all men," Wassu corrected. "And they need not be lost to you."

"But I cannot even return through the Mists of Shagrash-Mula, much less forge a way to the Over-lands!" Okona protested.

"True. From Massora one cannot build up. But it is possible for one from the Over-lands to descend to Massora, is it not?"

Wassu settled back upon his mat and said, "When your ancient forebear Lakosha departed from the ruins of the Stairway, he crafted for his children a mighty gift. But it was unfortunately not properly preserved by his descendants. Indeed, many things were not rightly preserved by them. This side of the Great Waters, even those who remember the most about the old days have forgotten or altered much, though some truth yet shines through. But as for the gift I mentioned, it was a song known as the Lay of Lakosha. Your people correctly remembered that it was from Lakosha's time but have forgotten that it was composed by Lakosha himself and have lost also its words, though you have correctly maintained that the song was of particular value. Indeed, it is, for it tells of some of the very things of which we speak. In its age-old rhymes, one may find a promise of a better Stairway being built and of a way for men to receive again the treasures of the Over-lands, to regain That Which Was Lost. The tune of this song you already know and have played many a time. It is the lofty ode with which you called from beneath the earth."

Okona's eyes grew wide. "Do you know of *all* my doings? It's rather unnerving, you know."

"I only know of them what I was told or that for which I was present. But hear me well, Okona. Music can speak of many things, wondrous things that words cannot. But even so, if it be bereft of words, it cannot tell man what he must know if he would be set upon the road to the Lands Above and not those Below."

In a voice barely above a whisper, Wassu began to sing.

"The upward road by man's hand laid has fallen down in fierce cascade,

The light is lost, the blessing passed; such heavy cost to down be cast!

But in ages hence, one hope remains, amidst the sea of tears and pains,

That what cannot from 'neath be wrought may be forged from above, and vict'ry bought."

"The broken Hand mayn't touch the sky, with whate'er might it so may try,

But the Hand above may yet reach down and grant to mournful men a crown,

So hark to the tread of the Over-lands' king; look for the light that he shall bring,

When he will come, who can say, but all must await that glorious day."

"Only when man may bathe in that light shall death be done and all set right.

Look to the West, from whence we have come, for there shall rise the Secret Sun.

Look to the West, from whence we have come, for there shall rise the Secret Sun."

While Wassu had been singing, the dim hut had seemed a realm unto itself, ethereal and exalted, but now the dwelling sank back to sultry Sarkanna.

Wassu solemnly folded his hands and said, "Those, Okona, are words from the Lay of Lakosha, rendered into Sakooma so that you might comprehend them."

"Thank you for sharing them with me," said Okona with much reverence. "But there's much I simply don't understand. And I still don't know how to evade this Second Sundering of which you spoke. Yet is that not why you have come—to warn me how to flee it?"

"Even the Lay of Lakosha, told in full, is not sufficient to tell you *that*. And I have come to warn you to flee it and to some extent how, though it is another who shall tell you how in full. Yet I repeat what I said before; you cannot grasp the Hand of Help until you've let the Hand of Harm go. Also, the shard of sunfire will only prove of any real use once you understand from whence all good things come."

Okona stared keenly at Wassu. "That, too, is something the Seer said." He paused. "Who are you? Who are you really? And where are you from?"

Wassu regarded him, unblinking, with cool, brown eyes. "Wassu am I, Wassu of the West. Let that be sufficient. But as for my proper home—well, it is far from here. Very far, one might say. But you have been on the edge of my lands several times, closer than you are presently anyway, though my realm isn't far from you even now. You're practically breathing it, after a fashion. You passed through curtains to its borderlands at Ponca Peak, in the Realm of the Kishikot and in Korashac. But Ponca Peak was nearest to it."

Okona scratched his head. "Do you know the Seer there?"

"We are acquainted," Wassu returned.

"Yahsi called him the true peril of Ponca Peak. Was he indeed perilous, and if so, why?"

"Tremendously perilous, as am I." His eyes flickered. "And if you could see either myself or the Seer as we are, you would immediately know why. There is no evil within us, only good. That is why I am clad as I am; the white is for purity and the red for fire."

He continued, "You fear much to say the names of evil ones who prowl my realm but you should fear more to ever use lightly the name of him who is purest. Know this, Okona: good is far more perilous than evil, but only to those who are defiled is it so."

"Am I defiled?" Okona inquired nervously.

"You are."

"How then can I be in your presence?"

"There is such a thing as mercy. Also, boundaries, veils, barriers and so forth are a mercy. But there is more mercy still when the defiled are made clean and the boundaries removed. So seek that greater mercy. Seek the Greater Hand! Seek Blessing itself. As I told you before, draw from the Well whence all good things come; it is narrow at the mouth, for there is only one place from which one may get the right water, but wide at the bottom, for the water itself is very deep."

Suddenly, Wassu rose and said, "Kiamosh did you and your people a great service by opening the Mound of Hamora. Let not his deed have been in vain."

"What do you mean by that?" Okona looked up at him, much disturbed.

"Sun must conquer Moon," Wassu briskly declared. And with that, he strode from the hut.

For a long time, Okona sat alone in the relative dark, thinking upon all that Wassu had said, his gaze lost within the glowing fire. But he came no nearer to comprehending the arcane matters of which the stranger had spoken. Despairing of further reflection, he arose and went out to sit with Orobec and his men, who were conversing by one of the cookfires near the front of the compound with other travelers from up and down the Kanno. After a while, Yahsi and Anisha joined them. Shoroba returned some time after that. Okona said nothing to anyone about his encounter with Wassu, though he hoped to discuss the matter with Yahsi later when they could do so in private.

The party passed the remainder of the day enjoying Quinoma Stakes and its environs, although Okona remained pensive and said little. That evening, Yahsi borrowed a harp from one of the traders and went off alone for a time (She had a song to craft before it escaped her, she said.), while the rest readied their supplies for the following morning. When Yahsi returned, Okona detected a peculiar look in her eyes, though he had no proper chance to ask if anything were afoot, for shortly after her arriving, the company gathered to hear her perform the tune she had composed. And all were much delighted, for it was a magnificent ballad about the adventurers' defeat of Kiamosh and the restoration of the Wakosi.

When Yahsi had concluded, she returned the harp with many thanks to the trader who had lent it to her, and the party went and offered their gratitude to the wardens of Quinoma Stakes for their excellent treatment during their stay. After that, they bedded down in the hut they had been apportioned.

At the first stirrings of dawn, the party arose and set out in a light morning rain for the southeast. That day and the next they traveled a total of twenty and eight miles through a wooded region known as the Pashola Timbers, arriving at Ohkasac Groves as the afternoon was waning. While the daylight lasted, they sang poignant elegies to their slain comrades buried there and laid blossoms and branches upon their graves. As Okona recalled the many carefree days he had shared with his departed companion Kimmanic, a barbarous blade of grief slit his heart, and he wept long and loud, even after the others had ceased their mourning.

In the evening, Yahsi made a brief trip to the nearby village from which she had been brought the signal drum she had taken into the north. Her intention was to return it to its owner, but she returned a while later with the drum and explained that the owner had demanded she keep it, since she had used it to such valiant purpose. So that night, she and Okona performed for the others several selections on flute and drum, songs which spoke of homecoming. And though the tunes were of the happy sort, Okona found that such music served rather to mock his heaviness of heart about the return to Takula than provide him any relief from it.

The next day found the company afoot early, for Takula Conflux lay less than two tens of miles from Ohkasac Groves. East along the Kanno they went, then curved southeast. They passed the tall, bright-yellow blossoms of Chennipot Chonka and continued south through the familiar country beyond. At last, in the midafternoon, Takula came in sight.

When they reached the gates, an exuberant cry rang out that the Hand of Hamora and its bearers had returned. With much excitement and fervor and with many Sakooma gathered around, the company was ushered to the middle of the central plaza. To the elation of Orobec and his group, Homino and Aywish and their bands were present, for they had arrived only a few days prior, having received Yahsi's message that the Hand was in the north (though it took messengers a fair while to track them down). They were going to depart for the north as well, but the messenger Orobec had spoken to at Quinoma Stakes had arrived before they left, bringing news that the Hand would be arriving at Takula shortly, so they had stayed to await its coming.

But the most delighted of anyone present was Dhagomi, who practically sprang down the wooden stairs of the high mound upon which his dwelling stood and rushed up to the companions.

"You have done it!" he cried. "Oh, praise, you have done it! May the Powers be exalted for their favor to us! And my Anisha, you're back safe and alive!"

He embraced her and showered upon her many kisses. Finally, he stood back and looked at her, then around at the others.

"Thank you, all of you," said the jubilant Sanno. "Thank you for your service to the Sakooma, for your valor in the face of peril and also for taking such excellent care of my daughter."

"Sir," Okona began. "We ..." his voice fell.

But Anisha seized the silence. "Father." He looked at her, and, with blank expression, she reached into Tencum's hunting bag, which was slung over her shoulder, and drew out the Hand.

Dhagomi's face was dreadful to watch. Okona cast his eyes down, as the Sanno crumpled to the ground, wailing.

Many were much taken aback, for they knew not why the return of the Hand should be anything but a cause for joy, but Orobec announced, "See you all the Sanno? He weeps for he knows aught which you do not. It is this—such is the Hand's magic that it cannot be returned to the Mound and our people made safe again unless the one who lays it there should die."

Those standing around covered their mouths and gasped. Many began weeping. And so the unbridled joy of Takula was swallowed up in inconsolable mourning.

Eventually, the Sakooma dispersed from the plaza, though still drowning in sorrow. Dhagomi took Anisha up to their lodge, while Orobec and Shoroba went to confer with Baneesh at the House of Flame and Fume. Yahsi wished Okona a good afternoon and looked as if she were going to say more but then decided against it. After she walked off, Okona stood alone in the empty plaza.

Looking about at the vibrant green mounds, the lad sighed, knowing this place, which had once given him so much joy, could never do so again. Glumly, he trudged off to the hut of some of his family's friends to ask if he might spend the night with them.

These friends welcomed him, so Okona spent several hours that afternoon resting in their hut. As evening approached, word spread throughout the compound that Dhagomi had an announcement to make. So Okona, along with the rest of those at Takula, gathered in the central plaza once more, and Dhagomi declared that Anisha had insisted on returning the Hand to its proper place the following morning, for it was not right that the unprotected condition of the Sakooma be prolonged any longer than it already had been. Everyone was grieved to hear this, of course, but admired the girl's valiance.

After the announcement, the people scattered back to their dwellings, but Okona stayed and spoke to Dhagomi about Tencum and the Stone of Sahku. He offered the Sanno the great stone axe, but he refused it, saying that it ought to go to Tencum's parents instead.

"What Tencum did was evil indeed," Dhagomi said, "but as it was he who killed this wicked Kiamosh, his father and mother have a right to that hallowed weapon before I do."

From Dhagomi, Okona learned that Tencum's family was actually visiting Takula presently, for they had received news at their village the previous day that the victory party would be returning. Thus, they had traveled to Takula to see its arrival. So Okona went to the hut where Tencum's father, Okamot, and his mother, Labona, were lodging, and presented them with the axe.

"I was there when Tencum struck the blow," Okona said, "and it was the mightiest I've ever seen."

"We have heard of the great wickedness Tencum did," Okamot said slowly, "for tidings of it have already gone throughout the compound. But you speak as one who honors him."

"Yes," Okona returned. "For his slaying of Kiamosh was worthy of honor, even if his other deeds were not. And it is Another's place, not mine, to separate the evil of Tencum from the good, for he was one man, not two."

"Here." He placed the axe in Okamot's open hands.

"Thank you." Okamot bowed.

When Okona returned to his friends' hut, he was delighted to find his family there. He learned that they, like Tencum's parents, had gotten word that the victory party would soon reach Takula and had come to see its arrival. Okona shared a meal with his family and spoke some of his adventures, but afterward, when twilight had fallen, he went out for a stroll alone by Takula Lake.

As he was pacing along the dark waters beneath the evening shadows of the hemlocks, he spied a dark figure a short ways down the shore.

"Anisha! What are you doing here?"

"Saying farewell," she returned, as he walked up to her. "And you?"

"Wishing I didn't have to," he replied, glancing sadly at Tencum's satchel hanging at her side.

Taking her by the hand, he said, "Anisha, why did you take the Hand?"

"I already told you. I love you, Okona, so I had to take it before you did."

"Joyfully would I have asked your father to approve the pledge we made in Korashac if things were not as they are. But now there would be no sense in doing so, for our love will be ever broken."

"Not broken, but buried. Preserved." She looked up at him. "For I shall tell all the people that I have granted my troth to you and that you would have certainly asked my father's permission if we had not been destined to be parted. From tomorrow on, the power that preserves our people will be a memorial to our love, not the black sorcery of Hamora."

"But that's all it would be," Okona said. "A memorial. Ought not love be living?"

Anisha turned to gaze upon the lake's starlit surface. "My fate cannot be altered. And I considered it well before I embraced it. I knew you would be devastated, and my father also, as well as many others. My father has taken it especially hard. I know it was unkind to leave without telling him, but at least he received news I was alive, though going into danger. And then he got word that I had survived, but just today learned I must die tomorrow. I haven't done right by him, and I apologized for it. Alas that so much sorrow has come of this affair!"

"But the chief thing is that our people shall be protected," she said. "And you also. I do not consider it foolish to have given my life so my dearest love might live, and all my people as well."

"B-but what if there were another way?" Okona stammered. "What if both I and the Sakooma and even you might be saved apart from the Hand? What if, even though we can't reach to help above, such might reach down to us?"

"What are you talking about, Okona?" Anisha said, searching his shadowed face.

To his surprise, the lad found himself replying, "What if Lanoka was right?"

Anisha shrank back, though still clutching his hand. "About the Hand? You're not serious!"

"Couldn't you just run away? You might always keep the Hand with you, and then you wouldn't have to die."

"And desert our people? Never," she returned, flinging his hand from her own.

"But what if the Hand really is evil? And what if putting it back into the Mound will only tighten the bonds of our slavery?"

"Okona, I don't know how you could even entertain such notions. Perhaps the Hand did have rather less than savory origins. Perhaps it is made of wicked substance. Still, we can use it for its good and leave it at that."

"I'd like to agree with you," Okona sighed, "but you remember what that Wassu fellow we met in the Washoma said? You can't take the hand of help until you've let the hand of harm go."

"That's enough, Okona." Anisha faced him firmly. "I understand that it's hard for you to let me go, but there's no sense in turning your beliefs about our whole world upside-down because of this."

She took his hand once again and looked up at him. "It's going to be all right. It really is. I simply must do my duty. I've got to make things right for our people. And you'll just have to accept what comes of that."

Still hand in hand, the couple turned to face Takula Lake and the silver moon high above.

"The water is magnificent tonight," Okona said after a while.

"Yes, as it was at the Song of the Summer Stars," Anisha remarked.

The two faced each other once more, and Okona said, "I suppose this is goodbye."

"Yes," she agreed, hanging her head.

Okona put his hand under her chin, lifted it, then said, "Thank you for what you did. It hurts like something awful now, but in days to come, I think I'll better understand. I just hate to lose you."

"We shall not be parted till tomorrow. Let that not sully tonight. At the moment, I'm the happiest a Sakooma girl could be, for I have everything I desire." Smiling, she placed her hand upon Okona's breast.

Tears sprang from their eyes, and Okona bent down and kissed her. Then they long embraced, as they had done in the blackness of Korashac.

At last, they gently let each other go, and as Anisha retreated eastward along the lake's shore, she called, "Goodnight, Okona."

"Goodnight, Anisha," he softly returned.

CHAPTER TWENTY-FIVE

THE TRUEST TREASURE

IN THE NIGHT THAT followed, Okona turned over and over upon his mat in the blackness of the hut, tormented by the slow, relentless approach of the morrow. His thoughts were ever harried by a host of questions and fears, and lurid visions of all the most dreadful parts of his adventures surged spitefully into his few intervals of slumber. In the crawling minutes he was awake, he strove in vain to understand all that he had seen and heard and most of all to decipher the mystic words of Wassu. But as dawn drew nigh, he at last gave up hope of vanquishing the impenetrable gloom that had enveloped him. Unable to hold back his stinging tears, he turned facedown and abandoned himself to a sea of despair.

But then, like a bolt of sun piercing smoke and storm, there came to him the peace he sought and the clarity for which he wrestled. He knew now what he must do. Okona closed his eyes, breathed deeply and found himself unafraid of the coming light.

Moments later, his father stirred and rose, and soon the others in the hut did as well. Not long afterward, Okona joined everyone for a brief breakfast. When they had concluded, together they departed for the Mound of Hamora.

Many were gathered north of the mound already, including Anisha's father, though the girl herself was not present. Just as Okona was walking up to the crowd, Yahsi was joining it from another direction.

"Well, Okona, are you ready for this morning?" she inquired, as their paths converged.

"I believe so," the lad stoutly returned. "But it certainly won't be easy."

"Behold! The Hand cometh!" called the Magic-maker Baneesh, clad in ceremonial garb, from the front of the company.

Okona turned toward the mound, atop which stood the Sanno's lodge. There, upon the highest step, stood Anisha, gazing out upon the plaza. Her sleeveless dress of deepest red clashed violently with the emerald hillside. And the Hand of Hamora, which she held before her, glittered coldly in the morning light.

Anisha descended the steps slowly, always looking straight ahead. Those watching neither stirred nor spoke. When the girl reached the mound's base, she turned toward the Mound of Hamora, and Okona was certain her eyes had fallen upon him for a moment before she began pacing forward. Anisha crossed over to the silent assembly, still moving in a most stately manner. The crowd parted for her to pass, and she halted at the front of those gathered, in-between her father and Baneesh. Finally, she turned to look upon her people.

Okona's stomach dropped, as he stared at the dark opening of the mound behind her, a veritable door into the blackness of the Under-realm.

"O Sakooma, O Star-Blessed Sakooma," Baneesh began, "before ye stands the noble Anisha, who journeyed far into the north to aid in the retrieval of the hallowed Hand of Hamora. She it was who laid hold of it after it had been severed from the vile Kiamosh, who schemed to slaughter us. While the Hand has been absent, we have been open to grave peril. Yet now it has come back, so we shall be saved, but only once it has been returned to its proper place. And, as by now you have heard, Anisha cannot return it there unless she herself perish. And thus we have come to a moment most solemn in our history, for this fair maiden is the very last in the line of

Hamora. And with her passing, we shall no longer have his regal blood walking among us. But at least we shall have his protection."

He turned to Anisha. "What you have offered to do, my dear, is a glorious thing: to give your life for your people. And you can be sure that this deed will ever be remembered and praised as long as there are Sakooma upon this green earth."

He placed his hands upon her head. "May you enter the Under-brakes with all the blessings Air, Water and Earth can bestow."

Then he removed his hands and stood back. "Now it is yours, my lady, to say your farewells."

Anisha turned to Dhagomi, who bit his lip to hold back his sorrow, as she kissed him upon each cheek. "Goodbye, Father," she said tenderly, embracing him. "Ever have you been good to me. And rest assured I carry my great love for you with me beyond the veil."

At last she pulled away and faced the people. "Goodbye, Star-Blessed Sakooma," she proclaimed. "May you prosper for ages to come, and may the mounds of Takula be ever green and glorious."

Then she cleared her throat and said, "Now, there is a matter of which I have already spoken to my father, but I would share it with all of you as well. Okona of Hachori, who played a tremendous part in the quest of the Hand, asked for my troth in marriage while we were away north, and I have given it to him. For of course my pledge to Tencum was annulled on account of whom he was revealed to be. And Okona would have asked my father to formalize my pledge but did not, as he knew we would be parted when I entered the Mound. But I want all of you to know I am glad that it was I who took the Hand and not him, for I love him dearly and happily consider my life exchanged for his."

"Okona," she said, "would you do me the honor of one final farewell?"

Okona stepped forward, and the crowd separated for him.

As he came up to Anisha, he swallowed and said, "Goodbye, Anisha. Now for the last time. I love you more than either words or song can tell. And that makes this all the more difficult."

Anisha's eyes began to water, and as she stared at him, clutching the wrist of the Hand of Hamora in her right hand, with her mother's silver bracelet upon her wrist just above it, the lad reached into a pouch at his waist. In a single, swift motion, he drew out the glinting shard of sunfire, which burst brightly aglow, and thrust it into the palm of the Hand of Hamora.

A great boom shook the whole of Takula, as a blinding blue light leapt from the Hand in all directions. Okona and Anisha were flung apart, tumbling to the ground. The shard of sunfire melted in the lad's hand into a glowing flame, yet without heat, while the Hand of Hamora smoked, hissed and writhed so violently that Anisha cast it away, crying out in pain. For a few moments it seemed all the sound and even physical depth had been pulled from the whole of Takula Conflux. But this queer condition was broken as a horrendous crack echoed off the mounds. The Hand of Hamora glowed so fiercely all had to shield their eyes, and a moment later, it exploded in a blue blaze of crystal fire. Darkness swept out from it in every direction, but the darkness quickly passed, and Takula was once again graced by the light of a fair summer morning.

Many of the Sakooma had cast themselves to the ground during this ordeal, but they now stood and looked at Okona in astonishment. The lad, just as astonished as they, stood up and stared at his tingling hand, where but a wisp of the sunfire remained, still burning brightly. Yet after a few moments, it evaporated entirely, and the lad immediately turned his attention to Anisha, who lay facedown and motionless some feet away. Rushing to her side, he bent down and laid his hand upon her back.

"Anisha!" he cried. "Oh, Anisha! Forgive me!"

Dhagomi rose, dashed forward and also fell upon Anisha.

"What is this you have done?" demanded Dhagomi, beside himself. "And what was the fire you held?"

"And where is the Hand?" cried Baneesh. "Stand, boy, and give account for yourself."

While Dhagomi turned Anisha over, Okona faced Baneesh, replying, "The Hand of Hamora is no more. And I was its destroyer."

"Why would you do such a thing?" Baneesh returned, practically hysterical. "And how then? How could a thing of such power be unmade?"

"The flame you saw was that of a shard of sunfire," Okona calmly replied, "which was given me by the Seer of Ponca Peak for this very purpose."

"To destroy the Hand of Hamora?" Dhagomi exploded, jumping up. "And kill my daughter?"

"I would never have slain Anisha except that she would have died in moments anyhow," Okona swore. "I love her tremendously and—"

Dhagomi slapped Okona across the mouth. "That is a lie! Anisha loved our people and would have given her life for them! But you—you have brought ruin and death to both."

"Not so, my lord," Okona soberly returned. "I have delivered the Sakooma or at least attempted it."

"Delivered them?" roared the normally imperturbable Baneesh. "Are you utterly mad?"

"Perhaps it must seem so. But I assure you, I did not act without cause."

"Anisha lives!" suddenly cried Orobec, who was standing near the front of the crowd.

Astonished, all turned to look upon the girl, who sat up, looking around dazedly.

"Anisha!" Okona shouted. "You're alive!"

Dhagomi grabbed his daughter and helped her to her feet. Okona sought to assist, but Dhagomi shoved him aside.

"Okona, what has—" she began.

"Have a care, Anisha," Dhagomi warned. "This lunatic just destroyed the Hand of Hamora and tried to kill you as well."

"You did what?!" Anisha exclaimed, staring at Okona, aghast.

"It is true I destroyed the Hand, but—"

"You ought to be executed right here and now," seethed Baneesh, and the people clamored in agreement. "Orobec, go get your spear!"

Orobec made to depart, but Anisha cried out, "Wait! Let me speak to Okona and him reply before anything is done. We have seen much together in the north, many strange things, and I would at least hear why he has done this and how before any judgment is made."

Orobec paused and looked at Dhagomi, who, while glaring fiercely at Okona, grudgingly pronounced, "Very well. But only because you ask it, my daughter. For no shred of consideration will I give to this wretched traitor from this day forth."

Okona took a deep breath, then faced Anisha. But he nearly quailed under the overwhelming hostility directed at him from everyone, including his family—indeed, all save Yahsi, who appraised him calmly, and Anisha, who was yet in some degree of disbelief.

"Okona, tell us how and why you have destroyed the Hand," Anisha directed, her gaze at him unwavering.

"As to the how," he said, "I used a shard of sunfire."

"Sunfire?" she replied, dumbfounded. "How came you by that?"

"It was a gift of the Seer of Ponca Peak. And I have a confession to make. It was what I took out at the Tongue of Tagwash that gave Kiamosh pause. He thought I meant to destroy the Hand and him along with it, though I swear I never would have harmed the Hand at that time."

"What changed your mind, that you were moved to destroy it now?"

"When the Seer gave me the shard of sunfire, he said it would only prove of any real use once I truly understood from whence all good things come. I do understand that now, and I can testify before everyone here that our real blessings do not come from the Hand of Hamora."

Okona spoke ever more earnestly now. "Anisha, I know you heard with your own ears the words of Lanoka, daughter of Kiamosh, for we were together when she told us the true history of the Hand, how it came from a vile pact between Hamora himself and a horrific being whose name I will not here utter. She told us also of what the Hand was made—moonblood—and how it served to bind the Sakooma under the power of the most wicked of all beings, for we have received his protection and blessing only at the cost of that bondage."

Okona turned to face the crowd. "I know what I did must seem terribly selfish to you all, and you must think me completely mad. But I swear that I destroyed the Hand to liberate us from this evil master, to release our fatal grip upon the Hand of Hamora, the Hand of Harm, and its grip upon us, so we might grasp the Hand of Help, from which all good things come. For we must abandon the Lesser Hand for the Greater."

"And what is this 'Greater Hand,' boy?" interjected Baneesh. "Speak no more in riddles!"

"That of Mahna Shuya," Okona asserted, gesturing skyward. "He it was who wrought both this world and those which preceded it, the First of Worlds and the World of the West. So our own stories say. Once men had traffic with his realm in the Over-lands. But the Stairway to the Sky was broken—by our own doing, I might add, again as our own stories say, for our quarreling with Mahna Shuya brought the Stairway to ruin. Yet he has continued to send many blessings upon us. And yet we have more often honored others, others whose power and goodness is far less than his. For our band did not triumph against Kiamosh by either the Powers of the Sakooma, nor those of the Shamoki, for the Wakosi is beyond their aid. It was Mahna Shuya who gave us triumph. Sometimes he aided more or less openly, like when he opened a way for us out of a dreadful prison of the Under-realm, but I believe now he was ultimately behind all our successes and every deliverance."

The lad continued, "Yes, we remember Mahna Shuya at certain times of year and in certain rites, but I am persuaded it is small thanks for all he has given us and done for us. So I urge you all to do as I have done; release the Hand of Harm, and even though we cannot reach to help above, know that it may reach down to us. Take the Hand that is extended to you."

Not a sound came from the assembly. There was only the gentle chirping of birds from far off on the green heights of Takula.

"One thing more would I learn, Okona," said Anisha after some stretch of silence. "Did you know I would survive the destruction of the Hand?"

"No," Okona quietly returned. "But I am overjoyed that you have. I knew that death was near for you, so I thought that if you must die, I should at least try to rescue our people. But I think you survived because the curse of the Hand—in its entirety and in all its effects—must have been lifted at its ending."

The lad faced the people once more and bowed his head. "I know it is better for one to die than many, for one to give himself so that the many may live. So I am resigned to whatever fate I am now apportioned. I expected to lose both my dearest love and also my life for what I have done, so any judgment less than that I will consider a great mercy."

Anisha turned to Dhagomi and said, "I beg you, father, kill him not. I do not ask thus because of my love for him nor because I agree in any measure with what he has done, but because he speaks the truth about the testimony of Kiamosh's daughter. If nothing else, for that alone, I can understand why he took the course he did. She was persuaded the Hand was utterly evil and ought to be destroyed, and I suspect Okona was inclined to believe her because she knew so much of lore and magic."

Dhagomi looked down, then over at Baneesh, briefly to Anisha and finally back at Okona. "Very well," he said coldly. "The lad shall not die. But he is henceforth banished from the lands of the Sakooma. And he may not even go to retrieve his own effects but must depart immediately. Also, any who see him upon our soil shall know him a marked man and consider it their duty to slay him. For he has done a worse thing even than Kiamosh, who only stole the Hand. Okona has taken it from us altogether and everlastingly."

"My lord, you are most gracious." Okona bowed his head. "I shall depart at once."

"Goodbye, Okona," said Anisha tightly, and walked off.

Those assembled began to disperse, and Okona was walking to his family to bid them farewell, but they turned and hurried away. Though it rent him in two, the lad knew it would be of no use to follow them or even to call to them. He looked around then for Yahsi, but she was nowhere about. So, sighing, he turned and strode toward the gate.

He had more than half reached it when a flute warbled from some ways off. The tune was not one generally known, but he knew it; 'Linger a Moment' it was called. He turned to look upon the lay of Takula; Yahsi was hailing him from afar.

Since no one was particularly watching him, Okona sat upon the ground to wait for Yahsi, who had hurried off toward the hut where she had been staying. The lad picked at the grass for a number of minutes and had waited almost as long as he dared when Yahsi came hastening toward him with several large items.

When she reached him, she said, "All these are for you." She laid down his pack from his adventures in the north and also the harp and drum, which she had brought upon their quest.

"Yahsi, I can't take these!" Okona protested. "Dhagomi said—"

"He said you mightn't go get your own effects. And you didn't. I brought them to you."

"But I can't take your harp and drum!"

"Okona, I shall be positively angry if you don't take them," Yahsi insisted. "I made the harp, after all, and the drum was honorably gifted to me. So both are mine to do with as I please, and I want you to have them. Now, remember what you've learned of this world, the world above and the world below. I think, now that you understand these things better and know what you do of Mahna Shuya, your music will be finer than ever. I couldn't be happier about your decision, by the way."

"Y-you mean," Okona stammered, "you really believe I've done the right thing by destroying the Hand?"

"Of course! I considered suggesting it to you rather openly when we parted yesterday but thought it'd be better if you came to that conclusion on your own."

"Well, I'm glad you and I had that talk on Bahska Lawn," said Okona. "For during the night, I made my decision after thinking about everything that had happened, along with things you said, things Lanoka said … and things Wassu said. You see, he talked to me at Quinoma Stakes a few days ago." Okona glanced rapidly around to see if anyone was watching them, but everyone seemed to have retreated to one of the compound's dwellings or else gathered in far-off clusters.

"He did, did he? Well, you know when I went off alone to compose by the Kanno that evening? I saw him there as well."

"Oh?"

"Yes, and we talked about you a bit. More on that in a moment. Anyway, your talk with him: how did it go?"

"He spoke of many things difficult to understand, but I think I grasp some of them a little better now. But I understand quite a bit more about what the Seer said after all this and also things you told me. For instance, you said going on this quest was one of the best things that could happen to me. So it has proved to be, for though

I lost everything—family, home, my dear Anisha and ever so much more—I have found the Greater Hand. I have found what I was not seeking. And Wassu spoke of drawing from a mystic Well, which I now believe to be the mercy of Mahna Shuya, and I hope I have found it."

Yahsi smiled. "You have. The Lay of Lakosha, the song of which I told you, and of which Wassu said he shared with you a part, speaks of a hope. And hark! This hope has already come. Lay hold of it, Okona! Though the Lay of Lakosha speaks not of its fulfillment, for it has come about since Lakosha's time, Wassu revealed it to me at Quinoma Stakes. Mahna Shuya himself, the mighty warrior lord of the Over-lands, has taken the same road as all men, from beginning to end. And by the hands of malicious men he has undergone the First Sundering so that those who hold fast to him shall not undergo the Second. But unlike every other who has passed the First Sundering before him, he has returned, never to undergo such again. He is the true Stairway to the Sky and the Secret Sun who has risen across the Great Western Water, and it is by him men who yet live may escape the pitiable fate of those held fast in the biting briars of the Underbrakes. He is the great fount of mercy, the remover of all defilement. For he has opened the long-barred road to the Over-lands for those who would remain loyal to him."

"Then he is the Truest Treasure," said Okona, "and gladly do I exchange all I have lost for him. And that includes veneration of the other Powers. I felt rather out of sorts during the offerings at Shakola Kora, and now I believe I know why. I think it is only right that, of the Powers, I should honor Mahna Shuya alone from this day forth, for he is the one who aided me from beginning to end in these matters. It was even he who got me to release the Hand of Harm. Ultimately, I can't take any credit for that; I didn't want to destroy the Hand of Hamora, after all. But thankfully, Mahna Shuya got the better of me. For Sun must conquer Moon. Anyway, what did Wassu say about me?"

Yahsi looked toward the center of Takula. Still, no one was paying them any heed, so she turned back to Okona and said, "He told me that if you were to destroy the Hand, I was to inform you he would meet you again where the Anoka meets the Southward Sea. You have more to learn and will need more guidance, and this will be provided. And a boat will be waiting for you at the Anoka's end."

"A boat? For what?" Okona squinted.

"I wish I could tell you more, but I know no more myself. Anyway, you'd better be going. You're supposed to be exiled, you know." Yahsi winked.

"Goodbye, Okona." She embraced him warmly, then stood back and looked at him in great satisfaction. "I couldn't be prouder of you."

"Farewell, Yahsi," said Okona, struggling to smile through his sorrow. "I expect we'll never see each other again."

"On the contrary. We most certainly shall."

Okona gave her a questioning look.

Yahsi merely smiled. She handed him the pack, which he donned, then lifted the harp in its bag and slung it upon his shoulder. Lastly, she handed him the drum and said, "Now, off with you. The world awaits."

Okona marched to the gate, where two sentries wordlessly opened the portals and watched him pass onto the road beyond, then shut the gates again.

The lad looked first one way down the narrow path, which led east some twenty miles to his home village of Hachori, then the other, which headed to the Kanno. Resolute, he turned toward the river and went on until the walls of Takula lay well behind him.

Okona walked several miles westward down the road before reaching a serene stretch of the woods graced by shafts of golden morning light beaming through the trees. And there, much drained by all that had transpired, he unloaded his burdens and sat upon a shaded stone bordering the road. For most of the morning he remained there, bathing in the gentle breeze and the song of a nearby brook and relishing the warm earth beneath his feet. At last, growing restless, he dug around in his pack. There he found food, his glittering stones and flakes of silver and also his flute. This he took out, commencing to softly play the Lay of Lakosha upon it. But after a few strains, he lowered the instrument and began to sing:

"Only when man may bathe in that light shall death be done and all set right.

Look to the West, from whence we have come, for there shall rise the Secret Sun.

Look to the West from whence we have come, for there shall rise the Secret Sun."

But the second time he sang "Look to the West," a soft, higher voice joined him. He turned, and there, to his complete wonderment, was Anisha, standing in the midst of the road, garbed in a simple brown traveling dress and laded with a pack and a large waterskin.

"Anisha!" He rose.

"Oh, Okona!" she cried, running and throwing her arms around him.

"Surely I'm dreaming," Okona exclaimed. "For you couldn't possibly be—"

"I am." She smiled. "I'm coming with you. Wherever you're going, I'm going too."

"But how? And why?"

"I decided you were right. Mahna Shuya, not the Hand of Hamora, is the Hand we need. I didn't want to believe what Lanoka told us about the Hand, but I know it's true. My heart just had to come around. I told my father, my relatives and my friends that I had concluded you were correct, and they all thought I was only saying such because of my love for you. And I do love you, but that's not why I changed my mind. The fact is that I believe it for myself. I told my father I wished to follow you wherever you went, and he was furious, but remarkably, he did not forbid me from departing. I'm not sure why, but I think it must be because he has despaired of everything now that the Hand is gone. You see, like the rest of the Sakooma, all his hopes were upon the Hand, so the world is simply empty for them now that it's destroyed, and nothing seems to matter."

"Anisha, you can't abandon your family at a time like this!" Okona protested. "Your father needs you now more than ever."

"You left yours," Anisha returned.

"Because I had to."

"Okona, releasing the Hand of Harm is something they'll have to do for themselves. I can't do it for them. At least Yahsi is still there. And she'll be trying to help others to see the light."

"Have you spoken with her, then?" inquired Okona.

"That's how I knew which direction you'd be going. For she assumed you'd be going down to the Kanno to follow it to the Anoka."

Okona shook his head. "I can't believe this. Everything is just so ... so ..."

"Wonderful?" Anisha laughed.

"Yes! For though I've lost everything, I've gained even more. I've you, for one thing, and tremendous treasure from the north, courtesy of our good friend, Shadoo, and a new adventure and ... and most importantly, the Greater Hand."

Okona replaced his flute in his pack, then loaded up his harp and drum. When he had finished, he reached for Anisha's hand.

"Anisha, where is your mother's bangle?" he asked perplexedly. Looking more closely at the spot it customarily rested, he inquired, "And your scar ... where's your scar? There's no trace of it."

She looked down at her wrist. "Oh, I didn't know it was gone! It was there this morning. I ... well, I gave the bracelet to my father. It was his wife's, after all. Also, he said if I left that I would be renouncing my claim as the last heir of Hamora, which I was more than willing to do. I know his blood runs in me, and that cannot be changed, but I wish not to tread in any way the path he did. I would rather be vulnerable to death than trust dark enchantments to protect me. For that is the error the Sakooma were committing with the Hand. I shall rather trust to Mahna Shuya than the likes of Bashula's Bangle."

She peered again at her wrist. "Perhaps with my giving it up, the scar has been healed, for I have separated myself from its magic. As it was an official heirloom of Hamora's line, and I was forever renouncing my right to continue such, perhaps I have been freed from its curse as well."

"By the way," she added, smiling at Okona, "because I renounced my claim to Hamora's lineage, my father said I am free to marry whom I will. Of course he knows I wish to marry you, but as I said before, I believe he has abandoned both me and everything else to whatever fate may befall us."

"And what fate shall befall you?" asked Okona. "To be wed to an exile?"

"Of course!" Anisha returned, grinning. "I'm glad you asked."

The two embraced and kissed, then set off westward down the road.

Some six and a half miles west of Takula Conflux, the pair reached the eastern bank of the Kanno and stared out at the wide river, glinting in the midday sun. From afar, they spied a canoe with a single occupant paddling down the current. The individual seemed to have spotted them and began making his way toward them. Shortly, they descried who it was.

"Wunko!" Okona called excitedly. "I can't believe it!"

The Tikkichaw canoed up to the bank, got out and stood looking at them in amazement. "I knew I was close to Takula but never would have guessed ... oh, it's grand to see you again!"

"How went your journey?" asked Okona.

"Well, after I left you, it took me another full day to get back down by the Tongue of Tagwash. And then it was three days more south and almost a full fourth before I came to Aska Karalonga."

"Did things there go as you hoped?" inquired Anisha.

"Better. The people there bore me no ill will, not even Trader Teepu, and they were very grateful for my offer of some of the glittering stones, which they happily accepted. Oddly enough, they seemed to be expecting something like the attack that happened that night as a result of their traffic in talismans. 'That's what comes of meddling in magic,' they said. So they didn't credit us for the trouble. I stayed a full day with Teepu and his family, and they treated me very well. Then he up and gave me a boat, saying that I had been so generous with my stones that it was only fair."

"Anyhow, I paddled for five days back to my quag, gathered my things and a fair amount of food I had stored up and left the next morning, which was yesterday. I went back to Talligo Spit, where I'd hid my own canoe, which I was rather attached to, and that's what you see me in now, of course."

"Where are you headed now?" Okona queried, glancing down-river.

"The Anoka," Wunko replied. "And from there, back home."

"All the way back to your kin?" asked Okona.

"All the way. I decided that, High Katchiwup or no, I'm going to face my family again, for now I've nothing to be ashamed of. If the High Katchiwup is still around and wants to throw me out again, so be it. After all, I've been exiled before," he laughed.

"Speaking of exile," Okona began hesitantly, "we're exiled as well, or at least I am. Anisha has come of her own will."

"What?" Wunko exclaimed. "What's all this about?"

Okona glanced at Anisha, then said, "Well, it's not easy to explain in a hurry. But the main thing is that I changed my mind about the Hand, deciding, based on everything I've learned, that it was evil. So, just this morning, I destroyed it."

"What?!" cried Wunko, with considerable animation. "After all that trouble we went through to get it? And how'd you destroy a relic like that anyway?"

"It would take a while to go through all that in full," said Okona, "but as to the how, I used a shard of something called sunfire, which was given me by the Seer of Ponca Peak. It was the thing I pulled out near the end of our fight with Kiamosh. Sorry I lied when you asked about it that night, by the way. But as for why, the Hand was evil to begin with, and it actually was keeping our people in bondage, so I had to destroy it. And when I did, what should I find but, to my great surprise and joy, that Anisha didn't die! However, since the Sakooma revere the Hand so highly, I was exiled for my deed. The fact is, I was lucky to be banished rather than executed. But it's a sore blow to reckon with that we shall never see these lands again."

Wunko shook his head. "That's a lot for an old Tikkichaw to take in, but I suppose it'll have to do for now. And you know, you may believe you'll never be coming back, but I never thought to return from exile, and look—here I am! Who knows where your paths will lead? Anyway, where are you two off to presently?"

"You'll never believe this," said Anisha, "but we're to go to where the Anoka meets the Southward Sea."

"You see, we've someone to meet there," Okona added.

Wunko's mouth fell open. "Well, then we're headed right nearly to the same place. Would you care to join me?"

"If you'd have us," said Anisha hopefully.

"Would I!" Wunko laughed. "Nothing could please me more. Hop in!"

Okona and Anisha loaded their gear in the canoe. Then Anisha sat in the prow, with Okona just behind her and Wunko in the stern. Wunko pushed them off, and soon they were drifting out in the the sun-graced river, winding through the green fields and forests of Sarkanna.

The river carried them swiftly southward, and high above soared a great eagle, its wings flashing gold in the sun.

THE END

PRONUNCIATION GUIDE AND INDEX

This pronunciation guide and index is included for those readers who would like to delve deeper into the lore of *The Hand of Hamora*. Accordingly, it contains an alphabetical listing of all (or most all) of the unique entities that appear in the text of this book. Each entry includes a page number reference, set within square brackets, which marks either the location of the term's first appearance in the text or the instance in which it is most clearly explained.

Due to its conciseness and suitability for accurately representing various phonemes, the IPA (International Phonetic Alphabet) system of phonetic transcription has been chosen to represent the pronunciation of the various entries found in this volume. Several tables of correspondence between IPA symbols and phonemes in the English precede the listing of entries. There is also a small list identifying grammatical abbreviations that are used in this index.

NB: Words or parts of words which are of English origin are not generally provided with IPA representation, as their pronunciation can be readily deduced without it.

Consonants

b - <u>b</u>ook, mo<u>b</u>

c - hear<u>ts</u>, va<u>ts</u>

d - <u>d</u>og, ma<u>d</u>

f - <u>f</u>ire, lau<u>gh</u>

g - <u>g</u>old, fla<u>g</u>

h - <u>h</u>ill, han<u>d</u>

j - <u>y</u>ard, <u>y</u>ore

k - <u>c</u>astle, la<u>ke</u>

l - <u>l</u>oss, ca<u>ll</u>

m - <u>m</u>ark, ra<u>m</u>

n - <u>n</u>ail, bar<u>n</u>

p - <u>p</u>ond, ta<u>p</u>

r - <u>r</u>ow, ba<u>r</u>

s - <u>s</u>oft, pa<u>ss</u>

t - <u>t</u>ale, ra<u>t</u>

v - <u>v</u>ale, ha<u>ve</u>

w - <u>w</u>orld, al<u>w</u>ays

z - ma<u>ze</u>, tray<u>s</u>

ţ - be<u>tt</u>er, li<u>tt</u>le

ʃ - <u>sh</u>ore, a<u>sh</u>

ŋ - ri<u>ng</u>, a<u>ng</u>er

tʃ - <u>ch</u>imney, la<u>tch</u>

dʒ - <u>j</u>ar, a<u>ge</u>

Vowels

ɑː - f<u>a</u>ther, c<u>o</u>t

ɛ - l<u>e</u>t, h<u>ea</u>d

iː - f<u>ee</u>d, l<u>ea</u>f

oʊ - sh<u>ow</u>, m<u>o</u>le

uː - r<u>u</u>de, t<u>oo</u>

æ - s<u>a</u>t, sh<u>a</u>ck

ə - <u>a</u>gree, s<u>u</u>ppose

ɪ - l<u>i</u>d, p<u>i</u>n

ɔː - f<u>a</u>ll, l<u>aw</u>

ʌ - d<u>u</u>ck, s<u>u</u>n

eɪ - p<u>ay</u>, r<u>a</u>ce

ᵊ - mutt<u>o</u>n, sudd<u>e</u>n

Vowels Followed by 'R' Sounds

ɑr - f<u>ar</u>, c<u>ar</u>pet

ɛər - b<u>ear</u>, wh<u>ere</u>

ɔər - b<u>ore</u>, <u>oar</u>

ɝ - b<u>ur</u>n, w<u>or</u>k

' - This symbol precedes the syllable
which is most strongly stressed. (e.g.
delectable - dɪ ˈlɛktəbəl)

Abbreviations

Sing. - singular

Disamb. – disambiguation

Agra Chalura [181] - ˈægrə tʃəˈlɜə

Aloobish [283] - əˈluːbɪʃ

Ambori Kamosa [148] - æmˈbɔːriː kæˈmoʊsə

Amwot [5] - ˈæmwɔːt

Anisha [2] - əˈniːʃə

Annamet [24] - ˈænəmɛt

Anoka River [71] - əˈnoʊkə

Anoka Valley [78] - əˈnoʊkə

Anu Ashori [2] - ˈɑːnuː əˈʃɔəriː

Ashori, The [9] - əˈʃɔəriː

Aska Karalonga [81] - ˈæskə kɑrəˈloʊŋgə

Aunt Kapicha [94] - kəˈpiːtʃə

Aywish [26] - ˈeɪwɪʃ

Babora [154] - bæˈbɔərə

Bahska Lawn [300] - ˈbɑːskə

Baneesh [8] - bəˈniːʃ

Banuma Creek [100] - bəˈnuːmə

Banuma Falls [100] - bəˈnuːmə

Bashula [283] - bəˈʃuːlə

Bashula's Bangle [283] - bəˈʃuːləz

Bemmica Beans [116] - ˈbɛmɪkə

Black Throat, The [217]

Bloodmouth Fall, The [181]

Bok Barusha [181] - bɑːk bəˈruːʃə

Bright Face, The [240]

Burrows of the Oolasheg [234] - ˈuːləʃɛg

Cannibals of the Quags (see Momagaw) [94]

Canoba Wood [284] - kəˈnoʊbə

Caverns of Oshaga [25] - oʊˈʃɑːgə

Chachuma [93] - tʃəˈtʃuːmə

Chadori [100] - tʃəˈdɔəriː

Chapimu [154] - tʃəˈpiːmuː

Chennipot Chonka [25] - ˈtʃɛnɪpɔːt ˈtʃɑːŋkə

Chiborka [173] - tʃɪˈbɔərkə

Chief Magic-maker [15]

Chief of the Kishikot [135] - ˈkɪʃikɔːt

Chief Troubler, The [176]

Chogrot [264] - ˈtʃɑːgrɔːt

Chogrot Creek [297] - ˈtʃɑːgrɔːt

Coil of the Omaka [249] - oʊˈmɑːkə

Coryoc [24] - ˈkɔərjaːk

Crossing of the Broken Crag [81]

Darker Lands, The [96]

Decrees, The [136]

Deggas (sing. Degga) [15] - ˈdɛgəz (ˈdɛgə)

Dhagomi [8] - dəˈgoʊmiː

Dome of Doom [221]

Dongo Rabbit [5] - ˈdɑːŋgoʊ

Edge of the Underbrakes [215]

Elixir of Nadula [148] - nəˈduːlə

Evening Leaf [97]

Eyes of the Midnight Owl [194]

Eyuja [7] - eɪˈjuːdʒə

Faithful Fifteen, The [287]

Faithful Forty, The [179]

Falcon Clan [91]

Falls of Time, The [291]

Final Bridge, The [293]

Kashamee River [89] - ˈkæʃəmiː

Kayuna [304] - kɑːˈjuːnə

Kidara Mountain [289] - kɪˈdɑrə

Kiamosh [195] - ˈkiːəmɑːʃ

Kimmanic [3] - ˈkɪmənɪk

King of the Elk (see Amwot) [5]

Kishikot [135] - ˈkɪʃikɔːt

Kniferoad, The [216]

Komakop [93] - ˈkoʊməkɑːp

Korashac Caverns [194] - ˈkɔərəʃæk

Korashac's Courtyard [206] - ˈkɔərəʃæks

Korba Landing [38] - ˈkɔərbə

Labona [330] - ləˈboʊnə

Lair of the Oolasheg [228] - ˈuːləʃɛg

Lake Oganosha [126] - oʊgəˈnoʊʃə

Lakosha [322] - ləˈkoʊʃə

Lalaska Point [98] - ləˈlæskə

Lands of the Living [194]

Lanoka [233] - ləˈnoʊkə

Lay of Lakosha, The [323] - ləˈkoʊʃə

Lesser Hand, The [340]

Light Beyond the Mists, The [10]

Linger a Moment [342]

Lodge of the Sanno [8] - ˈsænoʊ

Lord of Shadows, The (see Skaggish, The) [241]

Machakam [124] - ˈmætʃəkæm

Machila [244] - mæˈtʃɪːlə

Magic-maker [14]

Master Song-maker [9]

Mahna Shuya [301] - ˈmɑːnə ˈʃuːjə

Maskugi, The [242] - mæˈskuːgiː

Massora [17] - mæˈsɔərə

Matora, The [18] - məˈtɔərə

Maze of the Marauders [108]

Middle Realm [240]

Midnight Owl (see Navina Shoga) [194]

Mists of Shagrash-mula, The [10] - ˈʃægrɑːʃ ˈmuːlə

Mistwoods, The [249]

Momagaw [94] - ˈmoʊməgɔː

Moon-bit [199]

Moonblood [254]

Moon Owl (see Navina Kayu) [194]

Morning Herbs [89]

Mound of Hamora [8] - həˈmɔərə

Mud-Fiends [94]

Mushatuck (disamb., language) [27] - ˈmʌʃətʌk

Mushatuck (disamb., tribe) [26] - ˈmʌʃətʌk

Nadula Creek [148] - nəˈduːlə

Nadula Valley [154] - nəˈduːlə

Nasi [198] - ˈnɑːsiː

Nataki [179] - nəˈtɑːkiː

Navina Kayu [194] - nəˈviːnə ˈkɑːjuː

Navina Shoga [194] - nəˈviːnə ˈʃoʊgə

Nebara [249] - nɛˈbɑrə

Neck of Night, The [242]

Nightwater Stream [136]

Night-woman, The (see Oshaga) [25]

Noolaboo [124] - ˈnuːləbuː

North Beyond North [10]

Northern Eagle, The (see Torokay) [5]

Odamac [179] - ˈoʊdəmæk

Ohkasac Groves [33] - ˈoʊkəsæk

Oja [124] - ˈoʊdʒə

Okamot [330] - ˈoʊkəmɔːt

Okona [2] - oʊˈkoʊnə

Old Shadoo (see Shinnemah Shadoo) [172] - ʃəˈduː

Omaka, The [248] - oʊˈmaːkə

Oolasheg, The [18] - ˈuːləʃɛg

Orobec [26] - ˈɔəroʊbɛk

Oshaga [25] - oʊˈʃaːgə

Other-lands, The [128]

Over-lands, The [10]

Padooga Bird [95] - pəˈduːgə

Pagoma Rock [111] - pəˈgoʊmə

Pale Eye, The [240]

Pamori [301] - pəˈmɔəriː

Panni [7] - ˈpaːniː

Pashola Timbers [327] - pæˈʃoʊlə

Paths of the Powers, The [288]

Pillar of the Under-realm [211]

Piskah River [88] - ˈpɪskə

Pit of No Return [214]

Ponca Peak [47] - ˈpaːŋkə

Ponnicberries [2] - ˈpaːnɪkbɛəriːz

Powers, The [8]

Powers of Air, Water, and Earth [2]

Powers of Earth [197]

Powers of the Air [15]

Powers of Water [113]

Quagweeds [70] - ˈkwægwiːdz

Quinoma Stakes [318] - kwɪˈnoʊmə

Quompi [3] - ˈkwaːmpiː

Realm of the Kishikot [325] - ˈkɪʃɪkɔːt

Realms Beyond, The [63]

Redstone [83]

Rite of the Daughter's Blood [233]

River Anoka (see Anoka River) [71] - əˈnoʊkə

River Wakosi (see Wakosi River) [155] - waːˈkoʊsiː

River of Dreams [92]

River of Years [10]

Roamers' Refuge (see Ambori Kamosa) [148]

Sacred Tens [29]

Sahku [244] - ˈsaːkuː

Sakoom [244] - səˈkuːm

Sakooma (disamb., language) [71] - səˈkuːmə

Sakooma (disamb., tribe) [2] - səˈkuːmə

Sambo Creek [183] - ˈsæmboʊ

Samoolga [96] - səˈmuːlgə

Sanno, The [18] - ˈsænoʊ

Sarkanna [18] - sarˈkænə

Second Sundering, The [321]

Secret Sun, The [344]

Seer of Ponca Peak, The [74] - ˈpaːŋkə

Shadoo (see Shinnemah Shadoo) [172] - ʃəˈduː

Shadoo's Shelf [172] - ʃəˈduːz

Shadow-Stalker, The (see Waboka, The) [18]

Shagora Gorge [256] - ʃəˈgɔərə

Shagrash-Mula (see Mists of Shagrash-Mula, The) [322] - ˈʃægraːʃ ˈmuːlə

Shakeega [248] - ʃəˈkiːgə

Shakola Kora [152] - ʃəˈkoʊlə ˈkɔərə

Shamoki [26] - ʃəˈmoʊkiː

Shamuri River [248] - ʃəˈmɚiː

Sharapoc, The [18] - ˈʃɛərəpaːk

Sheelim [26] - ˈʃiːlɪm

Shinnemah Shadoo [172] - ˈʃɪnᵊmɔːʃəˈduː

Shinnemah's Kitchen [185] - ˈʃɪnᵊmɔːz

Shoggo [105] - ˈʃaːgoʊ

Shoroba [26] - ʃɔəˈroʊbə

Silent Walkers, The (see Jaggo) [50]

Singing Falls, The [148]

Sister Kwennitch (see Navina Shoga) [194] - ˈkwɛnɪtʃ

Sister Shukina (see Navina Kayu) [194] - ʃuːˈkiːnə

Sisters of Korashac, The (see Oolasheg, The) [18] - ˈkɔərəʃæk

Sisters, The (see Oolasheg, The) [177]

Skaggish, The [240] - ˈskægɪʃ

Slumberwood [297]

Song-maker [9]

Song of the Summer Stars (see Anu Ashori) [2]

Sorrequom Ridge [26] - ˈsɔərəkwaːm

Soul-Lodges [15]

Southward Sea, The [71]

Span of the Shimmering Nights (see Shagrash Mula) [10]

Stairway to the Sky, The [10]

Star Clan [38]

Starfly [38]

Stonearch Dell (see Shakola Kora) [152]

Stone of Sahku, The [246] - ˈsaːkuː

Storm-singer, The (see Kannikos) [47]

Summer Stars, The (see Ashori, The) [2]

Sunfire [58]

Sunflower Junction (see Chennipot Chonka) [25]

Sun-lord, The (see Samoolga) [96]

Swamp-Demon, The (see Sharapoc, The) [18]

Swamp Talk [72]

Taboba [296] - təˈboʊbə

Tagwash, The [256] - ˈtægwaːʃ

Takula Conflux [3] - təˈkuːlə

Takula Lake [2] - təˈkuːlə

Talligo Spit [82] - ˈtælɪgoʊ

Tannomet [26] - ˈtænoʊmɛt

Tarbomu [249] - tɑrˈboʊmuː

Tarrameg Nuts [33] - ˈtɛərəmɛg

Tarrameg Oaks [33] - ˈtɛərəmɛg

Tauboma Bank [304] - taʊˈboʊmə

Tauboma Creek [308] - taʊˈboʊmə

Tawassi [198] - təˈwaːsiː

Taygor [179] - ˈteɪgɔər

Teepu (see Trader Teepu) [113] - ˈtiːpuː

Tencum [7] - ˈtɛŋkʌm

Terrible Troughs, The [210]

Teshoga, The [15] - tɛˈʃoʊgə

That Which Was Lost [10]

Three Realms, The [240]

Thunder-Bear, The (see Matora, The) [18]

Tiba [296] - ˈtiːbə
Tigglesquat [67] - ˈtɪgᵊlskwɔːt

Tikkichaw (disamb., language) [72] - ˈtɪkɪtʃɔː

Tikkichaw (disamb., tribe)[93] - ˈtɪkɪtʃɔː

Tonga [3] - ˈtɔːŋgə

Tongue of Tagwash, The [256] - ˈtægwaːʃ

Torokay [5] - ˈtɔəroʊkeɪ

Toshigan Hollow [126] - ˈtɑːʃɪgᵊn

Trader Teepu [112] - ˈtiːpuː

Tumanila [148] - tuːməˈniːlə

Turtle Clan [38]

Twin Crones of Torment, The (see Oolasheg, The) [18]

Twin Terrors, The (see Oolasheg, The) [194]

Umarna [139] - uːˈmɑrnə

Underbrakes, The [178]

Under-realm, The [209]

Unlucky Eleven [29]

Unlucky Eleventh [31]

Upper Wakosi, The [177] - wɑːˈkoʊsiː

Vale of the Wakosi (see Wakosi Vale) [135] - wɑːˈkoʊsiː

Valley of the Singing Falls (see Nadula Valley) [144]

Valley of the Wakosi (see Wakosi Vale) [250] - wɑːˈkoʊsiː

Vannabish [71] - ˈvænəbɪʃ

Wabashi Igama Chika [71] - wɑːˈbɑːʃiː iːˈgɑːmə ˈtʃiːkə

Waboka, The [18] - wɑːˈboʊkə

Wakosi River [126] - wɑːˈkoʊsiː

Wakosi Vale [127] - wɑːˈkoʊsiː

Warlock's Hive, The (see Bok Barusha) [181]

Washoma, The [88] - wɑːˈʃoʊmə

Wassu of the West [97] - ˈwɑːsuː

Watamora [100] - wɑːtəˈmɔərə

Wayawoc Woods [124] - ˈwɑːyəwɑːk

Western Thunder, The (see Matora, The) [246]

Where the Wakosi Rises [163] - wəˈkoʊsiː

Window of Southsight [239]

Winged Watcher, The (see Ganoja) [78]

Wippikats (see Great Wippikats) [74] - ˈwɪpɪkæc

Wise-women [19]

Witch-man [180]

Wolmac [44] - ˈwoʊlmæk

Woods of Much Buzzing, The [71]

World of the West [10]

Wunko [70] - ˈwʌŋkoʊ

Wunko's Wash [77] - ˈwʌŋkoʊz

Xiku [71] - ˈʃiːkuː

Yagoni [17] - jɑːˈgoʊniː

Yahsi [3] - ˈjɑːsiː

Yakoba [117] - jɑːˈkoʊbə

Yaroka Falls [304] - jəˈroʊkə

Year of the Pale Sun [245]

Yuriba [24] - juːˈriːbə

Zaranga [71] - zəˈræŋgə

About the Author

JARRETT SKADDISSON

Jarrett Skaddisson is a native of the Midwestern US, an accomplished musician and composer and an avid linguist, philosopher, author, researcher, mountain climber, spelunker and tea enthusiast. He lived in the Orient for several years as a child and has traveled to more than 30 countries for mission work, performance tours and good, old-fashioned adventures. His favorite pastimes are reading, writing, making music, learning languages, eating exotic foods, doing improv comedy and voice-acting and engaging in a wide variety of shenanigans. He lives with his wife, Michelle, to whom he has been married for 18 years, their son, Fritz, who is an exceedingly happy, imaginative, energetic and hilarious seven-year-old, and their beautiful and exceptionally cute, silly and spunky three-year-old daughter, Nora. Jarrett can be contacted via e-mail at jarrettskaddisson@gmail.com. He is also the author of the immersive fantasy series, The Kingblade Chronicles. Information about and various media for the series may be found at thekingbladechronicles.com.